The Probability Matrix

AN ECHOES OF THE END NOVEL

Cover Artwork by Martina da Bologna
https://www.deviantart.com/martinadabologna
twitter: @scarlet_artist

Cover Layout by Erica Lynn Evans

Edited by Lily Ingersoll

ISBN: 978-1-963266-04-7

Visit the author on the Internet
https://www.therunespring.com

FOREWORD

If you are new to Ahlysim, I bid you welcome, though you may wish to begin your journey in The Arcangineers, where this story begins. If you are returning after a first expedition across Ahylsim, welcome back! This foreword is to give you a quick heads up on the language of Ahlysim. This being an alien world, you can imagine that the languages have been run through an epic magic translation device of babblefish-like capability to reach you in a form that you, as a human being of this Earth, can understand.

That being said, not everything makes it through translation. There will be some phrases, animals, plants, and other quirks that may be hard to understand. For many of these things, I have included a glossary at the end of the novel. While it is not a comprehensive resource, it should cover most of the things that are not obvious from context. I hope you enjoy the adventures of the Tier!

~ C.M.

<h1 align="center">PROLOGUE</h1>

"Subtle Chaos"

Lia's telepathic handshake buzzed in Ales' mind.

{Do you see it?}

They had been watching the Center for two days solid, barely moving, neither sleeping. The sprawling collection of beautiful norstone buildings was the only Center for hundreds of lengths in all directions. A waving sea of unbroken forest spread to the compass points as far as the eye could see. The Black Wilds surrounded them, and backing the city of Rihanna was the unassailable peak of the Rak Escarpment.

"I see it, Sister. The subtle chaos is clear. The Probability Matrix is there. The question is, how did they get it? There was only ever the one, and it was absolutely destroyed in the Cataclysm. There is no way it would have survived the explosion you described," Ales said.

{This One estimates that at the current rate, the Probability Matrix will cause a disastrous chain reaction in less than a cycle, two cycles at most, depending on the usage of the Matrix,} Kiltik spoke into their telepathic link.

Alessandra and Liassa moved back from the edge of the cliff. Kiltik was slightly closer, having made his way into the Center itself. Kiltik had requested that he be addressed with male pronouns on their travels through the Wilds, and was becoming increasingly human with each passing day.

{I can't believe they noticed it. It's quite subtle,} Lia said.

{People can become quite sensitive to the movements of the world around them when they are like the Ryhim. Their royal families have had the most stable and consistent rule in history since the Tier, if you are to be believed. When they suddenly begin to do things in ways that go against their long tested heritage, their people are going to notice,} Ales said through their mental link, including Kiltik in the conversation.

{This One questions if it is possible that the people tap their latent Tieran abilities for such things.} Kiltik noted.

{It is unlikely to be anything that complicated. While it is possible that from time to time anyone might vaguely tap into the

magic of the Vision, I believe it is likely that they simply noticed that many of their clans are being sent to places at times they are not supposed to be there. They are being asked to perform tasks they never have before. Things stand out in their memory,} Ales explained.

The Ryhim had an odd social structure. They did not have a King unless they were at war. During war, a King was chosen from among the clan chiefs to oversee the defense of the Black Wilds. The rest of the time, the royal families of each of the clans worked together to ensure that the Ryhim as a whole were supplied with all of the things they needed to prosper.

{This One questions how we might approach the problem.} Kiltik queried through their mental link. He still had not found a satisfactory way to communicate vocally. The Mind knew that its speech patterns were odd, but seemed unable to change them as of yet.

{I don't think we will easily find answers in the Center. We need to find out who this benefits. It's almost certain that the Invader is at work here. It's unlikely that for this scheme it will use someone as visible as the King, but it has to be someone who can influence the movement of the Clans. We will have to integrate ourselves with each of the Clans until we can piece together enough about what they have all been directed to do before we will see the whole picture,} Alex explained. Lia nodded.

{Once we can see the whole plot, we can see who it benefits. Once we know that, we will know who has the Probability Matrix,} Lia finished.

"Can you all stop that?" Ilsa asked. She watched them carefully as they came out of the woods into the massive clearing where they had made camp with Clan Mizami of the Ryhim.

"Apologies, Ilsa. Kiltik is still uncomfortable with speaking aloud. He prefers mental communication with us." Ales said. Ilsa looked over to the Mind. It had begun to take on the form of something like a katali in miniature, but had four legs rather than six.

"This One is aware that This One's speech patterns are still perplexing to those around This One," Kiltik intoned. Its voice was deep, and had an odd mechanical twang. Ilsa ran a hand over Kiltik's furless head.

"Can you feel that?" Ilsa asked uncertainly.

"This One is aware of touch. This One's approximation of the living body is quite accurate. The place you touch stimulates This One's positive sense receptors – what you may call This One's pleasure centers. This One… enjoys… this touch," Kiltik said. Ilsa rubbed Kiltik's dull silver ears a moment longer.

"So what is the verdict?" Warran asked.

"They are correct. There is something desperately wrong here in the Sea of Wilderness, as they call it," Ales explained.

"So we will be staying?" asked Cole. Ales nodded to him and they all settled down. Each one sat on mottled deep blue logs placed around the fire. Ilsa's parents and Queen Aisha Roa stopped at the edge of the firelight, as if to ask if they could join. Ales smiled and waved them in.

"This is as much your fate as ours. Clan Mizami have offered you sanctuary, and I suggest that you take it. Your family is still recovering, Aisha. King Roa will not wake for some spans yet, if I am any judge of such things."

"But it has already been almost a full cycle. Will he not need more healing?" Aisha queried. Ales shook her head.

"No, Queen Roa. All of the damage that remains is to his mind. The last transfusion of Structures we gave to him will complete his healing. He was badly damaged, but gods willing, when he wakes, he will be restored," Ales said.

Aisha bowed her head, "Thank you."

Ales went on, "We have to split up. If we stay together, it will take cycles for us to discover everything that is happening here. Warran, I think you will stay here with them. You have Kayna to look after, and we need you to continue your work. It is more important than anything that you finish. Kiltik, you will go stoneward with Ilsa, to Clan Navano. Find out what they have been sent into the mountains to do. Kiltik, you will have to look after Ilsa, as she is not fully up to Tieran strength." Ilsa looked offended for a moment before she realized it was not a jibe, but rather a statement of fact.

"The same goes for you, Liassa. You will go with Cole. Make sure he doesn't get himself killed. Go to Clan Byranti and speak with their Clan Leader. Angran has told me that he can make introductions for you to ease your job. However, I think you will find that worrying out what the Byranti are doing will be more difficult. Angran indicated that they are very reserved and do not easily reveal what is being done within the Clan to outsiders, so your job will likely be more difficult than that. Once each of us has a fair picture of what the Clans are doing, the plan will be to meet back up with Clan Mizami," Ales plotted.

"What will you be doing?" Lia asked.

"I'm going to investigate the Center. I don't think I will be able to find out where the Probability Matrix is or who is using it. The chaos is still too subtle. But with any luck, I can get the currents of the city – position myself so that when you return with your information, I will be ready to do something about it," Ales finished.

Everyone nodded and all but Ales and Liassa trailed away to pack their things to prepare for their various trips. Lia sat next to the fire arranging her six paws for comfort.

{I don't think it is good for you to be alone,} Liassa worried.

{I don't think it is either, but you saw it, Liassa. It is subtle, but if anything, Kiltik's estimate is conservative. If this is allowed to continue, this Center will descend into chaos and destruction. I will need to be the one to stop it.}

Liassa narrowed eyes at her sister. *{No,}* Lia growled at Ales when she gave Liassa a look that said she was in a mood to fight. She opened her mouth.

{No. We are done with that. You almost died, again. I lost you for three thousand cycles. No, you will not do this alone. You will not.} Lia showed her teeth in challenge. Ales leaned back away from her, not afraid, but startled.

{I am not a child!} Lia roared in Ales' mind. Ales flinched as the roar ripped through her mind.

"Alright, Lia," Ales whispered, "I'm sorry."

Lia huffed out a breath as if to say 'so there' before she settled her paws beneath her and lay down. "You will not be alone. Never alone. We were charged by the goddess to bring our people back to this world. We will not be alone. We will defeat the Intruder, and we will take back our world."

Speaking out loud was something Lia often avoided. Even though everyone here knew what she was, she found it to be unpleasant. She was not supposed to be human, and a human voice was one of the things she had left behind when she had become one of the Wild. Her baby blue fur rippled over strong muscles as she got back to her feet restlessly. She began to pace.

{Cole can do this job on his own,} Liassa concluded.

Ales frowned at the statement. Lia was right. Since he had accepted his place among them, Cole had learned more about the Vision than their other two new ones combined. He had learned with an intensity that impressed even Alessandra. He had become one of them, and only the lack of Cellstructs made him vulnerable in ways that Lia and Ales were not. He still had a dozen cycles of study to learn all of the nuances of his power, but they had focused on the combat applications of his powers so that he could more easily keep himself alive. One cycle was more than enough for him to learn that.

"Only if he feels confident can he do it on his own. Otherwise, you will go with him?" Ales tilted her head, making it a question. Lia just shrugged.

{I don't think so. It's time to throw him into the deep water and see if he can swim. We can't take him to the Abyss, but I think this may be almost as good.}

"One whole cycle. Is he really doing that well?" Ales asked. Lia made that same odd shrugging motion.

{He's doing at least as well as I was at one cycle, and I don't think this will be quite as dangerous as running the Abyss,}

An older man walked into the circle of their firelight. He was shorter than Ales, just over five marks tall, but his body was strongly muscled. He was clothed in tan, homespun cloth and his boots were thick hide, and well worn. Over everything, he wore a long, white fur cloak. His hair was an odd salt and pepper mixture in yellow and dark blue that Ales had not seen before, and his skin was a deep bronze. He had hunter green eyes with smile lines at the corners.

"Wind at your back, Angran," Ales welcomed. The traditional greeting of the Ryhim had become normal after almost a full cycle of traveling with them.

"And to you, honored Tier. Did you see what you hoped to?"

"We did, Angran. You and your elders were correct. There is something terribly wrong in Rihanna. I do not believe it is the Banners, but perhaps one of the royal families causing the problem."

"Is it one of ours?" Angran's expression turned very serious. Each of the clans had one family among the royals. If it was anyone in Angran's family, he would be upset.

"Perhaps. We will not know until we can find out exactly what they are attempting to accomplish. Only then can we trace it back to them." Angran watched Liassa for a moment. Lia sighed. She recognized the uncomfortable hiccup in someone's thoughts that marked a reaction to her speaking. Angran gave her an apologetic smile.

"I apologize, honored Wild one. I give you my word that I am unafraid. I know that you are not going to eat me." His smile mutated into something more genuine. "Will you be able to return things to the way they were?"

It was clear that he was concerned. He was responsible for the people of his clan, truly a big responsibility, as his clan was the second largest. They were ten thousand strong, and if they continued to be directed by the Probability Matrix, they would come to terrible harm.

"We hope so, Angran. Until that time, I can only suggest that you do not heed the word coming from Rihanna."

Angran nodded uneasily. "We will try, honored Tier, but Rihanna is our life. Without guidance from Rihanna, we risk contending for resources with other Clans."

"I understand, Angran. We will move as quickly as is possible. Can you provide the place we asked for?"

"That we can, honored Tier. In general, the Clans do not have such places, but we know of a place nearby that will suffice."

"Then we shall begin." Ales hoped that the subtle chaos did not become something more malevolent sooner than they could stop it.

PART 1

1

Ales tossed a fist-sized rock into the air and caught it while she watched the Guards at the center gates. These were not like the guards at Vilhena. No one but the Ryhim came to Rihanna. There were no menageries to hide within. She wouldn't be talking her way past these ones. Ales' hand whipped forward in a blur, sending the rock whistling through the gate at blinding speed. It shot through a murder hole in the guard house wall and bounced off one of the interior stone walls, slamming into one of the spears on the end of a large rack. A thunderous clatter of steel against stone erupted from within the guard house. The guards jumped, having never seen the stone sail by. They turned and rushed through the gate.

{Go!} Ales sent to Lia. They both shoved open their Constraints, ratcheting up their strength and speed. They rushed the gate and slipped through before the guards were ten marks away. It was not something a human could accomplish. The throw had been over a hundred marks.

{Great. Now we are trapped in here,} Lia intoned with amusement and sarcasm. Ales blew out a laugh.

"Please. You could steal the armor off their backs and they wouldn't notice. You don't even have thumbs. We could have walked right past them with Taking. That was just for fun." Ales grinned.

{So what are we doing here again?}

"No more lies, Lia. Never again. I don't think we will be able to find whoever is using the Probability Matrix without more information from the Ryhim Clans. However, it is a safe bet that the Intruder is behind this, so we will attempt to root out anyone who is infected. Primarily, though, we will attempt to counteract the effects of the Probability Matrix here in the Center. My hope is that we will draw the attention of the Intruder so that we may destroy its presence here."

{And what of the Core? It has been a cycle, and we are no closer to finding the truth of what happened to it.}

"I disagree. If we can fix this place and obtain the Probability Matrix, we can use it properly to get an idea of where to go next in our search for the Core."

{Is it safe to use it that way? Even for us?} Lia had always been better at using the instinctive abilities of the Tier.

"We can. You must be careful with what questions you ask. Be indirect. In other words, we have to ask questions that will not directly effect our movements. You ask it not where we will find The Core, but rather where we should look to begin our search for The Core. The more you take direction from the machine, the more catastrophic the eventual cost when it reaches the limit of its ability to predict the future."

{Where are we going to stay while we are here? This Center is strange. I somehow suspect that they do not have Wayhouses here. No one ever comes here except the Ryhim.}

"Which means," Ales held up a finger as they made their way through the dark alleys between buildings, "we will need a friend."

{Yeah. I'm just gonna sit over here and shut up now apparently. I mean, really, is there anything you don't have rigged?} Lia snarked. *{You probably have plans going down in other dimensions, I swear.}*

"Angran gave me the name of a relative of his who has a home here in the city. He has given us a token that will tell this relative that we need a place to live in the Center."

{Who's carrying the note on all of this?}

Ales switched to purely mental speech. *{We are. Angran says that we can pay him, and he will distribute the funds as is necessary.}*

{You know that the treasure room is not limitless?}

{Lia, what is stored in that room is a fortune unlike any other gathered in our history. There is enough gold alone in there to buy and sell all the kingdoms in the world. How did father gather it all?}

Lia lashed her tail once, but said nothing in response. Ales looked askance at Lia then raised a brow in question. Lia eyed her right back, and blew out a breath through her nose.

{He didn't gather it, you did.} Lia recalled.

{What?}

{Didn't you wonder why there was no Mind controlling your sleeping place? I'm surprised that you didn't notice the connection when you were last there.}

Ales paused for a long moment. Lia recognized the mental pause that came when one of the Tier queried their Structures for information.

{That's impossible. Where did they all go?} Ales asked, though it was clear that she already knew the answer.

{They got used up. We couldn't create more bondstructs after the cataclysm, and those that Father designed to mine all of those precious materials would not self-replicate for some reason. I believe that Father had an idea of how much he wanted us to have. As your Cellstructs managed them, they broke down and followed their recycling routines.}

Ales frowned. "Father couldn't have known what was going to happen," she intoned quietly, knowing that Lia would hear.

They walked through the back alleys of Rihanna. This place did not have the same sort of perfect layout as Vilhena. This great Center had been constructed by the hands of the people over hundreds of cycles, and while the original Center did have a symmetrical spiral layout that was clearly of Tieran design, the rest had been built by the people. It had a beauty and charm all its own.

{He didn't. The Mother informed him it would likely be far into the future before you would wake from your stasis. He wanted to leave you as prepared for this new world as you could be. So he put all of that in place before we even had any inkling of the cataclysm. We weren't sure any of us would be here when you woke. I only found out later that I would be able to stay.}

"So what was running the rest of the minor functions of the bunker?"

{Just a processing unit. He didn't feel right leaving something self-aware alone to manage everything while you were sleeping.}

"You work with Finding much better than I do. If you use the Circle of Finding, you should start to see the patterns of the Matrix going wrong."

{Yeah, but I don't know what I am looking for. How does the Matrix work? My education in temporal theory never really took.}

"It is actually pretty simple in an explanatory sense. The Matrix uses a low-orbit spectral sensory array to track everything happening in an area. Absolutely everything. Every gust of wind, every breath a person takes, every thought, every choice. Everything is a variable that it plugs into a calculation. Like a rock rolling down a hill, if you can track its path, know every bump it is going to hit, everything that will change its direction, and measure the exact force of friction on the rock, you can calculate exactly down to the atomic level where it will stop.

The Probability Matrix was designed to do that on a larger scale. The problem comes when you act directly on that information, and continue to do so. Over time, the Matrix is unable to cope with the repetitive intrusions into its calculations, especially if those actions are intended to steer the natural progression away from the original prediction. Because of this lack of ability to calculate the residual exterior variables, it is unable to warn the user of the consequences of their alterations. As such, it is only able to warn them that there will be consequences to their actions. Now think about what a normal person with no ability to gauge the exponential effects of a small decision applied to a large scale would do with that power."

{So what you are saying is that whatever outcome they are trying to achieve will likely happen, but the widespread consequences of that outcome will become more and more damaging?}

"Exactly."

{And how exactly are we going to counter that effect?}

"Well, countering the effect is not terribly difficult. Palial, the original designer of the Probability Matrix, found that you can examine the effects with the Circle of Repair. From that, you can determine how to counter the effect. The difficult part is finding whatever it is that the person using the Matrix is trying to accomplish here."

{And how large is "here"?}

"The spectral array had a coverage area of about forty thousand square lengths."

Lia goggled. *{So we are looking for one individual grain of sand on a beach. Great.}*

"Told you that I thought we were unlikely to be able to find the Matrix."

{So we are fire chasers, then?}

"Sounds about accurate. We find those infected by the Intruder's Cellstructs and observe them in an attempt to find a way to free them. We have to be careful, Lia. Remember the assassin from Vilhena? She was consumed when I attempted to access her Cellstructs. It had shoved structures into her body with no integration. However, if it is allowed to continue, I believe that it will eventually find the keys to integration."

{So what about using these?} Lia held up one of her front paws. It gave her an odd gait as she kept walking on the remaining five. She twisted the paw so the black metal of her Sparks glinted in the sunlight.

"They aren't going to be able to transmit properly through living tissue. They were designed for direct contact with the infected structures. They will be hit or miss at best."

{Are we sure that is what we are going to run into here?}

"We can be fairly certain that we won't run into the same things here that we did in Vilhena. The bondarmor is too noticeable. I think the Intruder is playing a more subtle game here."

They came to a central square, and Ales stopped short at the sight. It was a massive cleared area directly in the center of the Center. The outer edge of the square was paved in white cobblestones. There was not a single stone of any other color as far as she could see. It must have taken countless cycles to find each of the stones as not a single one was cut. An irregular line of grass made its way around the circumference of the square, never closer than twenty ticks from the edge of the square. The trees began near the edge of the grass, and continued in an even more irregular line. They were close-set, but far enough apart that one could walk between them if they desired. Ales looked at them in astonishment. The massive trees stretched into the sky, glimmering leaves of shining crystal spread in a canopy that nearly reached the edges of the square. They filled the square with curtains of refracted light. Their chiming filled the air with enchanting music.

Ales looked down to Lia. "Those are, impossible."

"They are no more impossible than you are, my Daughter," a slow deep voice said from the alley they had just exited. Ales and Lia slid back into the alleyway before any of the various people could notice them.

"Lightleaf trees only grew in the Union Grove in Ahal," Ales marveled.

"That is truth, my Daughter. However, the explosion that consumed Ahal took the single seed of life that each of my precious Lightleaves produced each cycle and scattered them to the wind. Two groves came to be from two of those seeds. This is one of them," Zezzhz explained. The god's burning emerald eyes looked upon the trees with pride.

"Do they facilitate…" Ales trailed off. It was too much to hope for.

"Light jumps?" Zezzhz grinned, his blazing smile projected the cool breeze of high places. "Of course they do. Like your connection to the Core, their connection is unique. Even an interdimensional transition cannot sever that."

{Do they know the purpose of the trees?} Lia asked.

"Not any more, my Daughter. For a time, when Kinas was among them, they did, but as you both know, the knowledge of how to communicate with the network must be passed from person to person. It can't be written down or recorded. A person must be guided by someone who knows. Over time, the knowledge was lost and passed into myth."

{So this is where Kinas ended up?} Lia wondered.

"He helped the Ryhim build this Center. Their entire civilization was based on his teachings. He was the longest-lived of the survivors besides you two. He lived here for eight hundred twenty one cycles before he passed back to the Core."

"This is the Nexus, isn't it?" Ales asked.

"It is what remains of the Nexus. We have lost much of our connection with this world, my Daughters. This holy place is not what it used to be. Kinas recognized it for what it was, and set the Ryhim to tending it."

"Apologies, Father, I did not presume to wrest information from you." Ales said.

"Were you asking questions which I could not answer, I would not."

"Then far be it from me to waste this chance to take advantage of your grace, Father. I have one more question. Am I correct in thinking that the Intruder is doing this?"

Zezzhz seemed to consider it for a long moment. "Yes, your assumption is correct. I dare not say more than that. This situation is too delicate."

{May I ask what destinations are still available to us?} Lia queried.

Zezzhz made a gesture towards the trees. "Go on and find out for yourselves."

Ales and Lia looked towards the trees. When they turned back, Zezzhz was gone. They exchanged a look.

"Perhaps we should find our place here before we rush out and touch what might be the most sacred things these people have?" Ales speculated.

{Or perhaps we should just use Taking to get out there without anyone seeing us.}

"I don't like doing that to people. I worry that we are damaging them somehow."

Lia let out an annoyed grunt. *{You do realize that they did extensive studies on this? Only if we use Taking to force an energetic stall of the synaptic processes do we risk damage to those looking on.}* Lia's eyes glowed, and Ales felt a slight desire to look away.

Lia's affinity for Taking had been well known. Among the Tier, it had been more of a legend. Unlike Ales who could make people not notice her and perhaps two others if they were close enough, Lia could make two dozen people vanish from every sense any normal person could bring to bear upon them. Ales made a minimal effort to focus, and the feeling faded.

{I want to know were we can get to in a hurry if we need to.} Lia padded out into the square and walked a meandering path towards the trees. Ales dogged her every single step. None of the hundred or so people walking about the square to shops and buildings of other import even looked in their general direction. They made it to the trees, and Lia dropped her focus on the Circle of Taking. Once they were between the trees, no one would be able to see them.

"You are impossible to deal with, do you know that, Spook?"

{Pride myself on the fact.} She put her front paws on one of the trees, her feline eyes widening as far as they would go. *{Ales, the endpoints...}* Lia found herself without words.

Ales put her hand against one of the trees, clearing her mind and allowing the synaptic connection to the trees to flow into her. She struggled to maintain her contact with the tree. The network was overwhelming. Lightleaf trees were connected to any exposed crystalline structure on the planet. They needed to be exposed to the light of the sun and to have a certain purity of molecular structure to be connected to the network. In their time, there had been perhaps four dozen endpoints in the entire world, but when she allowed the connection from the Lightleaf trees to flow into her mind, hundreds of endpoints appeared to her. It might even be thousands.

{This is my gift to you, my Daughters. I have prepared the jump network to be at your service. It is more useful than it was in your time. Take from the trees a single leaf. As long as the leaf is alive and viable, it will allow you to return to the tree you take it from as long as you can bring yourself into contact with one of the endpoint crystals.} The Father's voice in their shared mental link was startling.

{How much strain can we put on the trees before they will begin to die, Father?} Lia asked tentatively, her mindvoice concerned.

{The trees have grown here unused for three thousand cycles and more, my Daughters. Lest you begin to use the power of the trees to the same degree that they were used in your time, they will support your usage in perpetuity. We cannot direct you, but Avaara and I will do what we can to provide you with the tools to prevail. I think

that this will be the last I can provide you with without there being overwhelming consequences. However, properly utilized, it could be the solution to many future problems,} the Father's voice boomed.

Ales' face spread into a manic grin of terrifying proportions. Lia shuddered at that look. She had seen the kinds of things came out of that look. Corrupt governments had toppled after a look like that. Empires of tyrants had fallen after that smile.

{Thank you, Father. I believe this will be sufficient.} Ales practically purred.

2

Leaving the Lightleaf grove, they found their way to the street they needed. They followed it moonward into the city, about halfway to the end. Ales eyed the polished bondsteel gates and then raised a brow to Lia.

{*Should we knock or something?*} Lia asked.

Ales raised a hand.

{*You're going to break something, aren't you?*} Lia intoned suspiciously.

"Of course, not, Spook. I'll save the gratuitous destruction for some other time. Besides, it's all so breakable that it wouldn't be any fun at all. The only thing that wouldn't immediately explode if I touched it right is..." Ales waved a finger around at the wall and the house then stopped at the bondsteel gate, "the gate."

Ales carefully pushed it open and then fished in the inner pockets of her long coat for the letter. The cobblestone path lead through well-kept gardens. The front door of the house was a heavy wood bound with bondsteel. Ales narrowed her eyes at the door.

"More tree killers." She grumbled.

Lia looked up at her. {*I thought you were over this.*}

Ales just gestured wildly at the door. "It is still alive, Lia!" she growled.

{*So it is a new door. Can we move on?*} Lia's mindvoice was exasperated.

Ales stared at the door for a long moment and thought about destroying it. She could touch the right spot, and it would shatter.

{*Stop it. It is just a door,*} Lia scolded her.

Ales sighed in frustration. {*What do you expect, Lia? Are you telling me you think it is just fine to kill trees for this?*} Her mindvoice was laced in anger and frustration.

{*No, I don't, but if we want to restore our world, insults to our ways are something we must endure until they can be rectified. It isn't the time, Ales.*}

{You would think Kinas would have taught them better,} Ales growled.

{Do you see any bondstruct manufactories or builder constructs around here? No. We left them, Ales.} Lia's mindvoice was steeped in guilt.

{We left them to fend for themselves. We were chosen by our gods to protect our people, and we did our best. It wasn't enough. We gave everything to this world, but we left it in a state where it was vulnerable without us. These were some of the things they had to do without us to teach them better ways.}

Ales lifted her hand again and knocked gently on the door. They waited patiently, and after a few minutes, a young lady no older than Ilsa opened the door. She wore a simple dress of white that hung to her ankles, bound by a wide, dark green ribbon about her waist tied in a bow at the small of her back. Her lavender hair was knotted in a simple bun on the back of her head.

"Hello, young lady. I hope that we are expected here. You should have received a missive from Chief Angran of the Mizami informing the household that we would be arriving."

The young lady's deep red eyes were fixed on Liassa standing at the bottom of the stairs. She seemed stunned beyond her ability to speak. Ales waited patiently, and Lia sat down on her haunches, her ears swiveled up and forward in an attempt to look less threatening.

{Why is everyone so afraid of me? I'm not roaring or snarling. You can barely see my teeth. I even have my ears up! Three thousand cycles and I have never figured it out. I'm cute, damnit!} Lia sent, her mindvoice filled with annoyance. She wiggled her ears comically to illustrate.

{It is simpler than you seem to think. They are afraid because they can sense that you are more than you seem. It has nothing to do with your size, your claws, or your teeth. They are afraid because they know, subconsciously, that those are not the things that make you dangerous.}

"It is fine, young lady. She will not hurt you."

"Oh, I'm sorry. Yes, you are expected. You are Alessandra, and this is your... pet?" The girl's nervousness was clear in her voice.

"Her name is Liassa. We will need to speak to the Princess and Prince as soon as possible."

"Of course, Ma'am." The girl spread her dress in a little curtsey. She waved a hand for them to follow.

The inside of the house was not what Ales had expected. It contained none of the lavish decorations that she had seen in high houses in Vilhena. The walls were polished dark wood. There were paintings of beautiful landscapes in simple frames of brass decorating the walls. Some were portraits of people with the same yellow and dark blue hair that she had seen on Angran. Ales shuddered. Everywhere she looked, there was dead wood. She closed her eyes for a moment and spoke a short meditation to the Mother in her mind. She was rewarded with a feeling of warm support suffusing her from the Mother.

The girl led them between two large curving stairways. The wall between them had large doors within, which opened onto a wide hallway about ten marks long. They went through a door on the other end. This one opened into a large dining hall. Polished blue stone tiles veined with black covered the floor. Warm golden wood covered the walls. It was smooth and polished, without mark, carving, or blemish. Currently, there was a single, long table set up at the end of the dining hall. Seated at it, dressed in simple clothing, were the Prince and Princess of Clan Mizami. It was odd to Ales that they were not dressed more elaborately. Even among the Tier, your position was somewhat indicated by the way you dressed. It was never about showing your importance, unlike in Vilhena, but rather about everyone knowing who everyone else was. Help from a healer was easy to get when all healers wore their green finery when on duty. Perhaps that was just the point here. Perhaps they were not on duty.

"I present Alessandra and her pet, Liassa," intoned the girl.

The Princess had long yellow hair with highlights of blue. She was obviously the one related to Angran, as the Prince had brush-cut hair the same bright green of the feathers of a shardwing. The young lady curtseyed again, and then quickly left the room. She glanced back over her shoulder at Lia, who bared her teeth for a moment. The girl jumped and ran the rest of the way. Ales swatted at Lia, who ducked.

"Very mature," Ales chided.

"I was very mature the entire way in here. She still stared," Lia complained.

"We were not sure that Angran was telling the truth in his letter. We have told no one as per his request. That is not to say that someone carrying the letter could not have opened it, but the rider carrying the letter was a trusted member of our clan, so we think that your secret is safe for the time being. Depending on what you do, that may or may not remain true." The Prince's voice was calm enough, but his eyes were a bit wide. He put his spoon down into the soup bowl, and left it there unable to continue.

"Are there only you two?" the Princess asked.

"No, but for now, we will keep our fellows' identities to ourselves if it does not trouble you," Ales responded.

"That is your prerogative. So it is true, then? There is something wrong here in our clan home?" the princess asked.

"Might we sit?"

"Of course, of course. Apologies for our rudeness. I am Eilee, and this is Bahram. Please make yourselves comfortable."

"Thank you," Ales said. She pulled a chair away from the table and seated herself. Lia sat down next to Ales' chair, putting her head and shoulders above the table. With Ales sitting down, they were almost the same height.

"The Chief said in his letter that you would explain the trouble when you got here, and we should provide you with all assistance," Bahram indicated.

"And we will," said Lia. The pair clearly had prepared themselves well for the idea of one of the Wild, as they had no drastic reaction to her speaking. It warmed Lia to know that at least some people in this time would respect her for who she was instead of thinking of her only as an animal.

"We believe that one of the clans has acquired a relic from our time called The Probability Matrix. It was a device that had a limited ability to accurately predict future events. We believe that they are using this device to attempt to sway the movements and decisions of the Ryhim as a whole. Unfortunately, they are unlikely to realize that using the device in such a way will eventually cause catastrophic events to unfold all around them. When it was first invented, we thought to use it to prevent loss of life due to natural disasters, or to diffuse situations where war could result. It was a terrible mistake.

The device, when used to pursue a specific goal, causes an imbalance in the natural order of things. You will achieve your goal, but everything related to that goal that is not absolutely essential to its achievement will be pushed aside," Lia explained. Every Tier knew the story of the Probability Matrix, but very few of them actually studied the function of the machine. It was one of their greatest failures, and most of them attempted to avoid it.

"I'm not sure I understand. We sway events all the time with goals in mind. How come it doesn't do the same thing?" Eilee asked.

"It does, but not to the same degree. The Probability Matrix predicts the future in the same way you or I make decisions. When you are deciding where each of the clans will go at the next Rotation. you take into consideration as much information about all of the lands of the Ryhim as you can before deciding where it is best to send each Clan, do you not?" continued Lia.

"Of course. We would not send our clan stoneward if the reports from other clans were that the herds are not moving in those areas for instance," Bahram replied.

"Well, the Probability Matrix works the same way, but it has access to every single piece of information possible within a certain area. If it is centered here in your city, it knows everything that happens within the entire span of the forest, and then some beyond. Its knowledge is absolute, right down to the thoughts in your head and the decisions you make, as you make them. That is how it predicts the future. Give it a goal, and it will calculate exactly what needs to happen to achieve that goal, but it gives no thought to the side effects of what needs to be done to achieve that goal. If your goal were to destroy one of the clans, it would tell you how. It would not tell you how that would affect the other clans," Ales explained.

"Why would you ever build such an awful device?" Eilee asked, concern clear in her voice.

"Because in the right hands, used with proper restraint, such a device can do immense good. You have to use it in such a way that you are making the decisions rather than allowing it to make the decisions for you," Lia emphasized.

"I think that I do not envy you your positions," Eilee uttered quietly.

"That is actually quite odd to us, M'lady," Ales said.

"In our time, it was considered an extreme honor to be invited into our family. It is not an easy life, but we know we are doing good in the world," Lia explained.

"And some of you end up as animals?" Bahram asked carefully, knowing that he was asking a delicate question.

"What sort of answer are you looking for to that question, M'lord?" Lia asked evenly, without emotion.

"I'm not sure what you mean."

"I mean, you are not asking what you really want to know, because you are certain I will not tell you."

"Would you tell us how a katali became one of the Tier?"

"It is more accurate to say that one of the Tier became a katali, but that is a sad story thousands of cycles old," Ales said.

"I will tell it in exchange for a story from you. Tell us, if you can, how the art of using the Lightleaf trees was lost." Lia inquired.

3

Ilsa watched the guards patrolling the border of the massive field of semi-permanent structures that the locals called a camp. The word "camp" was clearly an understatement -- there had to be at least twenty thousand buildings standing in the foothills of the mountains. The Trasal Mountains comprised one of the most unforgiving environments on the continent. Traditionally, the Ryhim avoided the peaks as the mountains were unstable. While it was likely that mining the area would produce a large supply of rare minerals that could bring great wealth to Ryhim, the mountains had long been considered far too dangerous to mine. According to Angran, even Clan Navano, whose houses contained some of the most skilled miners and metal workers, had maintained for generations that mining here was suicide. The mountain range had many areas with open magma vents, and the ground shifted regularly due to tectonic activity. The mountains raised at least a few ticks a cycle as the tectonic plate that the continent sat on smashed itself into the one beneath the ocean on the far side.

Ilsa looked to Kiltik where they lay in the grass, "How do you think we should approach them? I somehow feel like you might frighten them."

"This One can change This One's form more completely. This One simply does not enjoy This One's appearance when This One takes a more realistic shape. Those ones will dismiss This One if This One appears only to be your pet. However, to be clear, This One would not be able to easily communicate if those ones think that This One is your pet."

"I think that for the time being, it is better if they do not know. They are already going to know that I am one of the Tier from my eyes. I can't hide them. I think that knowing that you are something out of legends they never heard of will be a little overwhelming. We don't want to throw so much at them all at once."

"This One concurs. What shape should This One take?"

"Can you make your body smaller?"

"This One can reduce This One's volume by twenty two cubic measures."

"Kiltik, please, I am still learning. Simplify?" Ilsa grumbled.

"Apologies. This One can become smaller by one half of This One's current size."

"Well, then you can take the shape of a hiluk, or..." Ilsa trailed off as she looked at Kiltik. "Actually, can you make fur?"

"This One can replicate fur or hair of any kind."

"Better for this area. A shuvoo. You know what that is?"

"This One is unfamiliar with the name of this animal. Can you describe it to This One?" Kiltik's speech patterns were improving, but he still hadn't much idea of how to use the first person.

Ilsa did not reply for a long moment. Shuvoo were smallish canid creatures that the Ryhim valued for their fearlessness and exceptional hearing. There were always at least a half dozen of the creatures with the various guards who kept the borders of their camps secure. After a moment, she saw one with red-spotted white fur. Its fur was long, hiding many of its features. The Shuvoo's ears were large enough that they seemed far too large for the size of its head. Adding to the size mismatch was a too-short muzzle with canine teeth long enough that they showed even with its mouth closed. The little animals had a wicked bite, and they would protect their masters with their lives.

Ilsa gestured towards it. "There. That is a shuvoo. Can you get that small? They only weight about fifteen sphere. You weigh much more than that."

"This One can shed weight to match the size of that animal if This One finds it necessary. However, This One's body is mostly empty space." With that, Kiltik began to shrink. His katali form melted away into that of an animal with black fur broken up by bright lavender spots. The spots, though, were perfectly symmetrical.

"Can you make your spots a little more random? Your symmetry is a little too perfect to be real," Ilsa suggested.

Kiltik bobbed his head, and the spots slid across his fur like water sliding across a piece of glass. One of the two spots surrounding his eyes vanished, leaving one eye surrounded in purple and one without.

"Let's go," Ilsa said as she stood up from where they had been hiding, making her way onto the road. As she moved, Ilsa's outfit swished, a sound caught all too easily by Kiltik's new ears. The ankle-length yellow skirt and white button up top was common among women of the Navano.

"This One's new levels of hearing are most annoying. Hearing is vastly improved due to the structure surrounding the auditory canal upon This One's head. This One can hear your skirts as if they were inside of This One's head," Kiltik complained.

"I'm sorry this is uncomfortable for you, Kiltik. Please remember not to speak once we are inside of the camp. Can you study the creatures there so that you can match their mannerisms?" Ilsa tried to move more smoothly for Kiltik's benefit.

"This One has already begun. This One believes that This One can replicate the sounds quite accurately." Kiltik said, before making a small growling sound followed by a bark. He kept the volume low enough that only Ilsa would hear. It was very close to the sounds that the real animal made.

"Good. If you need to warn me of something, make that sound. If you believe my life to be in danger, you can reveal yourself. I would rather be alive and have to explain what you are than take a bolt in the back," Ilsa advised.

"This One will defend you as necessary, Ilsa Family Katane."

Ilsa stopped on the road. The patrols had spotted them, but they waited for her to approach. "Why did you call me that? That's not my family's name."

"It is. Among the Tier, new Tier from the outside are supported by one of the already-existing Tieran families, of which there were hundreds. Traditionally, the new Tier would take on the family name of the family who spoke for them. Ales and Liassa brought you among the Tier.

Therefore, you are their sister, and a member of their family," Kiltik explained carefully.

"I didn't think that they meant it so literally." Ilsa began to walk again, and Kiltik trotted to keep up with her.

"Originally, there were under one hundred of the Tier – one from each race, creed, and sentient species that existed at the time of their origins. Once they were told that new Tier would not be born but chosen, they realized that if the Tier were to feel as if they were one, then new members would need to be made family. Truly family. You have not been through the family bonding yet, but you are our sister. They would treat you as such."

Ilsa realized that they had indeed treated all of them as if they were family. They had shared everything as soon as they could, and when one of the men among the Ryhim had been too forward with Ilsa, Liassa had come out of nowhere and scared the man nearly out of his skin, just like she would have expected a sibling to do. Ilsa and Kiltik finally moved close enough for the guard to hear them and hail them. Kiltik went silent.

"Whoa, stranger. What is your business with Clan Navano?"

The guard's eyes were dark, but Ilsa thought they were either brown or perhaps golden in color. Both guards wore hide armor over padded green coats and pants. Their boots were covered with black bondsteel disks, as were their gloves. They must have traded for worked bondsteel to make those. As far as she knew, they didn't have any way to make bondsteel anywhere outside of Vilhena. She looked up at the man.

"I am Ilsa of the Tier. I am here to speak with Triane, Chief of the Navano." Ilsa focused on her Tieran abilities and after a moment, her eyes began to glow faintly. The man stepped back quickly. She let the glow fade from her eyes and presented him with her most pleasant smile.

"I do not wish to frighten you, sir. I simply did not wish you to mistakenly believe that I am not who I say I am," Ilsa explained.

Kiltik sat quietly next to her, his tongue lolling out as he panted. She realized that he was almost indistinguishable from a real shuvoo now. It was amazing how quickly he had picked up the behaviors of the little animals. It hadn't been more than ten minutes. He noticed she was looking at him, and winked at her so quickly that if she hadn't known better, she'd have missed it.

"Will you please wait here?" requested the guard.

Ilsa thought it strange how quickly his mannerisms changed once he knew she was one of the Tier. However, she thought, she was, after all, a legend standing right in front of them. "I will."

The guard who hadn't spoken ran off into the camp.

"I was not frightened, only surprised," the remaining guard faltered.

Ilsa just grinned at him, "Of course you were. I just walked out of legend, glowing eyes and all, and cuffed you aside the head. You were going to be one or the other. I did apologize."

The guard blushed blue, then coughed and turned away from her. Kiltik gave her an odd look, as if he had no idea what was wrong with the young man. She knelt down and scratched Kiltik's head between his ears.

"I embarrassed him. He doesn't think he should be scared of a girl my age, let alone, one my size. I also think he likes me. At least, he likes the look of me," Ilsa explained in a whisper.

"This One does not yet fully understand This One's own emotions. This One does not comprehend the meaning of feeling embarrassed," Kiltik whispered back.

"It means that he feels awkward. Widely-held belief tells him that he should not fear me. He is, however, still afraid because his instincts tell him that my powers make me far more dangerous than someone my size and age should be." She stopped when she noticed that he was watching her out of the corner of her eye.

"Something wrong with me telling my shuvoo how patient and good he is being?" Ilsa asked aloud.

"No, ma'am," the young man responded stiffly.

The other guard came back through the crowd, moving much more slowly this time. With him, there was an older woman, about thirty cycles in age. Her light gray eyes peered out from beneath her faded purple hair. While her dress made her appear plump, her movements told Ilsa that there was no fat on this woman – she was powerful, both in bearing and physical endowment. She stopped in front of Ilsa and waved the guards away. They went reluctantly, obviously thinking that their leader should have kept them in case Ilsa meant her harm.

"You are what, twelve cycles? And they expect me to believe you to be one of the Tier?" Tirane narrowed her eyes, watching Ilsa. Ilsa bowed to Tirane just as Angran had taught her – she spread her skirts and bent at the waist briefly. It was a respectful gesture among the Navano.

"I did not come here to dance for you, Chief Tirane. I respect you, but realize that I demand respect as well. I am of the Tier. Question that at your own peril," Ilsa chided. She had only been one of the Tier for a cycle, but a cycle under Ales' tutelage had made her the equal of any ten men in a fight. It would be worse if she used the more advanced powers of her Vision to see the weaknesses in the things around her. She would not do so, however, unless her life were truly threatened.

Tirane snorted. It was an arrogant sound, but Ilsa could tell that Tirane was trying to bait her. Angran had told her that Tirane was an extremely skilled fighter, and had an excellent military mind. She defended her people with the minimum effort needed for maximum effect when outsiders tried to invade their lands.

"I am Chief here, girl, and I earned my place. Speaking to me like that is unwise," Tirane challenged, her eyes narrow.

"Chief Tirane, I have not come to be baited by your false bravado. I will not be drawn into a fight that will embarrass both of us, you more than me. Angran warned me that you would attempt something like this. I am not a threat to your people. Much to the contrary, I am here to attempt to help all of the Ryhim," Ilsa rebuked, barring her teeth in something that barely resembled a smile.

"Well you have a spine, girl. I'll say that." Finally, the woman made a preemptory gesture to follow, and walked away into the camp without another word. Ilsa looked down at Kiltik. He shrugged his little shoulders in a very human gesture, and trotted off behind the Chief. Ilsa followed as well.

4

"I will look like a Father-Cursed fool!" Cole growled as he examined the outfit that Angran's wife Tulan had brought for him.

"You look like an outsider to the Byranti. They have very strict rules about how outsiders are to dress when among them. The guards will not let you pass in your normal garb," Tulan explained.

Cole's eyes, one amber, one deep red, moved to her from the garment she was holding. Both eyes brightened with internal light as he looked over her. "They will let me pass regardless."

"True, but they will trust you more if you simply wear this."

Cole thought about it for a long moment. "You are probably right, Tulan, but I think I must decline your advice in this case. I think it is important that they know I am an outsider, and that I am outside of their rule. If I follow requests such as these, then they will feel they can simply ignore me."

"This is unwise. The Byranti elders are extremely conservative about the clan's traditions, and their tradition is that all outsiders must dress in approved garb," Tulan rebuked.

"Perhaps, but what do their traditions say of one of the Tier? How are they going to react to seeing one of us?" Cole asked. He began to put things into his pack.

"I'm not sure. The Byranti are the most skeptical of the histories. They believe only in their own traditions. They are solitary. Their clan is the smallest of the Ryhim, but they are one of the most powerful, because they make all of our medicines," Tulan said.

"Maybe that is the key to whatever it is they are doing. Ales seems to think that their part in this is the most important." Cole started putting on his padded hide armor.

"Do you always wear that?"

"For now, I do. There is bondsteel mail sandwiched between the hide and padding. It's quiet, and strong enough to stop a lancer bolt as long as it's not from a longbarrel. It will also stop a sword or a knife."

"Lancers are not common outside of Vilhena," Tulan pondered.

"Do you have one?" Cole asked.

"We keep more than a few," Tulan admitted.

"Exactly. It would be stupid of me not to wear it for comfort's sake, thinking that no one has a lancer just because they are uncommon."

"I meant more that it must be hard to be afraid for your life all the time like that." Tulan folded the robe she had brought with her, and put it on top of his pack. "In case you change your mind, honored Tier." She made her odd, bowing curtsey and slipped quietly out of the tent.

Cole grunted. He had insulted the woman by not taking her advice, and he felt like an idiot. It didn't matter that he was right. He had asked her to advise him. She had done so, and he had ignored her. He stared into the reflection of his eyes in the mirror, wondering if he had really changed or if he was still the same thief he had been a cycle ago at the fall of Vilhena.

"You're not," Warran said as he came bustling into the tent. He was fiddling with some small piece of complex machinery. His eyes were glowing brightly as he examined the thing critically. He reached into a tool pouch on his bed and took something out of it without looking. He jammed it into the little metal collection of gears and springs and began twisting it viciously.

"Can you stop that?" Cole asked.

"Sorry. It's hard not to see your thoughts. You live in the now. Everything is on the surface of your mind." Warran held up the device to the light. He turned it one way, then the other. "You are not the same person you were a cycle ago. The Cole I knew would never have done the things you've done."

"What in the abyss are you building?"

"I'm not sure."

"You're building it. How can you not know what it is?"

"Because this is something that no one has ever attempted to do before. I don't even know if it's possible."

"Then I guess the better question would be, what are you attempting to do?"

Warran opened his mouth to answer then closed it again without saying a word. Cole eyed him for a long moment.

"I wouldn't understand, would I?"

"I'm trying to find a way to explain it that you can understand. You know I don't think you're stupid, Cole. Even I don't understand everything I am doing. I believe there may be some divine intervention involved here."

"Box it for me?" Cole pressed.

"We think that this Intruder is some sort of machine intelligence like a Tieran Mind, but gone horribly wrong. I am building a device that will give off energetic pulses that can disable that machine intelligence. The issue is that it must be calibrated to affect only the Intruder. If I don't calibrate it properly, it could be devastating to Ales and Lia. Us, too, if I finish rebuilding Verdant first," Warran explained.

"How is she coming along?"

"It's hard to say. The device that Kiltik gave me for communicating with the Bondstructs telepathically is wondrous, but their minds are not like ours. It is hard to get a read on what they are doing and how far along they are in the process. I can only give them the instructions for the next step, and wait for them to notify me that they are ready for the next set of instructions. Building a system of synapses that apes an organic mind is an extremely complex process. It's like a jumbled net of hundreds of millions of wires suspended in a substrate that absorbs the discharge of electrical signals from those wires, and creates a semi-permanent pattern that can then be read by reactivating the wires in that area again. They can also be reset when memories are no longer needed by sending an opposing charge along those same wires.

That's an extremely simplistic explanation of what actually goes into building a Tieran mind, but again, even I don't understand all of what I'm doing. I'm simply acting as a relay for the information. Consider that we are on step five thousand thirty seven in a process containing seventy thousand or so steps. We usually finish between two and three hundred steps in a day. I would say it should be done in about seven rotations."

Warran eyed Cole, who had thrown his head back and was snoring softly. As soon as Warran trailed off, Cole's head snapped forward and he snorted.

"Why do I even bother with you? Obviously, The Father mistakenly filled that empty space between your ears with rocks instead of brains," Warran scathed.

"Honestly, Brother, I find it fascinating, but I don't think I am ever going to understand it like you do. So, I'll just do the dirty work so you can do the important work that I always knew you were meant to do," Cole said, before standing up and patting Warran on the shoulder. He shoved the robes that Tulan had left for him into his pack. Then, he shouldered the pack, and disappeared through the tent flaps.

Shortly after, Kayna wandered in through the same flaps. She looked up at her father.

"You hear all that?" Warran asked.

Kayna nodded. "If you're having trouble communicating, why didn't Kiltik stay and help rebuild Verdant?" Warran suspected she was far too intelligent for her own good.

"Because he's worried that if he leaves himself open to the degree necessary for him to communicate with the Core Fragment that contains Verdant's plans, he may be infected by the Intruder. Without Cellstructs, and because of our organic natures, that's impossible if we're the ones doing the rebuilding. Also, he said that the substrate had to be handled by living human hands to impart the proper elementary force charges to awaken a new Mind to life." Warran was concerned that he might have answered her in a way that she wouldn't understand.

Kayna thought for a long moment. "So he's worried he'll get sick if he does it, but you can't get sick from doing it."

"Yes, little one." He looked at the small table in the corner where Verdant's new shell was taking shape. "Would you like to help?"

Kayna looked at the shell too. "I don't know, Daddy. This is..." Her expression turned worried.

"Important?" Warran supplied. She nodded. He ruffled her hair affectionately.

"That's why I want you to help, Midget, because I think that someday you're going to be even better at this than I am. Besides, you've been watching me use this thing for a span solid. I know you want to try."

Warran unsnapped the thin silver bracelet from his wrist. It flowed like liquid mercury. The arms retracted in upon themselves until a polished silver marble sat in the palm of his hand. He fished the Core Fragment out of his pouch.

"Now just touch the bracelet to your wrist," Warran said.

Kayna turned the marble this way and that before doing as he said. The silver flowed out until it closed around her wrist with a click.

"Now, think about the next step in building Verdant and touch the fragment." Warran said as he held out the Core Fragment.

Kayna put her tiny hand on top of it. Her eyes went wide, and she pulled her hand away as if it burned her.

"It's alive!" She squeaked. Warran grinned, and Kayna stuck her tongue out at him.

"Yes, it is. Just remember if you don't tell it what you want, it's going to try and tell you everything it knows. So remember to think about what you want," Warran reminded. Kayna nodded, and then put her little hand on the fragment again.

"Oh, it's telling me how to explain to the bondstructs that the neural netting must be laid down in a random, non-repeating pattern."

"Oh Gods, Warran is that your daughter or your clone?" Cole's voice came from outside of the tent.

"You're just pissed because she's only a third your age and has twice your brains," Warran shot back in a sing-song tone.

A raspberry noise came from outside and trailed off as Cole walked away.

"Don't listen to him, Midget, you're perfect just the way you are."

"I know, Daddy." She grinned up at him. "Even Uncle Cole says so. When's he going to be back?"

"I don't know, Muchkin. There's a lot to do, but don't worry. Your Uncle Cole'll take really good care of himself," Warran soothed. Kayna took her hand off the fragment and watched Verdant's outer shell slowly merge closed at the top.

"The cube says the next step will take a few days." She held up her wrist with the bracelet.

"Keep it on, Muchkin. This is your job now. Think you can do it?"

She looked at the bracelet for a long moment before nodding her head. "I can do it, Daddy."

He put the Core Fragment in her tiny hands, "Keep it safe little one."

"I got a real good hiding spot for it. It'll be safe."

"I know it will." Warran said before opening the tent flaps and stepping outside.

"Is that wise, Honored Tier?" Angran asked. He was leaning against the tree next to the entrance of the tent. Warran held up his hand and shook his sleeve down, revealing another of the polished silver bracelets. He walked away from the tent.

"She is the next generation of the Tier, Angran, and I would take no chances with the life of my daughter in any case. As long as we are both wearing one of these, I know everything that is happening within a hundred marks of her through the power of my Vision," Warran said.

"But like all children, if you were to tell her that she would be unlikely to be happy about it," Angran chuckled.

"Of course she wouldn't. But unlike most parents, I also don't feel the need to scold her for every childish indiscretion. She is a child, and if I don't allow her to make some mistakes on her own, she'll never grow into the person she's meant to be. So, there's no danger of her finding out what I'm doing because I'll never feel the need to reveal it simply to satisfy a parent's protective nature," Warran explained.

"That is far more rational than most parents are capable of being concerning their children," Angran observed.

"I like to think I do well in that area. I need a more permanent space to work in, Angran."

"So Antieri Ales has informed me. I believe we have a place such as that."

"Cole is on his way, and with everyone else gone, it is time I got to work. Here is a list of materials I am going to need. Also, I will need an assistant to help me with my work. It must be a Fixer."

Warran held out a piece of paper. Angran took it from him.

"I will see it taken care of. Near the center of our territory, there is a storage structure built into a cave that we use for resupplying when any of our hunters are too far from the main camp to make it back. There is also a small semi-permanent camp nearby. There is more than enough space there for you to work, and only a few people know its location, which makes it ideal for your needs."

Warran fiddled with his lancer belt and pulled out a small cloth packet. He pulled a small, shining black disk out of it. Angran eyed it for a long moment.

"You know what this is?" Warran asked. Angran nodded.

"Powerful medicine. The Byranti would pay a fortune for it. How did you get so much?"

"I haven't the slightest idea. Ales gave it to me. She said it should be more than enough to cover any expenses you or I might incur."

"I agree."

Warran pushed the disk back into the cloth packet and held it out to the clan chief. He took it, and tucked it carefully into the pack hanging at his side.

"Angran, once we're gone, if anyone comes looking for us, be careful. I would not have you tell them anything if you can avoid it, but do not risk your people to defend us."

Angran stopped walking, and turned to Warran.

"Honored Tier, you have told me that the very balance of our world may rest on your success. I will protect my people, but I would not be much of a leader if I were to stand by and refuse you any aid you need."

Angran bowed, and Warran mirrored the respectful gesture.

"Thank you. We will leave as soon as those supplies can be collected," Warran said.

"Wind at your back, Honored Tier," said Angran.

"Father's Luck to you, Angran," Warran responded.

5

"The Lightleaf trees have been a mystery for centuries. The story goes that when Kinas left us, he took the knowledge of how to use the Trees with him, but if you have access to the royal libraries, you will find that the story is far more detailed. Kinas taught many of the Ryhim how to use the trees, and he taught us about the magic of the Nexus. As I am sure you know, the lands in this area change rapidly every few cycles, which is why the system of clans was established. The herds move, the plants change, the minerals shift beneath the land, so each of our clans has an area of expertise. Mizami manages the herds and crops. Navano are the miners and metal workers, so on and so forth. Much of the Wilds was seeded with exposed crystal so that we could easily move our clans to the areas where they needed to be, to continue producing a living.

However, after Kinas passed on, those of us who were skilled in using the trees to perform light jumps began to lose the talent for it. Less and less were the people able to sense anything when they touched the trees. We thought that perhaps it was because we did not tend the grove properly, or maybe that there was some secret that Kinas did not reveal to us because he did not think we would be responsible with such power. Regardless, as the number of people who could use the trees dwindled, the ability left us completely. We could not find any other children who could hear the call of the trees.

When it became apparent that we could no longer use the trees for travel, our lives became much more difficult. As we had depended on them as a way to keep track of the magical movements of our supplies, an enterprise in scouting such things sprang up right away. We really have no idea why the talent faded. We just know that it did," Eilee explained.

Ales rubbed her chin in thought and mumbled, "Belief."

"Hmm?" Eilee looked curious.

"You stopped believing. The magic of the Nexus is something that is natural. It is part of the Mother's connection to this world. You don't have to believe in her for that magic to continue to function, but the Lightleaf trees are different. They are a magic that comes from the Father, but they don't just teleport people at random. They aren't a functioning system unto themselves. You are calling to the Father for aid when you use their magic. They are inexorably tied to your belief in the Father. When your people stopped believing, the ability started to fade," Ales elucidated.

"But we know they worked in the past."

"Knowledge and Belief are two very different things. The trees worked because you believed in the Father, and by believing in the Father, his magic would hear your call. Without that belief, the connection does not exist. Knowing that the trees worked is not nearly the same as believing that when you reach out to the magic of the Trees, the Father will be there to answer."

"Can you use the trees?"

"Of course we can. We are of the Tier. Even the youngest of the Tier has an undeniable connection to the Gods," Ales explained

"You said that no one is born one of the Tier," Bahram prompted.

"We did, and they are not. We have children, and they almost always became Tier, but until they were old enough to choose, they only lived among the Tier. Becoming one of the Tier must be a choice," Ales continued.

"And how young does one make that decision?" Eilee wondered.

"Some of us younger than others," Ales confided with a small smile.

"But never until we were ready," Lia added. "Ales made that choice when she was eight, but I didn't choose until I was almost twelve cycles old. Some Tier did not come to us until they were much older – sometimes even as old as fifty cycles. Some children left us and never became Tier, though that was rare."

"So we could learn to use the Lightleaf trees again?" Eilee asked.

"You can, but it would require many many more of your people to believe with you. Our power as Tier is a little piece of the Mother and the Father. It is a power that is hard won, over many cycles of training. For you to be able to do the same thing, the Father must be able to spread the power out over many people. Otherwise, the damage could be deadly," Ales warned.

"And anyone can become one of the Tier?" Bahram asked.

"Yes and no. Everyone has the potential to become one of us, but it requires a certain state of mind. You have to be a very specific type of person, which is why even at our height, there was only one Tier for every four hundred or so people," Lia explained.

Bahram and Eilee exchanged an excited look.

"Still, it could be done. We could not only revive our lost belief, but restore the travel routes," Eilee blurted excitedly.

"Let's not get ahead of ourselves. You must understand that our world is very much out of balance. We would be overjoyed to see your people renew their connection with the gods, but that is not our purpose right now. We are too few to be starting revolutions just yet. We need time to bring Balance," Ales hedged.

"Then what is it that you need from us?" Eilee probed.

"Access. We need to see all the information passing from the Center to the clans – not just your clan, but all the clans. Angran said that you could point us in the right direction."

"All of the clans issue information to our outriding groups through the Central Office of Scouts. Our suggestions are reviewed against the most recent information before they are passed along to a scout for delivery. Only the heads of the scouts are privy to all of the orders from all of the clans. We could speak to them on your behalf," Bahram suggested. He finally seemed to realize that he had been eating when they started. He lifted his spoon, but put it back down when he realized the soup had gone cold.

Lia turned to Ales, and they exchanged a look. *{We can't pull them into this. We know where to start looking. We can just* *slip inside, and memorize the information.}* Lia spoke through their telepathic link.

"No, that will not be necessary. We can get the information without any further assistance. What we need now is just a place to sleep. We do not wish to stay here, but if you could recommend a place to stay?"

"What do you mean?" Eilee said.

"That is what we were afraid of. There actually are no wayhouses here, are there?" Ales asked.

"What is a wayhouse?" Bahram wondered.

"Gods, you never actually travel beyond your borders, do you? How do you have lancers but not know about wayhouses?" Lia uttered.

"No, we do not. We have everything we need within the borders of the Wilds. If we trade with outsiders, it is done by the outriders," Eilee shared.

"Nevermind, it isn't important. Are there any places in the city that the clan owns that are not in use right now?" Ales queried.

"Yes, the late-season storehouses are empty. Plenty of room," Bahram mused after a moment of thought.

"Is it a crowded area of the city?" Ales asked.

"Unfortunately, yes. It is a busy area near the outskirts of the city," Bahram affirmed, thinking they would be looking for someplace that would be isolated.

"No, that is perfect. It's much easier for people to lose us in a crowd," Ales stated.

"They won't be used for rotations yet, but they won't be very comfortable," Eilee said.

"You realize I spend most nights sleeping on a rock in the woods?" Lia lilted.

"Oh." Eilee's face was hard to interpret.

"No need to feel pity for me, Eilee. I knew I would be sleeping in trees and on rocks for the rest of my life when I chose this. The fur coat helps," Lia smirked.

"We will be just fine. Sleeping rough is not much of an inconvenience for an Arcangineer," Ales confirmed.

Eilee picked up a small silver bell from the table and rang it. The girl who had guided them to the dining room came scurrying in.

"Shia, paper and pen please," Eilee requested.

"Yes, ma'am," Shia affirmed. She left the room and came back in a few moments.

"The warehouse is near the sunward gate on Kiln Street. It has been locked for a rotation, but we have the guards check it out regularly. We will tell them that we are setting up some new thread makers in there to keep them from doing any checking," Bahram said.

"That would work perfectly. If you need to contact us, do not come to the warehouse. It could be dangerous if anyone sees you visiting. Eventually, whoever it is that is using the Probability Matrix will know who we are and where we are staying. It is likely that they will attempt to get rid of us. We can defend ourselves from such attempts, but with the Probability Matrix at their disposal, you would not be able to," Ales instructed.

She did not want anyone else getting hurt. Her instinctive desire to protect was running high. She knew that whoever was doing this was linked to the Intruder somehow, which meant they would have no regard for the lives of any who opposed them.

"Won't they know about this meeting?" Eilee asked. Clearly, she was concerned, but Ales did not think it was with the well-being of herself or her mate. No, she was concerned with the safety of her House.

"No. Our presence shields this area from the Probability Matrix. Not only that, the matrix is a black box. If they don't ask it the right questions, they will never know that there is a new danger to their operations," Lia reassured.

"Instead, if you need our attention, take this and hang it from your doorknob. We will know that you need us," Ales instructed, holding up a glimmering silver ball attached to a thin chain. She stood up from the table. They had a lot of work to do.

"Eilee, Bahram, thank you so much for your trust and help. We will do everything we can to help set things straight here." Lia said. She stood up, and stretched as only a predator can.

"Um… Before you go, is there anything that you can suggest we should do to help people believe in the gods again?" Eilee wondered.

"Do you believe, Eilee?" Ales probed. Eilee opened her mouth to speak, then paused and closed it again.

"That is where you start," Ales said, and followed Lia out of the room.

~ END OF PART 1 ~

"SEER"

6

Mina watched the cart go by, piled high with bluedrops. She licked her lips nervously, and fussed with her yellow skirts. She didn't need to steal one of those bluedrops, but she definitely wanted to, mostly to see if she could. She pulled up her skirts to her knees and ran after the cart. There were two large men riding with it, which gave her pause for a moment, but they weren't looking around at all.

Mina had almost caught up with it when she saw the woman. The woman seemed taller than she actually was, and had light blue hair that hung in a long braid to the middle of her back. Walking next to her was a massive Katali with fur the same color as her hair. Mina slowed to a stop to stare at the woman as she strode by. Mina had no idea why, but she was more fascinated by the woman than by the massive animal striding along beside her. Mina dropped her skirts and started to follow the tall woman through the crowd.

{There is a girl following us,} Lia noted telepathically as they neared the sunward gate.

{I saw her. She started following us after we passed that fruit cart with the bluedrops,} Ales replied.

{And why are we letting her follow us?}

They turned the corner onto Kiln Street.

{I'm not sure yet. I have a feeling we should meet this girl.}

Lia looked over her shoulder discretely to eye the girl.

{Oh, not her, Ales. She can't be more than six cycles old.}

{Same age as I was, Lia.}

{And you were the youngest ever by almost five cycles. She's just a curious little girl,} Lia said hopefully.

{I don't think so, Spook.}

Ales walked past the warehouse where they had been aimed and headed towards the sunward gate. She turned left down the alleyway between their new home and the building beside it. She stopped a few paces into the alleyway. Lia passed her and sat down behind her. They waited a few short moments before the girl came around the corner. She stopped short when she saw them waiting for her and immediately began to turn around.

"A moment, little one?" Lia said. Mina saw her speak, and froze. She turned slowly back and lifted a shaking hand to point at Lia.

"Did that katali just talk?" Her voice was small and quiet.

"She did. Against her better judgement," Lia replied.

"Don't listen to my sister. She's an ill-tempered monster. Come here, child. We won't hurt you. Why were you following us?" Ales noted the girl's fine dress. Clearly, she was not a child of average means.

"I don't know. I just saw you, and you looked different," Mina mumbled. Lia groaned and stormed away down the alley, grumbling to herself. Ales just smiled as she watched her go.

"Why is she so cranky?" Mina asked.

"Oh, don't worry about her. She's cranky because she was hoping I was wrong about you. Might I ask your name?"

Mina looked at her suspiciously for a moment.

"My name is Mina, and I'm the princess and scion of Clan Clai," she announced in a very proper, crisp voice.

"Hello, Mina. I am Alessandra of the Tier. Aren't you a little young to be out here on your own?"

Mina's face developed a very sour look.

"If I didn't lose my minders every now and then, I wouldn't ever have any fun at all. It would be books and writing and manners every day forever." Mina pretended a vomiting noise, and pointed her finger down her throat.

"I understand, but don't you think that maybe your minders just mean for you to know things so that eventually you'll be able to take care of yourself?"

Mina's sour look deepened.

"I suppose," Mina admittedly grumpily. Her cornflower yellow eyes darted up to Ales' face.

"You're not going to make me go back, are you?" She looked like she might dart away. Ales just grinned.

"No, because you're right. Sometimes, you need to have a little fun. But doesn't everyone recognize you in that dress?"

Ales realized that the color of the dress matched the girl's eyes. Mina looked at her dress, oblivious as to how much it made her stand out. It was a confection of yellow fabric with white frills and plenty of pink bows. The short sleeves were puffy and seemed to float around her arms. Petticoats beneath the skirt made it billow out like a bell around the girl's legs.

"No one usually notices." She shrugged.

The fact that she not only had noticed something different about them, but had also been drawn to follow them spoke to her potential to be one of the Tier. But her ability to move through a crowd in a dress so brightly colored and obviously expensive without notice made it clear that she had the unconscious skill of the Taker. Ales knelt down closer to the girl's eye level, though her less-than-tall height made her slightly shorter than the girl.

"Mina, do you know why Lia and I seemed so different to you?"

Mina shook her head.

"How much do you know about the Tier?"

"Just the stories in the house library. Old, old books that they don't let us touch. The bookminders read them to us with white gloves on."

"What do you think of the Tier in those old stories?"

The girl's eyes went wide as she started to realize where Ales was going.

"The stories say that they were heroes, but the bookminders say that the Tier are just old stories. And even if they aren't, they abandoned us to fend for ourselves. They took all of their magical secrets with them when they went." Ales nodded.

"But that's what your teachers told you. What do you think?"

"I think they were magic, and they did amazing things, but maybe the minders are right about them. They took their magic with them. Why didn't they teach it to us?"

Ales nodded once more.

"A good question, Mina. We did try to teach people about our magic, but magic requires a certain ability to believe in things, not just know them. Knowing is not enough. And lots of the Ryhim don't believe in things magical anymore." Ales hoped that the girl's noble upbringing would give her the mental facility to understand.

"What are we supposed to believe in?" Mina asked.

"Once, long ago, your people believed in the Gods. I would hope you would again," Ales explained.

"Father and Mother said that there are no Gods, that they are just stories like the Tier."

"Well, Mina, I can tell you that the Tier are quite real, as I am one of them, and if you want, you can be one too."

The girl's bright yellow eyes widened as she looked into Ales' two-color eyes.

"If you are a Tier, can you show me some magic?" Mina asked. Ales laughed at her obvious eagerness.

"Alright, alright."

Ales stood up and looked around the alleyway until her eyes found a window in the side of the warehouse. She raised a hand, her index finger outstretched. She reached out to one of the window panes. She touched it, and it exploded into fine dust. Ales drew her hand back so quickly that the void where it had been created a vacuum, pulling the dust into the space it vacated. The compact ball of sand fell into her hand. Ales looked down to Mina, her eyes glowing brightly with magical illumination. Then she turned her head and blew the dust off of her hand. Mina's eyes had gone almost impossibly wide. Ales laughed at the wonder in the girl's eyes. She hadn't seen a look like that on anyone's face in a long time.

"And I can do that?" Mina said, awe clear in her voice.

"Maybe. I can tell you what your talents might be if you choose to be one of the Tier, but for that, I would rather you come inside with me. It will make you queasy for a few moments." Ales moved to the warehouse door, unlocked it, and pushed it open.

"I don't know if that's a good idea," Mina said cautiously.

"Mina, I promise we mean you no harm, but if you feel that you are not safe, I invite you to bring me to your home. I will introduce myself to your parents and tell them what my intentions are concerning your future."

Mina screwed her face up into a brave, stolid expression.

"I'll come inside."

She lifted her little skirts and scurried through the door. Ales shook her head and headed inside. She had not been trying to manipulate the girl. The warehouse was surprisingly clean inside, with only a few small crates. Ales walked to the crates. A quick glance with her Vision showed her that the crates were packed with some sort of grain. She pulled two small crates from the stack and sat down on one of them. Mina looked at the crate for a moment, and then let out a put-upon sigh. She smoothed the back of her skirts and folded them beneath her before scooting onto the crate. It was a good sign. The girl could adapt if she was forced to.

"I'm going to look into your eyes with my magic, Mina. It's going to make you feel a little woozy, but it'll go away fast." Ales placed her hands on the girl's shoulders to steady her.

"Mmm K," Mina hummed.

Ales opened her Vision and gazed into Mina's eyes. A moment later, Ales drew back. The girl had four Circles, a very high number for any Tier. She usually expected two or three. Anything more than three was telling of what kind of Tier the girl would be. She had Observance, Finding, Taking, and Distance. Observance was her dominant talent. She was going to be a Seer if she chose to be one of them. Ales' own second most powerful Circle was Observance. She could see almost three full minutes into her immediate future if she focused on Observance. She never really used Observance on a conscious level. Like Breaking, it had become an unconscious effort that she left her Cellstructs to process for her. They delivered the information directly to her brain in an unconscious stream that primed her reflexes to be entirely precognitive during a fight. Mina swayed for a moment when Ales closed her Vision. Her little hand went to her head, and she let out a little groan.

"Oh, I think I'm gonna be sick," Mina rasped.

"You'll be fine in a moment. Take a deep breath."

Mina did so and steadied almost immediately.

"M'better," she mumbled.

"You're fine, Mina. Now, I think that we really should go see your Mother and Father. You are not in danger of having your Vision come out on its own. I would love nothing more than to make you part of our family, but you are very young, and these are very dangerous times for the Tier. I would speak with your parents so that they know when you get older you have the choice to be one of the Tier," Ales began before an ear-splitting crack rang out from outside and Lia roared at the top of her lungs. Ales reached out with her mind and made the connection with Lia.

{*I need help, Ales! People are going to get killed!*} Lia yelled into her mind.

"LIGHTEYE"

7

Jame watched the outriders move back and forth through their drills. It was important training for Jame and the other young outriders. Still, Jame was bored out of his mind. He had run these drills dozens of times. He had long since mastered the sword, bow, and stave. The only thing that still held any interest to him was training with lancers.

"What's the matter, boy?" a strange voice came from behind him. He turned to find the Tier they were escorting sitting behind him. The thief's two different colored eyes disconcerted him.

"I am not a thief, boy. Not anymore," Cole said.

"How did you know I was thinking..." Jame began but Cole waved him off.

"I'm not reading your mind, boy, just your expression. When people think someone is disreputable, they get a certain look about them, even if they try to hide it."

"I'm sorry."

"Don't be sorry, boy. Not long ago, I was just as disreputable as you think me to be. I have only been one of the Tier for a cycle. No more. I take no offense, but I am no longer that man. I'm still trying to find out who I am supposed to be, now. But I can see that you're bored. If you are so bored, you must have mastered all of these weapons. Care for a real workout?"

Jame eyed him warily.

"You'll use your magic to beat me."

Cole grinned.

"Boy, the day I need my power to beat a runt like you is the day I hang it up. If these eyes aren't glowing, then I'm not using my power. Besides, if I were to use my power, you'd never see it coming. So, do you wish to test your skill or not?"

Jame stood up.

"Fine, if it's a thrashing you are hoping for, I will deliver it for you, Tier. And my name is Jame, not boy."

"Staves, Jame. If we use swords, you are going to end up full of holes, and if we use practice swords, it'll be bruises. I am not your peer or your instructor. This is a test of your skill, not mine," Cole said confidently. He picked up a stave from one of the racks that the Ryhim had set out. Cole spun it deftly in his hands. He grinned and tossed the stave to Jame.

"If you can land a solid hit on me, you can have this."

Cole held up a gold piece. Cole had a feeling that it would be worth it to see what this young man could do. He wasn't sure what made him feel that way, but something had drawn him to this particular practice yard. There were three others besides this one. Jame spun the stave just as deftly as Cole had.

"I'll take your gold, old man," Jame challenged.

Jame drove forward, thrusting the stave towards Cole's middle. Cole stepped back and to one side, letting it pass by harmlessly. He stuck out one foot and Jame tripped over it. However, the young man was well trained, recovering deftly by using the stave as a crutch to keep himself from falling. Cole simply centered himself as Ales had taught him and waited for Jame to recover. Jame watched him for a moment. Cole just shrugged and beckoned him forward.

"Surely, you can do better than that," Cole taunted.

Jame, though, didn't let anger affect his control. It was impressive. He came forward more carefully this time. He whipped the staff at Cole's head. Cole deflected it with the flat of his hand. Jame spun the staff in a blur, swinging it towards Cole's shins. Cole hopped over the staff and Jame let out a little shout of triumph. He whipped his leg up towards Cole's midsection. Cole twisted his body in the air and pushed Jame's leg aside as if Jame were moving in slow motion. He landed neatly on both feet and Jame went stumbling past him.

"Apparently, you do not want that gold coin very badly."

Cole knew now that this young soldier was what had drawn him out of his tent and into the camp. Jame found his balance again, and a look of concentration came over his face. Cole watched him more carefully now. The staff blurred in his hands, and his movements became more fluid than they had been. Jame came at Cole. He swung the staff in a flurry of blows, darting towards Cole's head. Cole ducked beneath. The other end of the staff whipped around expertly towards his ribs, narrowly missing when Cole took a precise step backwards. Jame spun, swinging the staff in a wide arc, a maneuver that would have put a normal person off balance. The added momentum, if it struck, would be devastating.

Cole grinned and lifted a hand. His cycle of training had brutally drilled into him the ability to judge the speed and path of moving objects, even without using his Vision. He moved his hand backward just as the staff slammed into his palm. It still stung, but he suffered neither broken bones nor even pain for more than a moment. He grinned at Jame's stunned face.

"That's impossible," Jame said. He withdrew the staff, and Cole let him.

"Not impossible, just hard training. Training that I can offer to you, Jame. What you've just shown me tells me that you have the ability to be one of the Tier, if you so choose."

Cole didn't give him a chance to respond any further. He picked up his gold coin and walked away without another word. Jame watched him go, stunned. Banno, his commanding officer, came up next to him and watched Cole go.

"Did he just offer to teach you of Tieran magic, or are my ears feeding me false information?" Banno observed.

"I'm not sure *what* he just offered me."

"Perhaps, Jame, you should go and ask him."

Banno made a shooing gesture at Jame. He turned back to the rest of the troops and started shouting orders. Jame watched his back for a long moment, and then realized that the Tier had spoken to his commander already. Jame set his stave back in the rack, picked up his jacket, and ran off in the same direction that Cole had gone. It took Jame a few minutes to locate Cole's tent between two trees at the edge of the camp. Jame thought it was strange that the person they were meant to protect wouldn't be in the center of the camp. Having seen him fight, Jame wondered if perhaps he was the one protecting them. He stopped at the canvas flaps of Cole's tent, wondering how to interrupt the Tier.

"Come in, boy, and let us see if you have what it takes to be one of the Tier."

"BREAKER"

8

The two days that Ilsa had spent arguing with the Chief of the clan seemed like a pleasant memory compared to how they all looked at her as she walked through the Camp. The raw admiration they all showed for her once they had discovered she was one of the Tier was almost disgusting. Ales had warned her that this might happen, and she hadn't understood how people liking her could be as bad as people wanting to kill her. Now, she understood. These people thought of her as some sort of demigod; as a sort of direct line to their god and goddess. They thought that she was something she was not. She had spoken to the Mother and Father only once. She could feel their presence even now watching over her, but she did not know them any more than the rest of these people did. She was not any more special than them. She wasn't sure why they treated her like she was.

"You believe you are not special, and you think that makes you humble? Humility is not an excuse to make yourself less than you are, Ilsa." The voice was deep and patient.

Ilsa realized that everything around her had come to a stop. She looked around the camp, then took a step to the right and pressed her finger into a tent flap. The heavy, oiled cloth resisted her attempts to move it despite the fact that it hung loosely. Then, she saw him, a few marks away near a cook fire. His feet hung a few ticks above the ground. There, he hovered. Ilsa lowered her eyes and fell to her knees.

"Father, I'm sorry. I do not know how to be this." She gestured to the elaborate dress that the Ryhim had given her.

"Do not be sorry, Daughter. Be better. You were cautioned that when you became one of the Tier you would be both hated and admired. All of my children are unique creations, but there are some like you who have the potential to be more. I know that this is difficult for you, but these people around you do not know our presence like the Tier. They know only that you are closer to us than they are.

We do not expect you to fulfill their prayers, my Daughter. That is our choice. But we do expect that you receive them with grace. You do not think of yourself as a conduit to the divine, but that is exactly what you have become. Embrace the person you are becoming, Ilsa. Few things are more rewarding than being a source of hope for those around you." Zezzhz spoke with gentle reproach, and Ilsa felt the weight of his disapproval.

"But if I am to be a source of hope, I feel like I have to live up to those prayers. I'm not strong enough for that. I don't think I'm like Ales. She is truly special," Ilsa tried to explain.

"If Ales is as special as you think she is, do you think she could make such a catastrophic mistake as teaching someone who is not meant to be one of the Tier?" Zezzhz asked. Ilsa had no response.

"Ilsa, you have all that you need to accomplish wondrous things. Believe in yourself. Be the symbol that these people need you to be."

"I will try, Father."

"Good. Now rise and be aware. There is another in this place who would be one of you. This one in particular was newly made and will become a danger to himself and others if he continues to discover his powers without assistance."

Then he was gone. The sounds, smells, and movement of the camp resumed as if nothing had happened.

Ilsa sighed and slowly looked around the camp. Then, she closed her eyes and opened her Vision. In the cycle of training that Ales and Lia had put her through, they had taught her mostly of her Vision. However, there had been a few other lessons. The first and most important lesson was how to spot those with the potential to be Tier. There were many methods, and some of them were very subtle and complex.

Out of all of them, there was one surefire way to recognize someone with Tieran potential. It was the least pleasant way. When using her Vision, she could peer into the eyes of a person and see the shape of the magic within them. It was a method rarely used as it was extremely taxing. People without the potential had no protection from her sight. She could see into their very souls, and some of those souls were not good.

She forced herself to do it. Zezzhz was right. She knew what she was getting into when she made her decision. She would be better. So she walked and looked into the eyes of all that crossed her path. She saw the terrible things that some of them had done and had been forced to do. Then she realized, as she passed through the Center sized camp, that everyone was looking at her. Everyone had stopped what they were doing. They pointed when they thought she could not see, but it was with awe that they watched her pass.

She was about to close her Vision when one of the children ran out in front of her. She concentrated and pulled her Vision back so that she could more easily see the boy. In his hands he held a simple bundle of flowers. Tiny blossoms of blue, red, and yellow. In her Vision, she could see them bursting with the life of the Mother. Wherever he had picked these blossoms had been a special place. He held up the flowers shyly.

"Your eyes are really pretty, lady," he squeaked.

She knelt down and took the flowers from him. He had bright orange hair and beautiful ruby-colored eyes.

"So are yours. What is your name, little one?"

"Manat."

"Thank you for the flowers, Manat." Ilsa started threading them into her hair, behind her ears, and into her braids.

"Nat?" A young man's voice cut through the crowd of milling onlookers. Ilsa looked around for the source of the voice.

"Nat, where have you gone?"

A young man came out from between the tents. He was a little younger than Ilsa, perhaps ten cycles old. He had the same bright orange hair and ruby red eyes. Ilsa's eyes met the boy's and she was instantly drawn into them. The boy stumbled, and Ilsa darted forward on instinct. She caught him without ever losing eye contact with him. It lasted only a moment longer, and then she was past the knowing.

"Ohh, I feel so light-headed," the young man croaked.

"Take a deep breath. You will be fine. What is your name?" Ilsa asked. When he realized who he was leaning against, he stumbled backwards.

"Antieri. I am sorry. I didn't realize..." he stammered in apology. She held up a hand to stall him.

"It is I who should apologize. Your name?"

"I'm Juran, Antieri. I'm sorry if my little brother bothered you," Juran said.

"I hardly think he could bother me with beautiful flowers, Juran." Ilsa made a gesture to the blossoms decorating her hair. She closed her Vision and the glow faded from her eyes. "Is there someplace that we can go to talk?"

"You want to speak with me?"

"Please?"

"Of... course," Juran stammered. He made a gesture back between the two tents he had come through.

"Lead the way, Juran."

Ilsa followed him between the two tents on a meandering path through the camp. They were near the center of the massive camp when Juran finally pulled open the flaps on a large tent. It was made of a very thick, royal blue material. She stepped inside, and found that it was more than just a tent. It was a home. The dirt floor had been leveled, and an inventive interlocking wood floor had been laid atop. A system of moveable walls had been set up inside, dividing the space into many rooms.

"This is beautiful," Ilsa said.

"But you are one of the Tier?" Juran asked, as if she should have seen much more beautiful things than his home. He shooed Manat into one of the rooms and then pulled a sliding door across the opening.

"All the more reason I can appreciate such a simple and elegant solution to moving around so often. How often does it happen?" Ilsa asked.

"No less than two cycles, no more than four. It's less for some clans, more for others. The Byranti, for instance, usually only move once every eight to ten cycles."

The short hallway of movable walls opened up onto a living area. The furniture was very plush for something that was meant to be picked up and moved at a moment's notice. She sat on a couch that had a low, long table in front of it. Juran took a chair on the other side.

"Can I offer you some refreshment, Antieri?" Juran asked.

"Please call me Ilsa. I'm likely not much older than you. I'm not old enough or wise enough for titles like that, yet. Maybe one day I will be, but not now," Ilsa said, slightly exasperated by the whole situation.

"Truly?"

Ilsa nodded. "I'm twelve cycles and change."

Juran's eyes were a little wide with surprise.

"But you seem so..." Juran made an inarticulate gesture that asked how she had become one of the Tier at such a young age.

"A cycle of hard training under possibly the most powerful of any of the Tier ever to live has an effect." Juran nodded and it seemed that he truly understood what she meant. "Which brings me to why we are sitting here."

Juran tilted his head in question.

"Juran, the dizziness you experienced outside was because I was delving into your potential. I apologize for the discomfort."

"My potential?"

"You could become one of the Tier. I'm here to offer you that opportunity." Ilsa could see the effect of the news on him. His brain ground to a halt. His face went slack, and he seemed unable to process what she had just said.

"What?" Juran exclaimed, stupefied. Ilsa laughed.

"Juran, you have the inborn ability to be one of the Tier. You're what we call a Newling. You have begun to use your Tieran abilities without any sort of training. This is going to become very problematic for you in the near future if you do not receive training."

"How can you possibly tell all that with just a look?"

Ilsa raised her right eyebrow in question, and just pointed to her eyes.

"The magic glowing eyes didn't give it away?"

Juran laughed and shook his head.

"Fair enough. But what do you mean I am using my abilities?" Juran asked nervously.

"You already know what I am talking about, Juran. You have *Broken* things already." Juran's eyes went a little wide as he realized what she was talking about.

"How could you possibly..." Juran stared fixedly at her mismatched eyes.

"It's your choice, Juran. Even if I teach you how to use your abilities, you do not have to join the Tier. We just hope that you would. I will still teach you even if you ultimately decide not to."

"Really? Why would you do that?"

Ilsa tilted her head in an animal fashion.

"Why wouldn't I?"

"Well it seems like an odd pitch to me."

Ilsa chuckled. "It's not a pitch, Juran. I am just trying to help you."

"And what does that involve? Being one of the Tier."

Ilsa laughed. "Oh, Gods, Juran, you don't go for the small questions, do you? What do you think that one of us does?"

"I have no idea."

Ilsa shrugged. "I unfortunately don't have as many answers as you might hope for that question. We're meant to safeguard the world, and help those who can't help themselves. As long as we work towards those goals, the Tier can do whatever they want. What I can tell you is this. Only a handful of people ever get the opportunity I'm offering you, Juran, but it's a decision you must make on your own. I will start to teach you how to control your power tomorrow."

"How much of my time is that going to take?"

"Well it took me several rotations to learn how to work with my abilities, and I am still cycles away from having it all figured out. But I can get you to the point where you're not a danger to yourself and others. You haven't hurt anyone, have you?"

"No, just a few things I have picked up have disintegrated lately. I have no idea why."

"It's because you are possessed of a Tieran power called Breaking. It allows you to see and manipulate the weakest points on anything, no matter what it is. I have the same power, and it's difficult to learn how to control it. I can also tell you that you have at least one more power, but I can't tell you which one because it isn't the same as mine."

"Rotations?" Juran asked, somewhat alarmed.

"That's just to get the basics. Juran, this training is not optional for you. If I do not teach you how to control your Vision, there'll be consequences for you."

"I have a job, though. I have to provide for my little brother. I have responsibilities here."

"Aren't you a little young for that?" Ilsa asked. Juran looked sad, and Ilsa understood.

"Working the mines here can be dangerous. It's why we have long avoided mining these areas even though they have the most valuable deposits that never move. They are just outside of the area of the shift. Last cycle, while our parents were setting beams in a mine, a lava flow burst through the wall of the mine. We lost eight of us. Our parents never stood a chance."

Ilsa took a deep breath and looked up to the ceiling of the tent. This was going to be a very delicate situation. Juran would soon understand that if he had control of his Vision back then, he would have been able to see the problems in the mine at a glance. He would have been able to save his parents. She said a small prayer to the Gods for wisdom.

"I'm sorry, Juran. What is it that you do?"

"I'm currently studying with the Shapers learning to work metal."

"Your study to learn to control your Vision will not interfere with anything you are doing already. If anything, what I have to teach you will make your work at the forge that much easier. So, Juran, see you here at sun up?"

Juran turned and looked at the room where he had left Manat for a long time. "What's going to happen if I don't?"

Ilsa sighed. She had not wanted to do this. It was a terrifying experience. She stood up and rounded the low table between them. She opened her Vision and looked into his eyes. In her imagination, she constructed the image of a pair of eyes slowly opening just as Ales had taught her. She touched Juran on the forehead and his eyes brightened with internal light. One red, one bright with white light. It was an odd color for an eye. That bright white iris was going to make his eyes very startling. He swayed and groaned. His eyes darted around wildly as he tried to look everywhere at once.

"What did you do to my eyes? What is happening?" Juran asked frantically.

"This is what will happen to you if your Vision opens and you don't know how to control it. What you are seeing now is the main ability of your Vision. Once I teach you how to sort through all of this, you will be able to understand the world around you with this power. But without teaching, you could spend spans or rotations to just learn to open and close your Vision." She closed the door in her mind and the glow in his eyes faded. They both returned to their ruby red.

"That's going to happen, isn't it?" Juran asked.

"Yes. A Newling's Vision always comes out eventually," Ilsa said.

"How do you know I am one?"

"Everyone is born with the ability to learn to control their Vision, but a newling is born with their Vision partially open. Looking into your eyes with my own Vision shows me things about you. It shows us things about everyone, which is why only a very special few ever get the chance to be one of us. Everyone has the potential, but only those who will use it properly ever get the chance to learn."

"And you think I'm that kind of person?" Juran asked skeptically.

"I know you are," Ilsa reassured. Juran smiled. Ilsa turned and moved toward the exit.

"You believe in me more than I believe in myself. I'll be up with the sun, and waiting for you, Antieri."

"I will be here, Juran." Ilsa said and disappeared out of the flaps.

PART 2

9

Ales hustled Mina out the side door and back down the alleyway to the street. She trusted Lia to hold her own with whatever was attacking until Ales was sure the little girl was safe.

"Mina, you go straight home, and don't stop for any reason. We will come and find you soon. I promise," Ales said.

"I can run for the guards," Mina offered.

"No, child. Run straight home. Run!" Ales shouted the girl off. Mina lifted her skirts and ran off into the crowd.

Ales pushed open the first two levels of her Constraints. A deafening crash rang out from behind the warehouse. She opened her Vision and scanned through the warehouse, then beyond. It took a moment for her to locate Lia through the intervening buildings and people. She was two streets over, locked in a bear hug with another massive animal of some sort. Ales couldn't quickly sort out what it was beyond a large, furred predator. She didn't wait. Lia was shoving it back into the alleyways out of sight of the Ryhim.

Lia's mental voice rang out, {*Ales, this thing is strong! It's been enhanced somehow! It's in pain, Ales. Terrible, driving pain.*}

Ales felt Lia's own pain as the creature's claws tore into her side. Ales flung open three more levels of her Constraints and bolted down the alleyway. She blurred across the street, dodging between the Ryhim who stumbled in the violent gust of wind caused by her passing. She darted into the alleyway on the other side of the street, between two large storehouses. The corridor between the two buildings ended in a T against the back of another building. She turned right, knowing exactly where Lia was.

Halfway down the back alley, Lia was wrestling with the massive creature. It looked like a banic, but no banic had ever had black fur like that. Ales skidded to a halt on the cobblestones. There wasn't enough room in the alleyway for her to maneuver past Lia to get to the monster. It had a short, powerful muzzle with long canine fangs that hung well past the lower jaw in its rounded skull. It had no eyes, and two large tines stuck out of its head. It was definitely the remnants of a banic. Much like Lia, it had six powerful legs, but they were more powerfully built than hers. The only reason she was able to match its strength was the massive support she received from her Cellstructs. Two of her paws were braced against the banic's throat, holding its teeth away from her muzzle. Her second set of paws were pushing against its chest, and her rear paws were tearing cobblestones from the alley floor as she held the roaring, slavering monster back.

{Can you back out when I say?} Ales asked.

{Can we help this poor creature?} Lia grunted as the creature raked her with its claws again. Her wounds were healing almost as quickly as the thing could cause them.

{Let me knock it unconscious, and we will do everything in our power to repair whatever has been done to this animal,} Ales sent in reply.

{Alright, jump over to the other side. I will shove her back and you can take it from there.}

Ales took a few steps back. She jumped and braced her left foot against the left wall. She pushed off and planted her right foot against the opposite one. Ales kicked off and shot upward, flying over the top of the massive banic. She landed in a roll on the other side of the creature and rose to her feet, turning.

{Now, Lia!}

She opened her Vision, and red blotches blossomed all over the body of the banic. There were so many that bile rose in Ales' throat. It was disgusting to see a living thing so damaged. Lia heaved the creature off balance with a grunt, sending it falling backwards towards Ales. She jammed two fingers straight into the red dot at the base of the creature's skull. A shock shot through the banic's spinal cord, paralyzing it temporarily. Ales popped the remaining levels of her Constraints open. She caught the massive black creature and lowered it slowly to the ground with a grunt.

{Lia, if we are to save this poor creature, we will need to take a risk. I feel horrible for pointing this out, but dare we risk ourselves for this?} Ales asked.

{Yes,} Lia replied without hesitation.

{If we each impart half of our Cellstructs to this creature, it should be sufficient to both wipe out the crude Cellstructs it has been forced to take in, and heal much of the damage they have done to it. But this will leave us vulnerable until our remaining Cellstructs can replicate their lost numbers.}

{It would be better if only one of us were vulnerable for a few days. I will pass the banic the majority of mine. I can take in far more food than you can to replenish my Cellstructs,} Lia argued.

For a long moment, Ales looked as though she would object, but soon let out a breath and nodded.

{Will you stay by my side until you are replenished?} Ales pled.

Lia displayed her terrifying dagger-toothed grin and put her paw down on the beast's head. Ales' Vision spun down to the microscopic level so that she could see the Cellstructs crawling out of the pores on Lia's paw pads. Millions upon millions of the tiny ant-like machines crawled out of her skin and into the skin of the banic. Immediately, the black color began to bleed out of its glittering silvery fur. Lia walked on five paws, touching her lifted forepaw on the banic's back in several places. There, too, glittering silver fur began to emerge from the oily black.

{I will endeavor to stay by your side, sister, until I am stronger again.} Lia's mind voice was getting thick with exhaustion as her Cellstructs left her body in such massive quantities. She would lose access to the power of opening her Constraints.

{How much do you have left?} Ales seemed overly concerned.

{I'm not a baby. Can you carry it?}

{I can, but we are going to need to be quick. Go back to the warehouse and open the bay doors.}

Lia nodded and trotted off. She looked a little wobbly without any of her Cellstructs reinforcing her body. She steadied quickly, though, and sped up when she reached the end of the alleyway. Ales counted slowly to 200. Once she did, she opened her constraints to the fifth level. She bent her knees and pulled the banic up over her shoulders. She straightened up, but the banic's back legs still dragged on the ground behind her. It was of little consequence.

She started out at a jog, but by the time she reached the end of the alleyway, she had achieved a full run. She bolted across the road and into the alleyway on the other side. She darted around the corner, leaning her body further to one side to evenly distribute the banic's weight on her back. Thankfully, Lia had done as she was told, and Ales was able to run directly into the warehouse. The door closed behind her as soon as she was through. Lia had somehow managed to tie a length of rope around the warehouse door handle and pull it closed in her teeth.

{How in the pit did you tie that knot?} Ales' mind voice was amazed.

"Eh, after a few thousand cycles you learn a few tricks with these paws." Lia's voice held a little laughter at Ales' expression.

"This poor old girl is far from being healthy, but we have stopped the terrible process that was destroying her from the inside out." Ales put her hand on the banic's flank.

"Can we make her well again?" Lia asked.

Ales focused on her Vision and looked over the locations that Breaking told her were most damaged.

"I will. For this, Lia, we will call to the Mother if we must to save this tortured soul."

Ales ran her fingers through the glittering silver fur spreading between the banic's horns. She looked over the wounds the banic had suffered beyond the Cellstructs forced into its body. The steel tines that had destroyed its eyes were serving as some sort of antenna. She carefully pulled the tines free from the banic's eye sockets.

"I cannot heal her eyes without assistance from Verdant, but I can repair her damaged body beyond that. She has a punctured lung and a broken rib. Her heart is damaged, but can be repaired. You realize, though, that she is thousands of lengths from home, Lia. What are we going to do with her?"

She went to her pack and took out a roll of medical tools. Inside the roll were dozens of tiny, bright knives and some oddly-shaped pliers used to spread open wounds rather than hold them closed. She and Kiltik had spent an entire sleepless span creating her medical kit. The dozens of tiny coils of thread within it were especially difficult to make. They were not as good as healing threads made from Cellstructs, but the threads were made of Bondstructs that were able to knit tissues back together at the cellular level. It meant that the wounds would heal only slightly faster, and the healed tissue would only be as good as it was before the injury. She cursed the necessity of it. With Cellstruct thread, the wounds would heal within hours, and the cellular structure would be reinforced, leaving the injured area stronger than it had been.

"Can you keep her asleep?" Ales queried hopefully.

"Yes, there is enough of me in her to exercise minor control over her motor functions." Lia spoke softly because she could tell Ales was already beginning to concentrate on caring for the banic's wounds. Ales constantly insisted that she was a hack when it came to treating wounds, and it was true, but only when compared to someone like Haw.

Haw had devoted his entire life to healing people. He had been so exceptionally gifted that it was said that even death had bowed to his ability if one was brought to him quickly enough. Lia had seen it with her own eyes, seen Haw expertly cut into a dead man's chest and reach inside of him. Haw had pumped that man's heart manually, and then used an elementary force container to discharge elementary force into his body. A moment later, he gasped and his eyes fluttered open. Compared to a feat of science and skill like that, Ales was a hack.

Still, she took a razor and shaved away the banic's fur with clean swipes of the blade. She cut and parted the wounds with perfect, precise motions and applied the pliers. Then, she practically dove into the wounds with monomolecular thread. The banic was so large that Ales was up to her elbows in blood by the time she was done. Each wound was taken care of in mere ticks. Every bit of damage that the banic had taken was repaired in less time that it took to tell of it.

Ales stepped back and looked over her handiwork. By the time she had finished, only a few spots of black fur remained on the banic's beautiful silvery body. She was also breathing much more normally.

"Can you touch her mind?" Ales inquired. She did not have Lia's subtle touch with telepathy, and Lia's Cellstructs still suffused the banic.

"Yes, my Cellstructs have passed into her brain. She's scared, Ales. She doesn't understand why she can't see," Lia explained.

"Lia, I've neither the skill nor the equipment to repair her eyes. How much access to her mind do you have? Can you teach her things?" Ales was leading Lia somewhere, and it didn't take Lia long to get there.

"I'm not sure I can give knowledge like that. You know how long it took me to learn how to do that. Seeing with sound like that…" Lia shook her head. "I wouldn't even know where to start knowing how to convey that to someone else. I spent hundreds of hours walking around with my eyes closed before I learned how to listen for sound bouncing off things around me." Lia seemed genuinely distraught. She wanted to help so badly.

"You can try, Lia. It'll be at least half a cycle before we can even hope that Warran will be able to resurrect Verdant. He is beyond talented with Repair, but bringing a Mind to life takes both luck and skill." Ales implored Lia to try her best.

"Ales, this banic is very intelligent. She is calming, and she is grateful for our help. She remembers things about where they took her, what they did to her."

Lia padded closer to the banic. She gently ran her forepaw down the banic's horns.

"We'll take care of her, Lia, and we will use what she remembers to make sure this doesn't happen again." Ales touched the banic's horns as well.

{It's not far away, Ales, and there are more animals there. She remembers their smells.} Lia's mind voice was alarmed.

"How many, Lia? Are they all like her?"

{Dozens, Ales. She smelled dozens of others there. She remembers hearing their cries of pain. Many of them were predators. That's all she remembers,} Lia finished.

"Put her to sleep, Lia. Assure her that she will feel much better when she wakes up. We have work to do."

10

Ales leaned against the wall of what was shaping up to be their new home for the time being. The banic had been sleeping comfortably for almost a span. In that time, Ales and Lia had walked the Center, trying to get a better feel for the flow of the city. They found four locations that were not good places. Even in a city filled with only the Ryhim, there were criminal elements, but none of those places were the one they had been looking for. The place where the banic had been experimented on still eluded them. Lia had followed her scent to one of the gates out of the center and beyond, into the surrounding forest.

{She must have spent an entire span or more wandering around out there. I tried to unravel the trail, but she crossed her own path in the same spot dozens of times in dozens of areas. There just wasn't anything left by the time I was able to unravel it,} Lia complained. Her mind voice held barely-veiled anger.

{I assume you attempted a spectral light separation?}

{I've practiced it, but it's not as useful to me. I can't scope my Vision down past the molecular level. It makes it harder to follow a trail that way. This is probably the one and only time my olfactory senses are better than my Vision.}

Ales shrugged. *{You're probably right. I've never had a sense of smell like yours. There is precedent for this from others among the Wild.}* Ales watched the street with sudden interest.

{You're about to run off, aren't you?} Lia's mindvoice was exasperated.

Ales strolled out into the street without a backward glance. Lia watched her go, and then sighed. She crouched down and popped the first level of her Constraints. It was the only level left to her right now. Her Cellstructs were quickly replenishing themselves, but she was still weakened.

She leapt onto the roof of the adjacent warehouse. Lia glided across the rooftops. After Vilhena, they had agreed that it would be better for Lia to stay out of sight as much as possible until they could establish a better rapport with the guards and the various royal families. It had mostly been Lia's decision. Ales had argued that what had happened in Vilhena would have happened even if Lia had tried to stay hidden. Lia had been firm. If she hadn't been seen with the new ones, things would have been different when they left Vilhena. She would have been able to get everyone out without anyone getting hurt. Ales had finally relented and agreed that Lia could stay out of sight unless she was needed.

{*What did you see, Ales?*}

Lia sometimes wondered what it was like looking through her sister's eyes. Her ocular magics were dizzyingly more powerful than Lia's own. While she knew the doctrine of the Tier focused more on how you used your abilities than how powerful they were, it was hard not to think that Ales saw so much more than everyone else. She never seemed to miss even the smallest detail.

{*What we have been looking for all day. Residue,*} Ales replied.

She had melted into the crowd, and Lia was having trouble picking her out among the sea of heads wandering the market below her. She crept to the edge of the rooftop and inhaled deeply, catching all the scents on the air. Millennia of practice had made her nose almost as acute as her eyes. She caught Ales' scent from downwind. She turned her head slowly that way until she caught a glimpse of Ales' cerulean braids bobbing through the throng. She was drawing her Windblade out of her jacket.

{*Ales, what are you doing?*} Lia asked in alarm.

{*Nothing that requires that tone of voice,*} Ales replied.

Ales lifted the blade over her head and did something that Lia had only ever seen a half dozen Tier accomplish. She whipped it in a circle over her head and a small cyclone of air kicked up immediately. Dust filled the air in a massive cloud that spread outward from Ales to cover the entire street in moments. Lia opened her Vision and the cloud of dust became somewhat transparent to her eyes. Ales was darting through the crowd at a speed that beggared belief. Lia wondered why she didn't just use her Taker's powers to slip through the crowd unseen. She slid to a stop and watched Ales for a long moment.

Ales had never been comfortable with using Taking. As Arcangineers, they were responsible for researching the effects of their powers on the world around them. Taking was the most heavily researched of their magics. There was overwhelming proof that even if you used it to invade the minds of others like she had done in Vilhena, there would be no lasting damage unless you attempted to keep them that way for an extended period of time. But Ales was convinced for some reason that it was much worse than that. It was her curse. Ales was forever uncomfortable with how much power she had.

Lia pulled herself from her thoughts. Ales had shoved a young man into an alleyway, and the dust had begun to settle in the street. Lia backed up and tested her second level of Constraints. Her Cellstructs informed her that it would be at least two more days before enough of them had been regenerated to push her body that far.

She growled and lept off the side of the building, landing in the street as she opened her Vision. Lines appeared on the ground all around her, and she put her paws on the one that went in Ales' general direction. She walked through the crowd completely unseen. When she made it into the alleyway, Ales was holding the man by the throat. His feet were swinging a few ticks off the ground, and he was clawing ineffectually at Ales' arm.

"Even *I* can smell it on you. You have been in the place where they are turning animals into monsters, and you are going to tell me where it is." Ales' eyes were blazing with her Vision. She was furious. Lia slid into the alleyway.

{Ales?} Lia asked.

{Don't worry. He's foolish, but I will not hurt him. I'm just going to make him think that I will.} Ales' sending was amused. Lia let out a little sigh of relief.

"I...can't..." the man choaked out.

"Boy, I have broken better men than you over breakfast. Do not test me. Where?" Ales growled. The young man gasped for air and Ales loosened her grip, but not enough that he would fall.

"He told me that if I told anyone, I would die. He put things inside of me just like the animals," the young man quavered. Ales looked him up and down. She nodded.

"Yes it did. Unfortunately for it, and you, I have learned well how to deal with its crude attempts at Cellstructs. Death's embrace will not save you from me. Where is it?" Ales' glowing eyes reflected off of the young man's yellow ones.

"I don't know where it is. I was never there. He delivered the animals to me, and I let them loose in the forest. I can take you where I picked them up."

"Lead on, then. Do not think of running. I assure you that I am faster than you are," Ales snarled, dropping the young man to the ground.

11

They tromped through the woods. The boy, whose name was Iraine, had tried to run twice. Ales had just leaned against a tree and watched Lia slink off into the undergrowth in pursuit. She wasn't sure what he had been thinking the second time he had run off, after the first demonstration of how outrageously slow he was compared to a gigantic Katali.

"No, don't bother trying to run a third time. You're annoying my sister, and I fear that if you make her chase you again, she will eat some part of you that you will sorely miss," Ales said, and Iraine paled visibly. He stared for a long few moments at Lia, who bared her teeth at him.

"We're here," Iraine muttered.

The trees opened up onto a massive cleared area. It was too regular to be natural, and not large enough to support a real settlement of any kind. The collection of buildings, Ales knew, were storehouses that were only used occasionally, when there were overages of materials that the Ryhim did not want to keep in the city. They were currently empty, and while she knew this was not the place where the banic had been experimented on, it was an excellent place to leave such a creature to be released into the wild at a later time.

"I brought you, can I go now? He said I would die if I bought anyone else here," Iraine implored.

"It, Iraine. It was not lying. Whatever it was that you spoke with, it was not a man, even if it looked like one. Had I not interceded, you would be dead. You should get out of the Center. Can you get a position outside with your tribe?"

"I can."

"We will make sure you get there."

"I will take him. I'm sure you can investigate this without my help," Lia said.

Ales nodded, and they disappeared into the forest. Ales watched the warehouses for a long moment, but there were no signs of life at all. There was a high chance that this was some sort of trap, and after her near death encounter in Vilhena, she was wary. She had become much stronger over the last cycle.

Ales hadn't realized it when she woke from her sleep, but her Cellstructs had lost their ability to fully integrate with her cells the way they had before. Their overwhelming new power had fooled her into thinking that everything was as it had been before her long sleep. She knew better, now.

As the spans passed, she could feel the difference each morning as her Cellstructs regained full integration. Still, the power of the King's armor had been frightening, and they still had no idea what other machines of destruction the Intruder had constructed over the last three thousand cycles. After sharing their memories and making assessments on what both she and Liassa had gone through in Vilhena, it was clear that the difference between what they knew and what they needed to know was staggering. They had uncovered the bare tip of a horrific iceberg. They both hoped that Ales had not awoken too late.

Ales sat down cross-legged beneath the nearest tree to be fully hidden by the ragged line of shrubs between her and the warehouses. She opened her Vision and slowly began to pick her way through the things between her and the buildings. Eventually, she was able to see through the walls of the warehouse to the inside. There were crates inside, but they were lined with some dense metal that her Vision was unable to penetrate. It was likely bondsteel. Made using bondstructs, all of its molecules were perfectly aligned to create the nearly indestructible metal. This also made it very difficult to see through if she was not very close to it. There was too much interference from the other materials.

Finally, she pushed open her constraints to the fourth level. She left her Vision open and darted towards the warehouse. She invoked the Circle of Taking to make certain that no one saw her approach. The door had a heavy lock on it, but oftentimes a heavy lock was the easiest to bypass. Ales reached into the pouch on her belt and slid out two thin pieces of metal designed for lockpicking. It took only a moment with her Vision open to unlock the door. She slipped inside and closed the door silently behind her. There were four other large buildings just like this one, but none of the others contained anything of interest.

The crates had an interesting locking mechanism. The lid had an odd circular keyhole in the center. She could see the hooks built into the lid that had engaged into the walls of the crate. A few moments of fiddling with the lock disengaged the mechanism, and she was able to push the locks out of the way. She pulled open the lid. She narrowed her eyes at what she found inside.

Neatly cut cubes of Black Sol alloy filled the crate. She had never seen so much of the black metal in one place in all her life. Just one of these cubes was enough to build ten sets of armor like the one that Terran Roa had been forced to wear for most of his life. The horrors this box could produce were so numerous and disturbing that Ales did not want to think about it. Black Sol had been one of the great mistakes of the Tier, and they had taken that mistake to their graves. But somehow, the creature had used those two swords to reverse engineer the means of making more of the life draining metal.

Ales shivered and closed the crate again. She didn't want to look in the three other crates, but she did so anyway. They were all filled to the brim with the same gleaming black metal. Ales' eyes immediately darted around the warehouse. There was no way that this would be left here unguarded. She called up the Circle of Light and pushed her Vision into hyper-spectral frequencies.

At the corners of the warehouse near the ceiling, there were devices transmitting energetic waves. She recognized what they were for immediately. They were a type of monitoring device that transmitted images to a remote location, allowing the place to be watched from afar. Ales took a moment to consider her options. She could not possibly allow this metal to disappear into the possession of the Intruder, but she couldn't carry it all out of there on her own. The four crates had to weigh hundreds of sphere. She did not want to destroy the warehouse and trigger the need to rebuild the structure, and it wouldn't sufficiently slow down the Intruder, anyway.

She reviewed the memories that Liassa had given her about the land surrounding Rihanna. Nearby to the warehouses was a very deep lake. It was a little over two lengths away. There were four crates of the metal, and considering the length of the process and the materials necessary to make Black Sol, this was likely to be the full supply of the stuff in the entire world. With Rihanna being so well protected by the Ryhim, this would be the perfect hiding place. No one here would know what it was or its worth, so there would be no need to protect it.

Ales made a rude gesture at the monitoring device in one corner of the warehouse and then mentally commanded the fifth and sixth levels of her Constraints to open. She snapped the lid back onto the first crate and then hefted it onto her shoulder. It was large, but thankfully not so large that it was awkward to carry with her increased strength. Even with fast maevae, it would take them a lot longer to reach the warehouse than it would take her to deal with the Black Sol.

They would eventually figure out what she had done with it, but by then, she hoped to find a way to permanently destroy the stuff. The real question was how the Intruder had gotten the materials necessary to make so much. Some of the ingredients necessary to produce Black Sol alloy were near impossible to procure even for one of the Tier.

"It was not luck that we came here next," Ales said.

She paused for a long moment, and then he was there standing in the doorway of the warehouse, his diamond grin shining with pride.

"I must be losing my touch," Zezzhz said.

"Will you be guiding everything we do, Father?" Ales asked.

"Of course not, Daughter. This is only the most immediate danger that needs to be resolved. I only subtly influenced events so that your path to the Ryhim was the easiest to take. If you had chosen another path, I would have allowed you to take that one instead. I meant it when I said that the Lightleaf trees are the last advantage that we can give you. Anything from here on out is up to you. We may give you indirect advice on how to proceed from time to time, but we are pushing the boundaries of consequence with our interference if we do any more. We have not been so directly in contact with the world for hundreds of thousands of cycles, and the power that we have applied will not dissipate for hundreds of generations. But none of this is why you have called me here."

"It used to be that we could lock the Lightleaf network so that only those with the proper signature could use them. Is that still true?"

"These trees are just as those in Ahal. Further, Kinas spent his final Intervals making sure that nothing could possibly happen to them."

"I didn't see the other grove as an endpoint when I accessed the network. Can you tell me where the other grove is? Is it a place we can retreat to in the event that we need a safe harbor?"

Zezzhz frowned for a long moment and then shook his head.

"No, daughter, I cannot tell you that. It is something you must discover on your own," Zezzhz said, regret filling his voice.

"Do you mean for Rihanna to be a home for us?" Ales asked hopefully. Zezzhz just smiled.

"That, my Daughter, is for you all to decide." Zezzhz winked at her and then vanished.

Ales sighed and went through the open door. She started an awkward jog, allowing her Cellstructs to take over some of the controls of her body to ensure that she did not trip on her way to the lake. It didn't take her long to toss all four boxes into the lake. When there was still no response, she hid herself in the woods. She intended to wait until something happened, even if it took days. Thankfully, it did not take that long.

Two hours later, a large Hiluk came slinking out of the forest. It was far too cautious to be normal. Besides that fact, it was one of the mountain breeds. Its hide was black as night, which was beyond unusual. She watched the creature sniff around the warehouses. It wasn't going to be following her scent. She had used her Cellstructs to trap all of the scent molecules against her body, hiding her scent entirely.

The creature's tail did not wag, which was somehow disconcerting. She had never seen a hiluk that wasn't sleeping with such a still tail. She really wished that it had sent something that could answer questions. She watched the hiluk. It finally turned around and headed for the forest. Ales considered for a long moment whether it would be better to follow the animal or to wait and see if someone else came to investigate. She wished that she had not sent Lia to help the boy. She opened her mental link to see if perhaps Lia had come back, but there was no response. There really was no chance that the hiluk was going to lead her to anything important. At that moment, though, it was her only lead to anything, so she did the next best thing.

She used one of the things that she had taken the previous cycle to make, something that she had carried often. It was hard to make but worth the effort. She went back to the warehouse door and pulled open the flap on one of the pouches on her belt. She took out a glass vial and unscrewed the cap. The silvery powder inside had been given an elementary force charge. When she looked at it with her Vision, it glowed brightly. The force charge would transfer to anyone who touched it. It wouldn't wear off no matter how hard someone tried to clean it, and it wouldn't fade for cycles. She scattered the dust over the inside of the door and the ground outside. She didn't use it all. It was too hard to make to waste it. If anyone came to investigate, she would find them. She recapped the vial and then dashed into the woods to catch up with the hiluk.

12

Warran stared at the disturbingly black orb on his work bench with consternation. He could not imagine what was wrong with what he had done. He had followed every instruction in the memories he had been given from Verdant. Kiltik, after an entire rotation of combing through them, had confirmed that the instructions were complete. There were things in them that he did not fully understand yet, but he was sure that he had gotten everything of the mechanical workings of the Mind right. He had spent an entire rotation examining the memories before he had begun forming the thousands of paper-thin layers of substrate that would be the framework upon which he would be able to inscribe the channels for the neural network.

He had ruined at least a hundred layers of the substrate before he was able to successfully impregnate a single of one of them. The entire time, Kiltik's presence over his shoulder was unnerving. He had finally banished the Mind from his workshop. It wasn't that Kiltik had done anything threatening, or even impolite. He just felt so inadequate around the Mind who had completed the first 200 layers with perfect precision to instruct him on how it was done. The Mind had told him that he had to do the rest anyway, because if the substrate wasn't handled by human hands, it would not be properly infused with the right elementary forces to properly channel a Mind's life force.

Those were the parts that Warran did not understand at all. How was his handling of the materials imparting elementary forces? It made no sense to him. How was he supposed to know if he was doing it right? He opened his Vision and carefully ran his fingers over the black casing. The orb's internal elementary force locks, triggered by the correct pattern, sprang open. The bottom of the orb receded slightly into the casing, letting it stand steadily on the table. It was balanced in such a way that it would always return to this position, but to allow one of the Tier to assist the Mind within, a more stable base was necessary.

According to Ales, even the Minds could become ill in a way. The layers of substrate that acted as the repository for their neural network could degrade for various reasons. Sometimes, they would be replaced by a helpful member of the Tier so that the Mind could remain healthy. He didn't remove any of the layers then, though.

The top part of the orb split down the middle and the two halves retracted to the sides, falling slowly open to reveal the delicate bondsteel framework that held the layers of the substrate. In the case where they needed to be removed, there was a further trigger to allow the internal framework to be retracted as well. Warran didn't need to go that far.

He examined the layers of substrate through the framework. To his Vision, the Sol alloy lines running across the surface of the substrate glowed subtly with elementary force charges. Was that right? He wished that Kiltik had not gone with Ilsa. He had to awaken the Mind before he could transfer all of Verdant's memories into the shell. The resulting Mind would not be Verdant as Warran understood it. It would have all of Verdant's memories, and to some extent, it would be influenced by those memories. But this would be a new Mind. It would have to make its choices about whether or not to help the Tier. He was almost afraid of what it would say when it did finally awaken and then was infused with Verdant's memories.

"What's the matter?" His daughter's voice was a comforting sound.

"I've done everything I am supposed to, and it still won't wake up," Warran explained.

"Maybe it's still tired?" Warran grinned at that. Despite what she had been through she had not lost the innocence of childhood. Not yet.

"Maybe you're right, Midget."

He turned away from his work. She had grown over the past cycle, but she was still small for her age. Ales said she always would be small. She had explained something about her biological structure and how it predicted her bodily development. She had lost Warran within ten words. He was great with anything mechanical, but when Ales started talking, he felt like an idiot. It seemed that everyone felt like that around her except possibly Lia, but even Lia admitted that Ales was something special. Kayna climbed up onto the stool next to his. It was taller to accommodate her shorter stature.

"Maybe it's just afraid," Kayna said. She put her tiny hands on the outside of the case. "When you're little like me, everything can be scary."

Warran tilted his head and eyed the glowing pulse of light inside the casing. He remembered something that was in the instructions.

"Once the synaptic bridging grid is in place, all that is required to awaken the Mind is the presence of a sound, safe soul."

He had had no idea what that had meant when he read it. But now he did. The problem was that he wasn't that kind of soul. He wasn't sound or safe. Maybe one day he would be, but right now, he wasn't. He was still recovering from what happened in Vilhena and so was Kayna, though her recovery was going much better than his own. He could barely touch his irons without feeling that pain again. However, he did know someone that was safe and sound.

"Kavan."

Warran didn't shout, just raised his voice just enough to get the attention of the assistant the Ryhim had left with him. The young man was one of their best Fixers, and he had been overjoyed to be working with Warran. He was almost annoying in how helpful he had been. He had learned a great deal in the last few rotations, and Warran knew that he was hoping to be asked to become one of the Tier. Sadly, Warran knew that he did not have the temperament. He had an incredible thirst for knowledge that could easily turn into greed if he was given the power of the Tier. It was disconcerting how much his Vision let him see about a person if he looked into their eyes.

"Yes, Antieri?" Warran grimaced at the sound of the title, but he didn't correct Kavan. It had not done any good to try to get him to stop using it.

"I need to get a message to Rihanna. What's the fastest way?"

"By rakling. I keep a few messenger flits with me on extended trips so that I can get reports back and forth quickly from the forges when there are alloys of metals I want to report on, or when I come up with a better design for something we are already using."

Racklings were small winged lizards, sometimes called flits like any animal with the ability to fly. They were extremely intelligent. The flits could be very easily taught to seek a certain spot, and they would always find their way, as long as you left them out where they could see the terrain as it went by. They seemed to be able to remember landmarks, somehow. They were also extremely fast fliers, able to cover hundreds of lengths in a single day. Even more importantly, they were ideal as messengers because they could change the color of their skin, making them all but impossible to find when they choose to roost for the night.

From where they were, a rakling would get to Rihanna in about three days. Ales or Lia might only take a few hours to get back. He knew that Lia had run fifteen lengths in half that amount of minutes when she was going at top speed. She loved to run, and it seemed impossible to tire her. Warran took out a piece of paper and scribbled a note in Tieran asking Lia or Ales to pay him a visit. He added the names of the prince and princess of Clan Mizami. He also wrote "For the Tier" on the outside of the envelope in the Common tongue. He took the time to seal the note with a dusting of bondstructs.

He had not gained Cellstructs of his own, so he could not interface directly with the tiny machines, but he knew how to issue them commands. If anyone but Ales or Lia attempted to open the note, they would have to destroy it to get it open. Further, the bondstructs would send out a short-range signal that, if the Tier were in range, would alert them to the fact that a message meant for them had been opened by another. Writing it in Tieran was another measure of security. Ales had taught them all the language expressly for the purpose since no one had spoken, written, or read it in over 2,500 cycles. He handed the note over to Kavan.

"Send this to the prince and princess of your Clan. The fastest one of your bunch, Kavan. We still have a lot of work to do here, and we're short on time." Kavan turned away a little too eagerly. "And Kavan, do not try to open it. You wouldn't be able to read it anyway." Kavan looked offended for a moment, but then their eyes met, and Warran's unsettling glowing gaze bore into him. He went pale.

"Of course not, Antieri. I will send it post-haste." Kavan hurried out of the workshop.

"I don't like him. He's too..." Kayna made a little fidgety hand gesture.

"Nervous? Eager?" Warran suggested.

"Both?" Kayna's voice turned up at the end making it a question. Eager, she knew, but nervous, she wasn't exactly sure of. Warran laughed.

"A good guess, Midget. Nervous means he's worried all the time. Anxious is another word for it." His daughter absorbed new words like a sponge.

"Then I am right!" Kayna said proudly. He mussed her hair, and she smiled.

"Yeah, Midget, you are right. About the Mind, too. I think it's afraid to awaken into the world, and we can't make it feel safe enough to wake up. You're going to be an amazing Fixer someday."

"Nuh-uh, I wanna be a big strong katali like Lia!" she said excitedly, adding a little roar. Warran laughed and she giggled.

"So not a Fixer like your dad, huh? I don't think you can Fix things with paws." He said.

"Oh, well then maybe I will stay like this, then."

"Oh you think so, huh?" Warran chuckled.

She nodded.

"What do you say we take another look at the spark trap?" Warran asked.

Kayna nodded enthusiastically. The spark trap was the elementary force bomb that Warran had been working on since he had finished the mechanical part of Verdant's new housing. He had not been able to get the frequencies and output of the energy discharge tuned so that it would be enough to penetrate the armor or other protection that the Intruder could place around itself. But the real problem he was having was making the device durable enough to withstand the sort of trauma it would endure in use. It wouldn't be much good if it could be broken by a solidly thrown rock. Kiltik had left him a store of bondstructs made for various purposes. He had used most of those in the construction of Verdant's new shell.

Both he and Kiltik had decided that after what had happened with Verdant that each Mind needed new protection to keep them safe in case they ended up without a body. That was his third project, one that he had no idea where to start with at all. He had the plans, but they were out of his range of knowledge. There were ten books worth of knowledge stored in his head that he still had not absorbed, and he needed most of them to even begin to start on a machine that would be able to produce synthoid bodies like the one that Kiltik had constructed for itself.

He wasn't even sure it was a good idea to build such a thing. Kiltik's body had only been prevented from causing incredible harm because the Mind had been quick to contain the issue. If the Intruder got ahold of a machine that could build bodies like that, it could kill them all with it. He shook his head, looking at the half-built cylindrical chamber in the corner of the workshop. He decided it was best that it never be found.

"You know what, kiddo, we've been stuck in this place too long. We both need a break. It's early enough. Let's take a ride into town and find some other kids for you to play with. I'm sure those two boys you thrashed at Kep are dying for a rematch," Warran said, and Kayna's face lit up.

Kep was a children's game that Kayna loved because her mother taught her how to play it. It was a game children played the world over. Even the poorest child could play it because all you needed was a handful of rocks large enough for the game, though there were better ways to play it. You started by drawing a line in the dirt and then a circle a way's away. The more skilled the kids playing the game, the further away the circle was drawn.

Lots of kids played with a sack of colored balls instead. Most were made of heavy wood or stone, and kids got really attached to their Kep balls, believing that they were lucky. You would stand behind the line and toss the ball into the circle. At the end of the game, the kid with the most stones in the circle won. There were some small variations on the game. If you were able to play with colored balls, often the object of the game was to knock the other kid's balls out of the circle. Kayna was especially good at that version of the game, and Warran had seen her knock balls out of the ring from almost twenty paces away. No one could aim a Kep ball like his little girl.

"They don't stand a chance," Kayna said with a grin. They went out the door. Kavan was sitting in the little office that he had claimed when they arrived.

"Kavan, we're going to ride into town so Kayna can have some play time. I'll leave half the guards here with you. Did you send that message?" Kavan looked up from a notebook he was scribbling in.

"On its way. Will you be back tonight?"

"No clue. Depends on how much fun the Midget is having. We might spend the night under the stars."

Warran noticed what was on the notebook page Kavan had been scribbling on. It was a depiction of the chamber in his workshop.

"Kayna, why don't you go outside and tell Jak to saddle our maevae?" Warran said.

"Okie," she said, and skipped down the hall. Warran stepped into Kavan's office, his facial expression morphing into an angry scowl. Kavan looked pale. Warran held out his hand wordlessly. Kavan picked up the notebook and held it to his chest protectively.

"I warned you, Kavan, that when you came on to work with me, I would not allow any written notes or diagrams concerning my work. You were to assist when I needed your help, and you would learn some things in the process, but only the things you could retain by rote memory. Give me the notebook and any others that you have kept. Do not make me ask twice, and do not tell me there are no others. I will know if you are lying to me." Warran's voice was stern.

"I can't remember it all, Antieri, it isn't fair," Kavan protested.

"The notebooks, Kavan." Warran demanded, clearly becoming more agitated by the moment. Kavan handed over the one he was holding. He opened a drawer in his desk and took out two more, handing them to Warran.

"I trusted you, Kavan, and you were warned that it would not be fair. Who else has seen these?" Warran asked. His eyes were blazing brightly as he watched Kavan.

Kavan opened his mouth, fully intending on telling Warran that no one else had seen them. The words died on his tongue.

"I have sent copies of most of my sketches to the Clan Fixers in Rihanna," Kavan finally admitted.

Jak came in a moment later, having finished saddling the maevae. He immediately felt the mood of the room and his hand went to the hilt of his sword.

"What is it?" the barrel-chested man asked. He was imposing, and his tone brooked no argument, but even he shrank away from Warran's angry gaze.

"Jak, I will need a map of Rihanna and supplies for the ride. Kayna and I must go to Rihanna personally. You are to dispatch a rider to return with a brace of the Lance Guard from Angran. They are to guard this place. Their orders are to kill any who approach who are not one of the Tier. Take no chances, Jak. What I am leaving behind cannot fall into the hands of the enemy. Kavan has shared my work with others, and that means that this place is no longer safe. My workshop will need to be moved. Kavan is to be imprisoned until I or another of the Tier return to decide what is to be done with him."

Warran counted the flits in the cage in Kavan's office. There were two missing from the cage.

"What messages have you sent by rakling?" Warran asked Kavan, who had his mouth open to protest. He snapped his mouth shut.

"Kavan, you have likely put in danger not only my life, but the lives of the guards and that of my little girl. You could have learned things from me that you would not anywhere else. This is not a game, and you have treated it like one where the knowledge you can gain from me is a prize. You have brought shame on your Clan and family. Now, unless you are answering my questions, keep your tongue behind your teeth while I decide how to best diffuse this situation you created."

"One to the Prince and Princess like you requested, and one was a batch of sketches and specifications to the Fixers in Rihanna," Kavan admitted after a moment.

"Sit down and write a list of all of the Fixers who you can think of that might have seen the things you sent them. I assume that they were exact copies of what you have written for yourself in these journals?" Warran asked.

"Yes, Antieri," Kavan replied. He took out a clean sheet of paper and started scribbling down names. He was done within a few minutes.

"I'm sorry," he said as he scribbled.

"No, you're not. You're just saying those words because you think you should. You have no idea the scale of the damage you may have done. Apologies are immaterial at this point. Make up for it with actions."

Kayna came back into the hallway and looked at him imploringly. Warran gave Kavan one last glare and then closed his Vision before turning to Kayna.

"I'm sorry, Kayna. We have to go to Rihanna. Can you please get your bag and Daddy's bag?"

She looked sad, but only for a moment before putting on her brave face.

"Yes, Daddy."

Kayna headed down the hall past the workshop towards their rooms. Warran went back to the workshop. He opened his Vision and looked around. The shop had a variety of extremely dangerous traps that he had constructed over the last few spans. Anyone who came into the room after he set the traps would not survive the experience. Not only that, the traps reset themselves, and could only be bypassed by another of the Tier. He went to the back wall. The chamber he could do nothing about but arm the traps. The spark trap, though, he could address.

He moved to the back of the chamber where it had been carved from the rock of the cave. There, he put his hand on the wall. A thick slab of the rock slid aside. The space within had been carved out with bondstructs and reinforced by multiple layers of bondsteel. It was large enough to hold the spark trap and all of his coded notebooks.

He removed his belt with its holstered lancers. He belted them around his waist and touched the grips. He closed his eyes and pulled his fingers away from them. It almost hurt to touch them. He wasn't sure he could draw and fire even now. Ales had worked with him on how to prepare himself to endure the pain. He closed the panel and the locks engaged. If anyone tried to force it open, everything inside would be destroyed. He touched the outer casing of the fledgling Mind on his workbench. It slid back together and locked into place.

"I'll keep you safe," he promised.

He carefully nestled it into a padded satchel that he had made specifically to hold it. He slung the bag over his shoulder and went back out, arming the traps behind him. He locked the door shut and sighed. Kayna pulled the door to their rooms closed. She was carrying two packs that were far too large for her little body. Warran took his and slung it over the same shoulder as the new Mind.

Kayna had changed into her divided riding dress. It was one of the things Ales had bought her and she loved it dearly. It had skirts that hung to her ankles that were divided in the front and back to let her comfortably straddle a maevae. The fabric was thick, warm, and soft. It had long sleeves and a thickly padded hood that attached with snaps. The hood made it extremely comfortable to sleep in. It was gray, and had long sleeves with blue trim at the cuff, collar, and hem.

Blue was Kayna's favorite color. She had braided her hair, and tied it off with a blue ribbon.

"Did you wash up?" Warran asked. She nodded.

"Daddy, would it be ok if I did want to be like Lia?"

They walked out towards the cave entrance. He took a deep breath, trying to come to grips with the idea that his daughter was considering being a different species. Finally, he just laughed.

"I think that I'll love you no matter what you want to do, half-pint."

They stopped outside where the ten guards Angran had sent with them were waiting.

"Jak, no one is to be allowed into my workshop. The defenses have been armed, and anyone who is not one of the Tier cannot enter without grievous consequences." Jak nodded.

"I will make sure that it is kept secure, Antieri," Jak said.

"I'll return as quickly as I can. Until then, clear the building, Jak. Get everything that isn't in the workshop onto a cart. Please ask the men to pack the things in our rooms carefully."

"As you wish, Antieri."

Warran pinched the bridge of his nose.

"Gods, would you all stop calling me that?" Warran grumbled before he raised his voice again.

"Linten and Hagar will be going with you. They are saddled and ready," Jak said.

Warran frowned, but it was pointless to argue. They had their orders to protect him and his daughter.

"As long as they don't slow us, that is fine."

"We will not," Hagar said. He led three maevae out from behind the bluff.

"Maybe it would be best if the girl stayed here?" Linten suggested.

"I'll not be leaving my daughter behind. Besides, she'll ride you and Hagar ragged. Trust me, if anyone slows us it will not be my daughter," Warran said.

They nodded and eyed Kayna skeptically. Warran just grinned. They would learn that lesson the hard way. Kayna swarmed expertly up the stirrup strap and slung herself into the saddle of her sleek blue maevae that she had named Bluedrop. She gave the soldiers a waiting-on-you look.

13

Ilsa eyed the Clan Chieftess narrowly across the table. The woman had been a source of ire from day one in the camp. Kiltik sat in Ilsa's lap, and she knew he was listening to everything. He had been amazingly helpful in getting information, but hadn't said a word the entire time. Each time, he had just listened, and then they would speak later. He was a wellspring of knowledge, and she had apologized to him for underestimating him early on in their time with Clan Navano. They had become fast friends, and she had learned a great deal about Tieran history from him that Lia had not had time to teach her. He had taken very well to wearing the form of the shuvoo, and no one in the camp thought he was anything more. Not even Juran had guessed, and he was quickly picking up his abilities as one of the Tier. She wasn't sure he would ever be able to tell until she told him. Even with her Vision, it was hard for her to tell the difference between Kiltik and a real shuvoo.

At first, she had thought that she and the Chieftess would be able to become friends, but after an entire rotation, it had become extremely obvious that she was just stalling for time. Ilsa knew that she had begun moving things out of the mine as soon as Ilsa had arrived. Juran had told her what was going on, but she had not wanted to be so blatant as to simply go around the Chieftess and find out for herself.

"I have been unfailingly polite, Chieftess, but my patience is at an end. What were you sent here to do? These mountains have dangerous levels of volcanic activity below the surface, and for intervals, your Clan has stubbornly refused to mine them because of the lives it would cost. Suddenly, you have broken that prohibition. Why?" Ilsa asked. Tirane's face slid into a scowl.

"Who do you think you are, girl? You are what, twelve cycles old? How dare you attempt to pry into our affairs?" Tirane growled indignantly.

Kiltik jumped out of Ilsa's lap a split second before she shot to her feet, her eyes burning with the light of her Vision.

"I am Tier!" Ilsa shouted, raising her fist and smashing it into the thick wooden tabletop. The table shattered like glass. The pieces of the table sprayed the walls and floor with detritus, but not a single piece hit Ilsa or Tirane. Ilsa held her balled fists at her sides and went on.

"I am putting myself in harm's way because elders of other Ryhim clans think there is something wrong. I am charged by the Gods to find out what." Ilsa pointed an angry finger at Tirane. "You will answer me, or I will find the answers for myself. The choice is yours!" Ilsa roared.

Tirane's eyes had grown wide with fear. Ilsa frowned and her Vision faded. She spun on her heel and stomped toward the tent's exit. She didn't feel shame for scaring the woman. Tirane had lied, stalled, and placated her for spans, and Ilsa had still tried to politely coax the chieftess to help her. Her anger was justified. She could not waste any further time here.

"Wait." Tirane's voice wavered, but it gained strength when she spoke again. "For intervals, we have been protected by the Black Wilds. The forest has never been a hospitable place for those who do not understand the magic it holds. But a few cycles ago, a party of soldiers from far Moonward breeched the forest and attacked Rihanna. We can only guess it was a probing attack to see what our defenses were like, as no further attacks have followed. The men wore odd armor, and had weapons made of dull black metal. The armor was impervious to any damage that we could do to it. It was a nightmare.

Finally, we were forced to burn the attackers to death after we forced them into an old warehouse on the edge of Rihanna. It cost us over a hundred warriors to do it. Some of our best. After it was over, our Searchers began to comb the old tomes from the time of Rihanna's building. Back to the knowledge that Kinas imparted when he lived among us. There, the Searchers found and deciphered plans for weapons that required the forging of Sol alloy. But the alloy requires the purest ore, and Kinas speculated that the ore would be found in the mountain borders of the Wilds. We were sent here to find what was needed to make the metal. That is why it is worth braving the dangers of the mountain," Tirane explained.

From what Ilsa knew, Sol alloy had been the precursor to bondsteel, and was very difficult to make. Black Sol alloy had been extremely dangerous. It allowed machines to draw living energy from humans and animals. Unfortunately, she was out of her depth here. She needed more information. She had no idea if there was some difference between Sol alloy and the black version of the metal. This was going to require a long talk with Kiltik to understand what her next move should be. Her tension drained away and she sighed.

"Tirane, I realize it must seem like I am trying to pry out information that I could use harm the Ryhim, but I promise you that nothing could be further from the truth. So I'm going to give you the chance to ask me any questions you would like, and I will answer if I can."

Kiltik made a soft sound of warning that was just loud enough for Ilsa to hear.

"I apologize for the table."

"I apologize for my disrespect. I worry for my people, and you seem like a blessing that could be too good to be true."

Ilsa reclaimed her seat, and Kiltik jumped back into her lap. Ilsa made an uncomfortable sound from his weight, but he quickly arranged himself to spread it across her entire lap. He had actually shed a great deal of his weight after the first time someone had tried to pick him up and found that he weighed at least five times what other shuvoo weighed. Now he was much closer to the fifteen sphere that he should have been. He said that the bondstructs would be just fine in an inert ball inside of their tent until he needed them again. It wasn't like anyone was going to carry away the compacted 150 sphere of weight easily.

"Why are you here?" Tirane asked.

"I'm here because the Tier have been charged by the Mother and Father with returning the full protection of the Tier to the world. We have found that there is something terribly wrong in Rihanna, and that it is affecting you all. I cannot say more than that until we know more about the threat," Ilsa explained.

"And you think that something we are doing is part of that threat?"

"I'm not making accusations. I think that what you are doing here might be part of the threat, but I can't know for certain until I consult with my sisters and brothers. The problem is from what we can see the problem is affecting all of the Ryhim everywhere. We are few right now, and so I have been sent to gather information and confer with my sisters and brothers before we decide on a course of action to help." She went on before Tirane could speak again. She was putting together the events as she went along, and the picture she was painting did not please her. "I think that if there is something wrong that you are likely participating unwittingly."

"So you think we are stupid?" Anger filled Tirane's voice.

"No, Tirane, and you don't think that's what I think, either. I think that someone you should be able to trust is using that trust against you. It's making you angry, and it should. But I'm here to help if I can. If you want my help, I need you to believe in me."

"I cannot just trust you because you say you are one of the Tier. We no longer know what the Tier stand for," Tirane said hesitantly.

"What would prove to you that I am working for your benefit?" Ilsa asked. Tirane sighed. "Before you speak, remember, I am working at the direction of the Gods. I may simply proceed at my discretion. I'm offering to ease your mind, but I can't wait for your trust forever. At some point, I must think of the greater good." Tirane stiffened, but then looked at the shattered fragments of the table littering her tent. The tension fell away.

"We have long since lost our faith in the gods, Ilsa. I have a hard time believing anything you are telling me, but I remember the legends. The only thing I can believe right now is that you are who you say you are." Tirane gestured at the shattered table. "But short of a conference with the Gods themselves, I can't see how I can just trust you with the secrets of my Clan. I am going to have to ask you to leave our camp."

Ilsa ground her teeth. She truly was not cut out for this. She disliked what she was going to have to do to deal with this impasse.

"I cannot leave, and if you attempt to force me to leave, there will be consequences that you cannot imagine." Tirane opened her mouth, but Ilsa spoke over her. "It is not a threat, Tirane, it is a certainty. Not only am I tutoring one of your people in his Tieran abilities, as you well know, but many others look to me for guidance at this point. Since you will not be convinced to listen to reason by me, I will send for my sister. Perhaps she can convince you."

Ilsa did not want to have to call for Ales. Ales would not take no for an answer. It would not be a pleasant experience for Tirane. She noticed Kiltik looking up at her, and she shook her head. Kiltik jumped down out of her lap, and she followed him out of the tent. He looked around to make sure that they were alone, and then looked up to her again.

"This One may have been able to convince That One to assist us," he said.

"I'm sure she would have been startled by you, but she is too paranoid. She is not going to budge. It's going to take something more, and I'm not sure how to do it. Niether of us is experienced enough in dealing with people like the others. Cole, Ales, or Lia may have been able to push her over the edge. I need time to think about how to approach her again."

As they approached the ring of tents surrounding the low hill where Tirane had made camp, Kiltik stopped speaking. They made their way through the tents towards the tent they had been given. It was close to the edge of the camp, but Juran had showed her how to set up the screens as well as hang carpets to make the interior portions of the tent soundproof. It was amazing how well it worked. She sat down on the couch, and Kiltik curled up next to her. He had adapted extremely well to the shuvoo body over the last few spans. His floppy ears lifted, and he picked his head up, staring off towards the sunward side of the tent.

"Hear something of interest?" she asked. After another long moment, he shook his head and put it back on his paws.

"Just someone passing close to the tent. A boy that cuts between all the tents all the time. It took This One a moment to catch his scent. You wish to know more about Sol alloy?" Kiltik asked. Ilsa nodded.

"Sol alloy was a secret of the Tier. It was an attempt to create a material that would resist the stresses that use by someone with the physical prowess of the Tier would apply to it. This One has detailed information concerning the manufacture of Sol alloy. Bondsteel was created to be given to the world in place of Sol. The benefits of materials of highly increased strength are undeniable. Sol alloy is more durable than bondsteel, but the Tier found it unsuitable to release knowledge of its creation to the world as it is a key component in the manufacture of Black Sol alloy. The danger that Black Sol presents to the world was too great to allow knowledge of either material to be released," Kiltik explained.

"So if that was the case, why would Kinas leave behind knowledge of how to make the stuff?" Ilsa asked.

"This One does not believe he would. This One suspects he may have mentioned the metal as aside to the creation of bondsteel, but This One finds it impossible to believe that Kinas would have left behind specific knowledge of the creation of Sol alloy."

Ilsa looked thoughtful.

"You can help them make bondsteel?" Ilsa asked.

"Creation of bondstructs and materials using bondstructs is This One's primary function."

"And how would bondsteel weapons perform against armor made of Sol alloy?"

"The difference in durability between Sol alloy and bondsteel is extremely subjective. The true difference is in longevity. Bondsteel requires more maintenance than Sol alloy. Sol alloy is entirely impervious to all environmental damage. It will not wear down over time due to exposure or use. Bondsteel can be weakened by exposure to water and other sorts of environmental damage. However, properly maintained bondsteel weapons would be just as effective against Sol as weapons made from the same."

"Then you would not have objections about helping these people learn how to create bondsteel?"

Kiltik lifted his head and let his tongue loll out of his mouth in pleasure, a behavior he had certainly picked up from the other Shuvoo.

"This One thinks that you are cleverer than you give yourself credit for, Ilsa Family Katane."

14

Ales crouched outside of what she was sure was not the end of the line. The hiluk had been extremely paranoid in its flight through Rihanna. It had doubled back at least a dozen times, trying to foul its scent trail. It had tried to spot followers, but Ales had run the entire time using Taking. There was no chance that the creature had seen her. She had managed to get near enough to the hiluk to tag it with the energetic powder, and it was a good thing she had. It had slunk into a sewer pipe below a house on the northern edge of the city. She could not fit down the pipe, and even if she could, she wouldn't have followed the poor creature. There was only one person who could safely follow that pipe. Unfortunately, he was five hundred lengths away. She sat atop the roof and watched the pipe for hours before Lia finally appeared next to her.

"This is growing more and more complicated, and I am starting to fear that splitting our forces was not the correct plan," Ales said. Lia settled herself next to Ales. She eyed the pipe with suspicion.

"I think you were right to do it. We need more information about what the clans are being asked to do before we can discover who might be holding the matrix. Maybe it is time to put the Lightleaves to use after all," Lia said.

"I think it might be as well. We should go together, though. I'm starting to get a terrible feeling about all of this. I think that maybe this is a trap being laid specifically for us, now."

"They must have been at this for cycles though to have built this sort of dissonance using the matrix." Lia was far from an expert in temporal prediction theories, but she knew it would take a long time to cause a visible problem like the one they were seeing.

"I agree. They can't be using the matrix against us, but that doesn't mean that the Intruder couldn't have altered its plans. There are numerous ways it could have found out where we were headed after what happened in Vilhena. We got away fairly clean, but we both knew that wouldn't protect us forever."

"You're making me worry about our new brothers and sisters, Ales."

"I don't think that we have much to worry about yet, but I could use Kiltik to follow this trail the hiluk has left behind. We need to know where it went." Ales pushed herself to her feet and strolled across the rooftop towards the center of Rihanna.

"It's been a long time since we traveled by light jump."

"You're not going to throw up, are you?"

They both hopped off of the rooftop, and landed softly in the alleyway between two large houses.

"I hope not. I rather enjoyed the last thing I ate, but I do not think it would be quite so appetizing coming out."

It was a common reaction after a light jump. One's body was disincorporated into particles of light and then traveled as energy at nearly the speed of light to the end point crystal, where the energy was then converted back to physical matter. Each end point crystal was imbued by the will of the Father with the magic necessary for the conversion. As long as it was regularly in full sunlight, the Father's magic would continue to be injected into the crystal. For a few moments as one's body was rebuilt and their life energies were reattached to the body, internal senses were completely scrambled. If one was not used to the sensation, it could easily cause someone to lose their meal.

"How is our patient doing?" Ales asked.

Lia switched to speaking mentally. *{Almost back to full strength, and as usual, you were right. She is quickly learning how to navigate by hearing alone. Do you think she could be one of us?}*

Ales shrugged. Without her eyes, it was hard to make a determination about her in that respect. It was not unheard of for one of the Tier to come from among the non-human population of Ahlysim.

"Hard to say until we can restore her eyes, but you would know better than I would. You were responsible for inducting at least two dozen non-humans into the Tier in our time," Ales said.

{I haven't been able to speak with her enough. There are not enough of my Cellstructs left in her to speak anymore. I am almost back to full strength, as well.} Lia explained.

"I'm glad to hear that." Ales ruffled the fur between her sister's ears, and Lia made a rumbling purring noise.

{You worry too much,} Lia said.

{I worry exactly the right amount, thank you very much,} Ales said through their mental link.

They passed people in the market square, several blocks away from the Lightleaf grove. It was clear that they knew who and what Ales and Lia were. Many made formal bows as they passed, but almost everyone who saw them greeted them in some way or another.

They passed the warehouse they had been using as their home, and Ales peered in through one of the windows. They had blacked it out, but it was no obstacle for her Vision. The banic was sleeping soundly. Boxes and crates had been setup on the warehouse floor in a haphazard pattern. Lia had been using it as a sort of obstacle course for the banic. There was no telling how long it would take for them to restore the banic's eyes so Lia had been teaching her methods for navigating by sound and smell. Unfortunately, she was apparently left to her own devices at this point without Cellstructs of her own to allow them to communicate more readily.

Ales was about to turn back to the path when her Cellstructs chimed a warning inside of her mind. A glowing red arrow was overlaid in her sight, pointing back towards the banic. She turned back towards the window, and the arrow resolved itself into the shape of a small creature not bigger than the palm of her hand. It was right next to the banic. It was no normal animal for her Cellstructs to identify it in red like that.

Ales took a step back to give herself room and drew a small metal spike out of one of the inner pockets of her coat. She pushed open the first level of her Constraints. Her muscles tightened with increased strength. She whipped her hand forward, and the spike punched through the glass of the window. It shot across the room, and slammed into the wall next to the banic with amazing force for such a small item. The sharp spike passed through the plank of the wall with ease, and skewered the tiny animal inside of the wall.

The banic shook itself awake. It tilted its head one way, then the other. It snuffled at the air, and then turned towards the wall where the bondsteel spike was sticking out of it. Ales wrenched open the door, and hurried inside. Lia did not ask questions but followed right behind. Ales put a comforting hand on the banic's head. She spoke softly into its ear. That was one of the few things Lia had been able to impart to the banic in their short time, a basic understanding of their language. Ales spoke Tieran.

"Everything is fine. I did not mean to startle you, but something dangerous is here. We are dealing with it. Please go back to your rest," Ales whispered. The banic settled back down, eager to return to sleep.

Ales slid a Sol dagger from a sheath on her belt, and opened her Vision a little further. It made it easier to see through the wood. The tiny creature was still alive, so her shot had been good. The tiny spike had driven itself through the little vark's pelt just above the shoulder. She could see that the small carnivorous rodent was absolutely brimming with crude Cellstructs, just like the ones they had cleared from the banIc.

Varks were not very smart, but people thought otherwise, because their paws had opposable digits that allowed them to get into many places that other rodents could not. It struggled violently. The spike had gone into the wall at a downward angle, though, and had forced the tiny creature into an awkward position where it had no leverage to pull itself free.

Ales pushed open the second level of her constraints and made three quick slashes at the wall with the dagger. It bit deeply into the wood, and a section of the paneling fell away, leaving a hole the size of one of Lia's paws. The tiny black vark snapped and made shrieking noises at them through the hole. Ales reached in and pinned the small creature to the outside of the wall. She pulled the bondsteel dart out of the wall to free the creature. Then, she put a finger against the tiny hole in its pelt. Cellstructs poured from her fingertip and into the rodent. Ales had always been extremely accomplished at taking over structures that did not belong to her, and unlike the previous times she had dealt with the creations of the Intruder, this time she was prepared.

She Cut her way into the crude Cellstructs, accessing their information storage units. The information that she pulled out of them was impregnated with something terrible. It was some sort of energetic infection that attempted to spread itself to her Cellstructs. She slowly sat down on the floor, focusing all of her attention on the battle raging inside of her mind.

She dove into a space within her mind. It was a large white room with six sides. Each of the walls acted as a window onto different parts of her mind. One wall displayed all of the information coming from her Cellstructs. She didn't really have a body when delving inside of her own mind, but she projected one to make it easier to focus. She pointed at the wall that displayed her Cellstructs, and the other walls went blank for a moment. Then, that wall split out into multiple streams of information one on each wall. She could see three of the walls at a time. While she was inside of her own mind she could do almost anything, but splitting her focus six ways was inefficient. The walls were covered with glowing writing and figures.

Ever-updating information about what was happening with her Cellstructs flowed across the walls. One of them was lit in red. Red was a warning color in her mind, and so that meant something was going wrong there. As things went more out of control, it would deepen in color from red to dark red, and then finally it would go black if she completely lost control. It wasn't headed that way yet. The infection was contained in the Cellstructs that were best adapted for storing information. These were centered in her brain.

She looked at one of the blue walls. These displayed the information from the Cellstructs in other areas of her body. She waved her hand at one of the walls to bring it to the position directly in front of her. She requested that they move to her brain and move all of the Cellstructs from her brain into her chest. They reacted quickly, flowing into her bloodstream to move them. With that done, she waved her hand at the red screen to move it back to the forefront of her attention.

The information and figures moving across it told her that her Cellstructs were on even footing with this infection. She couldn't let that balance stay that way, so she mentally connected to the Cellstructs fighting the infection. The information started to flash across the display much more quickly now that she had directly focused on them. The information she had pulled from the vark was like a sphere of glass with a smaller sphere within. She could sense that there were multiple spheres layered inside one another, protecting the information and attacking her. Her Cellstructs were simply surrounding the information with energetic defenses.

She directed the rest of her Cellstructs to make links with the ones already holding the infected energy at bay. Every bit of information stored inside her mind was a bit of elementary force. All of those bits of energy vibrated with an extremely complex pattern of frequencies. Every living thing had an impossible to duplicate organic pattern.

The pattern in the crude Cellstructs that had been controlling the vark was chaotic, but artificially generated. That meant it had to have some sort of pattern or it would be unusable even for the intruder. Her initial attempts to read it sounded as if someone were clawing a chalkboard inside of her skull. Her Cellstructs were attempting to decode the chaotic pattern of noise that made up the energy trying to infect her. When she allowed her Cellstructs to connect to the power of her own mind, the chaotic noise began to resolve into a pattern. It was a long, complex repeating pattern but the pattern was there. The various layers of defenses that surrounded the information she wanted were actually vibrating with different distinct patterns that were combined to create the turmoil in the pattern.

Once her Cellstructs recognized the pattern, they began to construct an energy opposite to the pattern. It took a long moment, and Ales lost track of time as she allowed her

Cellstructs to mine her own personal mental energy reserves to construct the counter pattern. When it was finally finished, her Cellstructs relinquished control to her, and she mentally forced the counter energy against the energetic shell protecting the information she wanted.

As soon as the counter touched, there was a violent reaction, and the elementary force shells shattered. The energy dissipated into its harmless base elementary force components. They looked harmless, but her paranoia told her that it might just be what she was meant to think. The white hexagon room returned, and she swiped her hand at the red wall which was now displayed in orange, which was slowly transitioning to purple. It would return to blue now that the threat had passed.

The wall shifted to give her access to the latent Cellstructs, and she set a portion of them to monitor her energetic structure for the next two spans. By then, her own elementary force would overtake any possible contaminants remaining in her pool of personal energies. If something bad was going to happen, it would happen by then. That done, she pulled back from her mental space to reality. Lia was lying next to her in the darkness, her large almond shaped eyes glowing brightly. One orange, one gold.

"Are you well, Sister?" Lia asked.

"The mental energies from the vark were protected by an elementary force construct that attempted to infect me. Why do you look so concerned?"

Ales remembered the part in the middle where she had lost track of time and queried her Cellstructs for the actual time. They reported to her that it had been almost three days since they had begun the process of decoding the energies.

"Oh gods, I'm sorry, Lia. The construct was multi-layered, and it required mining my own mental energies to build the counter structure. I allowed my Cellstructs to do the mining while I put myself into a sleep cycle. I thought that would take a few hours at most, not days," Ales said.

A chime sounded inside of her head indicating that the information had been integrated into her memories. Her

Cellstructs directed her to the information, allowing her consciousness to access the memory of the tiny creature. That was what had been there, the memories of the animal, such as they were.

"Was it worth it?" Lia asked.

"Very much so. I know where that Hiluk was going," Ales said grimly.

~ END OF PART 2 ~

Juran stared at the metal in the burning forge, waiting for the color to change to show that it was at the proper temperature. Kiltik had produced bondstructs that would help with the alignment of the molecules in the steel to ensure that every single bit of it was without flaw. They had cleared away everyone in the forge except for Juran, who was the only worker in the process of becoming one of the Tier. He would be able to teach more people, but he needed Kiltik's help to learn how to make the material the first time. Kiltik had taken on the form of a human about Kayna's size. He was rapidly assembling an unrecognizable tangle of gears, wires, and other mechanical parts. Kiltik had started to give Ilsa traditional Fixer training at the same time that he had started teaching Juran about bondsteel.

"Why doesn't he have Repair? He seems an ideal candidate for it," Ilsa asked.

"This One hasn't the slightest idea. You would have to pose your question to Fahmor, if we ever find That One, or if it interests you so, pray to the Father for guidance on the subject. He may choose to answer your questions," Kiltik replied. He had not stopped working on the forming machine on his workbench.

The Forge was one of the only permanent buildings in the camp surrounding the foot of the mountain. They had grumbled about relinquishing it to her use alone. Once Ilsa had offered to teach them how to make bondsteel, Tirane didn't hesitated to dump the other fixers out on their ears. She noticed Juran was pulling the glowing metal out of the forge. Kiltik got up from where he was sitting and moved to the anvil. Juran put the glowing metal on the forge and lifted a hammer. He pounded the metal until it started to resemble a sword. When the color started to darken, he slid it back into the forge as Kiltik watched.

"Keep on with that until you are prepared to temper the metal for strength. The difference between regular steel and bondsteel happens during this treatment process. You will use bondstructs during this process to remove impurities in the metal, and to align the molecular structure to remove all possible flaws. You will need to instruct the manufactory as to the disposition of the item that the bondstructs are being created for. Once the bondstructs finish their work, the durability of the resultant metal will be such that further shaping of any sort will be impossible without degrading the structure of the metal in a way that is detrimental to the end result," Kiltik explained.

"Kiltik, I do not think either of us understood half of that." Kiltik turned his featureless face to Ilsa.

"Gods, you are creepy like that. Can you please form a face?"

The featureless head tilted one way, then the other. "This One has no need for facial features," Kiltik said.

"For me, please."

Kiltik shrugged. Faint facial features formed on the blank slate of his skull. A moment later, a nose, mouth, and eyes formed on the face. They were not completely human, but it was much better than the blank slate. His lips moved properly when he spoke, which helped even more.

"This One is simply attempting to imply that bondsteel is of such strength that further shaping through the use of increased temperatures will not be possible without causing irrecoverable damage to the object."

Ilsa was disassembling a lancer that she had built herself with a little help from Kiltik. For some reason, it wasn't working properly. She thought that something in the trigger mechanism wasn't coming together right when it was activated. She had read and re-read the document that Kiltik had given her about the chemical work necessary to create the solar cells, but it still looked like a foreign language to her. Kiltik was next to her now, reading the document as well.

"This One apologizes, Ilsa. This One is producing more basic documents so that we can increase your knowledge to the point where you need to be to complete your work to your satisfaction."

Ilsa sighed. She wished that she had been learning from her Father all this time.

"Do Tier have some sort of increased learning capacity, because I feel like what you are talking about is cycles worth of work."

Kiltik hummed. "Not in the way you are thinking, Ilsa Family Katane. Because you lack Cellstructs, you cannot retain information the same way the Tier of old would. However, even without Cellstructs, you will retain everything you learn with perfect clarity, up to the capacity of your brain's elementary force structure. You are able to grasp any subject that you have clear interest in without limit. Unlike Ales and Liassa Family Katane, you are only able to process a single data stream at any given time."

Ilsa banged her head gently on the desk.

"So I can read all of this, and I'll learn it as quickly as I can read it, but only as quickly as I can read it."

"Is that not what This One said?"

Ilsa just groaned without lifting her head. Kiltik went back to his work bench and started assembling the machine he had been working on at high speed once more. He had told them both that the machine he was working on to manufacture bondstructs for the Ryhim would be about the size of the back of a wagon when he was finished with it. They wouldn't really have to do much in terms of learning how to operate the machine. What he would have to teach them is how to communicate to the bondstructs making up the machine what they wanted to do.

Kiltik and Ilsa had spoken at length on how the machine would function. Kiltik assured her he would hide traps inside of the machine so that it would immediately destroy itself if it came into the presence of the Intruder. He was also building a mechanism into the device so that it would contact Kiltik and the Tier with Cellstructs if anyone attempted to disassemble it to learn its secrets. They had told no one that they were including the failsafes. Kiltik had warned them that the machine would be complex beyond their ability to understand without assistance from one of the Tier, and attempting to disassemble the machine would destroy it.

Juran had taken the steel out of forge, and was shaping it carefully with a hammer. The sword blade was curved slightly, with a single edge. He had hammered the blade wider near the middle extending to the end, and there was only a small tapper at the other end for the tang. The tang was almost the full width of the blade. Juran quenched the blade into a barrel. He pulled it out quickly and looked down the length of the blade to check that it had stayed straight. He slid it into the jaws of a vice and adjusted it carefully. Then, he put the tang into the vice and left it standing there, straight up and down.

"So what are you trying to learn?" Juran asked. Clearly, he had been following their conversation. She could see white starting to bleed into the red iris of his left pupil.

"Like you, I have three Circles of power to learn. I have trained extremely hard to learn Breaking because it is dangerous without training, but I am also a Fixer and a Finder. I still have a lot to learn about those powers. Kiltik is attempting to teach me the basics of the Circle of Repair. I'm doing a poor job at it. Repair is an odd power. I look at the lancer and I understand the parts. I see how they are supposed to fit together, but I'm missing basic knowledge to go with that understanding. I can build the lancer and it will work, but I don't know *why* it works. So I am going to have to start from scratch. You'll have similar things to learn about your powers, depending on what they are. I'll teach you enough about Breaking to keep you safe, but if you want to know everything that I know, you will have to decide to come with me," Ilsa explained.

"I can't. I have Manat to take care of. Maybe when he can take care of himself, I will be able to," Juran said. Manat was learning writing and numbers with the rest of the children in the camp, and they had minders, but that wouldn't always be the case. They didn't have anyone else.

"I can't make you come with me, Juran, and I can't make you decide to be one of the Tier, but I can tell you that I don't think you'll be happy doing anything else. You can talk to Ales when she gets here. Perhaps she will have the solution to your problem," Ilsa suggested as she put the lancer back down on the workbench.

"Come on, let's have a look at this blade you're making."

Ilsa opened her Vision and went to the workbench, where he had left the blade clamped in a vice. Juran knew his work, as the blade only had one flaw, right near the transition from blade to tang. The flaw was tiny, and while Ilsa could have destroyed the blade with a touch, she didn't think it was possible for anyone else to strike on the flaw properly. Ales had explained that the flaws Breaking showed them were usually not easy to exploit. It could happen by accident, but without the Vision, it was nearly impossible, especially on things that were well made. This blade was very well made, indeed.

"Alright, this is a good time to practice using your Vision."

Under her instruction, and armed with the knowledge that Ales had given her about a Newling's Vision, she had been able to work him through his issues with opening and closing his Vision in one short rotation instead of double that time. Juran closed his eyes, and took a deep breath. When he opened them again, his irises glowed with magic. One red and one white. He looked at the blade and shook his head.

"I don't see anything like red spots," Juran said.

"It's alright. You need to learn to focus on what you want the magic to tell you. Now, I will help you work into calling up the Circle of Breaking. You will be tempted to touch the markers that show the weak points in things. Do not touch them. Breaking is useful in numerous ways, but it not only shows you the weak points, it guides you to using them. When you touch a Breakpoint, it begins a destructive chain reaction," Ilsa explained.

"But didn't you say that Breaking was good for fixing things and healing?"

Ilsa nodded. "I did, but only in the sense that it can show you what needs to be fixed. It isn't used to fix or to heal, only to aid you in knowing what is wrong when you are trying to do those things." Ilsa pointed at the blade he had hammered out.

"So to call up the Circle of Breaking, or any of your Circles, you have to convey your need to your Vision. Just like when you open or close your Vision, you have to create a mental image that is used specifically for triggering the Magic. Doing that is slightly different for everyone in the case of Circles, but the general rule for the Circle of Breaking is to construct an image of something that you recognize as being broken and seeing the places it is broken. The idea that the image creates can then be used to tell your Vision that you want to be able to see those broken places in other things."

Juran pinched the bridge of his nose.

"Do you realize how hard it is to do what you are asking?"

"More than you can possibly imagine. It took me three spans just to form that image."

"Why me? Three spans of unbelievable headaches, and now more mental acrobatics. I'm not smart or overly skilled. I'm a metalshaper."

"You're asking the wrong person for that. I had the same question when I first started going through the training you're undertaking. I chose you because I was told by my Vision that you were worthy of being Tier, and because you needed to be taught about your Vision. There were never many people who gained the Vision who did not become Tier, but they were out there. Maybe you are one of them. But as I understand it, they went out into the world and did nearly as much good as the Tier themselves did. Everyone has the potential to learn of the Vision.

However, not everyone can bond with a Tieran soul. Our souls are our own, but to activate the power of the Vision, we need something more. Upon opening your Vision for the first time, your soul is bonded with the spiritual energy of one of the previous Tier. It comes to you from The Core. But, like me, you are a little different. You were born with your Vision open. They call us newlings because the Tieran spirit that bonded with us was new, made from The Core."

"How can anyone tell?" Juran focused on the blade and tried to concentrate on building the image in his mind that Ilsa described.

"Liassa, my teacher, tells me that when we are more experienced with our Vision, we can see the difference because the Tieran Spirit carries with it the memories of the Tier it has bonded to in the past. I honestly can't tell that you are a Newling or not. I was visited by the Father just before I found you. He told me that you are a Newling."

Ilsa left her Vision open and walked over to where Kiltik was working at a blurring pace. She watched for a long moment and tried to call up the Circle of Repair. Her personal image to trigger that Circle was still incomplete, but her ability with it partially came to her. She couldn't understand everything Kiltik was doing, but she could see how the final machine would function. Her Vision made it clear that it would fabricate the microscopic machines using some sort of molecular bonding process. She couldn't get more than that, so she closed her Vision.

"It's right there," Juran whispered. He lifted his hand, reaching towards the blade. Ilsa stepped quickly up to him and grabbed his wrist as his fingertip neared the transition between the sword's blade and the tang.

"But it's flickering," Juran said, and the glow faded from his eyes.

"That's because you still have a long way to go before the image fixes itself in your mind as being the trigger for the Circle. I have the same problem with Repair right now. We will both get there," Ilsa encouraged.

Kiltik lifted his head from his work. He stood up, backed away from the workbench, and then began to change. His silver skin darkened to black, fur sprouting as he shrank. What looked like a stream of sand ran away from his body. It collected into a perfect sphere of what looked like silver metal. It rolled into a small crate beneath the work table. In less than twenty seconds, he had retaken the form of the black shuvoo with lavender spots. A few moments later, there was a knock on the outer door to the forge. They exited the forge room and closed the door behind them.

Kiltik let out a short stream of barks, like most shuvoo would when someone came too close to what they considered their home. Ilsa put her hand on the doorknob, and was about to open it when Kiltik let out a deep growl. This was also a typical noise for the shuvoo he was pretending to be, a warning. Ilsa took her hand away from the handle, and then Kiltik spoke in Tieran.

"Down!"

Ilsa dove to one side of the door, and Kiltik tackled Juran to the ground. An ear-shattering explosion rang out, and the door disintegrated into a cloud of deadly splinters.

Mina's family had not been pleased with her when she had brought home Ales and Lia. Ales had had a long talk with them, but her mother had flatly refused to listen to the idea of Mina possibly becoming one of the Tier. Finally, Ales seemed to lose her patience. She had told her mother without any reservations that the only person who would decide whether or not Mina would be one of the Tier would be Mina.

"Mina?" Her older brother's voice came through the door of her room.

"The Lady is busy with her studies, Taylon." Mina's minder for today was the elderly bookminder that kept Clan Clai's libraries. Mina never could remember her first name. She insisted on being called Minder Mest. Her family had been responsible for keeping all of the libraries of Rihanna for the last hundred cycles. Taylon opened the door to her room and stepped inside.

"She can finish with her studies after I have spoken with her Bookminder. Please leave us alone," Taylon said. Minder Mest scowled, but she nodded. She left the room and slammed the door.

"You okay, pipsqueak?" Taylon asked.

"I'm okay, Tay. Mom will get over it. I don't know why she was so angry,"

"She was so angry because you are the heir to the clan."

"Well maybe I don't wanna be," Mina grumped testily.

"Mina, being the princess of the clan is important. We need someone who is properly trained." Taylon tried to persuade her to see sense.

"I'm five, Taylon, and we have a sister who is three. Let her be the princess. You know I hate doing all these things." Mina waved to the book in front of her, the notepad next to it with rows of neat figures penciled into it, and lifted the skirt of her bright blue dress to show the pile of petticoats beneath it that made it puff out around her legs like a bell when she stood. "Well, the dress is okay, I guess." She liked her dresses. They made her look pretty.

"Mina, the Tier abandoned us. We lost almost everything because they left. It took an entire interval for us to put it back together after the Last Tier died. You don't even know if they really are Tier." Taylon had studied the old books too.

"I'm not stupid, Taylon, and Minder Mest read all those old dusty books to me too, about how we all couldn't use the Lightleaf trees after he was gone. Doesn't mean it was his fault. Alessandra said that we stopped believing in the Gods, and that's why they stopped working," Mina grumbled.

"What gods, Mina? They're a myth."

Mina just shook her head. "Leave me alone, Taylon. I don't want to be the stupid princess. I'm five, and mom has been trying to make me the princess since I was three. Same thing every day. Read this, Mina. Do those figures, Mina. Always stand straight, and don't embarrass us, Mina. I hate it. Just let me finish my work so Minder Mest will leave me alone too." Mina snarled at him and kept scratching down numbers on the notepad.

Taylon threw up his hands and stormed out of the room. Mina continued to add figures on the page, making sure the columns of numbers added up properly. She put the pencil down as soon as she was done, and got up from the desk. Minder Mest would be angry that she had not stayed, but Mina knew her answers were right so she went out of the library through the side door. Once she had gotten into one of the side hallways, she went to the end of the hall and peaked around the corner.

Bookminder Mest was coming up the hallway from the other end. Mina pulled her head back around the corner quickly and waited until the door to the library opened. Mina lifted her skirts a little and ran down the hallway as fast as she could. She needed to get back to her rooms and change her clothes if she wanted to get away to play. She got around the corner and slowed down. To get back to her rooms, she would have to pass her mother's sitting rooms, and her mother would definitely hear her if she was running. She crept slowly by.

"The predictions are always right. The machine never lies." Her mother's voice came through the door to her study, and it drew Mina's attention. She paused by the door to listen.

"Then how did the Tier get into Rihanna without us knowing about it?" The voice was male and deep. Mina didn't recognize it, but they were talking about the Tier.

"I don't know. When I ask about the Tier, the machine seems unable to answer. The display just cycles over and over again until I ask another question. I left it for four days, but it never answered about the Tier." That was her mother speaking.

"He will not be pleased that they have been able to enter without our knowledge. We are in control of the Ryhim," the man's voice came again. Mina was good at remembering voices, and she was sure she hadn't heard this one before. What she did know was that what the man said was wrong. Each of the Clans of the Ryhim had a prince and princess, and each pair was part of a council that made decisions about where each of the clans was to make their home until the Wilds changed again. Mina wasn't sure what to do with this information.

"He can't blame us if the machine does not tell us what to do about them," Mina's mother said.

"He can, and he will. We need to fix this problem before he finds out that we have it." There was a sound of chair's scraping on the sorstone floor.

Mina hurried down the hallway as fast as she could without making noise. She sniffed back tears, because she had liked Ales and Liassa. She didn't want them to get hurt, but her mother thought that they were dangerous. She loved her mother, even if they didn't get along very well, and had no idea what to do with what she had heard. So she decided to go to the only person she knew she could trust.

She passed her room and headed towards the kitchens. Ahldal was from another of the clans, and served a dual purpose in their manse. He was not the master of the kitchens, though he was the best cook in them. He was also responsible for making sure the pantries and coldboxes were stocked, so he shared an office with the mistress of the kitchens. Almost no one knew who he was, and he liked it that way. He had once been a scholar among the royal family of another clan. When his clan had found that he was sharing their library freely with everyone, his family had disowned him.

She waited until she heard the door to his office close before she went to the door down the hall from the door to the kitchens. She opened it a crack and looked inside. When she saw the small office was empty except for Ahldal behind the large desk, she slipped inside and closed the door behind her. She turned the lock, and Ahldal waited for her to turn to him before he spoke.

"If I am any judge of it, it appears as if you, little Flower, have a problem," Ahldal said warmly.

Mina climbed up into one of the two big armchairs that he kept in front of the desk for visitors. She had told him all about the Tier as soon as she had had a chance. Ahldal had believed her. He had pulled down a book from his shelves that had been penned in his own hand, his own personal research about Kinas and the Tier. He had told her that being taken into the Family of the Tier was an honor higher than any other. She didn't completely understand what he meant by that, but he had said she would one day, when she was older.

"Dal, I just heard something in my mother's sitting rooms by accident. I was going to my rooms and I heard her talking when I passed. I don't know what I should do," Mina said.

Ahldal frowned, "We have talked about eavesdropping on people, Mina."

"I wasn't! It was an accident, Dal!" Mina shot back angrily. She hadn't been listening on purpose.

"Fair enough. What did you hear?"

Mina took a deep breath and relayed everything she had heard. When she was done, Ahldal sat back in his chair.

"Little Flower, you have stumbled upon something very dangerous, and in all honesty, I have no idea what should be done with it."

"Do you believe in the Gods, Dal?" Mina asked quietly.

"Very much so, Mina. My family is the only one that I know of who continued to pass down the knowledge of how to use the Lightleaves, and when I touch the trees in the Travler's Grove I can feel their power. Even if I cannot use them. I may be the only one left who can. But the Gods would not want you to put yourself in danger. You are too young for this. Do you know where the Tier are staying?"

Mina nodded.

"They were in a place down by the sunward gate, but Ales told me that if I needed her, I could just draw a symbol on the wall by the gate with a piece of chalk and she would see it. I can show you if you have a pencil and paper."

Ahldal opened a drawer in his desk, and pulled out a sheaf of paper. Mina stood on his big chair and held out her tiny hand for the pencil. He handed it to her, and she scribbled down the symbol Ales had taught her.

"What am I supposed to do, Ahldal?" Mina asked.

"Nothing, Princess. Please just keep to your studies, and don't tell anyone else about this."

"Mmkay. Thanks, Ahldal." She jumped down out of the chair, and he got up as well. She threw her arms around his waist, and he put his arm around her squeezing her comfortingly.

Jame ran for his life. Lancer bolts zipped by his head, and he tried desperately to crouch as far down as he could while maintaining speed.

"Father's Stones, have you never done a dishonest thing in your life, boy?" Cole shouted as he ran just ahead of Jame.

"Can't you use Taking to get us out of this mess?"

"Not when they are looking right at us, idiot. Run!"

If Jame didn't know any better, he would think Cole was enjoying himself. They had both worn hooded cloaks with face masks so no one in the camp knew who they were, and no one would, as long as neither of them opened their Vision. Finally, they made it around an extremely large family tent. Cole opened his Vision and called up the Circle of Taking. A glowing blue line appeared through the tents, and Cole immediately ran that way as fast as he could. Jame, still panting from their run, almost didn't catch up to him before he rounded the corner of the next tent over. It wasn't long before they had gone through so many twists and turns that no one would ever catch up to them. They whipped off their cloaks and Cole stuffed them into the pack he carried slung over his shoulder.

"Doesn't that thing get heavy? How can you run like that with all that gear on?" Jame asked.

"A lifetime of not wanting to die because I got caught. How did you get caught back there?"

It had turned out that Jame had two Circles. Taking, and one that Cole did not recognize, which meant it wasn't one of his. When they had arrived at the Byranti camp, it had not been a welcome arrival. The Byranti were suspicious, and Angran had not had many contacts in their Clan. For some reason, their place as physicians and medicine makers had made them snobbish. Cole shook his head.

He had spoken with their Clan Chief, and he had provided proof that he was one of the Tier. So while he tried to negotiate with them to help find out exactly what was going on in all of the Clans, Cole had decided to use their camp as a proving ground for Jame. He had gotten through the exercises to open and close his Vision much more quickly than Cole had. Then, Cole had tried to teach him how to call up the Circle of Taking. The problem was that Jame had serious trouble with handling more than one stream of thought at a time.

"I lost my grip on Taking. The image just..." Jame made a fluttering motion with his hand.

"Got fuzzy?"

"Yes." Jame said, disgruntled.

"Don't worry, it will get easier. The more you practice, the less you'll have to focus to hold the image. Eventually, it'll become instinctual to you."

"Did we actually get what we went in there for?"

Cole slipped a small black book out of his pack. "Of course I did. Your little episode of almost getting yourself killed gave me plenty of time to pick every lock on every desk in the entire building." Cole grinned when Jame made a rude gesture at him.

"They really move every ten or twelve cycles and rebuild all this somewhere else?" Cole asked. Jame nodded in response. Cole opened the book and started to page through it.

"These are all of the orders from Rihanna, from the Princess of Clan Byranti."

Cole thumbed through the book. Much of it was mundane, but bits and pieces were odd. He wished he had Lia's abilities as a Finder. She would be able to decipher this with just a glance.

"So what are they doing?" Jame asked. Cole continued to page through the small book.

"I am not entirely sure, but look at these shipping numbers. Whatever this is, they are making and moving quite a bit of it. This marker here I have seen somewhere before."

Cole put the book down on the camp table. Their tent was a motley collection of essentials, and apparently it was not sufficient for talks with the Bryanti's Chief. They had insisted that he come to the one permanent building at the center of the camp.

"I don't know what it means, but I know it is an herbalist symbol," Jame said.

"Well, we can't show it to anyone here. Our relationship with the Byranti is not good, and I have no idea how we are going to make it better. Angran's mate told me that they would be hostile to outsiders, but their hostility to me has been far worse than what Tulan described."

They had spent three span just trying to get a meeting with the Clan Chief of the Byranti. They had been stonewalling the entire time. They had completely ignored the fact that Jame, a member of the Outriders, was ready to speak for Cole. Even with proof that he was one of the Tier, they had tried to send them away. Once they had finally spoken with the Chief, it had become abundantly clear that the Chief had known they were coming somehow, and had no interest in trying to speak with them. That left only a couple of possibilities as Cole saw it.

Either the Chief saw the return of the Tier as something that would destabilize his control of his clan, or the Chief was in league with whoever it was among the Ryhim that had the Probability Matrix. He hadn't told Jame about all of his suspicions yet. Jame believed that the Chiefs of the Clans were good people, and until he was ready to see the world more clearly, Cole did not want to poison him. He wanted to ease the boy into the world as it was.

"We could take it back to the Outriders. I'm sure one of the Fixers there will recognize the symbol," Juran suggested. Cole shook his head. He had a feeling that there was something they were meant to do here, and if they left it would go undone.

"No, and before you say you can go back on your own, no. You are at least two rotations away from being able to properly control the Circle of Taking, and it will be bare minimum a full cycle before you are fit to be let out of my sight or the sight of another of the Tier.

"Another one of your mysterious feelings?" Jame asked.

"Maybe. Look at the notes here in the margin. Can you read this?"

Jame shook his head.

"Well, I can. These are coded notes. Not many folks could read these. I can only read them because I spent a few rotations working with a crooked merchant in preparation to steal..." Cole paused, and smiled crookedly. He opened his Vision and ran his finger down the page.

"Well, that doesn't really matter. The point is, I recognize the merchant coding system here. The code is personalized, so I can't read it all, but with a little help from my Vision, I can read enough. Someone who writes in this notebook is wondering why they are moving so much of whatever that symbol is. Someone who should normally know why," Cole explained.

"Yeah, but who? I mean, almost every Clan has a book like that. They're not a secret, and a dozen important people in a Clan make notes in it from time to time. It is so that everyone who needs to know can stay up to date on the happenings within the Clan."

"The problem here is your people don't have much contact with the world outside of the Black Wilds. I don't know what your merchant system looks like. And do you people even have criminals?" Cole asked. Jame burst out laughing.

"Father's Stones, of course we have criminals, Cole. There are almost five million Ryhim in the Wilds. We do not allow outsiders to live here, and there are enough Outriders that anyone trying to stay within the confines of the Wilds is found within a few days. But there are plenty of dishonest Ryhim who trade beyond our borders and smuggle goods back into the Wilds."

"And the Merchants?"

"Well..." Jame said hesitantly. "There are some. There is trade between the clans, but it is mostly managed in Rihanna by the Princes and Princesses of the Clans. It's complicated."

"I've been meaning to ask you that. You have a Clan Chief, and then each Clan has a Prince and Princess that represents the Clan in Rihanna?"

Jame nodded. "Ultimately, the Clan Chief is in charge of everything, but the Prince and Princess of the Clan work with the ruling families of the other Clans to make sure that each Clan is where they need to be in the Wilds. This way, each Clan is where they need to be to support their specific needs."

"Ales explained that this forest is a sort of conduit of the Mother's power, and so it is almost like different areas of the forest are in different seasons."

"That's a good way to describe it. The forest periodically changes around us overnight. It is surprisingly polite about it. It never happens when we are near the end of a harvest. We will finish a harvest, and when we wake up the next morning, our fields will be gone. The forest will have filled them in with trees. The Outriders send word to Rihanna when it happens. So within a span, we are already moving to where the new fields have appeared," Jame explained.

"So the other Clans?"

"Same for them. Navano has it the hardest. They have to remove all of their mining tools from the mines at the end of every day. The mines just fill in overnight. It won't trap anything living. A long time ago, they tried to keep the mines in one place by keeping miners working at all times. It doesn't work. They will find themselves ejected from the mine one way or another. Never anything harmful, but there were accounts of someone appearing in the forest outside of the mine mid-swing of a pickaxe."

"Then most of the trading is actually worked out in Rihanna by the Prince and Princess?" Cole got a thoughtful look on his face.

"Yes, what are you thinking?"

"They do most of it there, but who does it for your Clan out in the Wilds?"

"Well, for the Mizami, most of the trade goes through Chief Angran's mate, Tulan. Usually, it is a member of the Chief's family that handles trade, but it isn't always like that. There are lesser merchants who trade their goods to other clans. They keep strict records of what they are trading, and it is all reported back to Tulan."

"Then that's our starting point. We need to find out who controls trade among the Byranti. Whoever that is, they are the one most likely to have made these notes. They will talk to us."

Mina peaked into the room where she had heard voices talking about Ahldal and then opened the door fully. It was a place off of the kitchens that she hadn't known was there until she had sneaked into the kitchen for a snack and heard the people talking. She had hidden inside an empty cupboard until they had left. She pushed open the door to the side room, one she had never gone in before. Inside, the room was dim. The glow bulbs had been turned down low. She reached up to the knob and turned them up.

There were three long, wooden tables in the room, and it was terribly cold inside. Along one side of the room, large sides of meat hung on hooks. Mina had seen what meat looked like before it was cooked, so that did not scare her. The room was extremely clean and the walls were covered in metal panels. A man was laid out on one of the tables. He was on his back, and she recognized his clothing. He looked like he was sleeping with his hands folded on his chest. It was Ahldal, but he looked wrong. His hands were pale, and there was a red stain on his tunic, down the side of his chest. The table was high and she wasn't tall enough to see much beyond that.

"Dal?" she asked quietly. She touched his hand, and it was so cold. It was nothing like the hand of the man who had hugged her and comforted her days earlier.

"Ahldal?" she asked, a little louder this time, but he still didn't respond. When she shook him, his arm fell limply to one side of the table. That was when she knew that Ahldal wasn't there. He was gone, and he wasn't ever coming back. She stumbled back, utterly stunned, and tears gathered in her eyes. Ahldal was the only person she ever trusted in her whole life. He was the only person that would help her with what she had heard her mother saying.

She was completely alone now, and the horror of that idea overwhelmed her. She slid down to her knees, and when her rump hit the floor, tears began to stream down her face. She did not sob. She had never been a loud crier. Now, more than ever, she didn't want anyone to hear her and know exactly how much she hurt on the inside. She put her hands on her face and tried to rub the tears away but they just wouldn't stop.

She had not felt alone since the day Ahldal had found her crying in the stoneward gardens. He had made her smile with a silly song about laughing so hard that you cried. She realized that she didn't remember the words to the song anymore. That was when she let out a single tiny sob. Just once, before she caught her breath and got control of the noise.

She tried several times to stop crying so that she could get off the floor and leave. She did not want her mother or her minders to find her here. They would not approve of her kneeling on the floor and dirtying her dress. That was what they would say to her, even though the stone floor here was scrupulously cleaned. Even though she had just lost her best friend. She had no idea how long she had been kneeling there venting her grief when the door creaked behind her.

"Mina?" The voice was Ellent, who was in charge of the kitchen when Ahldal wasn't around. That meant all the time now, she supposed. The plump woman bustled into the room, her fiery red hair pulled back into a pony tail flying behind her.

"Mina, what are you doing in here?"

That was when she saw Mina's face. Ellent had known that Mina spent a lot of time in Ahldal's office reading his books, but she hadn't known how close the two were. Mina had been careful not to tell anyone. Her mother would have found it improper for the scion of the house to befriend one of the servants. She realized right then that she loved her mother, but she didn't really like her very much.

"Oh, child, you shouldn't have seen this," Ellent said.

"He was my friend," Mina said softly. She sniffed loudly, but she didn't think she would ever stop crying at this point.

"Come on up. You're mother will have my hide if she finds you freezing in here."

She gently helped Mina to her feet. For a moment, Mina thought that her legs wouldn't hold her, but then she steadied.

Ellent gently ushered her out of the freezing room and into the warmth of the kitchen. She picked Mina up and sat her down on one of the tall wooden stools that the cooks used while they prepared food for the Manse. She opened one of the large ovens and took out a tray of bluedrop rolls, rolled pastry dough with bluedrop jelly in the middle. They were Mina's favorite. Ellent took one, hot off the platter, and put it on a small plate for her. She set it down on the counter next to Mina and smiled at her.

"Now let it cool for a few minutes. When you are done eating it, you'll feel better," Ellent said.

She put a small silver fork on the plate next to the pastry roll. Next to that, she put down a clean white towel. Mina took the towel and wiped at her face with it. She didn't think it helped very much, because she could still feel tears running down her face when she took her first bite of the pastry. It was still warm, and that was how they were best. Before she knew it, she was putting the last bite of the pastry in her mouth. She remembered Ahldal letting her watch him make the pastries early in the morning before everyone else was awake. Ellent was right, though, she did feel a little better. She still felt absolutely dismal, and still thought she might cry at any moment, but she had stopped. She climbed down off the stool and straightened her powder blue skirts. Ellent turned from the stove where she was preparing a soup.

"Better?" Ellent asked.

"A little."

"Well, run along, then, before anyone sees you in here and both of us are in trouble," Ellent said as she made a shooing motion with her free hand.

Mina left the kitchen. She wandered the manse for a long time, lost as to what to do with herself before returning to her rooms. There was only one thing she could do now. She would have to try to chalk the mark on the wall herself and wait for Ales or Lia to come and help her.

<h1 align="center">PART 3</h1>

18

Rain pelted the oiled coat that Ahldal had donned before slipping out of the manse. He had no idea what he was doing, but he knew that he had to do it. Mina had heard something that the Tier needed to know, but there was no safe way for the girl to relay the message but through him. He had chosen the rainy day on purpose. It was an excuse to keep his hood up, because if anyone saw him doing this, it could be disasterous. He exited the sally port in the manse wall like he had done hundreds of times, and then locked the door behind him. They never kept guards on the door. It was thick bondsteel that had been there for two thousand cycles. Rihanna had been just a collection of manses surrounding the inner Center in those days.

Ahldal went down the street, and as he passed the wall, he reached out towards it. He chalked the mark that he had practiced two hundred times. He had chosen a black piece of charcoal to make the mark, and it was almost the same color as the dark brown brick of the wall. If Ales truly was one of the Tier, though, she would see it just fine, even if no one else did. He continued on his way towards the sunward gate. No one would think twice about him making his daily trip to the market. He got to the market without much trouble, dodging a large group of children who would have likely attempted to pickpocket him. There wasn't much crime in Rihanna, but it was still there.

"Hello, Dal! How does the day find you?" Stoker was his source from Clan Mizami. All of the cooks in the city had one, if they were worth their salt.

"Wind at your back, Stoker," Ahldal said.

"And you. I take it you have come here because the gantha herds have been producing stringy roasts?" Stoker said knowingly.

"No, not at all. You warned me, and the price was right. Besides, the day I can't best a stringy roast is the day I retire."

Ahldal chuckled. He reached into a satchel at his side and pulled out a square glass bottle with thick sides. It had a green bundle of leaves with a green fruit in the middle painted on the side. Stoker's eyes went a little wide.

"No, you couldn't have," he said, his voice filled with awe.

"Oh, but I did. You don't know what I had to give up to get this bottle. You know Braem only makes a hundred of these a cycle and they are likely spoke for through the next, oh, I don't know, forever? Someone in Vilhena pays him a thousand pieces of gold for five of these every cycle."

The bottle was filled with a green liquid that Braem called Green Candy. In Vilhena, they called it Aluvian Starn after the sweet green fruit that everyone thought that Braem put in the stuff. The liquor inside had a subtle fruit flavor that seemed to change the longer you kept it in your mouth. No one had ever been able to figure out exactly what he did to make the delicious alcohol. There had been more than a few attempts to find out, but Braem never wrote his recipe down. He said he would teach it to his sons on his death bed, and not a moment sooner.

"So do we drink it... or sell it?" Stoker asked.

"Drink it, man! We drink it. I traded him an entire sphere of maan spice for this bottle."

Maan spice was impressively hard to gather. It added a savory flavor to any dish. Ahldal was the only person that anyone knew of who had been able to cultivate the plant that the spice was made from.

"He's going to use that in a liquor?" Stoker asked, surprised. Ahldal nodded. He motioned for Ahldal to follow him into the back of the store. His daughter was storing meat in the cold room.

"Niki, go watch the shop while Dal and I enjoy a drink."

"All right, Da!" the girl said cheerfully. Her pink pigtails bounced as she went out to the shop front.

"That hair of hers, she looks more and more like Hila every day," Ahldal remarked as the girl went by them. "How old is she now?"

"So much that it hurts me to look at her sometimes. Twelve Cycles. Almost a woman grown."

Stoker twisted a corkscrew through the black wax covering the cork. Once the seal was broken, he stripped away the wax. He pulled the cork from the bottle, and the fruity smell of the liquor wafted up from the bottle. Stoker opened a small cold box in the wall next to his desk. He took two glasses from a shelf, and dropped a couple of cubes of ice into each one. He carefully poured two fingers of the green liquor into each glass. He carefully corked the bottle, and put it on the shelf next to the other bottles of liquor.

"Don't get the idea that you're keeping that bottle," Ahldal said cheerily.

"Never! A single drink of this is worth more money than I will take in this entire rotation." They raised their glasses in toast, and then each of them took a sip.

"Gods, that man is magical." Stoker's sublime smile told the whole story. Ahldal had similar thoughts. Outside of some of his most practiced dishes, he had never tasted anything so fine in all his life.

"If you came down here just for this, I would understand, but I don't think you did," Stoker said. Ahldal sighed, and nodded.

"I wanted to know if you had seen them?" Ahldal asked. Stoker took a few minutes to process the question. Then he realized there could only be one "them" that Ahldal was asking about.

"I have." Stoker took another sip.

"What do you think of them?"

"I think they are the real thing, Dal. You heard about the incident with the banic?"

Ahldal nodded. "I did. It nearly killed a guard on its way into the center. Scared a dozen people half to death. They say that people have seen the Tier walking the center with the animal, and it is all silver-white. They said it was black as slate when it attacked the guard."

"The katali spoke to me, Ahldal."

"One of the Wild? I didn't know they could speak." Much like Ahldal, Stoker had had an excellent education. He was a relation of the royal family of Clan Mizami. It afforded him access to the royal libraries. Stoker had always been an avid reader. That was how they had become friends.

"I don't think they could, but regardless, they are something, Dal. Why are you asking about them?"

"Probably better if you didn't know."

Stoker made a sour face. "Fair enough Dal, but you're worrying me."

"I know, but I think what I have is dangerous, and you have Niki to think of." Ahldal finished his drink and handed the glass to Stoker.

"On second thought, I can't imagine wanting to share that with anyone but you, my friend. Hold onto the bottle for me?"

"Sure. I won't touch a drop without you." Stoker held up the remainder of his drink to the light. "It really is something."

"It is."

"Be careful, Dal." Stoker finished his drink and stood. He offered his hand, and Ahldal gripped it.

"I'll try."

Ahldal left the shop and headed for home the usual way. The twists and turns of the path back to the manse were old hat now. When he rounded the corner that would take him back to the royal quarter, the blade went into his chest so quickly that he never even felt the pain.

19

Lia started awake. She did not move her body, only her eyes. Ales was asleep on the cot next to her, but something had awoken her. She just wasn't sure what. There was nothing in the room, so she arranged her paws beneath her and stood.

{Ales, something is wrong,} Lia spoke into their mental link. Ales' eyes slid open, and she turned them until she was looking at the door to their quarters.

{What is it, sister?} Ales asked.

{I'm not sure. Something is shifting. Can you sense it?}

Ales sat up and swung her legs off her bed. Her eyes began to glow softly as she called up her Vision.

"It's the chaos, Lia. That is what you are sensing. It's getting worse, much worse. Someone has just done something that could have rectified the problem, and someone else has stopped them."

Ales got to her feet and started to dress. Liassa slipped out the door and across the warehouse floor. The night was cool, and she could tell from the smell that the rain had stopped not long ago. She stepped into a puddle, and then shook a paw reflexively to get the water off.

{Catch up with me when you get your pants on. I'm going to make a circuit and check our monitors,} Lia said, and darted up the fire stair on the side of the building.

{Right behind you.}

Ales finished dressing and pulled her coat on. She lifted her Windblade from the rack next to her bed, then slipped out of the warehouse and into the night. The center of Rihanna never really slept. There were many things that happened at night, so there were always people on the street. Repairs to the public areas of the center were done in the night, which, considering the size of the center, were needed almost all the time. They had installed the monitors to keep an eye on certain areas of the massive place.

{I miss having a dozen Tier for an operation this size,} Ales said into her mental link with Lia. *{If our brothers and sisters were still here, we would have this issue taken care of by now.}*

{Sad but true,} Lia replied.

Ales slid her Windblade into her coat. Thankfully, there were no real crowds at night, but that didn't stop people from noticing her. Finally, she opened her Vision and called up Taking to make people stop paying attention to her.

{Ales, the monitors are missing. I'm up to seven missing signals out of the forty or so monitors.} Lia's mindvoice seemed a little breathless, which meant that she was running at top speed.

{Calm down, Lia. It isn't like we hid them extremely well. If anyone recognized the devices, they would probably take them. It isn't as if they are common, and a Searcher would know how to repurpose them.}

{No, there is a pattern here. Someone tried to make this look random, but the pattern is there, I can see it.}

Ales climbed the fire stair to the roof of the warehouse, and then darted across the rooftop. She pushed open two levels of her constraints and lept from the rooftop across the width of the street. She landed as lightly as she could, and then bolted toward the moonward edge of the city. The jumps between rooftops were much shorter, and she quickly converged on Lia's position. Lia had stopped, and was waiting for her on a rooftop in the Merchant Row area of the center.

"Alright, show me, Lia."

Lia opened her Vision and her mental link with Ales. Ales sat so she could give her full attention to the link. Lia passed the memories of the last few minutes to Ales.

"You were always the better Finder, but you're right, I see the pattern as well. They were trying to hide which monitor was important," Ales said. She sorted through Lia's slightly frantic memories, and sighed when she opened her eyes again. The glow of her Vision faded.

"And whoever it was did a good job of it, too. No indicators at all?"

{None that I could find. Maybe you can do something more?} Lia asked.

Ales shook her head. "I can try, but I don't think I will pick up anything you haven't already. You don't give yourself enough credit. Your Finder magic has always been more than a match for mine and any other Tier I could name. Even our mother said that you were the most talented Finder in generations. Stop second-guessing yourself. I'm not one of the gods."

{Thank you, Ales. I am just worried. I feel like this situation is getting out of our control.}

"You're right. It's time that we use the Lightleaves like we planned to days ago. It's time to consolidate our forces and find out exactly what is going on here."

Ales stood up and jumped from the rooftop. She had shuffled through the images from the monitor, and seen something that made her think they should check it out.

"But before we go, there is something from the monitors we have to investigate," Ales said.

{You saw the murder as well?}

"I did, and considering the time, it is likely the murder is the event that woke you. I believe that whoever took the monitors mistakenly thought that it would prevent us from seeing the images they captured."

The time the monitors caught the murder coincided with Lia being woken from her slumber. Ales allowed Lia to lead the way. She used Taking so that no one saw them as they made their way to the streets that ran between Merchant Row and the Royal Quarter of the city. They found the body right where it had fallen. Ales stood back and allowed Lia to walk around the body first. Her animal senses would allow her to get a better feel of what had happened here. Lia was careful not to actually touch the body. She would leave that for Ales. She snuffled about the body, and then her nose got very close to his chest.

{I have his scent, and the scent of the thing that killed him. It was careless when it pulled the blade free from his chest. The sword splintered a rib and stuck in this poor man's spine. Whatever killed this man touched him here, and it was not human. Not even alive. The scent is synthetic, a man made oil of some sort,} Lia informed.

Ales moved closer and opened her Vision to glean what she could from the body. The face had been mutilated beyond repair. Clearly, someone didn't want this man identified. Ales studied the mangled flesh and ordered her Cellstructs to take images of the face as she fastidiously turned his head left and right to record every bit of the destroyed features.

"This was done after he was dead, mercifully."

She lifted his hands and examined his fingers. She tilted them left and right. It was too bad that no one in this time had realized that each person's fingers had patterns that were absolutely unique to that individual. The knowledge lost in the cataclysm was incalculable. They needed The Core back. The libraries at Ahal needed to be recreated. It would take an interval easily, even with hundreds of bookminders to do the job. Perhaps if they were successful, they could rebuild the dissemination system that had been in place at Ahal.

"I want to find out who this man is. It will be a good exercise for Ilsa for training the Circle of Finding. We'll tell the guard about the body," Ales said. She requested that her Cellstructs take the jumbled images, use them to establish patterns in the flesh, and recreate the man's face. His nose had been removed, but her Cellstructs calculated how it should look based on the rest of his facial features.

{Going to draw for us?} Lia asked.

"Looks that way. Let's go collect our wayward sister and brothers."

{Everyone will know that the trees can still work if we use them now.}

"Good. I want them to know," Ales grinned.

20

True to Warran's word, Kayna had ridden them all ragged. Kayna was an absolute natural on a mavae's back. Not only that, she had managed to perfect the art of sleeping in the saddle, which always baffled Warran.

"Gods, does she never stop?" Hagar complained.

"I seem to recall someone complaining that I would slow you all down," Kayna's little voice said. She did not open her eyes. Warran chuckled.

"My daughter can sit a saddle even in her sleep. She can ride for as long as a mavae will carry her," Warran boasted.

"How does she not have saddle sores? I know I do," Linten complained.

"Your guess is as good as mine. My ass feels like someone has used it for hammer practice," Warran chuckled. "How far out from Rihanna are we?"

"We should be there around falling," Hagar said. His mavae stopped abruptly and tossed its head restlessly. Warran immediately opened his Vision and glanced around. Hagar's hand touched the hilt of his sword.

"Keep going," Warran said amiably.

"How many are out there?" Hagar asked, gently spurring his mavae forward.

"Three, but I don't want them to know we know. Just move up around Kayna slowly, please. I don't want them to have a shot at her," Warran warned.

"If you can see them, can't you just kill them?" Linten asked. Warran shook his head.

"I can't or I'll be useless for hours at best. Also, we don't know their intentions. They may be just as afraid of us as we are of them."

Warran's Vision zoomed through the trees. Hagar and Linten moved up on either side of Kayna. He got a good look at one of them. He was holding a long barrel pointed right at Hagar. Warran drew both of his lancers in a blur. The irons barked four high pitched discharges so fast that Hagar could barely tell they were not one sound.

"Hagar, protect my daughter. Linten, there is a man down forty marks from the path on the left. I will take the right," Warran ordered.

He lept from his saddle and darted into the underbrush. His first shot had shattered the long barrel, and his second had taken that man in the left leg just above the knee. He had fallen from his mavae. The second man had taken a bolt in the leg as well, but he had kept his saddle and was galloping madly away. Warran lifted his lancer and fired three quick shots. A branch snapped off of a tree and smashed into the man's chest as he rode. He flipped backwards off of his mavae and landed face-down in a heap. The mavae never stopped. Warran scowled down at the first man he had shot.

"Who are you?" Warran demanded, his Vision blazing brightly. The man opened his mouth, and Warran aimed his lancer at the man's eye. "You pointed a lancer at my daughter. If the thought of lying crosses your mind again, you will fervently wish I had killed you."

"I'm Otten of Clan Hanoi," he snapped. Hanoi was the scout Clan. They had started the Outriders, which had members from all clans.

"And why are you here, Otten of Clan Hanoi?"

"We were told that there were interlopers that fit your description that had killed a Scout to enter the Wilds. We don't take chances with invaders," Otten growled.

"By whom?" Warran demanded.

"I don't answer to you," Otten spat.

Warran crouched beside the man. He examined the man with the Circle of Repair. He slid his lancers back into their holsters, one at the small of his back, and one on his left hip.

"You seem to mistake your situation, Otten. You tried to kill my daughter. I suspect you were just following orders, but you will tell me who was responsible for those orders," Warran threatened. The man looked at Warran's glowing eyes and shivered. Hagar came through the woods and stood over Warran. When Otten's eyes fell on Hagar, they went wide.

"Standard Hagar?" Otten asked, confused.

"Scout Otten. Can you not see that you are annoying the honored Tier? I suggest you tell him what he wishes to know before you raise his ire further." Otten's face changed from anger and confusion to awe.

"Yes, sir. The orders came down from Command Larand. They have the proper dispatch codes." Otten pointed to his mavae's saddle bags. "They are right in there." Hagar opened the man's saddle bags and took out a sheaf of papers. He handed them to Warran. Warran quickly scanned the pages and then crumpled them in his fist.

"These came by rakling?" Warran asked.

"Just this morning."

"Hagar, these orders did not come down the chain of command." Warran examined the paper with his Vision. "This paper came from the stock in my workshop."

"Which means we have a traitor in our midst," Hagar said.

"Kavan," Warran growled angrily.

He knew he was jumping to a conclusion. The writing on the order was not in Kavan's hand, and he had no association with the Outriders, so he would not have the Outrider dispatch codes. But somehow, Warran knew that Kavan was responsible. Ales had taught them over their cycle of hard training to trust their instincts. She said they wouldn't always be right, but it would be a close-run thing. Warran eyed the hole in the man's leg. The bolt had gone through and through, and his shot had gone exactly where he had placed it. Otten would heal up just fine. Even the bleeding had nearly stopped already. No shattered bones, and he had missed all the tendons as well. Otten would have no lasting damage from the bolt as long as he didn't try to push himself.

Warran checked on the other two men he had shot. The one he had knocked off his mavae with the fallen branch was in worse shape than Otten. The bullet that had gone through his leg was the exact same wound that Otten had, but when he had flipped backward off his mavae, he had smashed his head into a tree branch. He was not in any danger of dying, thank the Gods, but he had a concussion. He wouldn't be ready to ride any time soon. Kayna's mavae was waiting on the road when Warran went across to check on the third man.

"Kayna, can you please circle around and collect their mavae? Linten, please go with her," Warran asked.

"Okay, Daddy." She gently spurred her mavae into the woods. Warran went to check on the third man. He, too, was unconscious, but despite his identical lancer wound, he was in better shape than the second man. He didn't have the concussion, and was already stirring. Warran threw the man over his shoulder and carried him back to the other two men so Hagar could watch over them while Warran figured out what he wanted to do next.

"Hagar do you have the authority to override these orders?" Warran asked.

"Of course. These orders are from the Command level. Do you feel that their injuries are punishment enough for their stupidity, honored Tier?" Hagar asked. Warran sighed. He looked back at Otten.

"Scout, were you or were you not acting solely on these orders?" Warran asked. Otten was still slightly dazed, but he seemed to come closer to sense and realize his position.

"I was, honored Tier. We were told that your party were interlopers who had killed a Scout to gain access to the Black Wilds." Warran could see through his Vision that the man was telling the truth.

"And you, scout?" Warran asked the third man.

"Aye, honored Tier. We were following orders, and we were told that you were armed and would attack on sight."

The second Scout was still unconscious, but Warran could see that he was stirring. But unless that second man had an ulterior motive, Warran was convinced that these men could be trusted.

"Alright. Bandage up their injuries and take command of these men, Hagar. We need to get to Rihanna today. Things are going in a direction that I find entirely too unsettling. I think that we were expected more than Ales and Lia thought," Warran observed. Hagar looked at him curiously.

"Just suspicions, Hagar. I don't have any evidence until I speak with my Sisters," Warran said. By the time he had finished questioning the third man, Kayna was back, having corralled all of the mavae.

"I apologize for the bolt holes gentlemen, but I have missed all the vital parts of your legs, so while it will be extremely uncomfortable, you will suffer no lasting damage from your injuries. Please mount up. I have tasks for you. I assure you, the Standard will support my authority to give you these orders."

Linten crouched next to the second man to make sure he didn't try to get up when he opened his eyes.

"That I do." Hagar followed Warran's lead. Warran went to his mavae, and took out a sheaf of papers and a writing board. He sat down on the ground with it in his lap and started scribbling notes. While he scribbled, Hagar spoke with the scouts, and Warran heard each of their names.

"Are these men fast riders, Hagar?" Warran asked.

"Until I met your daughter, I would have said any of the Outriders are unmatched in the saddle."

Scout Otten was the first to get to his feet. He tested his leg gingerly, and grimaced. It was painful, but Warran had not lied. There was nothing that made him think that his leg was going to buckle under gentle use.

"You'll be fine, all three of you, in a few spans. Just don't try to do any acrobatics, and your wounds will heal as if you had never been shot," Warran said. He set out a small candle in a glass jar and took out some blue sealing wax. He folded the two notes so they could not be opened without breaking the seal. Then he dusted each one with what looked like black sand.

Hagar's eyes widened. "Are those Bondstructs?"

"Yes. What I'm writing in these notes is sensitive, and I would rather they be destroyed if they are opened than allow anyone other than the people they are intended for to read them." Warran pressed his thumb into the hot wax, leaving a recognizable print.

"If anyone but the person I intend to opens them, they will simply disintegrate." Warran held out one to Otten. "This one is to go to Ilsa. She is currently with Clan Navano. Deliver this with all haste, Scout Otten." Warran took a small satchel from his pack. It clinked heavily with coins. "Take this for any issues that you run in to. There are one hundred pieces silver inside."

Otten's eyes widened. A hundred silver pieces was almost a full cycle's wages for him. "You may keep what you do not spend, but if it will allow you to arrive at your destination faster, I fully expect you to spend every single coin." Warran handed the second one to the man who had been on the other side of the road along with an identical coin satchel. His name was Scout Ilben.

"Scout Ilben, you ride to Clan Byranti. When you arrive, you will need to find Cole. I honestly don't know how you will achieve this, as Cole is good at staying hidden if the does not want to be found, but that is your task. Deliver this to him. Both of them are of the Tier and have eyes of two colors like mine." Warran handed over the second letter. "I am confident that if you ask about them, it will not be long until they find you. Scout Haftan, you will come with us. You have a mild concussion and I want to keep an eye on you so that I can make sure you recover properly."

"Help them get mounted, Linten," Hagar said, and the men moved off to collect themselves and get mounted.

Hagar spoke in a low voice, "How did you do that? I've been shooting lancers every single day for fifteen cycles. No man could make four shots like that."

Warran just grinned. "I've been shooting since I was old enough to hold a lancer. You can't fix what you don't understand, but one of the abilities of my Vision allows me to instantly judge distances and angles with absolute precision. So aiming a lancer with accuracy beyond the abilities of any normal man is a simple matter. If I can see an object, any object, no matter how small, no matter how fast it is moving, I will hit it. With the normal powers of my Vision, that's nearly anything. Even other lancer bolts. But if you think my abilities to shoot with a lancer are something, you should see Ales do it."

"If you can do that, why didn't you just kill them? I'm glad you did not, but no one would have thought less of you if you had."

"Because I can't, Hagar. There are consequences to using powers like this. The first time I killed someone using my Vision, I wasn't prepared for those consequences, and I'm still not prepared. Just hurting someone was bad enough. I can't kill right now. I don't know if I'll ever be able to kill again. And maybe that's alright. Just be thankful I could stop them without killing them, because for my daughter I would destroy myself."

"I think we would all do that for our children," Hagar observed. He swung up into the saddle, and Warran went to where Kayna was holding the reins of his mavae.

"Ready for a real ride, Midget?" Warran said affectionately, and her face lit up.

"Yes!" she said and turned her mavae. The creature sensed her excitement and danced in place, ready to run.

"Let's go." He swung up into his saddle and spurred his mavae up to gallop. Kayna was right behind him, shouting her pleasure at being able to go so fast. Warran kept his Vision open, scanning the forest to make sure there were no more surprises.

21

Ales and Lia made their way into the Traveler's Grove. The trees pulsed softly with internal light, giving the grove a dreamlike quality. Ales looked up at the branches closest to the ground. They were at least fifty marks up, and climbing a Lightleaf was extremely difficult. Their bark was slick like glass, and the trees themselves were extremely tough, so Lia's claws would not be able to penetrate the bark enough to give her sufficient grip.

Ales pushed open her constraints to the second level. She lept into the air and put her foot against a trunk. She pushed off and upwards, towards another trunk. Again, she hit the tree and pushed off. After three jumps, she was high enough, and she snatched four leaves from the branches. She landed heavily, and her feet sank a few ticks into the turf.

"We will have to see if carrying this inside of your pouch will be sufficient to allow you to access the power of the network." Ales tucked one leaf into her belt pouch. Lia sat down and tilted her chin up to give Ales easier access to the pouch around her neck. Ales slipped three of the beautiful crystalline leaves within. She put her hand against one of the trees and Lia reared up to put her paws against one.

"The Navano first. The endpoint crystal there is the closest to the camp," Ales said. She settled her day pack on her shoulder.

"Agreed," Liassa said.

Blinding light filled the Traveler's Grove. Surprsingly, it didn't hurt their eyes. The glow grew and grew until it filled the courtyard around the grove. It became so bright that it could be seen from anywhere in the city, and some distance beyond. People in the Center and for lengths around it stopped to stare at the glittering rainbow of light cascading into the sky. None of the Ryhim had seen that light for two long intervals.

Ales and Lia appeared next to low pillar of crystal about knee height and as big around as a large bluedrop tree. Ales stood very still and took deep breaths to settle her churning stomach. Lia looked absolutely dreadful. She was standing with all six of her legs sprawled as wide as they could go while still standing. She was panting and making unhappy, groaning noises.

"Are you..." Ales began.

Lia shook her head very slowly. "I'm not going to. I've got it under control." Lia's panting slowed a moment later, and she straightened herself up slowly.

"Father's stones, that is worse than I remember." Lia swore. "It feels like someone stuffed me in a barrel of rotted fish and rolled it into the Abyss."

Ales made a face and groaned. "Thanks so much for that image." Ales grumbled. "It'll get better the more we do it."

"I know, but right now, I feel like my stomach is running laps around my ass." Lia groaned. She finally lowered herself daintily into a sitting position. "I'm going to sit right here until it returns to its proper place."

Ales lowered herself to the ground, as well. "I think I will join you in that." She finally sighed when her stomach settled back into place.

"Gods, I need lisan root." Lia still looked a little green. She put her nose to the ground and started to sniff around the floor of the woods. She padded into the underbrush, and then Ales heard the frantic scrabbling of Lia digging.

Ales pulled herself to her feet and opened her Vision. She knew Lia would eat the root raw without a second thought, but she would enjoy a tea more. She examined the lay of the land, and then walked off moonward towards the likeliest place she would find water. It wouldn't take Lia long to dig up the fresh root, so Ales called out to her.

"Don't eat it raw, you beast! I'll start a fire and brew you a tea!"

Lia just grumbled in reply. It didn't take Ales long to find fresh water. The spring feeding the tiny creek was clean, and Ales filled the bondsteel canteen that Kiltik had made. When she returned, Lia was lying miserably next to a small pile of dirt with several thick roots running through it. Ales wasted no time building a small fire and cleaning off the roots. She put her canteen directly into the fire and took out a small brewing kit. The various pieces were in oiled hide pouches to keep them clean and dry. She took out a tiny mortar and pestle and ground up one of the fresh roots. The sharp smell of the root filled the air, and it seemed to settle Lia a little.

"Are you going to be alright, Spook?" Ales asked.

Lia nodded, "It's not as bad as the first time, but it is close."

"I would say it was something to do with you being one of the Wild, but Tredic traveled with me all the time, and he had no reaction to it at all. He never understood why the rest of us felt ill after a jump."

Ales finished brewing the tea and took a collapsible cup and a bowl out of the bottom of her pack. She poured the tea from the travel pot first into the bowl, and then the cup. She put the bowl down for Lia so that she wouldn't have to get up. Lia just breathed in the scent for a long moment.

"Oh, that's better." Lia sighed. She made quick work of lapping up the tea. By the time Ales had finished her own tea and put everything away, Lia had filled in the considerable hole she had dug. She came back into the clearing just as Ales was settling her pack on her shoulder again. Lia tilted her head and spoke into their mental link.

{We are not alone, sister,} Lia said, having picked up the scent of a human nearby.

{We are very close to Clan Navano's camp. I suspect that Clan Navano's Outriders have seen our fire or the flash of light from the endpoint crystal,} Ales replied.

She opened her Vision and scanned the forest. After a moment, she called up the Circle of Light. She swept her gaze around the forest, and stopped when she saw three men moving in from roughly stoneward. She strode off in that direction and Lia disappeared into the trees moonward. She would circle around behind them just in case it wasn't what Ales thought.

Ales invoked the Circle of Taking and walked until she was almost right on top of the men. She watched them creep through the underbrush. The men knew their business. Their clothing was made of mottled grey and dark blue fabric that let them blend in with the forest. Each was solidly built, and they all had similar bright silver hair beneath their hunter's hoods. She didn't look too closely, but she thought they were all brothers.

Ales fingered the lancer she carried at the small of her back. She was prone to using her Windblade, but the lancer was an elegant weapon that allowed her to strike at long distances with extreme precision. It was both amazing and unsurprising that weapons were one of the few things that found their way through the ages since the Tier had been destroyed. The lancer was a scaled-down version of the weapons that were posted at the borders of Ahal to protect the kingdom. She didn't draw hers, but she kept her hand behind her back near it. It was extremely unlikely that any of these men could outdraw her, even without her constraints open.

She pushed open the first mental block, and her muscles tightened with power. She released Taking, and to the men, she would have appeared out of thin air. The first man jumped back, but they were clearly impressively trained, as the other two moved left and right to avoid each other. Each man reached for the iron on his hip. Before their hands had moved even a fraction of the way to their weapons, Ales had drawn hers. She fired three shots into the ground, missing each man's left foot by only a hair's breadth.

"Now, now, gentlemen. There is no need for weapons here. Clearly, had I wanted you dead, you'd never have seen me." That was when they saw her luminous eyes. Each one gulped audibly, and Ales chuckled.

"You've seen eyes like these, have you?" Ales smirked.

"Yes, honored Tier. One of your number is currently staying with our Clan," the first man said. He rubbed his arm in remembrance of an old pain.

"Oh, not just seen them. She has thrashed, you hasn't she?" Ales said with a grin. The first man nodded.

"Us and five other men twice her size. It was a learning experience, honored Tier. She said she learned to fight from her sisters. Are you those sisters?" the man asked.

"We are. I'm going to put this away now. As I said, no need for weapons. We only need speak with our sister Ilsa," Ales said. The men exchanged a glance and then relaxed.

"How did you know we were here?" Lia said from behind the men. They all jumped, and their hands darted for their weapons when they spun to face Lia. They froze when Lia's glowing eyes pierced them.

"We were on patrol when we saw a bright flash of light in the woods, honored Wild. We came to investigate," the first man stammered. The other two men seemed to have chosen him as the speaker of their small group.

"It is alright, dear Boy. I am used to people being startled at a talking katali," Lia said, and when she gave her feline grin, the man shivered.

"I apologize, honored Wild. It is disconcerting."

"I understand completely." Lia chuffed in her equivalent of a laugh.

"Can you lead us to our wayward sister?" Ales asked.

"Of course, honored Tier. Please follow us," the young man said. They turned almost simultaneously, and Ales gave Lia a look.

"You're bound triplets, aren't you?" Lia asked.

"Uh, yes we are," the first man said.

Bound siblings were a real rarity in the world. They were always born together, and they shared an interesting mental link. They couldn't speak mind to mind like Cellstructs allowed the Tier to, but it was similar. They got impressions of what the others were thinking. Twins were the most common example of the ability. Triplets were extremely rare. But that was why the first man was the one doing all the talking. There wasn't really much need for the other two to speak when they were all together.

"I'm Tash," the first man said. He pointed to the left. "This is Alish." Then he pointed to the man on his right. "And this is Desh, though almost no one can tell us apart, so we have gotten used to answering to each other's names."

"We can tell you apart quite easily," Ales said.

"That would be refreshing," quipped Desh with a chuckle.

"Come to think of it, Ilsa could tell us apart too. Could you perhaps teach everyone else that trick?" Alish asked.

"If only it were so easy," Ales said.

It was thankfully a short walk back to the camp of the Navano. The guards had some questions for the three brothers, but once they pointed back to Ales and Lia waiting patiently, Ales called up her Vision, causing her irises to flash with internal light. This ended all questions. Desh and Alish separated from Tash. They went back to the forest in perfect lockstep, disappearing into the underbrush to finish their patrol.

"I will take you to where Ilsa is staying. My brothers are going to finish our patrol," Tash said.

The silver-haired man led them on a winding path through the camp until they came to a more permanent structure than the heavy tents surrounding them. It was not a large building, but it was two floors of sturdy logs. Ales started at it with annoyance.

"Lovely," Ales said with a frown at all of the dead trees.

"The inside is much nicer," Tash said.

"Don't mind her, Tash. My sister has issues that she will eventually get over, like adults do," Lia said, and grinned when Ales turned her scowl at her.

"Careful making a face like that. You'll cause everyone in forty paces to stroke out in fright," Ales retorted.

They both laughed, and Tash shook his head in bewilderment. He pushed open the door and invited them to enter. Ales went first, and Lia followed. Ales heard the sounds of a hammer striking metal. Lia and Ales followed it through a largish antechamber with large sheets of metal on the walls. Each sheet of metal had a beautiful scene etched into it. They followed a hallway to the left until they came to the forge. Hammering metal on the anvil was a young man with one red eye and one white. Sitting next to him on a chair was Ilsa. Her face was bruised on one cheek, and her leg was bandaged.

"What happened to you?"

Ales opened her Vision and examined her. The leg was not broken, but many of the muscles had been damaged. Whoever had treated it had done a good job. Not as well as Ales could do herself, but it would heal up just fine. Sitting in Ilsa's lap was a small canine-looking creature that Ales did not recognize, but her vision told her that the creature was Kiltik in a different shape than usual.

"Someone tried to kill us, and I didn't dodge quite fast enough. Kiltik was displeased that he had to fix my leg in such a hurry, and did not have the proper tools to do a very good job of it," Ilsa explained.

Ales reached down and ruffled the fur between Kiltik's large ears. "You did fine, Kiltik. I have examined the wounds, and while I may have been able to repair them a little more neatly, they will heal without any lasting damage."

He leaned into her petting. "This One thanks you, Ales Family Katane." The words sounded a bit odd coming through the canine muzzle. Ilsa lifted Kiltik and put him on the desk. She levered herself up, and threw her arms around Ales.

"I'm so glad to see you. I feel woefully inadequate to the task of training Juran, and he has Circles that are not all the same as mine. Ales, Lia, this is Juran," Ilsa said.

"Hello, Juran. I am Alessandra, and this is our sister Liassa."

Lia was barely able to sit down in the cluttered room. Juran left the still cooling sword blade clamped in a vice on the workbench, and then his eyes went extremely wide when they fell on Liassa. He gave a panicked shout and jumped backward. Ales darted forward in a blur, tangling her fist in the straps of the thick hide apron he was wearing. She dragged him forward before he could stagger back against the glowing mouth of the forge. When she had him righted on his feet, she spoke testily.

"That was incredibly stupid of you. You are a metalshaper. You should know by now how dangerous fast moves are in a forge," Ales chided. She pulled him across the room and planted him in a chair next to Ilsa.

"I promise you, young newling, I will not eat you. Humans taste awful," Liassa said.

Ales opened her Vision and looked into Juran's eyes. Juran blinked, and then held his head. Ales closed her Vision. "You possess Breaking and Distance, and your Vision is quite powerful. You should be able to see all the way down to the atomic level,"

She turned her eyes only and peered into Ilsa's eyes. Ilsa didn't get dizzy this time. Lia had explained it was because she had full control of her Vision, and it only happened because when you were untrained, one of the Tier looking into your potential forced your mind to function beyond its normal capacity.

"And you have come along nicely as well, Ilsa. I can see that your studies as a Fixer have progressed quite well. We need to speak in private once we are done here."

Ilsa lifted an eyebrow in question. "What's the matter?"

"Nothing that requires sharing with anyone but you, Ilsa. I can see that there is a lot to go over here, though. Go with Liassa. She can do what needs to be done while I attempt to help your young apprentice with a question he seems to have." Ales lowered herself into a chair.

Ilsa grabbed a crutch from where it was sitting next to her chair and wedged it under her arm. She had been avoiding going outside to prevent advertising her weakness. She was far less weak than most people would think, even with her leg so damaged. She had her lancer at the small of her back, and there were three knives on her person that she could throw with speed and accuracy. She followed Liassa out of the building. Kiltik climbed down from the table and into Ales' lap.

"Who picked this form for you, Kiltik? I can hardly think you chose something so adorable on your own," Ales asked.

"This One took this shape at Ilsa's behest. It has proven to be most advantageous in gaining the trust of the Ryhim. These Ones seem to find the shape of this animal to be comforting."

"How did you get so small? Your mind vessel is too large to fit inside of this small form, if I am not mistaken."

"This One recalls that you have not seen this one's mind vessel since before the Cataclysm. This One spent several intervals reconfiguring This One's mind vessel into a more compact and far more durable structure."

Juran watched the exchange with interest. "He will not talk to me like that."

"This One apologies, Juran of Clan Navano. This One has a long history with Ales Family Katane. This One does not wish to make you feel unwelcome. This One enjoys your company as well as any other. This One is shy because This One does not have much in common with humans. This One will endeavor to improve in the future."

"You must understand, Juran. Minds like Kiltik did not always have bodies, and were only able to speak with Tier for most of their existence. Once we were gone, they were unable to communicate with anyone, and even those that found them only wanted to use them for personal gain. But we are not here to talk about him."

Juran leaned his head back and sighed. "How do you know that?"

Ales just chuckled. "Because, dear boy, I am one of the Tier, and a fully trained Arcangineer. It is an ability that we are taught. I don't know your exact thoughts, mind you, just enough to know that you are carrying around a question that you want to ask me."

"What's going to happen to me if I don't choose to be one of the Tier?"

"Whatever do you mean?"

"Well, Ilsa said that she would not be able to stay and teach me forever. She said that if I didn't choose to be one of the Tier and go with you all, she would probably only be able to teach me just enough to control my Vision."

Ales nodded in response. "I see. Ilsa is quite right. Long ago when there were many Tier, in the situation where someone would not or could not choose to be one us, one of the Tier could be dispatched to oversee their training until they gained mastery of their Vision and their Circles. Unfortunately, this is not that time.

We are in a precarious situation. We will quickly grow the number of Tier available, but we are a long way from being able to even begin to do such things again. The time has already come where she must come with us because her assistance is needed elsewhere. However, it is thankful that the situation has changed in a minor sense. We are now able to travel more quickly and freely. We will not abandon you, Juran, not even if it were to kill us. But tell me, what is it that would keep you from joining us?"

"I would be honored to become one of the Tier, but my brother is far too young and has no one else to care for him."

"Ah, I understand. That is extremely important, but if that is what is holding you back, Juran, we can make certain that he is placed with someone who can take good care of him. We can conceivably come back and teach you, but considering that someone attempted to have you and our sister killed, I would much rather you be with us where we can defend you ourselves."

Juran looked uncertain.

"Make no mistake, the choice is yours, Juran. I meant it when I said we would not abandon you. I'm just hoping to help you make the best choice for yourself and your brother. Unfortunately, your natural talent with the Vision makes you a target. So we must do something to rectify that situation." Ales sighed. She stood up from her chair, and Kiltik jumped out of her lap.

"Consider, Juran, what it is you really want to do and we will go from there. But for now, I really do have to catch up with my sisters. I have to be present for what happens next. Kiltik, would you like to come, or are you going to stay here?" Ales asked.

"This One will stay and protect Juran. This One does not like the idea of That One being alone for any length of time."

"I'm That One now?" Juran asked with a little chuckle.

Kiltik opened his little muzzle, and Ales shook her head.

"He was attempting to be funny. He achieved mildly amusing," Ales said, and then laughed at Juran's sour expression.

"You'll be fine with Kiltik here for now. But if he tells you to duck, you should probably duck." Ales grinned. She opened the door, and Juran's words followed her out.

"I'm sure he'll just tackle me like last time," Juran chuckled.

22

Lia led the way out of the camp and into the woods. The mass of colorful semi-permanent tents was quite the sight, and it proved to be a bit of a maze. However, on the way in, Lia had memorized their path through the tent city. After a half an hour of walking, they came to the small clearing where the endpoint crystal stuck up out of the middle of a boulder.

"I have something for you, and I suspect we need to talk about what is happening here," Lia said.

"Why are you two here?" Ilsa asked.

"Because things have begun to take shape in Rihanna much more quickly than we thought they would and we need extra hands to start mitigating the situation," Liassa explained. She sat down next to the boulder.

"So we have to leave already?" Ilsa asked. "I've barely had time to help Juran learn to open and close his Vision. He needs more training."

"And we will make sure that he gets it, Ilsa, but it does him no good if we don't get the situation in Rihanna under control. I am sure that our sister is talking it over with him right now."

"She was, but then she decided that she should be here to share this moment." Ales' voice came out of the woods, and a moment later, she appeared at the edge of the small clearing.

"What moment?" Ilsa asked.

"Presents first," Lia said. She ran her paw over the bag around her neck, and one of the crystal leaves from the Traveler's Grove fell out onto the pads of her paw. She proffered it to Ilsa.

"This is a leaf from the Lightleaf grove in Rihanna. You should attach it to a necklace or something that will allow you to keep it on your person at all times," Ales said.

"It's beautiful, but why would I need to keep it on me?" Ilsa asked.

"Because the Lightleaf trees are living magic, Ilsa. With a leaf from them, you can use a crystal exposed to sunlight or moonlight like this one..." Lia made a gesture to the endpoint crystal sticking up out of the flat boulder, "to instantaneously travel from the crystal to Rihanna, or from Rihanna to any endpoint crystal in the world," Lia revealed. Ilsa's mouth made an O shape and she took a deep breath. She looked at the little crystal leaf in her palm in awe and reverence.

"Gods, those stories were true?" Ilsa asked, a little breathless.

"Those particular stories were true. We never believed we would ever see Lightleaf trees again. The only grove of them in the world was the Union Grove in Ahal. It was destroyed in the cataclysm. Only because the Father intervened did a new grove grow," Lia said. She tilted her head and got a thoughtful look on her feline face.

"I see your brain finally caught up with what the Father said," Ales grinned.

"He said there were two groves. So why can't we sense the other one when we access the Lightleaf network?" Lia asked.

"An excellent question. I suspect he is shielding it from us for a reason. We will discover it in time. Right now, this is more important."

"Agreed." Lia looked expectant but Ales shook her head.

"She is your pupil, Lia, and you taught her well. This is your honor," Ales said.

Lia's ears laid back in embarrassment, but she turned to Ilsa. The young woman was looking a little bewildered.

"What is this about?" Ilsa asked.

"We told you that there was an important formal ceremony that would make you one of the Tier. You've achieved the level of proficiency, and had enough time to consider your decision. It is time for you to decide. Are you ready to be a part of our family?" Lia asked.

Ilsa looked back and forth, and then she looked at her feet. "I made that decision the first time I saw those men attack you in that alleyway. Yes. What do I do?"

Lia made a gesture to Ales. Ales took out a small, bright knife. She made a cut on the palm of her right hand with her left. She commanded her Cellstructs to leave the cut open for the moment. She held out the knife to Ilsa, handle first.

Ilsa took the knife awkwardly because of her crutch. She looked uncertain for a moment. Then she understood, and made a small cut with the knife on her right palm. Ales smiled, and took the knife back. She set it aside, on top of the pillar of crystal rising from the flat boulder. She held up her hand with the fingers spread, and Ilsa interlocked her fingers with Ales', mingling their blood together.

"Ilsa, you come to us from outside, seeking a place among the Tier. We the Tier grant you a place in our family. Blood to blood, we make you our sister. With these words, you take your place among us," Lia pronounced in a very formal tone. Ilsa realized that she was expected to repeat after Lia.

"Of my own will, I take my place among the Tier," Lia began.

"Of my own will, I take my place among the Tier," Ilsa repeated.

"I shall protect those who cannot protect themselves."

"I shall protect those who cannot protect themselves." Ilsa felt something happening, a warmth that grew inside of her as she said the words. It seemed to pour into her through the cut on her hand.

"I shall gift defense to the defenseless."

"I shall gift defense to the defenseless."

"I shall free those who have had freedom taken from them."

"I shall free those who have had freedom taken from them."

"By my will, I am bound to the Tier forevermore."

"By my will, I am bound to the Tier forevermore," Ilsa finished, and when she did, she felt an overwhelming sense of belonging. It was how she felt when she was embraced by her parents, but somehow more than that.

Ales put her free arm around Ilsa's shoulders and pulled her forward until their forehead's touched. She gently pulled Ilsa down so they were both on their knees, so Lia could comfortably join in their embrace. Then she could hear Ales and Lia's voices in her head.

{Welcome, sister, to our family,} they welcomed her simultaneously. Their welcome felt so impassioned it brought tears to Ilsa's eyes. They stayed like that for a long time before Liassa finally, reluctantly, pulled away. Ales helped Ilsa back to her feet and picked up her crutch at the same time. Ilsa wiped the tears from her face.

"You didn't tell me this was so..." Ilsa trailed off.

"Intimate? Overwhelming? This is why we don't have anyone say the words until they have had a cycle, or sometimes even more, to really let sink in what a commitment being one of the Tier is. Once you say the words, you are permanently blessed by the gods with certain protections. Your eyes can never be damaged in such a way that they will not heal just as they were. There are others, but there is no need to go into them now. But there is no turning back. You may one day be called upon to sacrifice yourself for the good of others, and your pledge will compel you to do so if you falter, as we warned you during your training. Though we know of no one who has said the words that has willingly gone against their pledge. If you were unwilling, you would not be able to say the words," Lia explained.

Ilsa looked at her hand, and the cut had closed as if it had never been there.

"Am I always going to be able to hear you in my head?" Ilsa asked.

"Not from this bonding. It is a very brief effect of your bonding to our family. Once we are able to give you your own Cellstructs, you will have a permanent mental link." Ales said. "But no matter what happens, the most important part of this bonding is that you will always know that you are not alone. Even when you are physically alone, you will be able to feel your bond to us."

"We should be getting back," Lia said. Ilsa took a step, bracing herself with her crutch, and then she paused.

"It feels better. A lot better." She lifted her crutch and held it horizontally in her hand. She took a tentative step. Ales smiled.

"You have chosen to give your life to being one of the Tier. There are many benefits to that commitment. This is one of them. Your body will never age physically. Even Tier die eventually, but you will never feel the pains of old age. You will always perform at your physical peak. Your body will heal at an accelerated rate, as well. Not like it would with Cellstructs, but our Cellstructs are an enhancement of the natural magical protections given by the Gods," Ales explained.

Ilsa's eyes were a little wide, and she looked down at her leg.

"It'll still take a few days to heal completely, and you're probably a span away from any acrobatics without hurting yourself," Lia cautioned.

"It doesn't hurt anymore, though, not at all," Ilsa said wonderingly.

"It does, but you don't have to feel it anymore if you don't want to. The bonding opens your mind to the ability to control your subconscious bodily processes. This is yet another small part of why we wait so long for you to say the words. If you are not sufficiently trained, you could cause yourself unintended damage by ignoring pains. Not being able to feel the pain is not the same as the pain not existing. Pain tells you that your body is damaged in some way, so it is important to know it is there. The bonding allows you to processes pain differently. You can still feel it if you think about it. In reality, you can feel it more acutely than anyone else, but it is no longer just a warning that you are damaged. It is a tool that you can use to understand your body." Ales explained it all as they neared the edge of the camp.

"This is what you meant when you said torturing a Tier is pointless," Ilsa said.

Ales nodded. "Yes, we are the masters of our bodies and minds. Even if you are on the verge of death, you can retreat into your mind to protect yourself from anything that is happening to you physically," Lia explained.

"This is a lot to take in. Have you done this with Cole and Warran yet?" Ilsa asked.

Ales shook her head. "Not yet. They are not ready. Well, maybe Cole is, but Warran needs more time. He has not yet overcome the damage he did to himself by killing those men unprepared. But he will, and when he does, we will enact the bond with him as well."

They made their way back through the tents. Lia made a soft growling noise as they neared the forge.

"Yes I see them, sister, but I don't think they will be foolish enough to attack us. Why don't you go ahead and follow them when they depart. Perhaps we can discover who thought it might be a good idea to kill our sister and her young apprentice," Ales said. Lia nodded.

"What is it?" Ilsa said.

"It's nothing. When we passed the guards coming back into the camp, someone began following us. They are quite good at following people. They have changed who is doing the following three times to attempt to disguise the fact that they are following us."

Ilsa looked more alert.

"Just keep asking your questions. Lia and I will take care of this idiocy. You have more that you want to know."

"How do we protect ourselves from what we feel when we hurt someone?"

"That is an extremely complicated question, and it varies from Tier to Tier. For myself, I use my anger to bull through the emotional pain until I have time to process it. But the basic idea is the same. The first step is in being certain that you have no other choice. If you must do harm to other living things, then you must be certain that it is for the right reasons." Ales sighed. "I would do anything for a copy of the Beholder's Way right about now."

"It's a book?" Ilsa asked.

"It's a book that lays down not only the commitments of being one of the Tier, but also explains that as long as you keep the core ideals of the Tier at the foremost when making your decisions, you only really have to justify your actions to yourself. That is why Warran is having such a hard time with what he did in Vilhena. He did the right thing, for the right reasons, but no amount of us telling him that is going to help. He has to justify it to himself. He thinks that maybe those men were just doing what they thought was right, too,"

Ilsa nodded in understanding.

Ales continued, "But he is wrong. Those men knew that what they were doing was wrong. Could they have conceivably thought that Warran was some sort of criminal in secret? Sure. But Kayna was five cycles old, and not a street urchin or a thief. But even if she was either of those things, children do such things out of necessity. It is incalculably rare for a child of her age to be themselves responsible for such actions. His Vision told him that they knew she was blameless, but they were going to imprison her at the King's behest anyway, simply because it was the King who had told them to do so. Even a King should be questioned, Ilsa. Blind obedience out of loyalty is not an excuse for such unbalanced actions. Once that happened, those men became responsible for their actions, and instinctively he knew he had to stop them, even though they were not threatening Kayna directly."

"But isn't death a little bit harsh as a punishment?" Ilsa asked.

Ales nodded. "An excellent question, and maybe it is, but consider this. Someone, like those guards, who unquestioningly obeys the orders of another man for their own benefit is just as responsible, if not more so, for those actions than the man who gave the order. If that order leads to the death of another for reasons of expediency or personal gain beyond the necessary, is it not just that the punishment for those actions be equal to the act itself?

Ilsa, everyone wishes to believe that there is good and evil in the world, but how humans define those things is generally related to their own desires. We do not have the luxury of deciding like that. With the power we are given, we must view things objectively. Death itself is not evil. Killing others is not inherently evil. It happens in nature all the time. Some must die so that others can live. My own sister must kill other animals and consume them to survive. She is careful to choose those who are close to the end of their natural lifespan, because she believes that all things deserve to enjoy the length of a full life.

But true evil is not measured in life, death, or even in pain, but in senseless destruction. Those who are intentionally disharmonious with the world from the willful enjoyment of that dissonance. That is the purpose of the Tier, to try and spread as much peace and harmony in the world as we can. It is delicate, and there are always going to be counterarguments to anything I say as justification for our actions, but this is part of the reason for our oath and the magic we bind ourselves with. We are forced to observe our actions through the lens of objectivity."

"But aren't we all fallible?"

"We are, but our abilities grant us a greater measure of knowledge than others. It is up to us to use this knowledge to make the decision that brings things back into balance. And when it comes to taking the life of another, we are not so fallible. Our magic screams at us when there is no other choice. Do not mistake what I am saying. There are often times that there are possible alternatives to killing, but sometimes killing is the only correct choice. Warran knows that now, which is why he should recover.

That isn't always true, though. The damage done to his psyche is factual not just sympathetic. He was forced to understand the judgment he visited upon those men, and unprepared as he was, it damaged him. For others, it is not so simple. Sometimes, while necessary, the damage is too profound to be endured." Ales turned to look pointedly at Lia as she nosed the door open. They entered the forge, and Lia closed the door behind them.

"This is a lot more difficult in an existential sense than I thought it would be," Ilsa said.

"It becomes a lot less complicated when you learn to trust your instincts, both magical an otherwise. Our Gods are about making our world as bountiful and harmonious as it can be. You are interested in the same. If you were not, you would not have sought us out so fervently."

Ales turned to Lia when she finally settled herself on the floor in the much larger workroom outside of the forge. "Did you find where they are hiding?" They had brought in several chairs and a table.

"I feel like I have been the subject of some lesson," Lia said.

"Just a small one, Spook." Ales held up her hand with a thumb and forefinger pinched together.

"I didn't follow them all the way back, but I have their scent, and I followed them far enough to know that I can easily find them again," Lia said. Juran and Kiltik came out of the forge. Kiltik hopped up onto Ilsa's lap.

"Congratulations, Sister," Kiltik said when he finished settling himself on her lap.

"Thank you, Kiltik." Ilsa scratched idly between his ears.

"Whoever that was, Ales, they were not the same person that planted the explosive," Lia informed.

"How do you know that?" Juran asked.

"Various ways. Scents combined with careful use of our Vision, and many intervals of experience between us," Lia replied.

"I think whoever was following us just now was working for the Chieftess of the clan. I caught a woman's scent on them, and I can smell the same thing on you slightly, Ilsa. When was the last time you met with her?" Lia asked.

"A few days ago."

Lia nodded. "The scent is about that old."

"So perhaps you should tell us exactly what you have done here?" Ales asked.

23

Cole watched Jame slip out of the tent without a single shout of alarm to be heard. He had been much more serious about his Taker training over the last span since he had gotten them caught. Cole wished he knew what Jame's other Circle was. He might have at least been able to get him started on training his other talents if he knew what it was. Jame walked nonchalantly back to where Cole was leaning against a mavae hitching post.

"It's back where it belongs. I almost lost my hold on Taking for a moment when a guard came around the corner and looked right at me. He startled me. But other than that, it went smoothly," Jame said.

"Good work. While you were in there, I made some polite inquiries about who we would talk to if there was an issue with a merchant in the camp. Told them that one of the Menders sold me a pain salve that did not work. Apparently, they take such claims very seriously around here," Cole said with a grin.

"How do you lie like that?"

"With lots of practice. I don't think you will ever get it, Jame, and you should be thankful you cannot. Being a bad liar is a gift in your life."

"Seems like it helps you often enough."

"Speak nothing but the truth, Jame, and no one can ever catch you in a lie." Cole opened a small notebook bound in blue hide. "It seems that the Menders control all of the merchant traffic among the Byranti. We need to find Alicrom, the Prime Mender, because he is the one who made those notes."

They walked away from the meeting only to be followed by one of the guards. Cole frowned when he spotted the man who switched with the guard that followed them away from the building. That meant it was a team of men following them.

"Are you sure you can't read minds?" Jame asked.

"Not the way you are thinking. Ales and Lia can do it much better than I can. I can just tell for certain when people are lying and when they are not... for the most part."

"For the most part?"

"Well, I can't tell if one of the Tier is lying, but the rest of us that are left are terrible liars, except for Ales. In truth, even Alessandra doesn't lie, she just doesn't tell the whole truth all the time. Most of the time, it is better to just accept her omissions, because if she doesn't tell you, you are better off not knowing." Cole let the men follow them through the maze of tents.

"Gods, this is going to be the rest of my life, isn't it?"

"If you want to be one of the Tier, that is quite likely," Cole said, amused. "At least it will never be boring. Besides, they've been following us all over for days. Why is it bothering you so much now?"

"I just want to be able to relax at least some of the time," Jame grumbled.

"Do you want to stop and thrash them so they stop following us? Or would you rather do something more fun and more productive?"

"All of those sound like excellent options." Jame grinned.

"I get the feeling that these morons are under orders to see who we are talking to here to make sure we don't get any important information. Too bad for them we already know who we really need to talk to. So why don't you lead these dipshits on a merry little chase while I run down the Prime Mender? If they get a little battered in the process, well then maybe that will teach them a lesson about following people. Just don't get yourself killed."

Cole returned the grin. Jame's mismatched eyes lit with merriment. "That does sound like fun."

"Don't kill any of them, either," Cole chuckled. He opened his Vision, and even Jame lost track of where he had gone.

Jame kept on walking as if nothing had happened. He kept an eye on the one following him. Cole stuck his foot out in front of the man following Jame. He immediately went down face-first into the dirt. Cole bent and let out a peal of cackling laughter right in his ear. The man lifted his head in confusion, but saw nothing. Cole stepped back from him, and slipped between two large tents. They would find his apprentice was more than they bargained for, and by the time they decided that chasing Jame wasn't going to net them any useful results, Cole would have already gotten what they needed.

Cole doubled back to the building that they had just left. If the Prime Mender was writing in that book regularly, then he would have to show up there at some point. The problem was that Cole had no real idea what the man looked like. Mender was a title held by Fixers in many countries where they specialized in fixing the human body. Usually, they dressed in blues and whites to indicate their profession.

Cole did not have to wait long. A middle-aged woman dressed in the most exquisite set of Mender garb he had ever seen appeared from the jungle of tents. The skirt was knee length and hemmed in a blue vine pattern that had sapphire gems sewn into the fabric. Her spotless white blouse buttoned up the front, and each of the buttons was also a carved sapphire. She had glittering emerald eyes and long hair that matched them. She had it pinned up out of the way. She was wearing a pair of spectacles that had extra lenses on little tiny metal arms that attached to the temples. Cole stepped into her path and altered his focus on the Circle of Taking so it encompassed both of them. She startled when he appeared in front of her, but not nearly as badly as he expected her to.

"I apologize for startling you, but I suspect that someone is attempting to keep me from speaking with your Prime Mender, Alicrom. If you could point me in his direction?" Cole asked.

"And who might you be?" the woman asked him. He noticed that she had an emblem sewn onto each of her shoulders.

"My name is Cole, and I am one of the Tier."

She inspected his mismatched eyes his irises still glowing with power. "Well, Cole, you have found him." She spread her skirts and gave a small bow of respect. "I am Prime Mender Alicrom." She gave him a sardonic grin.

"Then I owe you a second apology. A poor assumption on my part. Be assured that no one will see us. If you have some place that we could speak in private?"

"I do. My quarters inside should be safe to talk in."

"Please lead the way, Prime Mender." Cole bowed, and swept his arm out toward the building. He kept a hold on his power until she closed the door behind them.

"Are you truly one of the Tier?" Alicrom asked.

"I am, Prime Mender, and I am here to try and help you. Your Chief, though, was not willing to accept that I am who I say I am."

"Our Chief is a buffoon, so that is unsurprising. Please, Antieri, call me Ali," she said as she dropped into a comfortable looking chair tucked into a corner of the room between two book shelves.

"Only if you call me Cole. I don't much care for titles."

She smiled at him. He took out a small black notebook that looked identical to the one he had had Jame return. He sat down in the other chair between the bookshelves. There was a small table between them, and he laid the notebook out on it. He flipped pages until he got to the one where he had seen the coded merchant marks. Alicrom's eyes narrowed when she saw the notebook.

"Where did you get this?" she asked. Cole just made a little gesture to his eyes. "Gods, where do I even start? I never thought I would have an opportunity to voice my concerns."

"But you are the Prime Mender. Doesn't that title mean something?"

"It should, but something has happened in the Royal family of the Byranti. People who don't tow the line now tend to go missing. I was preparing to attempt to go to another Clan with my concerns," Alicrom explained.

"How long has this been going on?" Cole finally found the page with the notations and the strange symbol he didn't recognize.

"About six cycles, ever since Chieftess Allial passed on and Chief Gregon took control of our Clan. We moved here about four cycles ago, when our foraging grounds moved. But once we did, the Chief had this building constructed. There are levels of the building dug out below ground, and there are laboratories down there with Searchers and Menders who are not allowed to leave. All I know is that they are producing a massive amount of Sarsan Tar, and I have no idea how."

"I am not a Mender or a Fixer, Ali. You'll have to elaborate for me."

"Sarsan Tar is generally refined into Black Sarsan gum and then dried into a storable substance. It is a nerve stimulant that can be extremely dangerous if not properly combined with other herbs to modify its effects. Properly used, it can work small miracles with many diseases of the mind, and it can also stimulate nerve growth."

"You're still flying a little over my head, but I think I understand. Why is it so hard to believe that they are making a lot of it? It sounds useful."

"Because the tar is made by distilling the sap of the sarsan shrub. Then, it is combined with the powdered bones of a specific poisonous serpent. The Sarsan Shrub is extremely rare as it doesn't seem to grow under any specific conditions. We have been trying to figure out how to cultivate the plant for intervals. It's never been done that I know of, and if someone had managed to do it somewhere, the Outriders would have found it by now. In my entire life, I have seen perhaps two whole spheres of Black Sarsan Gum, but the shipping logs say that we have shipped at least fifty spheres of the stuff in the last two cycles." Ali laid it all out for him, and he made a wordless sound of thought.

"Why would you need so much?" Cole asked.

"Properly utilized, it can cure a number of illnesses that have no other known treatments. It can stimulate nerve regeneration. It can cure paralysis and neural degeneration. We never really have enough of it. But the fact of the matter is, if someone like me discovered a way to cultivate sarsan shrubs, they would tell other Menders about it at least."

"Which means if they are keeping it a secret, either they are greedy or they have another use for the stuff," Cole said thoughtfully.

"What else could they be using it for?" Alicrom asked.

"That is certainly the question, but I am out of my depth, here. It is time that I spoke with someone who can unravel this mystery properly."

"But you are one of the Tier."

Cole grinned at her. "I am newly minted, and still have a long way to go to complete my training. But I am not alone. No one will have seen you come in here with me, and no one will see me leave. It will take a few spans, but I will return soon with help. We will help you, Ali. Until then, just go about your business. If you think that you are in danger, I urge you to come to Rihanna and find me."

Cole reached into the satchel he was carrying and took out something that Ales had made them over their cycle of training after Vilhena. There had been dozens of little bits and pieces that she had crafted to help Warran come into his abilities as a Tieran Fixer. This was one of them. It was a small, circular pin that could be worn on a coat or lapel. It was about twice the size around as Cole's thumb nail. It was made of bondsteel, and etched into the surface was an ancient symbol, three circles of carved vines overlapping one another. The pin was a distress call for the Tier. It glowed brightly in Cole's sight, and any Tier who saw it would know that the person wearing it was asking for help.

Cole held it out. "Pin this where it can be seen on your collar or coat. Walk the streets of Rihanna wearing that pin, and it will not be long before help comes to you."

Ali took the small pin and held it up to the light. "This is beautiful."

"Tieran Fixers have a talent for making beautiful things."

"Oh, and one more thing. I suspect more than a few of your guards are about to come in rather battered from trying to chase down my young apprentice. Treat them gently, Mender? They were just following orders, no matter how misguided."

Cole flashed a grin at her, and then he constricted the force of his Vision so that he was the only one left within its power. She looked up at the book cases around her, and when she looked back, he was gone. She blinked, not knowing why she had been compelled to look up at her books just then. She looked down at the pin in her hand and frowned.

"Well, I was probably going to get myself killed trying to go to the other clans anyways."

She slid the pin into the front pocket of her skirt. She started to pack some of the things she would need to get to Rihanna.

25

Getting into Rihanna had turned into a small ordeal. For some reason, the Outriders were being denied access to the city. Apparently, everyone was up in arms due to a murder in the Center, which had everyone on edge. Kayna sat on her mavae not far away and Hagar argued with the guard at the moonward gate. Finally, Warran tired of listening to them bicker and climbed down from his mavae.

"Enough." Warran's voice cut through the argument like a hot blade through butter. He opened his Vision just enough to make his irises glow with latent power. "Hagar is a Standard in your military and I am of the Tier. We have been entirely reasonable, and you are blindly following orders that clearly do not apply to us. I must speak with my fellow Tier. They are in the Center. Move or I will move you. Either way, the result will be the same," Warran growled.

The men looked for a long moment as if they were going to protest, but then they met his eyes again. There was no question that Warran was telling the truth. They quickly stepped aside.

Warran's group wasted no time making their way to the Clan home of Mizami. Warran knocked on the massive wooden door and waited patiently. After a few minutes, the door swung open. There were two people behind it. One was a tall thin man dressed in a crisp black outfit: a button up shirt with a formal jacket open in the front over the shirt and matching slacks. Next to him was a young girl, perhaps eight cycles old. She had on a simple white dress with long sleeves and a skirt that hung to her ankles. A wide green ribbon was tied around her waist with a bow at the small of her back.

"Hello. We are attempting to learn where we can find Alessandra or Liassa of the Tier," Warran said. The man and the girl exchanged a glance. Then the girl ran off into the house, her skirts bouncing.

"Please follow me. Standard Hagar, please bring the mavae to the stables around back and join us in the meeting hall?" The man in black bowed, and Hagar returned it. Warran was not surprised that the man knew Hagar as they were both Mizami.

"Of course, Headman," Hagar replied. He held out a hand to help Kayna dismount, but she just stared at him like he was an idiot. She swung out of the saddle and slid to the ground with a grace that made them all look like stumbling fools. She dusted off her knee-length riding dress a little, and then blushed when she saw everyone was watching her. The headman made a little throat clearing noise.

"Yes, this way please," he said and turned on his heel. Warran followed him, and Kayna grabbed her small pack from next to her saddle bags, slinging it over her shoulder. She followed him inside and then stopped and pushed the big door closed. Then she ran to catch up with him.

"I look all dirty from the road," she said, fussing with the divided maroon skirt of her dress as if she could shake the road dust loose that way.

"It's fine, sweetie. No one will notice, and we'll get you a bath and some clean clothes soon," Warran said.

"Okay," Kayna said, and then returned to her normal taciturn self.

Warran frowned. It had to be the new place that was causing her to retreat, because over the last cycle, she had become much more communicative than she had been since her mother had passed away. Still, she was smiling, so Warran didn't worry too much. His eyes fell on the wide blue cuff peeking out from the sleeve of her dress and he sighed in annoyance. With Verdant's help, they could erase the slave mark she had been branded with. It never seemed to bother her very much, but he caught her fingering the cuff sometimes like it hurt her. It made him wonder if she knew how close to disaster she had come.

They walked through a long wood-paneled hallway and came to an intersection. The headman went to the left, then the right, stopping at the third door on the right. Through the door was a nicely-appointed sitting room with a number of comfortable chairs arrayed around a large round table. A large stone fireplace took up much of one wall. The stone around the hearth was carved with animals. Above the fireplace, a large tapestry emblazoned with the Clan coat of arms was hung. A thick rug had been placed beneath the table and chairs. Four well-padded chairs flanked the large hearth, there to accommodate smaller meetings.

Two of those chairs were occupied. The woman in one was definitely part of Angran's family. She had the same yellow hair, feathered with light blue highlights, as Angran. The last letter that had come from Ales had told Warran their names.

"I assume you are Eilee and Bahram. Ales described you after she and Lia settled here," Warran said. They looked a little surprised, but also a little pleased.

"We are they. And who might you be?" Eilee asked, looking at Kayna.

"This is my daughter, Kayna. She's a little shy around new people," Warran explained. Kayna wasn't precisely hiding behind him, but she had stayed a few steps back, putting him between her and the hearth. She spread her skirts and bowed politely.

"It's a pleasure to meet you both," Kayna said, but Warran could tell they wouldn't get much else out of her.

"You can sit at the table and read your book, Midget," Warran said affectionately. She nodded and went to the table to do as he suggested as he sat down across from the pair. "Can you tell me where Ales and Lia have been staying?" They exchanged a glance, and Warran understood. "You're wary of revealing anything to me, not knowing precisely who I am. Ales and Lia left with you a polished silver sphere on a thin chain that would act as an emergency beacon. May I see it?"

To Warran's surprise, Eilee took it out from a pocket in a satchel by her chair. She handed it over to him. Warran opened his Vision and turned the sphere in his hands before moving it between a finger and thumb. He turned the sphere with his free hand so his fingers slid over the surface. He turned it this way and that. Then, he held it on the palm of his hand.

A line appeared on the surface of the sphere, and it began to unfold much like a flower opening. It unfolded smoothly until it was a flat sheet of metal held between his hands. There were words on the metal sheet. How the thing was made was entirely beyond Warran. Ales had told him that eventually, he would be able to understand how it was made, and even make one himself. The words on the sheet could be understood by literally anyone who would look upon it. The message was simple:

To whom it may concern: Any of those who are capable of unlocking this message are confirmed as one of the Tier and can be trusted implicitly.

Warran put the note down on the table, and it immediately started to fold back up into the silver sphere. Eilee reached out for it, but Warran spoke.

"I wouldn't do that if I were you," Warran warned, and Eilee pulled back her hand. "If any but one of the Tier touches it before it has fully closed, it will disintegrate."

"How do you know when it is fully closed?" Bahram asked.

Warran just pointed at the note, which had almost fully returned to being a sphere. When the last flap curved itself around the sphere, a bright white line of light appeared along its edge and then vanished. Warran held the sphere out to Eilee. She took it carefully and put it back into the satchel next to her chair.

"They have been staying in one of the empty Mizami warehouses near the sunward gate. Hagar knows the Center well. We can direct him and he can take you to them," Eileen said.

"It's very much appreciated. If I can offer you any assistance in return, please don't hesitate to ask."

Just then, the door opened and Hagar, along with Linten, slipped quietly inside.

"Princess, Prince," Hagar said. He and Linten bowed to each of them.

"Standard Hagar, would you be so kind as to take the honored Tier to the winter storehouse nearest the sunward gate?" Eileen asked.

"It would be my pleasure, Princess."

"What are your talents, honored Tier?" Bahram asked.

"I am a Fixer," Warran said. It was not exactly a polite question, but he had offered them his services to repay them for their help.

"Would it be possible for you to repair this?" Bahram stood up and took down a dark wooden box from the mantle above the fireplace. He opened the box, and within was something that Warran thought he would never see. It was a Stoe Model Zero. The old lancer was one out of very few that Stoe himself had designed, built, and tooled from scratch. It was absolutely stunning. Polished lacal wood grips contained carved silver inlay in the shape of the Mizami family coat of arms. The brushed finish on the barrel glinted in the light from the fire when Warran turned it in his hands. He opened his Vision and looked at it.

It was immediately clear that the internal components of the trigger mechanism had been separated due to some sort of strike or drop. The strike plate had broken away from the trigger bar, causing the spring to force it up against the outer wall of the strike well. That was extremely dangerous, because if it shifted to rest against the contact plate and you put a solar cell into the weapon, it would quickly overheat and explode. It was amazing that the weapon had survived this long. There were damping mechanisms inside of the trigger assembly to prevent this sort of damage.

"How did this happen?" Warran asked.

"A freak battle accident. The person wearing it on their hip was knocked from their mavae and rolled down a hill. The lancer was caught on a small tree branch and then crushed under them. It snapped the tigger off, and I have never trusted a Fixer with it," Bahram explained.

"May I ask who this belonged to? This was hand tooled by Bas'ter Stoe himself. From everything I have ever heard about these, there were only ever two dozen made, if that. The rails in this are the second most powerful set I have ever seen."

"It was a gift to the Clan Chief of Mizami for providing Bas'ter with safe passage to the other side of the Wilds," Eilee explained.

"I will repair and return this to you. It will take a little time," Warran said. He held the lancer out to Kayna. She jumped up from her chair, and came over to the group of chairs. She took it carefully from his hand looking it over. She went back to the table, and slid it carefully into the satchel she was carrying. Eilee looked a little apprehensive about the girl carrying the iron. "Don't worry. The iron will be perfectly safe with her," Warran said. Bahram gave him a questioning look. Warran smiled in return.

"My little girl is a born Fixer, and she has probably fired more lancers than everyone in this building combined, save for me." Warran chuckled when they looked shocked. "I promise to return it to you in perfect working order. I will even provide better solar cells for it. For now, I do need to speak to my sisters. Thank you for your hospitality."

"If you can repair my forefather's lancer, we will consider it more than a fair trade for our hospitality," Eilee smiled. "Hagar can show you the way back outside."

"Wind at your back, Prince, Princess." Warran bowed.

"Wind at your back, honored Tier, Outriders," they returned.

Thankfully, the stable hands knew their business well because the mavae had been washed and watered by the time they returned to the the stables. They were fresh and danced in their stalls with silent anticipation.

"If we didn't have our packs, we could just walk. We are not far from the sunward gate," Hagar said.

"It's no trouble to the mavae."

The architecture of the Center was a confection of flowing stone. The perfect radial symmetry of the building layout itself made it completely clear that it had been laid out by one of the Tier. Each of the four arms of the spiral was a curving street leading precisely sunward, moonward, stoneward, and bloomward. The expansion of the Center didn't follow the same perfect pattern, but the inner Center that was designed to conceal the Traveler's Grove was mathematically flawless. It was a feat of engineering that even Vilhena did not match.

Each of the buildings from the original city appeared as if it had been carved from a single block of stone. Each building climbed between one and three stories. Regardless of the size of the building, two elaborate carvings of the stonebark tree stood sentry on the entrance. The rest of the flowing bas relief carvings were done in such a way that the façade of the building looked very much like you were looking into the forest from the edge of a clearing. Warran had rarely seen such beauty in his life. He guided his mavae closer to one of the buildings and touched the carving of the trees. They felt as if they really were tree bark.

"Who maintains all of this?" Warran asked when he rejoined them on their walk down the street.

"Clan Clai is responsible for maintenance of the Center, and they provide all of the Bookminders for the libraries, but these buildings maintain themselves," Hagar replied.

Once they passed the first wall, the buildings became much more mundane. They were still well-built structures of wood and stone, but they lacked the graceful elegance of the buildings within the original Center.

"Here we are," Hagar said, turning his mavae down an alleyway. He dismounted and moved to the door.

"Bad idea," Warran said. His Vision was still open, and he was peering through the walls of the warehouse. Hagar dropped his hand from the door knob immediately. "Did you think that they would leave their sleeping place undefended?"

"Point taken."

Warran examined the defenses on the door through the wall. It had been rigged so that any who opened the door would be jabbed with a barbed dart covered in some sort of poison that Warran did not recognize. It probably wouldn't kill, just incapacitate. Still, he didn't feel like being knocked unconscious. He picked the lock on the door and then slid his tools back into his coat. He held out his hand. "Your sword, please, Hagar?"

Hagar drew his short sword and flipped it in his hand, holding it out hilt-first to Warran. Warran took it and turned the door knob, using the sword to push the door open. He tilted the sword's blade up at just the right moment, and the dart pinged loudly off the steel, burying itself in the wood of the door.

"It would be best if everyone waited outside. There's a large animal inside. I think it's likely friendly, but it doesn't know us, so I'll see if I can make introductions," Warran explained.

Warran closed the door behind him and walked across the warehouse. It was clear that the animal had been blinded but its other senses worked just fine. He could see the functioning of its mind as it roused itself from sleep. It pushed itself up onto all six of its massive paws. Warran switched to Tieran.

"I somehow suspect that if you're still here, there's a reason. I'm going to assume that you can understand me, and if you cannot, then I can run for my life before you attempt to eat me."

The Banic crept slowly closer. Warran stood extremely still while it sniffed him all over then pressed its massive head into his stomach, being careful of its horns.

"Oh good, not eating me is good." He put his hands on its head and scratched it between its horns. "I never thought that I would ever see a Banic. You're far away from your home, aren't you?" The banic backed away from him and nodded. "I have some friends with me. They won't hurt you."

The banic sneezed and then turned back to its sleeping place. It settled back down, but its ears twitched as he opened the door.

"Is that a banic?" Hagar asked incredulously once he could see the animal.

"It appears to be so. My guess as to what has been going on here is no better than yours. We'll need to wait to speak to Ales and Lia," Warran said.

"Then wait no longer," Lia said from the doorway. "I see you have met our patient, though I suspect she will not be our patient much longer if you are here." Lia finished.

"Is Ales with you?" Warran asked.

Lia nodded. "And Ilsa as well. We have a lot to discuss. I'm glad you found your way here," Lia said.

Ales, and Ilsa came in a few minutes later, having made a sweep of the perimeter. They were trailed by a young man and a boy younger than Kayna.

"Well, that is one less we have to chase down," Ales said.

"Where do we even start?" Warran asked.

"With asking your guards to leave," Ales suggested not unkindly. "I do not wish to be rude, gentlemen, but your minds are not shielded from the Probability Matrix and what we will be discussing here will be dangerous for an unprotected mind to carry about."

Hagar bowed, and Linten followed suit.

"Of course, honored Tier. Will we be needed further?" Hagar asked.

"I think that we will be fine from here, Standard, though I would appreciate it if you would stay within the limits of the Center if possible. If it becomes necessary to split up again, your services could be quite helpful, as I am sure they have been up until now."

Warran followed them outside. He helped them pull the saddle bags from the mavae that had been carrying them for him.

"Thank you for everything you've done, Hagar. I have something for you and Linten." Warran took from his saddle bags two dark metal boxes. He held one out to each man.

"We did our duty, honored Tier. We need no reward," Linten said.

"All the more reason you are going to take these, Linten," Warran said. Hagar opened his mouth, and Warran simply stared him down. "These are not just for you. They are for the good of all of the Ryhim. Take them."

Hagar took one of the metal boxes and opened the lid. Nestled into a cavity lined with short black fur was an amalgamation of brushed bondsteel and polished wood. The lancers were compact and square-shaped, unlike anything that

Hagar had ever seen. He picked his up and sighted down the square barrel.

"Beneath the fur are the designs for these lancers, their clips, and their solar cells. They'll use standard bolts and will fire off more than a hundred without the need to swap a solar cell. They are the best irons I can make, and I think that your people will need them. I know you can't manufacture bondsteel yet, but you can buy it from Vilhena to make these in quantity. The key is the magnetization process for the rails inside of the lancer. It's also described in the plans. I expect that these plans will make their way to each Chief of the clans," Warran explained.

Hagar seemed stunned as he placed the lancer back into the metal box. "Are you sure about this, honored Tier?"

Warran put his hand on top of the metal box.

"These weapons are a promise of protection that the Tier will be able to provide one day. Until we can be what we once were, you'll need to defend yourselves. This is the best way I know how to make that possible." Warran lifted his hand but left his fingertips on the box. "If I find that you've attempted to profit from these, you'll find my displeasure to be overwhelming."

Hagar shivered a little. "I understand. I will see to it that the plans go where you intend them to."

Both men swung into their saddles and rode out of the alleyway. Warran returned inside.

"That was well-handled," Ales said when he returned.

"I'm glad you approve," Warran replied. He had been a little worried she would be angry with him for giving them more powerful weapons.

"One day, they may not need such powerful weapons, but until we reach that point, the best we can do is arm them to defend themselves." Ales waved him into the circle of boxes that had been set up inside the circle of glow lamps.

"We apologize for the lack of accommodations. We have been busy here," Lia said.

"It took us four days to get beds in the workshop. I slept on a rock so we could use our blankets to make a bed for Kayna."

Warran chuckled, and then an odd look crossed his face. "Strangely, I slept just as comfortably as I ever have."

"You'll get used to being one of the Tier someday." Lia's voice held a note of amusement.

"So who wants to go first?" Ilsa asked.

Warran reached into a pack at his side and pulled out a black sphere about half the size of a man's head. "She's finished, but I haven't been able to wake her up. I think that her spirit is afraid to return."

Ales tilted her head thoughtfully, and looked at the black sphere that was meant to hold the newly-awakened spirit of Verdant.

"You are not far wrong, but I hope that you didn't think I could make her feel safe enough to awaken," Ales said.

Warran's face fell.

"Not me, Warran. I am a warrior. I protect with violence. My own countenance is not nearly of sufficient peace to make this fledgling life feel safe. Only one among us has that sort of peace to offer."

They all looked at each other, then heads turned to Lia. Ales smiled at her. "My sister protects by giving others the skills and confidence to protect themselves. She spreads peace of mind to all of those around her, just like she will to this one." Ales gestured to the small black sphere in Warran's hands.

Lia looked a little shocked, but she took a pair of steps into the circle and reached tentatively with her front right paw. Her paw was so large that it engulfed the small sphere. She turned her leg, and Warran let the sphere fall into the cup of her paw. She held it there for a long moment and then opened her Vision.

Lia looked into the sphere and saw the arcing elementary force that had collected in the sensitive Sol alloy poured onto each of the thousands of layers of substrate within. She leaned back so that she could sit steadily on four paws instead of six, allowing her to cup the sphere between her two enormous front paws. She concentrated on trying to project the peace that her sister claimed that she had. She could feel something happening inside of the sphere, and suddenly she had to close her Vision because blinding light filled the inside of the orb. Lia blinked a few times, and the glow faded from her eyes. She looked down to the orb, which now had lines of green light running over its surface. She opened her mental link, and was immediately greeted with a telepathic handshake from the budding new Mind.

{Hello, little one. What is your name?} Lia asked.

{This One is called Icci,} the mind replied in a hesitant, distinctly female voice that reminded Lia very much of Verdant.

{We are glad to know you, Icci. My name is Liassa Family Katane. I am an Arcangineer,} Lia responded. She felt Ales' mental handshake with the new mind. *{This is my sister Alessandra Family Katane.}*

There was a long pause before Icci responded.

{This One knows the Tier, and the Arcangineers. This One has many memories of This One's previous existence. This One fears that This One does not fully understand all of This One's memories,} Icci said hesitantly.

{In your previous existence, you choose the purpose of helping we among the Tier to maintain and improve our Cellstructs. We hope that you would like to continue in that purpose?} Ales asked.

Another, much longer pause ensued. Lia and Ales both held their breath while the newly-minted Mind made her decision. When the Tier first constructed the Minds, they had known that the artificial intelligence would outstrip Tieran abilities in some ways. That was the reason they were constructed, after all. They were given memories concerning what they were intended to do. What the Tier could not have known was that each new Mind would be a new life. Verdant had been the first and oldest of the Minds. It was she who had made it clear that she was unquestioningly alive, and that any others like her would be as well. That life necessitated that they be given a choice about what they were to do with it. So Ales and Lia waited for her to choose. Finally, she spoke into their mental link again.

{This One wishes to continue in This One's purpose, but This One fears that it will take many spans for This One to obtain full

reconciliation with the memories that This One's previous existence donated to This One's existence. This One apologizes, Arcangineers,} Icci said meekly.

{Not at all, Icci. You are our family. We know that you will need time to reacquaint yourself with all that your predecessor knew. Though, we would ask if you could assist us with a few pieces of information.} Ales requested.

{If This One can be of assistance, This One would be overjoyed to do so.}

{Our Fixer would like to begin building the equipment necessary for you to create Cellstructs for those among us who do not have them,} Ales explained.

{This One can give the schematics to the Fixer, but operation of this machinery is beyond This One's knowledge, currently. This One can endeavor to reacquaint with this knowledge. This One is feeling quite overwhelmed, currently. This One feels that rest is necessary. Please request that the Fixer touch This One's outer casing so that This One can pass the knowledge requested to That One.}

Ales held out her hand to Warran, and when he put his hand in hers, she guided it to touch the outside of Icci's casing.

"Open your mind to her. She will make the connection for you," Ales explained.

Warran nodded, and a moment later, he took a deep breath. He wobbled and almost fell before steadying himself.

"That is uncomfortable, but certainly convenient. This should take no more than a few days to build," Warran said.

He took his hand away, and Ales carefully took Icci from Lia's paws. She made a nest of a blanket on one of the crates and placed Icci into it. She wasn't really fragile like the Minds used to be. When they had been stored in Ahal, there had been no reason to reinforce their outer casing to mitigate massive damage. They had not been terribly fragile, but this new casing had been backed with Sol alloy to reinforce it. This made Icci nigh on indestructible, but Warran had managed to go a step further than any of them had ever thought of doing.

Because of the high energy environment inside of the casing, Structures could not be placed inside. What Warran had done was to give the outer shell its own self-replicating Bondstructs. This meant that any damage to the outer casing would be immediately repaired.

"She needs a body to defend herself," Ales said wearily.

"One step at a time. I have provided her with all the protection that I can right now," Warran said.

"Just an observation," Ales said, rubbing her eyes with one hand. "Now that that is done, we all need to compare notes about what we have found."

26

Cole sat at the edge of the forest, watching the Byranti camp. He had sent Jame ahead because he didn't want the boy to be here for what he had to do next. Jame didn't need to know that one of his people was betraying them to the Intruder. He didn't need to know that a Clan Chief, who was supposed to be the most trusted of all the Ryhim, was betraying them to the creature that wanted to destroy their world. Cole wasn't one hundred percent sure that was the case, which was why he hadn't told all his thoughts to Jame. Cole couldn't leave him to just continue destroying everything. It was time that the Chief be given a choice. Cole slid down from the back of his mavae and patted the beast's side.

"I won't be long, Wander. Stay nearby and I will be back," Cole said.

Mavae were far more intelligent than anyone gave them credit for. They knew their names, and they understood what people were saying all around them. Wander tossed his head and his antennae twisted this way and that. He was searching for water nearby. Cole walked off towards the camp, trusting that the mavae would see to its own needs. He had been well trained.

Cole did not like what he was going to do this night, but he knew that it needed to be done. Cole opened his Vision and took hold of the Circle of Taking. Even without his Vision, he doubted anyone would have seen him. He slipped between tents like a ghost. He had long ago mastered the art of keeping his steps silent. As he neared the building at the center of the camp, he became increasingly alarmed at the increased number of guards that were now surrounding the building. He had a very bad feeling that he was expected, and what he was going to find in that building wasn't going to be pleasant for him. It was of little consequence.

He waited until the door opened and a Mender came out. He walked right past the guards and slipped through the door before it could close again. Moving down the wood-paneled halls was slightly more challenging than getting through the camp. The halls were wide, but every door was flanked by at least one guard. Eventually, Cole became agitated by having to push his ability to attack the minds of the guards so they would not see him pass. He stopped outside of a door he knew had someone behind it and waited. Eventually, the man inside came out and Cole slipped through the door. He slipped across the small office to the window and unlatched it.

He leaned out to look up the side of the building. There were sufficient hand holds for his purposes, so he climbed out of the window. He stood up on the ledge and slid the window closed with the toe of his boot. He crouched on the narrow ledge and then jumped to the next window ledge up. He caught the ledge with his fingers, but didn't pull himself all the way up. He swung himself back and forth to give himself some lateral momentum. Then he did something that before his cycle of training under Ales, he could have never done.

He yanked himself upwards mid-swing, throwing himself to the next window ledge over. He caught the next ledge, and after he had steadied, he pulled himself up enough to see into the window. The room inside was empty, and so he pulled himself up onto the ledge. Cole focused his mind and opened his second circle.

He still didn't have a great grip on using Observance. The Circle allowed him to see a very short time into the future. He pulled himself up onto the ledge and peered at the small balcony. Instantly, he knew that if he pulled himself up onto that balcony, he would trigger an alarm of some kind. He could see himself standing there as a bell went off loudly inside of the building. He released the Circle of Observance and the knowledge it gave him.

Cole eyed the heavy wooden platform and the tall metal railing that surrounded it. He opened the Circle of Observance again, and could feel a small point of pain gathering between his eyes. He wasn't practiced enough in using two circles at once. This time, he intended to jump to the balcony and grab the edge of the platform instead of the railing. The alarm would not go off. He watched a bit longer until he saw himself pull up onto the railing. The alarm sounded immediately. It was the railing that triggered the alarm.

Cole released the Circle again, and focused on the walls between him and the office of the Chief. He could see the man sitting inside. He could also see that he had four guards in the room with him. Cole grimaced. He didn't want to hurt those men unless he knew that they were part of this. He looked up at the roof. The eves hung out a few marks away from the walls of the building. Cole bent his knees and launched himself into the air. He caught the edge of the roof with little trouble, and pulled himself up onto it. He didn't make a sound, but once he was on the roof, he stopped to take a breath. Breaching the building was starting to tax even his current level of physicality. He drew both of his lancers and checked his hold on the Circle of Taking. It was as solid as ever.

He dropped down from the roof and bent his knees at just the right moment to absorb the impact. The whisper of his boots landing on the balcony barely reached his own ears. He made certain that he did not touch the railing. The balcony doors were closed, but they were just frames around two large windows, which gave him line of sight to the guards arrayed one on either side of the door and one on each wall.

He focused on the Circle of Taking with the intention of disrupting the guard's ability to see anything out of the ordinary. He could see when the power hit them. They didn't exactly freeze, but there was no way for them to know that anything out of the ordinary was happening. It would last about an hour, unless someone physically touched them to break the illusion he had pressed into their minds. He swung open the doors and walked into the room. The man looked up immediately, and Cole released the Circle of Taking. He held his lancer pointed directly at the Chief's head. The man opened his mouth to shout, but Cole spoke before he could.

"That's going to hurt you a lot more than it does me," Cole said quietly. He slid the lancer in his right hand back into the holster behind his back. "Considering what I have discovered about you, Chief Gregon, we are going to have a talk, and whether or not you walk out of this room alive is going to depend on what you have to say."

"How dare you come into my home and threaten me, boy," Gregon growled.

"How dare I? You are betraying your people. Either you do not know what it is that you are doing, in which case you are simply a fool who does not question what he is told, or you know precisely what you are doing and you are willing to murder those that you were meant to protect for your own greed. Which one of these is it, Gregon? Answer me truthfully because I assure you, at this moment, your life depends on it," Cole snarled.

He had rarely felt this angry in his entire life. He wasn't sure what made him feel like this, and he thought for a moment that he would have to ask Ales if it had something to do with being one of the Tier.

"I have no idea what you are talking about," Gregon said.

Cole could see that he was lying. He pulled the copy of the book he had made and held it open towards Gregon.

"Lie to me again, and I'll kill you," Cole said flatly. Gregon's face paled when he saw the book. "You didn't see fit to ask your Searchers how they were producing fifty times the amount of Black Sarsan Gum every rotation as they had produced in the last twenty cycles?" Cole barked the question.

"Why would that matter to me? They had some sort of breakthrough. It was good for our Clan, and all the Clans."

Cole narrowed his eyes. That was the truth. This man didn't care how they had done it, but Cole wasn't sure yet if he knew what he was doing or not. Gregon looked like he was about to shout again.

"And you did not think it was strange that suddenly you were being asked to move to an area in the Black Wilds that clearly were not your normal foraging grounds? It didn't occur to you that if you were not making the other medicines that the Ryhim needed that it would do harm to them? The stores are running low, Gregon, and you have been ignoring your duties to the other Clans. Ignoring your duties to your own Clan. Children have been lost for the lack of medicines that your Clan is normally responsible for." Cole watched his mental functions through the power of his Vision. There was clear surprise in his mind. "So you are just a fool. If you were to die, who would take your place?"

The man looked a little green. "The Prince and Princess are still too inexperienced to be fully in charge. It is likely that it would pass to a new family. Prime Mender Alicrom would likely take my place as Chieftess of the Clan," he said, shaking a little.

"Stop being an idiot, man. I'm not going to kill you. You are not the source of this problem." The man once again looked as if he might shout, so Cole amended his statement. "I'm not going to kill you as long as you keep your mouth shut while I think about the best course of action for both of us."

Cole grimaced. There was no end to this kalec hole. If Alicrom would benefit from leading Cole to believe that the Chief could be responsible, he wasn't sure he could trust her. He mentally reviewed his conversation with her. Ales had schooled them thoroughly on their ability to tell truth from lies. She had explained that while all Tier shared this talent, some were better at it than others. Cole had been surprised to learn that there was so much variance in the talents of the Tier. Still, he was certain that Alicrom had been telling the truth. She had not slipped a lie past his talent. Even now, he could see the inside of her mind as she spoke.

"Would Prime Mender Alicrom be a good candidate for taking control of the Byranti?" Cole asked. When the Chief opened his mouth, Cole could see the lie brewing in his mind.

"No, don't answer that, I already know that she would be a better choice than you."

Cole pinched the bridge of his nose in frustration. This was not going at all as well as he had thought it would. He had been certain that this man was actively engaged in betraying his people. Clearly, he was not deceitful enough for that. Either the Prince and Princess of his Clan were the ones allowing this to happen, or someone who advised them was.

"Listen to me, fool. I am going to tell you what to do, and you are going to do it, or I swear I will return for you." Cole let the threat hang in the air for a moment. "You will take on Prime Mender Alicrom as your personal advisor. You will consider her advice on every single decision, and you will protect her as if she were your own child. If any harm comes to her, I will see to it that the same harm visits you."

Gregon went even paler than Cole thought possible, and he swallowed audibly. He seemed to finally realize the situation he had put himself in.

"Of course, honored Tier."

Cole went back to the balcony. "Your guards will come to themselves in a half an hour, or you can simply touch them and they will come out of their daze, though I suggest you leave them to come out of it naturally. It will be less jarring to them."

He took his grappling attachment and slid it onto his lancer. The hook unfolded, and he hooked it over the edge of the roof. He pulled on it to make sure it was set, and then jumped over the railing. The grapple lowered him safely to the ground. He touched a spot on its side, and the hook folded up and dropped from the roof into his hand. He let the thin cable retract into the attachment, and then slid the hook back into place. He took it off of his lancer, and then turned and left the camp.

When he returned, it took him a few moments to find Wander. The mavae was lying on its side, which was odd for one of them. He approached tentatively so as not to scare the beast. That was when he spotted the feathered dart sticking out of the creature's hind quarters.

He immediately drew his lancers, but it was too late. He felt the prick of the dart where it penetrated his shoulder. His Vision open, his eyes immediately tracked the exact position the dart was fired from. He whipped his lancer up and squeezed the trigger. The whining discharge of the lancer filled the air. He saw the bolt hit a hooded figure in the head. The figure collapsed, and there was a shout from another person. His eyes went blurry and he lost his hold on his

Vision. Whoever had shot him was dead, but it was too late to keep him from passing into unconsciousness.

27

It had taken them almost an entire span to work out a plan of action. Ilsa had spent much of that time trying to find out where the murdered man had come from. Her Finding had told her that he belonged somewhere in one of the homes of the royal families, but none of the ones she had checked had known him. They all seemed to think that they should recognize him, but none could place him. There were more families to check with, but that had to be put on hold for other tasks.

It took another span to find a place that was safe enough for the children and less trained Tier to live while they were trying to set the Ryhim to rights. They finally decided that, disruptive though it was, they would all have to move to someplace more comfortable and secure. They had consulted with the Prince and Princess of Clan Mizami to find an appropriate place that was utterly unrelated to the Clan in any meaningful way.

They had said that a Fixer's workshop and attached residence was available. More importantly, the residence was maintained by all of the clans, and had just emptied as the Navano Fixers had recently finished constructing the latest mining machine. Since it was one of four such facilities in the center, it was unlikely to be needed anytime soon. For the most part, the Fixers that Mizami employed were not necessary within the city, unless there was some large project that required the resources of the Center to accomplish. They had moved into the place and had paid Clan Clai in gold through an anonymous intermediary for the use of the building. Their stores had become much more accessible since there was an exposed crystal near the bunker where Ales had slept away the ages recovering her shattered mind.

They returned to Warran's workshop and found that the place had been abandoned. Just inside the entryway to the workshop was a corpse that turned out to be one of the Outriders. Warran had been furious because he was certain Kavan had forced the man to try and breech the defenses he

had left behind. It was obvious that they had been
unsuccessful.

He and Ales made several trips to take everything from the
workshop. Something about the mechanics of the light jump
made it impossible to take more than their body weight in
non-living material with them. They had disassembled the
chamber that would be used to generate a body for the Minds
and reassembled it back in the workshop. Kiltik said that the
chamber was necessary in order to generate bodies like his
own more quickly than an interval. None of them had a
hundred cycles to wait to make Icci and the other Minds safe.

Ales initiated the light jump that would take her close to
Clan Byranti. After an entire cycle of trading notes and
making assumptions about the geography of the world, as it
had changed in the last thirty three hundred cycles, Ales and
Lia had gained a fair idea of most of the places that the crystals
went, though Lia had not spent much time on the far
moonward continents.

Lia hadn't been far moonward for three hundred cycles.
She'd explained that her recovery from the events at Ahal had
caused her to go through cycles of recovery and dormancy.
Every time she believed that her mind had fully recovered, she
would find a new pocket of devastated memories that needed
to be rebuilt to make her whole. It meant that her knowledge
of the world was somewhat broken, relegated to the intervals
when she had been able to function normally. There were
large gaps in her knowledge of what might be near by to the
light jump endpoints.

This one, though, was right. She could see the perimeter of
the Clan camp. There was a steep hill carpeted with massive
stonewood trees between her and the camp. Her stomach did
a little flip from the light jump, but nothing more. From her
vantage point, she could see a large, more permanent building
surrounded by the tents. When Cole's apprentice Jame had
arrived in Rihanna and started looking for them, he had been
extremely worried that his master had not caught up with him
on the road. Ales was worried, too, but Jame had not been
able to tell her why Cole had sent him ahead. She was here to

find out why. She found two Byranti patrols on her way to the camp, and slid between them with a small application of the Circle of Taking. Getting through the camp proved somewhat more difficult.

There were armed guards in two rings around the camp. The circular patrol of the inner circle was counter to the outer circle, which meant she had to dart through an opening with Taking in full effect to get through unnoticed. Jame had not described anything like this when he had told her about the camp's security. Still, it was of little consequence. She navigated the labyrinth of multicolored semi-permanent pavilions that made up the camp. She approached the building from the back side, where she could see the two balconies that Jame had described to her. She decided that making an entrance was going to be the best.

Ales pushed open the first three levels of her constraints, and her body responded. She bent her knees and launched herself into the air. The balcony was more than sturdy enough, but even so, when she landed, it was with such force that it felt like the whole building shook. She opened her Vision and pushed open the balcony doors, striding into the office as if she owned the entire building. She looked at the two guards, her eyes flaring with power, and they backed down immediately. There were two other people in the room. One was a woman in Mender's garb and the other was clearly the Clan Chief. When he saw her eyes, he went completely pale.

"Oh Gods. Please don't kill me," the man quavered.

Ales frowned, and realized that if she wanted to know more, she was going to have to be here longer than she wanted. She couldn't wait for that now.

"I'm not here for you. I'm looking for Cole."

The woman seemed far more composed than the Chief. She spoke first.

"He left here two span ago. We have not seen him since. I would like to see him again," she said.

"And you are?" Ales asked.

"I am Prime Mender Alicrom. I'm in charge of all of the Menders of Clan Byranti."

Ales nodded. "Do you happen to know which way he went when he left the camp?"

The woman shook her head, but she got a thoughtful look on her face. "I'm sure the Outriders saw him leave. He didn't make a secret of it." She looked to the guards at the door. "Bearer?"

"Yes, Prime Mender. I will check with Standard Venti." He saluted with an arm across his chest and then departed.

"He will be back in a few minutes. May we ask a few questions while he is gone?" Alicrom asked.

Ales thought for a long moment, and then nodded. "You can ask. I don't promise answers."

They exchanged an odd look, and then Alicrom shrugged. "Cole mentioned that there was something wrong in Rihanna. Can you give us a better idea of what?"

"Not right now. More and more, it has become clear that unraveling the mystery of what is happening here in the Black Wilds is just as complicated as we thought it would be when we originally started," Ales said, then continued before they could say anything. "All I can tell you with certainty is that there is something wrong. If I were to tell you any more, it would not help you to understand, and the knowledge could put you in danger. I could advise you to stop delivering shipments of Black Sarsan to Rihanna, but that would quickly result in drawing extremely unwanted attention to you."

The Bearer came back into the room with another man. The man, an officer considering how crisp his uniform looked, had faded yellow hair. He saluted with his arm across his chest.

"Honored Tier, I am Standard Venti. How may I be of service?" The Outriders had been the most rigorous in using proper honorifics for herself and the rest of the Tier.

"I am looking for my apprentice Cole. I am sure you or your Outriders have seen him. He is about your height, stocky build, light grey hair, and his eyes are two colors like mine but his are amber and red."

"He left bloomward two span ago. That would put him taking the canyon road to Riahana. I can take you to the place where he was last seen," Venti offered.

"That would be most helpful, Standard. Please wait for me outside the building and I will be right along."

Venti saluted again and left the room. Ales turned back to the Chief and Prime Mender.

"I need to know how much Black Sarsan have you sent to Rihanna since the new production levels were reached."

"Nine hundred twenty sphere," Alicrom said.

Ales closed her eyes and grimaced. "Well that solves one mystery." Ales frowned. She wanted to disrupt the production of the substance, but she didn't want it to blow back on these people.

"There is something else, honored Tier," Alicrom said.

She opened one of the desk drawers and took out a folded piece of thick paper with a blue wax seal. She handed it over to Ales. The wax had a fingerprint embedded into it, and Ales' Cellstructs informed her that it was Warran's.

"The note arrived with a Scout, sent from another of the Tier. He was told that if anyone but Cole opened it, the note would destroy itself," Alicrom explained.

Ales examined the paper and put her thumb over the wax seal. A moment later, her Cellstructs made the connection to the bondstructs that impregnated the wax seal. The seal crumbled into dust, leaving the note to be unfolded. The note would have told Cole what they had discussed with Warran when he had arrived in Rihanna, that Cole should go to the Center because it was very likely that the Intruder had more of a presence here than they had first anticipated.

"Please send your guards away. I need to speak with both of you briefly before I go."

Ales decided it was time to be proactive. They still did not know who was using the Probability Matrix, but with this revelation about how much Black Sarsan the Byranti had been producing, it was enough information to start disrupting what was being done to the Ryhim. The men left the room, and she waited until they had emptied the entire floor. She opened the

Circle of Light and examined the energetic spectrum around them. There were no energetic transmissions of any sort leaving the building, so they were not being monitored. That was good, at least.

"I am telling only you two this because I want you to trust the Tier, and I promise you that if you reveal this to anyone else, it is very likely to draw deadly attention to you. Your production of Black Sarsan Gum absolutely must be disrupted. It is being used to produce an extremely dangerous substance. But I do not want you to stop producing it. That, too, will draw the kind of attention that could kill you. We will locate and destroy the source. No one who is working at this task innocently will be harmed. There may be casualties, but I assure you that any casualties will be people who are committing treason against the Ryhim. I can also promise you that we will be able to provide you with proof of their treason when this is all over." Ales turned towards the balcony, and Prime Mender Alicrom cleared her throat. Ales turned back.

"Are they actually real?" Alicrom asked. She had a desperate look on her face, as if she had been waiting all her life to find out the answer to this question. She wanted to know if the Gods were real. It was clear that, unlike most of the Byranti, she had been a devout worshiper and wished to know if her worship was being heard.

Ales considered the question. It was not always wise to fulfill the desire for that knowledge. Some people had a hard time coping with the idea that their Gods would hear their prayers but not answer them. The truth was that the Gods answered all the prayers that they could without causing serious issues. She decided that it would be better in this case not to answer completely.

Ales gave the woman her warmest smile and fingered the symbol of the Mother and Father pinned to her coat. Then she turned back to the balcony and strode through the doors. She checked below to make sure that no one was under her, and leapt from the balcony. She landed, bending her knees slightly to absorb the impact. Her improved strength allowed her to easily absorb the fall. Standard Venti nearly jumped out of his skin when Ales landed. She dusted off her jacket and then grinned at him.

"Please lead the way, Standard," Ales said.

The man composed himself, and coughed a little.

"Yes honored Tier." He took her in the opposite direction from where she had come into the camp.

28

Lia watched the people move through the streets of Rihanna from her perch high above the Center in the canopy of the Lightleaf trees. She and Ilsa had improvised a small, comfortable platform there for all of the Tier to be able to observe the city. It had become a necessity because the dissonance from the use of the Probability Matrix was becoming extremely evident.

In the last two spans, they had seen a catastrophic collapse of a new building the Ryhim had been constructing through a series of events that would have not occurred were it not for the Probability Matrix being active in the Center. It had killed twenty two people. That was when Lia had the idea of constructing the platforms in the Lightleaf trees so they could try to use their Vision to see the problems before they happened. Since then they had been able to avert over twelve disasters like the building collapse. Ilsa hung her legs over the edge of the platform and watched along with her. Her abilities with Repair were far more adept for this task, but she required help getting up to and down from the platforms.

"There," Ilsa said. She pointed towards the edge of the Center at a spot about halfway between the stoneward and sunward gates. Lia looked towards where she was pointing and opened her Vision. The Circle of Finding didn't show her anything right away, so she decided she needed to get closer to the problem. She stood up slowly, causing the hanging platform to shift slightly, but not enough to dislodge Ilsa. Ilsa carefully got to her feet. They had improvised three handholds tied around Lia's collar to give anyone on her back a solid place to hold on. Ilsa grabbed a handle and swung up onto Lia's back.

"Hold on tight," Lia said and felt Ilsa take a tighter grip on the handle. She jumped from the platform to a branch below, then again, to a limb on the opposite tree. She repeated the process until she was about fifty marks from the ground. After that, there were no more branches. She felt Ilsa bending over so she was laying almost parallel to Lia's back. She gripped the hide handles on either side of Lia's neck. Lia pushed open her first level of constraints and leapt from the branch to the tree opposite. She pushed off the trunk, twisting in the air so her paws hit the opposite tree and then bounced back and forth between the trees until she landed on the ground. Ilsa slid from her back and flopped on the ground, lying on her back.

"Soon, you'll be able to do this on your own. Warran is working as quickly as he can," Lia apologized.

"No, it's alright. I'm not bad, just my stomach is still catching up. You're so fast. You seem faster than I remember," Ilsa said.

"I am. Icci has been working with my Cellstructs, trying to fine tune them for better integration. She's been quite successful."

"How does that all work?"

"It is honestly beyond my knowledge to a certain extent. I was never a Structure Designer of any sort, but it has to do with how well your Cellstructs are accepted in your body on a helixical level. The deeper your Vision runs, the better you can see your own helix structure and communicate to your Cellstructs how to adjust their makeup so that they are compatible with your body.

The average Tier had Vision like mine, so making personal adjustments isn't a perfect process, because we can't see our own helix structure perfectly. Ales can see right down to the sub-atomic level, which is why her Cellstructs have such a perfect picture of her helixes. This means that they can go anywhere in her body without being detected as something her body should attack. That is how it should be. My Cellstructs, on the other hand, are specialized for the areas of my body they work in. It gives me less flexibility in terms of how much I can use them to strengthen my body because I can't devote all of my Cellstructs to any single task like Ales can. But Icci had the novel idea of having Ales view my helixes with her Vision and then save a memory of that viewing for Icci to analyze. Then she helped me reset my Cellstructs so they integrate with my body a little better."

Digesting the information, Ilsa got up. They started out of the grove, heading in the direction where Ilsa had seen the problem cropping up.

"How much knowledge did we lose?" Ilsa asked quietly.

"More than all the libraries in the world combined. If we can't return The Core to this dimension, it will be gone forever. When Ahal was alive and well, we could do things that were beyond imagination," Lia said.

Lia had left her Vision open when she descended from the trees, and as they wended their way through the Center, people stared at her glowing eyes as she passed. As they got closer to the area of the center that Ilsa had pointed to, Lia started to connect her Cellstructs to the monitors she had placed in the area. The real-time images of the places the monitors were watching started to stream into her mind. She stopped at the mouth of an alleyway that would take them into the newer parts of the Center.

"Ilsa, on my back now," Lia said.

The images showed her that they were surrounded by dozens of animals, large and small. Each one had a pitch black coat and two metal tines driven through their eyes. Lia shook away the mental images and focused on her own senses.

"You are not ready for this yet. This is going to hurt you," Lia warned, but there was no time. The alleyway filled with the growls of all the animals as they closed in on them. Ilsa swung up onto Lia's back.

"I can fight," Ilsa said.

Lia tilted her head just enough to see the hard look on her face. "It will hurt, and you will have no armor against it. These animals are innocent," Lia said apprehensively.

"I will survive it." Ilsa's voice had hardened.

She drew the lancer from behind her back in her right hand. She held no weapon in her left hand, but with the Circle of Breaking, it was a more potent weapon than any sword or dagger. She could kill with a touch if she was quick, and she was. Ales had made sure she was well-trained in the use of Breaking.

Lia backed them both into an alleyway. Men and women shouted in alarm as the animals moved toward them. They must have come from all directions. The alleyway would keep it so that they could only be attacked from the front and back. They could come from above if the Intruder had taken any flying creatures, but Lia would protect them from that. A pack of four hiluk approached, their dark blue skin identifying them as a northern breed. They were a larger breed. Not much danger to Lia, but Ilsa touched her flank.

"Switch with me. I can stop them without killing them," Ilsa said. Her Vision was blazing brightly.

Lia did not hesitate. The girl was young, but during her training, she had never once overestimated her abilities. She spun in the alleyway, giving Ilsa just enough room to slip past her. Ilsa darted forward, and the hiluk were eerily silent as they attacked. The alleyway was not wide enough to allow all four hiluk to come at her, and their claws scrabbled on the stone as they came forward.

Ilsa slid her lancer into the holster at her spine, and her free left fist slammed into the side of the head of the first one on the left. Anticipating its fall, Ilsa rolled ontop of its unconscious body. The other hiluk in the lead turned to snap at her, but missed. The hiluk behind the one she had knocked out leapt at her, but as she rolled, she lifted her knee. It collided with a bright red dot on the side of the hiluk's head, sending it stumbling over her. Its whole body flipped over her as she rolled through its legs.

She came to her feet. The first hiluk had been bowled over by the second one she had knocked out. The last one, though, was right on top of her. Her Vision helped her direct her hands, shoving the hiluk's powerful muzzle away from her throat. She turned her body, putting her weight behind the thurst. The hiluk's head slammed into the wall of the alley with a sharp smack. It collapsed to the ground.

Lia had been engaged by some larger animal. It wasn't another Banic, but Ilsa didn't have time to see what it was. The last hiluk darted forward, the nightmare ruin of its eyes replaced by steel barbs lunging towards her stomach. Ilsa turned her body to let the animal pass harmlessly. She punched it on the vulnerable red dot at the back of its skull. It hit the ground, out cold.

Ilsa finally got a good look at what Lia was holding back. It was a bull gantha. The claws of four of Lia's paws dug into the cobblestones as she held the gantha at bay with her other two on its massive rack of horns. Lia was inspecting the gantha with her Vision, but then she seemed to reach some sort of decision. She twisted her body sharply. The gantha's head twisted brutally and its thick neck let out a series of pops.

"These are too far gone, Ilsa. The Creature has sent its castaways against us. They are extremely damaged. Look inside of them. They are already dying. There are more coming, a lot more."

Ilsa focused on one of the hiluk and she could see that Lia was right. They were going to die anyways, and they had been driven mad with the pain of what had been done to them. Death was a mercy, but Ilsa grimaced because this was going to hurt her as much as it did them. "I can do it," Lia said.

Ilsa shook her head. "No. I am Tier, and I will be an Arcangineer one day. This is my responsibility."

It was not only that. Ales had been right. She could feel her Vision urging her to be merciful to these poor animals and take their bodies to release their spirits from the torment they had endured. She crouched and gave the hiluk the gentlest deaths that she could. She used Breaking to know exactly where to strike to end their lives. When she stood up, she staggered from the pain. It hurt more than anything she had ever felt in her life. Her broken arm in childhood had been like a pinprick compared to this screaming horror. She collapsed to her knees, and Lia carefully scooted her up against the wall of the alley so she could keep an eye on both ends of the alleyway.

"Ales did not exaggerate how much this hurts," Ilsa groaned. Her grimace turned to an angry scowl a moment later. "It did this to these animals just to attack us." Her anger was apparent in her voice, and Lia sighed in relief. Righteous anger was one of the few shields that she had against the pain of feeling a death that she caused. She drew her lancer again and set herself. "Let's finish this. We need to make sure that none of these poor animals kill anyone. Can you find them all? My grip on Finding is still pretty poor."

"Yes. Stay behind me and watch my back end. I'll take care of most of the work, but this will be much easier on them if I know my butt is covered."

The pain of killing was an old friend to Lia, now, and she found her anger much more easily than Ilsa had. She didn't show it to Ilsa, but she was utterly furious that the Intruder would do this to the animals. Lia killed for food, but when she did, there was no fear, no torture, and barely any pain. She ended her hunts so quickly that no animal even realized she was there before she killed. This was far different. The creature had infected these animals with unbound Cellstructs and then had accelerated their ability to multiply until every moment was unbearable torture to the animal. Lia was going to free these animals from this monster, and then she was going to find it. That was a kill that she would not feel at all.

Lia followed the alleyways in the direction that they had been going. From the smells, she knew that the gantha had been the largest animal they were facing. At one point, she heard a couple of lancer discharges behind her and Ilsa swore a few times. The pinging sounds of bolts bouncing off cobbles told Lia why she was swearing.

"Don't waste bolts until they get closer. Using a projectile weapon in a real fight takes more practice than you have, and you are more than fast enough to shoot when they get closer," Lia advised.

Lia had to kill seven more smallish predators to reach the building that Ilsa had seen. When they reached the street outside of the warehouse, Lia froze at the exit of the alleyway. Ilsa almost bumped into her, and then looked past her. Standing in the street, as black as the night sky, was another Katali. This one, though, was not dying. This one was a horror, with black metal spikes running down its back, and the structures that made it so black were not Cellstructs. They were bondstructs crawling across its skin. Ilsa, though, lifted her lancer.

"No. This one we can save, if I can best him. If we can get the spines out of his body, we can heal him. The Bondstructs on his body are controlled through the spines, and so is he," Lia said quietly.

"I'll give you a head start. Just stay still. The shot is going to go right past your ear."

Ilsa took careful aim and squeezed the trigger of her lancer. The bolt zipped past Lia's ear and pinged off one of the spikes. The spike flew free of the Katali's body, trailing blood behind it. The massive feline roared and charged them. Ilsa ran to one side and Lia darted forward. She dove beneath the black katali's charge, raking her claws at his legs. Her claws cut through the blanket of bondstructs and his pelt, leaving wet, ragged cuts across the fronts of his legs. She took out his other four legs, then immediately rolled, latching onto his side with her claws and pulling herself on top of the black katali. She grabbed the largest of the seven spikes remaining along his spine. She hoped that if she pulled out enough of them, it would paralyze him, but they had been very carefully placed so that when she removed them, they did no damage to the spine. They were set up to connect to the peripheral nerves around the spine. Removing them would be painful, but not paralyzing.

The black katali rolled violently and lashed its claws across Lia's face. It knocked her away, and she lost vision in her right eye to the claws. She jumped back and roared angrily. She dodged a second swipe of his claws and moved back for the long moment it took her eye to knit back together again. The black katali snarled and dove at her again. She sidestepped him and then drove her shoulder into his side to roll on top of him. The bondstructs on his body were clearly attempting to attack her.

Spines formed and drove into her flank, leaving behind tiny machines that tried to bore into her body. Her Cellstructs, while not as physically durable as bondstructs, were more numerous. As long as she was healthy, destroyed Cellstructs would be replaced almost as quickly as they could be destroyed. It meant that within moments, her wounds were healed and the bondstucts had been pushed off of her body.

While she had him down, she latched on to another of the spines with her teeth and ripped it free. That was when everything went utterly wrong. The katali rolled over fast and latched onto her head with his claws. He wasn't as big or strong as she was, but before she could react, he smashed his head into her muzzle. Her mouth dropped open, and bondstructs flowed off of his body into a seething cloud that surged into her open mouth.

Then Ilsa was there, balancing on the katali's shoulders. She raised her fist and smashed it into the back of the large feline's skull. It collapsed unconscious, but it was too little too late.

Lia rolled onto her side and coughed blood. It felt as if a tornado of razor sharp metal had been augered down her throat. The bondstructs were eating her organs faster than her Cellstructs could repair them. The last thing she saw was Ilsa ripping the spikes free from the no longer black katali's back. Its natural coloring was a bright yellow with a rainbow smattering of spots in green, pink, and light blue. Ilsa was fishing something out of her small pack when bloodloss overcame Lia's consciousness.

29

Cole woke from his drug-induced slumber. Wherever he was, it was pitch black. There was no light at all, but that was of little consequence. He sat up and took stock of his surroundings. Smells came to him first. He was in some sort of dank stone chamber. Water dripped somewhere nearby, but it was infrequent, so it was not some sort of leak. Probably condensation. He did not open his Vision because if they kept it this black inside, it was likely that they did not know he was awake.

He took stock of his body. He had not been injured in any way but pride. His hands and arms had been bound behind him at wrist and elbow. Whoever had done it knew what they were doing. He wasn't going to be freeing himself easily, but that wasn't the same as not at all. Cole had spent many rotations of his life learning how to escape from bonds of all sorts. These would be troublesome, but given a couple of hours, he would have them off. They had not bound his legs, which was foolish.

He rolled himself to his feet, and then realized he was naked. He grinned at that. If they thought that leaving him naked was going to hamper him, they were sadly mistaken. He felt his way around the chamber. He found the cot first then continued to follow the wall around the circular room. He found the door next. It was steel, without handle or keyhole as far as Cole could tell. The cell was well made, and would hold him for a day, or perhaps two, under normal circumstances.

Knowing it was unlikely that anyone had a way to see him, he opened his Vision and looked about the cell. The first thing he noticed was that he was underground. Looking through the stone wasn't revealing anything until he got to the side of the cell with the door. Outside was a stone hallway and a guard. Cole rolled his shoulders a little. Then he turned to examine the cot. The cot was made up of metal pipes that had been put together with bolts. Cole eyed it with glee. The edges of the pipes' ends had been finished by the smith. The bolt edges had not.

Cole sat down and began to work the knots of his ropes against the bolts holding the cot together. It took him less time than he expected to cut the ropes on his elbows. He turned his body and rolled backwards, swinging his arms below his rear. He nearly had to pull his arms out of their sockets to give him enough room to get his hands past his feet so they were in front of him again. Still, he managed it. His teeth showed in a grin as he quickly worked the ropes against the bolts of the cot. They parted for him within a few minutes. He rubbed his wrists and elbows. He was more furious that they had taken his things than that they had kidnapped and imprisoned him. He was going to tear this place apart.

Cole went to the door and thought for a long moment about what to do. He could see the locking mechanism inside the door. It was impossible to unlock it form the inside under normal circumstances, but he was far from normal. Stripping him naked had been smart of them, but not smart enough. He had asked Ales for this device, and she had made one for each of the Tier who did not yet have enhanced strength or the ability to counteract poisons.

He held his right thumb against his left forearm for a long moment. He felt a buzz beneath his finger, and it appeared as if part of his forearm had peeled away. It hadn't. The sleeve was made of bondsructs that had bonded to his skin. It was impossible to detect it unless he released it. A roll of lockpicking tools was secreted inside of the one on his left arm. There was nothing to pick here, but among the tools was a vial filled with bondstructs. The tiny machines were dormant and needed heat to be activated, but not much. They were instructed specifically to disable locks.

He dumped what looked like a dollop of fine black sand into the palm of his left hand. He flipped the lid on the vial closed and slipped it back into the sleeve, which he let seal back to his skin once more. He bent his head and breathed heavily on the black sand. It spun into a small vortex in the palm of his hand as the heat from his breath activated the tiny machines. Cole cupped his hand and pressed it against the crack between the door and the wall. He watched with his Vision as the group of tiny machines sieved inside of the lock. They destroyed the pins inside of the lock and turned the tumbler to unlock the door with a soft click. Cole just grinned.

Cole watched the guard for a long moment, but the guard had not heard the lock slip open. He had two lancers on him. One was a longbarrel like nothing Cole had ever seen. It had a massive clip of bolts and an even larger solar cell. The other was the average single-handed iron. Cole anticipated that the guard would go for the lancer on his hip first. He pushed open the door and watched the man jump up from the stool he had been sitting on. Cole was about to rush out of the cell, but to his amazement, the guard did not shout.

The guard drew the lancer and moved towards Cole's cell. He came into the cell lancer first, and Cole grabbed his wrist, sliding beneath the man's arm before standing up and yanking the wrist down. The man's elbow snapped like a dry branch. Cole pulled the lancer out of his hand and spun in a blur, smashing the grip of it into the side of the guard's head. The man crumpled to the floor unconscious before he even had a chance to scream.

Cole considered shooting him for a long moment, but then sighed in annoyance. He had no idea if this man was guilty of anything. Unfortunately, the man was the wrong size for Cole to take his clothing, far too small to fit Cole. So, he took the lancer belt with its clips and moved down the hall. He kept his Vision open, and it wasn't long until he was watching through the walls as a second guard came around the corner. Cole put the barrel of the lancer against his eye as he turned the corner.

"I'm gonna be real clear here. If you make a sound above a whisper, you can expect me to over react," Cole warned. The man nodded. His eyes wandered down to Cole's private parts. "Are you really eyeballing my family jewels when I am debating whether or not to discover what your head will look like with a nice hole through it?"

The man's eyes snapped back up to his face. He opened his mouth, and then saw Cole's finger strain on the trigger. It was not enough to fire the iron, but it was close. The man shook his head fervently.

"Where am I?" Cole demanded, and that was when the man finally realized his eyes were gleaming with internal light. "Yes, I will know if you are lying. Where am I?"

"You are in a prison house outside of Rihanna. You were brought in by Outriders from Clan Clai as an outsider who had committed crimes against the Ryhim."

"Where are my possessions?"

"They are in a lock room near the warden's office."

"If you were to take me there, how many guards would we run into along the way?"

"Three, and there is a locked gate between here and there."

"How long have I been here?"

"A few hours, I would guess. Not a full day, but I did not come on duty until after you were brought in. That was around falling."

"Good, very good. I do not know why I am here, and I do not know if you are in any way responsible for my imprisonment. I committed no crimes, and I was here to help the Ryhim. I do not want to hurt anyone here. However, I will do whatever it takes to recover my possessions and leave here in one piece," Cole said irritably. "You will take me to this lock room. No one will see me along the way, and neither will you, but rest assured, I will be right behind you. Any attempt to tell anyone of my presence will have consequences."

The guard nodded, and Cole took the lancer away from his eye. He followed the guard along the rough-cut granite hallways and through a door into a stairwell. They went up three flights of stairs, and it dumped them into another stone hallway, which lead in the opposite direction as the one they had gone through.

They passed the first guard standing outside of what was clearly an office door, going by the name etched on the door. Cole watched as they exchanged salutes, but nothing in the functioning of either man's mind indicated they had alerted each other of anything. Cole walked past and followed the man as he turned left and walked down the hallway all the way to the end. He turned right, and they came to a heavy locked gate. The door was made of bondsteel, and had a small window with heavy metal bars set into it. The guard knocked on the metal door twice, and a man's eyes appeared through the bars.

"Need to drop some things in storage." The guard said it smoothly, and the door was unbolted a moment later.

"Don't be too long. Warden is in a foul mood and doesn't want anyone in there," the door guard growled.

Cole followed the guard through the door and down the hall. This hallway ended in another thick door, and on the right hand side was a similar heavy door with a barred window. The guard pulled a key from his belt, and unlocked it. Cole followed him inside, and he closed the door behind them. The guard opened his mouth to speak, and Cole released Taking so that the guard could see him. He quickly held a finger to his lips to quiet the man.

The large room was filled with rows of racks containing hundreds of items – lancers, knives, swords, books, and clothing, anything anyone could ever need. He took an iron grip on the Circle of Taking in his mind and looked into the guard's eyes, disrupting the man's mind. He would awaken in about an hour. Cole went through the neatly organized shelves until he found his clothing and armor.

He dressed quickly, but to his annoyance, he couldn't find his lancers. He found his short sword, throwing knives, and dagger, belting them in their places. Most annoying, though, was that the book was missing. It didn't matter much he had sent a copy with Jame anyway. His lancers were a massive loss, and he was certain that they would end up in the possession of some upstart Prince. He slipped his long coat on, and found that it still had all of his tools in it, at least. He shook his head and sighed. There was nothing more he could do here.

"You'll be fine in about an hour," Cole whispered.

He focused on Taking again. He opened the door and walked into the hallway. The guard holding the door looked up and then stared when no one came out of it. Cole went to the other side of the hall and waited a long moment. Finally, the guard did as expected and crept down to the room. Cole slipped past him and slid a set of lock picks out of an inner pocket of his coat. He slid the picks into the lock and went to work on it. When the man started shouting an alarm, Cole ignored him.

It took him only a few seconds to pick the lock, and he was past the gate. An amazingly loud klaxon began to sound from the Warden's office and Cole paused. He thought for a moment that he should speak with the warden because it was possible that was where his lancers had gone, but right then he was ill-equipped to call the man to task. He decided that escape was the better option, for now. If the man truly had his lancers, he would have much better chances to call the man to task for his theft.

Cole moved to the stairwell and found that door to be locked as well. He paused for a long moment and examined the building with his Vision. He noticed that the building was more advanced than he had originally judged. Most of the doors and cells had elementary force conduits run to them through the walls. That meant that it was likely that the warden could lock down the entire prison at the flip of a switch. Cole assumed that he had done so.

Annoyed, he looked around for the best way out of the Prison. Unfortunately, the entire building was well-built stone which meant that his Vision could penetrate only a single floor before its density made it impossible for him to see further. Luckily, he spied something on the next floor down that drew his attention.

Guards were amassing in a single room. It was very likely that the guard room would have a map of the building. Cole picked the lock on the stairwell door and moved down the stairs. He waited for all of the guards to tromp out of the room before slipping into it. He heard the click of the door locking behind him as it closed automatically. Sure enough, on the wall was a map of the facility. It was massive, with hundreds of cells and dozens of corridors. It was smartly built such that many floors and stairwells did not provide an exit from the building. He quickly memorized the map and chose a circuitous route to the exit. Taking the most direct exit would be exactly what they were expecting.

He went down a stairwell on the opposite end of the hallway from where he had come up onto the floor. It took him back up one floor, and he took a left out of the door. The top floor had been built with three walls down the middle, separating it into five large sections. The section he was in now had a stairwell that would take him down two floors. He went to the end of the hallway and took a right. He picked the lock on the stairwell door. Following the stairs down two floors, he emerged into a little-used floor of the prison.

This floor was the only floor not divided into confusing sections in the whole prison. It was labeled the exercise hall. They probably only used it on days when prisoners could not be released into the yard. Cole idly wondered why the Ryhim needed such a large prison facility. He took a left out of the stairwell door and then followed the long hallway to the far end of the building. He took another left and went to the end of that hallway as well, which ran along the entire length of the building. At that stairwell door, two guards were posted. Cole rolled his eyes. He grabbed the longbarrel that the guard had leaned up against the wall. The two men startled, and both went for the lancers holstered on their belts. Cole released Taking and appeared, holding the longbarrel pointed at them.

"Please don't make me shoot you," Cole warned. He made a gesture towards their lancers. Each took theirs out of their holsters and tossed them down the hall, past the door. He gestured them back in the other direction. The hall was just wide enough, and he saw that one of them was going to try to attack him. "You're not going to win if you do that," Cole said, and the man paled. He leaned the longbarrel up against the wall and picked the lock. He side-eyed them, and his glowing irises seemed to ward off any other ideas of attacking him.

The door clicked open, and he pushed it into the hallway. He picked up the longbarrel and shot it at the stone floor just inside the doorway. The bolt created a divot in the stone. Cole slammed the door and wedged the barrel of the long lancer into the divot, jamming the butt of the iron underneath the door handle. A moment later, someone hit the door. Cole ran down the stairs two at a time. It took him down two more floors, and he picked the locks on two doors. He was finally outside.

The rear courtyard of the prison was covered by patrols, and opening the door drew the attention of almost fifty guards. His solid grip on Taking kept him invisible to them all. He couldn't maintain this kind of activity for very long, but it would hold for long enough for him to get away. He ran for the wall with everything he had. The wall itself was fifteen marks of thick stone. He reached into his coat and produced his grapple. Normally, he would need his lancer to fire it, but he pulled the hook from the end as he ran.

He pulled about twenty marks of line out of the grapple. He wasn't sure he would need it, but it was better to do this safely. He ran at the wall as fast as he could. As he had practiced hundreds of times, he threw the hook towards the top of the wall. He ran up the wall and yanked the line as soon as the grapple passed the top of it. The hook sprang open and caught the top of the wall. His weight jerked the line taut. It was unfortunately very thin.

Cole looped the line around his hand and it bit into the skin of his hands violently. Cole ignored the pain and pulled himself up onto the wall. He picked up the hook and ran to the other side of the wall. The forest, Cole noted, was only about fifty marks from the wall. It was a short run, and that was a good thing because he was about to lose his hold on his Vision. He swung himself down off the wall and hooked the grapple at the top. The line made deep cuts in his right hand as he lowered himself to the ground. He tugged the line, allowing it to recoil back into the housing of the grapple. That was when he lost his grip on Taking. He turned to bolt for the woods, and something hard smashed into his head with brutal force.

30

Ales had followed Cole's trail for two days before losing it on the Balang River. Whoever had grabbed him had taken him onto a boat, and the ever-moving water made it impossible to track him across it. That didn't mean she had no idea where they had taken him. The Outriders had been extremely helpful in that regard, so she knew that whoever had taken him had not left the Wilds with him. Not only that, but they had been careless. Cole had pulled the dart out and tossed it into the grass nearby for her to find. That was how she had made it to the Outriders.

Her Finder abilities had clearly marked the dart as something that was used by them. The ones she had spoken to hadn't known exactly who among the Outriders used the darts. What they had known was that the darts were made exclusively in Rihanna. When she had returned to Rihanna, though, the workshop was deserted. Kayna, Manat, and Icci were the only ones left in the building.

"Daddy said he was going to take the Lightleaf trees to Navano to fetch Kiltik. He took the banic back to its home like you asked him to. He came back and got Juran so that Juran could fetch more of their things. He'll be back soon. Ilsa and Lia went out to the platforms to watch the city," Kayna informed.

Ales sighed. She had not wanted to send the banic away, but Lia was extremely reluctant to confirm that the banic was meant to be one of the Tier for some reason. Until they knew for sure, it wasn't safe here for the massive creature.

"Did you find Uncle Cole?" Kayna asked.

"Not yet, but I will find him. That's why I came back. Do you know where Ilsa and Lia have gone?"

Kayna shook her little head. "Just out to the high up platforms."

"The high up platforms?" Ales asked, confused.

"They put them up high, high in the trees after you left to find Uncle Cole so they could see the whole city."

"Has anyone bothered you since they left?"

"Nuh-uh. I'm just teaching Manat his numbers," Kayna explained when Ales looked at the sheets of paper on the table where they had been sitting.

"No more playing with the tools when your Dad isn't here?" Ales asked suspiciously.

Kayna blushed a little and shook her head. After they had set up the workshop, they had returned a few hours later from a supply run to find Kayna had taken apart one of her Father's lancers and was working on putting it back together. She hadn't done anything dangerous, though. She was surprisingly mature and meticulous when it came to the workshop and had taken all the proper precautions for working with the lancer.

The issue was that Manat had been in the shop with her, And unbeknownst to Kayna, he had found a box of elementary force rails. Inside the box, they were perfectly safe, but without the shielding built into a lancer or the box, they would be dangerously attracted to any metal in the shop. Fixers had been seriously injured and even killed on a few occasions by elementary force rails from lancers zipping across their workshops when proper precautions weren't taken. Luckily, they had come in before he had gotten the box open. Kayna had been distraught and promised not to go in the workshop without supervision again.

"I won't take Manat in the shop again. I promised," Kayna said.

"No, it's alright, Kayna, I'm just having a little fun with you. I know you wouldn't ever put someone in danger on purpose. I'm going to go have a look around and see who I can find. Will you be all right on your own until I get back?"

Kayna nodded and went back to her chair, helping Manat scratch numbers down on a sheet of paper. Ales went to the door, and when she was about to reach for the handle, it burst open. Ales took one perfect step back, and her Windblade came out in a blur so fast that it looked as if it had appeared in her hand by teleportation. Ilsa was standing behind the door. Her arms were covered in blood up to the elbow, and it was spattered liberally over her knee-length green skirt as if she had been kneeling in it. The black metal bands of her Sparks covered her knuckles, and they, too, were spattered with gore. She was panting and looked exhausted, like she had run a great distance to get here.

"Oh, thank the Gods. I can't move her on my own and she is hurt badly. I can't tell if she is healing. I can't tell if I got them all. I think I did. I had to leave her." Tears streamed down Ilsa's face, but she had them under control on some level, because they didn't stop her from speaking clearly.

"Ilsa, take a few breaths while I get my things," Ales soothed.

Ilsa's fists uncurled and her Sparks clattered to the stone floor.

"Kayna, please take Manat and go into the play room," Ales asked.

Kayna nodded. Ales turned and disappeared through another door. Ilsa stood there panting, trying desperately to process what had happened. Ales was back within a few moments. She tossed her small pack to Ilsa, who caught it on reflex alone. Ales turned, and knelt down in front of her.

"Climb on and hold on tight around my neck."

Ilsa slung the pack across her body and climbed onto Ales' back. Ales grabbed her legs in a piggyback carry, lifting her effortlessly. She opened the door, exited, and locked it behind them.

"Where are we going?" Ales asked.

"It's about halfway between the stoneward, and sunward gates," Ilsa said.

"I'm going to go extremely fast, so don't let go, whatever you do."

Ales' muscles bunched, and Ilsa could feel the power in her body. Then everything was a blur as Ales ran. The sound of the wind was deafening.

"What happened?" Ales asked in a yell.

"Lia is hurt badly. I had to leave her because I couldn't lift her and she couldn't walk herself. Left here," Ilsa shouted back, and Ales darted to left so quickly that she almost lost her grip. "Right here, and go three streets. Then follow the road until you hit the square. She is in an alleyway near the building, on the bloomward side of the square."

Then, Ales was running with such speed that her boots shattered the cobblestones. Suddenly, they were standing over Lia's prone form. She had rolled onto her side, and blood was leaking slowly from her mouth. Her fur was soaked in her own blood. Ilsa jumped down off Ales' back and checked Lia quickly.

"It's better than it was. The bleeding was so bad when I left. She woke up for a minute when I shoved my Spark down her throat the second time." Ales stared incredulously at Ilsa for a long moment and then she shook her head. Ales bent over Lia, and her Vision blazed in her eyes.

"Gods, what have you done to yourself, Lia?" Ales mumbled.

{Was trying to save him.} The mental reply was weak, but it was there.

Ales quieted her mind, and then was inundated with a short flood of memories of what had happened. Ales pet Lia's head and watched the activity in her body. She was very close to death. The bondstructs had been instructed to try to get inside of her body where it was easier to attack vital organs.

"Will she be alright?" Ilsa asked. She was kneeling heedlessly in the pool of blood.

"She will recover, but she wouldn't have if you hadn't been so quick thinking, Ilsa."

Ales could see Lia's Cellstructs even now knitting up the wounds to her internal organs. They had concentrated on protecting her heart and lungs to keep her blood pumping and body warm. It had not been without cost. Her stomach had been utterly destroyed, allowing acid and bile to pour into her body cavity. Then they had gone to her liver, which had spread even more toxins throughout her system.

"It was the only thing I could think of to stop them, but I had no idea if it would hurt Lia's Cellstructs," Ilsa said.

Ales nodded. "It was very brave of you to shove your arm down her throat like that. They could have attacked you, too. She could have bitten your arm off when the discharge went through her. But if you hadn't gotten the Spark inside of her like that, it might not have shut down the bondstructs."

"I didn't think. I just knew that her body would block the discharge some." Ilsa rubbed her arms self-consciously. "I didn't even think about her jaw clamping down. I just knew I had to help."

Ales took Ilsa's right hand and guided it to the soft fur on top of Lia's head. "You saved your sister's life, Ilsa."

Ales smiled briefly, but then anger spread across her face in a wave that flattened her features into an icy plane. It was a cold, dark rage that made Ilsa lean slightly away from her. She could feel the black hatred coming off Ales like the heat from a fire. She had seen her father angry enough to do violence a time or two when people did stupid things with lancers. That anger was like a glass of water compared to the ocean when stood next to what she felt coming off Ales. It was the kind of wrath that would raze cities to the ground, leaving not one stone standing atop another.

"Ales?" Ilsa asked, and her frightened voice seemed to give Ales what she needed to tuck away that black place inside her, where all private things were hidden. The anger faded from her face and she sighed.

"It's alright, Ilsa. You never have anything to fear from me. But when I find the thing responsible for all of this, it would probably be best to be somewhere else."

Ilsa laughed.

"Did it work?" Lia whispered.

"It worked," Ilsa said. "He is in better shape than you are."

Ales turned her head to peer at the katali they had been fighting. It was breathing, and given time, it would heal up just fine, but it was frightened and hurting. It didn't seem to have the same sort of intelligent reaction to its injuries that the banic had. That enforced the idea that the banic was meant to be one of the Tier.

"How long before you can move?" Ilsa asked.

"Days." Lia groaned unhappily.

"She is right. The damage was widespread, and a lot of her Cellstructs spent themselves destroying the bondstructs that got into her body. You spent two rotations working with Warran to make your Sparks fit better and easier to use in a fight. Then you go out without them?" Ales scolded Lia.

"I didn't think I would need them here," Lia whispered.

Ales sighed. She wanted to be angry with her sister for being so careless. She was just happy she had survived.

"Rihanna is not treating you very well, sister," Ales said. Lia made a soft chuffing sound, though the laugh cost her something. "Ilsa, I need you to make another run back to the shop. Hitch up the mavae and bring them back with the cart. We need to get Lia back so she can recover in safety. Then we are all going to bend our collective abilities with Finding to the task of understanding what is happening here so that we can stop it. This has gone quite far enough."

Ilsa stood up. She unslung Ales' pack and handed it to her. She started to walk away when Ales caught her arm.

"Ilsa, if anyone or anything gets between you and your task, you use whatever means necessary to remove the obstacle. Do you understand?" Ales asked.

Ilsa nodded. She checked the lancer in the holster at the small of her back. Ales let her go, and she ran down the street as fast as she could. It was not as fast as Ales would have liked, and she cursed herself for not being there when King Roa had destroyed Verdant. If they had been able to give all of the new Tier Cellstructs, none of this would be so difficult.

"It's getting ready for something much bigger than we thought," Lia said.

{Don't speak. Give your body time to repair itself.} Ales used their mental link.

{Insight. Finding gave me insight into what is happening here. That empty building where you followed the hiluk with all those odd chemical smells. Then the attack tonight. All those animals infected with Cellstructs not their own. It is using Rihanna as a test bed for trying to give normal people our abilities with structures but leave it in control of them. That's what the Black Sol alloy is for. Intruder is using it to tap into their nervous systems,} Lia said, but even her mind voice was slurring.

She made just enough sense to get Ales' own Finder abilities going in the right direction. She closed her eyes and her mind voice trailed off into incoherent mumbles.

{Sleep, sister, and I will watch over you until you wake. Thank the gods you don't have to feel this,} Ales said.

31

Warran slipped the braided loop of cord over the end of the curved metal stave. The bow was a weapon that hadn't been used for hundreds of cycles, and when Ales had asked him to construct her one, he couldn't imagine why she wouldn't just have him build her a longbarrel. She had explained to him that the bow gave her several advantages that no lancer could match. She could make her own ammunition out of materials she could find almost anywhere without specialized tools. There were a litany of other reasons she had given him as well, but he had just ignored most of them. There was, after all, no point in arguing with her.

He had just finished stringing the weapon when he heard footsteps from the hallway outside of the workshop. Ilsa entered the workshop, still covered in bright azure gore. Warran set the bow down carefully on its stand and turned to see who had come in. Warran drew in a sharp breath when he saw her.

"What in the howling abyss happened? Are you hurt?" His concern was apparent.

"No, it's Lia's blood," Ilsa said. Warran did not look comforted at all. He just made a face and held out his hands, demanding an explanation.

"She'll be fine, but we have to get her back here so she can recover. I don't have time to explain it all now."

Warran nodded and strapped on his lancer belt. "Explanations later. What do you need from me?"

"We need the cart and mavae hitched up, and likely, you'll need to carry me out to the cart, since I'm about to pass out from exhaustion." Ilsa sat down hard on one of the numerous stools dotted around the workshop.

"Oh gods, what happened to you?"

"Get working. I'll talk while you help me get this done." Ilsa took a few deep breaths and then pushed off the stool to get back to her feet.

"I used my Sparks to save Lia from the Intruder's bondstructs that had gotten into her body through her mouth.

I had to push my arm all the way down her throat. Twice." Ilsa shivered.

She followed Warran out towards the stables into a walled courtyard. She stumbled at the exit to the courtyard, and Warran was there instantly. He bent down and scooped her off her feet. He carried her to the small cart that they had held onto in case they needed to move anything large, like a massive katali. He put her up in the seat and then went to work, hitching up two of their mavae. He was quick to complete the task, but Ilsa was already asleep by the time he finished. He got up into the seat and reluctantly shook her shoulder. She started awake with a shout of dismay. Warran cringed at her reaction. She turned her wild, tearfilled eyes to him.

"Oh, I'm sorry, Warran." She wiped her eyes and tried to smooth her features.

"You will talk to Ales about how you're feeling when this is done tonight?" Warran asked. She looked a little horrified. She swallowed and then nodded. "No one should have nightmares that fast, Ilsa."

"I thought I was ready, but I can still feel it, and it hurts. How could I do that to anything alive?" Ilsa asked quietly.

"You already know the answer to that question."

Warran flicked the reins. The mavae responded and pulled the cart through the gate that Warran had opened while Ilsa slept. He stopped them just outside and got off the cart to close the gate. Ilsa looked down at the cobblestones, and then back at Warran.

"Warran, why is the cart floating?" Ilsa asked.

Warran grinned wildly. "Because I took off the wheels and built gravitonic generators onto the bottom. Much smoother ride, and it can be pulled over any terrain without worrying about breaking a wheel or axle."

Ilsa stared at him incredulously. "I'll ask later. Head toward the corner of the Center between the stoneward and sunward gate."

It did not take her long to guide him to where she had left Ales and Lia. When they arrived, Ales was standing protectively over Lia's prone body. Her Windblade was out, and there were glowing lines of molten rock in the cobblestones. Burning cuts were driven through the stone walls of the buildings around them. Ilsa and Warran stared openly at the half-destroyed alleyway. Ales was quivering with barely contained rage. She had a few tiny cuts that were already closing. Ilsa didn't think that anything had gotten past her. She thought that it was more likely she had been struck by the exploding stone. Of whatever had attacked her, there was no sign at all.

Warran knew that with sufficient strength, the Windblade could generate lines of superheated air more than hot enough to cut through nearly anything. Lia had explained that Ales was the only known Tier that could swing the blade with enough speed to do it. She had also explained that Ales rarely did it because it was so dangerous.

"What happened?" Warran asked. He drew his lancers, and his eyes blazed alive with his Vision. He peered around, but found no threats. The male katali had been pulled into the alleyway, and was unconscious next to Lia.

"It sent more animals to attack us, and I have had quite enough," Ales snarled. She slid her Windblade back into her coat. "If you see anything moving in the shadows, put a bolt into it."

Ales moved to where Lia was lying and squatted down. She slid her arms beneath Lia and lifted her blood soaked body from the ground. She carefully carried Lia to the cart and laid her down in the back. That completed, she turned back to the alleyway for the other katali, and as she was walking back in, the loud bark of a large hiluk pierced the air. She looked up, but before she could do anything about it, Warran drew one of his lancers and fired in a motion so smooth that even Ales found it impressive. Clearly, he had taken to the Circle of Distance nearly as well as anyone she had ever seen. Ales eyed the glowing blue pods holding up the cart.

"Where did you get the Sol alloy to make these?" Ales asked suspiciously.

"Kiltik helped me with it. The coils don't take much of the metal, as long as you aren't trying to lift anything too heavy with them. Kiltik explained that you used to have massive vehicles with much heavier coils than these." Warran turned the mavae around.

"Yes, with light propulsion units. Very useful when there were large conflicts that required our assistance for mass quantities of injured people. We could keep entire medical facilities in them. Bring a hundred of them to the scene of a battle and everyone would survive. No use in longing for the past. We will make it come again. You have done an excellent job."

Ales looked back over her shoulder. Ilsa was sleeping with half of her body on top of Lia's side, which rose and fell much more smoothly than before. She got a worried expression on her face after a long moment of inspecting the girl with her Vision.

"What is it?" Warran asked.

"Just, something that I recognize. I think our Ilsa may take to the Wild eventually, which is not a shame, but she won't have much use for her Fixer talents if she has paws or hooves." Warran seemed concerned, but Ales just shook her head.

"It's nothing, Warran. It's just a good possibility. I recognize the patterns of emotional energy in her mind. It's the same sort that Lia had after her episode with Queen Yrsin. She coped with the emotional pain for a few cycles before she admitted to herself that she was losing her sanity to the question of whether or not what she had done was necessary. It was, mind you. Even the Mother herself confided in me that she couldn't have made any other decision." Ilsa would be their sister no matter what, and that was something far more precious than what shape she wore.

"I still don't understand how that helps."

"You don't need to understand it, Warran. Just know that it keeps them with us instead of letting them go mad."

"What are we doing here, Ales? We aren't getting any closer to finding the Core."

"I know. I suspect Lia and I were drawn here because we need a home. We can't just keep running about undefended, Warran. We need a place that we can fortify, defend, and feel at home; a place that we can safely train new Tier. I have no proof of it, but this place is uniquely connected to both the Mother and the Father in ways that only Ahal had ever been."

Warran nodded when she finished. "I think maybe you are right, but don't you think that the Ryhim will be upset if we attempt to take over their country?"

Ales shrugged indifferently. "I don't want to rule anything, Warran. I'm only hoping that if we bring their home back into balance and offer them some of the knowledge of the Tier, they will take us in. Eventually in the cycles to come, the Ryhim will likely be assimilated into the Tier. But I would never permit anyone to be forced out. Obviously, I haven't worked everything out, but we will do it when the time comes."

"So where do we go from here, then?"

"I think Lia got it right. I think that perhaps the Intruder has discovered something about the Nexus that allows it to grow mass quantities of the Black Sarsan plant. This means it has deciphered the helixical coding that prevented the plant from growing en masse. It has started to use this as a place to test out new versions of Cellstructs because it is close to its source of Black Sol alloy, which is necessary to create such things." Ales clutched the reins so tightly that he feared that they would snap from the pressure.

"So how is it hiding all this from us?" Warran asked.

"That's something I can only hope that Lia can tell us when she awakens. Now that we have the idea, though, I will attempt to use Finding while she recovers to gain some more insight. But while I have the Circle, I have never understood it like Lia does. Intuition like that just isn't my area of expertise. I don't have the collected thought process that Lia does. She is so calm. Finding is my weakest power. I worked diligently for almost thirty cycles to master it. I never could get there, but I use it the best I can. I can, if necessary, put myself into the proper state of mind to use it properly, but it is usually much easier to ask Lia to handle it."

Warran looked back at Lia. "Perhaps it is time to do that?"

Ales grinned and nodded. "Perhaps it is, but it takes me several days to calm my thoughts like that, especially considering how furious I am right now. By that time, Lia will be healthy enough to do it. Frankly, I think that finding Cole is much more important. I want to have all of us back together before this goes any further. Finding Cole is far more important than determining how we are to stop what is happening here."

Warran stopped the mavae outside of the stable yard gate. He climbed down from the cart and placed his thumb against the metal plate in the gate. To most people, it would seem as if the metal gate didn't have any sort of lock or handle. The metal plate was designed to read their helixes so that they could open the gate while anyone unauthorized would be kept out. Once they were inside and the mavae had been made comfortable, Ales woke Ilsa and helped her get to bed. When she came back, Lia was awake again.

"Go back to sleep. You are safe," Ales said.

"You think that the Intruder has Cole, don't you?" Lia asked.

"Yes, almost without a doubt, the creature has him. He would have gotten here by now if that was not the case."

"You will find him?"

Ales nodded. "I will find him, alive or dead."

"He is alive. Cole will always survive, but he doesn't have the protections yet. You have to find him."

"If you insist on talking, please use our link. You are still healing," Ales said with deep concern.

{Mother Hen,} Lia accused. Her mind voice seemed much stronger than it had been when Ales had found her.

{Some of us have to watch out for the rest of you self destructive children.} Ales chuckled. Lia gave her the scary feline grin, and Ales frowned unhappily. Lia still had bright blue blood on her teeth.

{My grin never annoyed you before,} Lia said, her mind voice a little upset.

{It isn't that. You still have blood on your teeth. Would you like some lisan tea?}

{Yes, please.}

{Go back to sleep. I will wake you after I have things ready.}

Lia closed her eyes and Ales sighed. She went inside, and it seemed that somehow, Warran had known what she would want because there was already a kettle on the stove. The gas burners had clearly been going since he had come inside, because steam was already coming from the kettle's spout. Warran sat at the small table fiddling with something that Ales couldn't see past his body.

"How did you know?" Ales asked.

"You have brewed a tea for Lia every time she was uncomfortable for any reason the entire cycle we travelled together. It wasn't much of a guess."

Warran got up and turned, holding something in his hands. It was an oddly curved-collection of three pieces of metal with a braided cord strung between the inside of them. Warran held it up, and the two bars of metal unfolded. They clicked loudly when they opened, stretching the cord between them. Locks slid into place, further reinforcing the position of the unfolded staves. Fully assembled, it was clear to Ales that it was a bow. He held up a quiver of twenty or so arrows with metal shafts.

"I finished this for you. I made it as light as I could manage. The string is a braid of Sol alloy impregnated with a core of self-replicating bondstructs. I doubt you could cut it even with a sword, but it will repair any damage to the cord or the bow itself. The grip has a small gravitation unit built into it. The arrow rest is actually a cushion of gravitational force that will adjust based on the weight of the arrow. Even minor exposure to sunlight will recharge the unit in a few minutes. This way, when you release a shaft, no matter how fast it is moving, the fletchings will not be torn away. I also doubt anyone but you could draw this monster at its highest tension. You should be able to link with the bondstructs in it and change the tension at will. It starts out at a thirty sphere pull, but can go all the way up to four hundred. At that weight, though, you would need bondsteel or Sol alloy shafts to stand up to the force of being fired."

"I realize that simple wood shafts would not stand up to anything past eighty or so sphere of draw weight," Ales said as she examined the weapon. "This is masterful craftsmanship."

"Thank you. What could you possibly need that for? That would put an arrow through a stone wall. I doubt anything but Sol alloy plate would stop a shaft fired from this thing at its highest draw weight."

"To make an impression." Ales grinned at him. "A lancer can have some of the same effect, especially one of your long barrels. However, there are several things I can do with an arrow that you cannot do with the tiny bolts in a lancer."

Ales lifted the bow and drew the string back to her cheek. He could tell from how far the limbs bent that she had pushed it to the highest draw setting. She lowered the draw slowly.

"I can draw it at the third level of my constraints now," Ales commented.

The kettle whistled, and Ales pulled it off the burner. She turned off the burner and began to fix the tea for Lia. She opened her mental link to Icci, two floors above her.

{Hello, Ales. This One is pleased that you have returned. This One has splendid news.} Icci's mind voice was a higher, softer echo of Verdant.

{It's good to be back. Can you please run a diagnostic on Lia's Cellstructs and tell me what would be best to accelerate the replenishment of her stores?} Ales asked.

{This One would be delighted to perform this task. This One is happy to report that Ilsa's Cellstructs are fully prepared for introduction into her system,} Icci said with pride in her mind voice.

Ales let out a sigh of relief. *{How long will full integration take?}*

{This One is content to report that with the study of your own personal Structures, This One has been able to reduce the the integration time to a single span. This One notes that this is

dependent on Ilsa being able to eat a sufficient diet to support the replication of her new Structures.}

"So what exactly did Lia say?" Warran asked as Ales fixed the tea.

"Exactly what I told you. She was too damaged to say much more than that. She barely had any internal organs left," Ales said.

Warran changed topics. "Can we give the kids Cellstructs next?"

Ales frowned at the sudden change of topics, then shook her head. "Sadly, we cannot. People without the Vision can only have Cellstructs if they are born of a woman who already has them. Otherwise, you must have the Vision to make minor adjustments to your Cellstructs periodically or your body will reject them. You will be up next, then Cole, when we find him."

Warran frowned. "I don't want to lose my little girl, Ales," he said quietly as he went back to the table.

"I know what you are thinking. If it is possible for them to do this to Lia, they can get to your little girl. But they won't. I haven't told you this, but I am fully aware of the danger that our little ones are in. Our world is not a kind place right now. We came here because we need a home, but more importantly, some of our new members will have children. They, more than us, will need the protection that a place like this can provide. I am drawing on the knowledge of what I know of the protections children had when Ahal was alive. I will make our children safe, Warran, and you will help me do it. Everyone will."

Ales poured the steaming tea into a bowl. She went out the door to the courtyard, and was back a moment later. She sat down at the table.

"Lia will be well enough to come inside soon, but she will not be doing much but sleeping for a few days to repair that damage. So for now, I will share my findings with you, and we together will begin to decipher what we must do to make this place safe," Ales said.

Warran nodded, and Ales began. She laid out what she knew. She started with the fact that the animals had been infected with Cellstructs that were made with a basis of Black Sol alloy.

"I've been meaning to ask. Why are there different types of Structures?" Warran asked.

"The specialization allows them to work more efficiently. Bondstructs, in a pinch, can do some of the things that Cellstructs can do, but because they are bondsteel-based, they can't live inside of our bodies. Our systems are sensitive to things that do not belong inside of them. Cellstructs are carbon-based, and the carbon is coated in a helixical casing that matches our own structure. To our bodies, the Cellstructs are a natural part of our own systems. Your helixes are fairly static, but over time, the chemical processes of our bodies change. We can talk about that later, though. This is more important.

Next is the fact that they are using the Probability Matrix to collect the elements necessary to forge massive quantities of Black Sol alloy. This tells me that whoever is using it is working for the Intruder, whether or not they know it. Somehow, I suspect if they knew what the Intruder was trying to do, they would not be so sanguine about helping it. So our next course of action must be to find the place where they are making the Black Sol alloy. I suspect we have spooked them by following that hiluk back to where they had been, but I can't imagine they would chance moving their operation too far away from their source. Especially since I have destroyed their supply of Black Sol."

"So our task is to find where they are resupplying," Warran said.

Ales nodded. "It is likely that when we do, we will also find the facility where they are infecting these animals with Cellstructs. This must be stopped, Warran. We cannot allow the Intruder to perfect this technique, or we may never be able to defeat it."

"Is that even possible?"

"It is. There is a reason that we destroyed all knowledge of Black Sol alloy. The only reason we didn't make it entirely impossible to make the metal is that Black Sarsan is an important key ingredient in a number of medicines. Unfortunately, they cannot be made any other way. Even what we did doomed a lot of people to mental instability and death over the intervals, I am sure."

"What do you mean?"

"After we decided that Black Sol alloy was too dangerous to allow into the world, we engineered an infection that rewrote the helixes of all of the Black Sarasan plants in the world. It made it so that the plant would only grow under very specific circumstances, and every subsequent plant spawned from the seeds of a previous plant would require different circumstances. To ensure it didn't die out completely, we also made it so the plant would grow much larger seed pods, and that the seeds would be extremely enticing to animals that could spread them," Ales explained.

Lia entered slowly through the door, carrying the large wooden bowl in her mouth. One side of her body was a filthy, bloody mess of fur that stuck out from her body like a crazed pin cushion. Her ears were laid back unhappily, and she looked on the verge of collapse. She put the wooden bowl down and looked up at Ales.

"More, please, and can you open the door to the bath house for me so that I can soak this mess out of my fur? I fear if I use my standard methods of cleaning myself, I may be sick, which would not be good right now." Lia looked as if she were walking very carefully, like everything hurt at once. The truth was that she didn't feel the pain, but her Cellstructs were continually giving her updates on how to move so that she did not disrupt the healing process.

"It's a good thing they have bathing pools here, Spook, or you would be stuck in the cold river. Head to the bath house. I will bring the tea there," Ales said. Lia made her slow way down the hallway towards the other end of the house.

"She doesn't look at all good," Warran said after she was far enough down the hall that she wouldn't pick out what he was saying.

Ales' hands clenched into fists as she watched her sister disappear down the hallway. "No she does not. She is not," Ales said angrily. She picked up the wooden bowl and filled it with more of the tea. "Think about what you would do to find the place where all of this could be hidden while I help her clean up."

Ales stormed down the hallway, trying to calm herself. Lia was sitting disconsolately outside of the door to the bath house, staring at the doorknob with her Vision open.

"Stop that," Ales scolded her.

{I can't help it,} Lia said with a little feline smile.

Ales sighed and turned the doorknob. The door was just barely wide enough to permit Lia inside, and she walked through it very slowly, as if she was worried about bumping into the door frame.

{Are you healing that slowly?} Ales' mind voice was worried.

{No, not really. Most of my organs have knitted up at this point. My liver took it the worst, and my Cellstructs are doing double duty filtering my blood and piecing it back together almost cell by cell. But a lot of the connective tissue that holds everything in place was torn, so I am trying to move as carefully as possible so that I don't re-tear anything,} Lia said.

"Ah, I see."

Lia stopped and stared at the long step down to the bottom of the bathing pool.

"Would you like some help?" Ales asked, setting the bowl of lisan tea next to the pool.

{I am consulting my Cellstructs right now.} Lia turned in a circle and backed up towards the pool. She stopped at the edge, considering for a moment.

{Let me help you,} Ales said. She stripped out of her jacket. A moment later, her dark blue shirt and black pants joined it on the floor. She laid them aside and got into the pool. She pushed against Lia's rear end to allow to her to ease back into the pool without actually holding any of her own weight. Lia

laid down in the pool and left her chin on the edge. Ales started to gently scrub the blood and offal out of her fur. It took a long time for the filtration system to return the water to clear from the deep blue it became.

{I am glad I don't have to feel how much this hurts, but I hate feeling so powerless. You would never have gotten into a situation like that.} Lia's mind voice sounded very depressed.

"Don't idolize me like that, Lia. Please don't. I have made my fair share of stupid moves, and my powers couldn't save me from being an idiot, either. You did what you thought was right. You saved that katali, and your little mistake has given Ilsa confidence that she would not have gotten any other way. She didn't freeze. She was right there when you needed her. Sometimes, Lia, you need to take risks. Sometimes those risks are not going to work out in your favor," Ales consoled, carefully running her fingers through Lia's fur to comfort her. Lia began to purr.

"What was Finding telling you at the end there?" Ales asked.

{A lot. We know that they are making Black Sol alloy here. That requires Black Sarsan to be used in the making and quenching of the metal to be viable. Together with the massive crates of it you threw to the bottom of the lake, they would have to be growing a lot of Black Sarsan, which means that somehow, the Intruder has deciphered the helixical code we wrote into the plant so that it can't grow it en masse. Considering this is the only place in the world that has the changing conditions necessary to grow large quantities, and the fact that the Probability Matrix has been placed here to facilitate keeping it all a secret, it makes sense that this is where the Intruder would also choose to do its research.} Lia's mind voice became pensive. *{The only thing Finding didn't tell me was where it was all happening. None of the places we have been seem connected in any way.}*

"If that is true, though…" Ales' eyes went wide. She stood up, still naked, and didn't bother grabbing a towel. She jumped out of the bathing pool and snatched her Windblade, sending a prayer to the gods that she had not realized this too late.

{Where are you going, sister?} Lia's mind voice was alarmed.

{I don't have time to explain. We are safe enough here, but Finding just pointed out that if the Intruder has been here that much longer than we originally thought, then it likely has eyes literally everywhere. Every tiny animal in the city could belong to it.}

Lia still looked confused.

{Mina. The girl is completely undefended!} Ales was almost to the door when Lia's words caught her.

{The few moments it takes you to dress will not mean you are too late. If we have figured this out too late, then it is already too late even now.}

Ales grunted angrily, but she knew Lia was right. She took a towel from the shelf and hurried to dress herself.

~ END OF PART 3 ~

Juran had just clamped a blade in the vice on the workbench when Ales came into the forge room. "How far along did Ilsa get with your combat training?"

Juran shrank back from her a little. Ales scared him. He wasn't sure why the others couldn't feel how close she was to violence all the time.

"I understand that I scare you, Juran, but I do not have time to address that right now. How far along are you?" Ales asked.

"Not very far. I'm fair with a sword, but I'm a terrible shot with a lancer, and my hand to hand combat..." He hesitated for a moment. "She thrashes me ten out of ten matches."

Ales chuckled. "Nothing to be ashamed of there, Juran. She is gifted. I'll let you watch her spar with me soon. It'll make you feel better." Ales winked at him. "Alright, finish up and get your sword. I don't think anyone will be stupid enough to attack us here, and if they do, there are defenses in place. But Lia is recovering from her injuries right now. Ilsa is exhausted, and Warran is going out to take the Lightleaf trees for a quick jaunt to pick up some things that we are going to need soon. I want you prepared in case anyone tries to get in here. If they do, wake Ilsa first. Lia will help if she absolutely must, but it would be better if she didn't have to."

Juran took off his heavy hide apron and hung it on a peg next to the forge. He belted on a beautiful looking sword. It had a swept basket knuckle guard and a slightly curving blade. It was his first perfectly made bondsteel piece ever. He wanted to make something out of Sol alloy, but he had yet to be able to get the alloy to join properly.

"I'll do my best," Juran said.

"Don't get distracted," Ales warned.

Juran nodded and followed her out of the forge. Ales took something small and blue out of a pocket. She went down the hallway from the forge and up a set of stairs, and then opened a door into Ilsa's room. She hadn't wanted to delay this long, but while she was getting dressed, Lia pointed out that it would be best to fortify their defenses here before she left. She shook Ilsa gently. Ilsa opened her eyes and groaned.

"I'm sorry to wake you, little sister, but it will be best if we do this now."

Ales held up the tiny blue sphere. Ilsa immediately opened her Vision and wished that she hadn't. The tiny blue sphere glowed like a tiny star. She closed her Vision immediately.

"What is that?" Ilsa asked.

"This is your cellstruct infusion. Once you take this and make sure you get plenty of food for the next few days, you will have all of the protections that Lia and I enjoy," Ales explained.

Ilsa took the small blue sphere from her and examined it.

"It's amazing that this tiny thing can do all of that," Ilsa said with wonder. She put the tiny sphere on her tongue and swallowed it.

"Go back to sleep. Don't be alarmed when they start speaking with you when you wake up. They don't speak in language, but you'll have a whole new stream of information that they'll be giving to you. Sleep, now. It will help them spread faster. Your apprentice will watch over you," Ales said. Ilsa nodded and put her head back down on her pillow. Ales closed the door behind her.

"I don't know what I am supposed to be doing here," Juran said when they got down to the kitchen. He unhooked his sword from his belt and leaned it against his chair. Ales could see that he was still scared of her and frowned.

"Juran, you are supposed to do the best that you can. None of us are going to ask more than that of you."

He finally raised his eyes to meet hers.

"Since we all have other tasks, and Kiltik has gone to the Darkhold Monastery to confer with Giri, you must be our last line of defense. Just follow your instincts and protect everyone here as best you can."

Ales took something out of her pocket and handed it to him. It was a broken piece of metal that he recognized from his last attempt at forging a Sol blade.

"To occupy you, use Breaking to peel away the outer layer of sorion and examine the surface of the steel. You should be able to tell why the two metals are not melding nicely," Ales said, handing over the piece of metal.

Juran took it and looked back up to her. "You know about metal shaping?" Juran's skepticism was clear in his voice.

"I'm a Fixer, Juran. Of course I know how to shape and work with metal." Ales chuckled. "If you haven't figured it out by the time I get back, I will give you a hint."

Ales opened the door and left. Jame had not spoken a word the entire time. He looked so grim and Juran had no idea why. He got to work using Breaking to peal back the layer of sorion metal to try and figure out what he was doing wrong.

Jame followed Ales into the night. He could tell that Juran was scared of Ales right up until the end. Jame was scared of her, too. She wasn't much like Cole at all. Cole had been confident, and he could be scary when he needed to be, but just standing near Ales, some primal part of his brain told him that she was dangerous in ways he could not even begin to understand.

"I assume that you know how to ride?" Ales asked.

"I do." Jame went to the stables and pulled the door open to reveal a sleek black mavae with white spots on lower parts of her legs.

"Good. You know how to get to the Clan Clai mansion?"

"Yes. Why? Aren't we going together?"

"Yes and no. I may just be overreacting here, but I don't know what I am running into, and you are not ready for this yet." She held up a hand to forestall his protest. "I am not questioning your ability against normal foes, but I may not be going up against normal foes. So to be clear, I want you there because you are clearly a gifted fighter and I can use someone to watch my back. But if I tell you to run and get help, you will run. Do you understand me?"

"Alright. I will do exactly as you say, nothing more, nothing less."

"Good. I am going to go ahead. Do not enter until I come out to fetch you. Just watch the building. Circle it and make sure no one leaves. If you see someone with a well-dressed girl of about five cycles, stop them, Jame, and make a lot of noise doing it."

He nodded, and she darted away at a speed that made it seem as if she had literally vanished. Jame goggled and opened his Vision to look around, but she was long gone.

"What have I gotten myself into?" he wondered aloud.

He gently spurred Stars out of the gate and then turned the mavae so that he could push the gate closed. It latched, and a hum of elementary energy current filled the air. He hadn't noticed the sound before. He reached out to touch the gate, but something warned him that he shouldn't.

He examined the gate closely, and through his Vision, he could see some sort of fuzzy moving snow on its surface. It moved like a swarm of angry blurwings. He shook his head and turned away from the door. That was why they said that if he wanted to get back inside, he should put his thumb against the plate in the middle of the door. It was the only spot on the door that didn't have the snow.

Jame spurred Stars down the alleyway and into the street. The twisting labyrinth of streets that made up Rihanna had always been a little confusing to him. They had taught him about the street markers and the layout of the center, but it had never been like finding his way through the Wilds. That seemed natural. The center was just odd to him. But as he looked around with his Vision open, the center seemed to glow with inner light, so many colors that he had never seen before.

There were shades of the entire rainbow here. Bands of light ran down the middle of the road, and suddenly he understood that each band of light could take him to a different place in the city. Then he saw words running along the lines of light, and he began to grasp how they worked. His Vision seemed to be speaking to him inside of his mind, and suddenly he knew exactly what he was seeing. Kinas had been a Lighteye like him.

Ales had explained that Lighteyes could lay down permanent messages in light just by the force of their magical tethers to it. Any Tier who had the circle of light could see the messages, but only a Lighteye could actually make them. He had asked Ales what her talent was, and after a long moment of consideration, she had told him that she was a Destroyer. She had said that she was the only one. After that, she would say no more on the subject. He had spoken to Lia, but she had just frowned and shook her head when he told her what Ales had said. She had explained that not every Tier would gain a talent for a Circle like he had, but almost every Arcangineer had one.

Ales was what they called a Breaker. She understood how to break things, but also could use Breaking as a way to mend things more quickly than others. Lia had told him that she would explain it the best way she could, but only those with a talent for a Circle could truly explain it. She said that strangely, every new Tier they had found so far had a Talent. Lia's talent was for Finding, so she was known as Finder. She was good with the Circle of Light, but she was not a Lighteye. What she could do was see connections between seemingly unrelated things and events that no one else could possibly see. When he had asked if Tier could have more than one Talent, she had told him that it was extremely rare. Lia herself had two Talents, but Ales had Four.

He focused on the bands of light running through the middle of the streets. Though he could see more bands of light around some of the buildings, the streets were the important ones to him right now. At least, until he saw a band of light that ran off to one of the buildings. He realized that he could perfectly tell that one band from the thousands of other tiny lines floating just above the street. He understood then that those with the talent to fully control a Circle could perform true magic, bending reality to their will in some way. It was the only explanation for the fact that the bands of light behaved the way they did and that they remained here for thousands of cycles after the person who had laid them down had died.

He would have to ask Lia about it when he got back. He didn't dare to ask Ales. That feeling puzzled him. He knew without a doubt that she would not hurt him, but some primal part of his brain told him that she could literally undo everything around her with little more than a thought and a twitch. It was stupid, because he didn't think anyone short of the Gods had that power.

"Oh but she does, young man," a deep, cultured voice said from beside him.

Jame nearly fell out of the saddle in surprise. Floating in the air next to him was a shining figure that appeared to be an odd statue of a man, made of slabs of gemstone. The glorious statue floated more than a mark off the ground, and Jame's eyes went so wide that the statue threw its head back and laughed. The tinkling sound of his gemstone hair filled the air as he finished.

"You do not have to be so awed, Child. This will not be the last time we speak." Zezzhz chuckled.

"I am short of words just now, Father," Jame said.

"Fair enough, Child, then I will talk. I cannot offer you any true assistance, but I can offer you some advice concerning Ales. You truly have nothing to fear from her as long as you stay on your path to becoming one of the Tier, but your instinctual wariness concerning her is not wrong. Ales has never shown the extent of her abilities. She fears her own power, so she is always holding back."

"You're not making me feel better, Father. I don't want to be afraid of her."

The Father rolled his eyes.

"I am not here to make you feel better, Jame. I am attempting to make you understand. Ales is a protector above all things. She fears her own power because she fears that she will one day be careless, and she will destroy something that she meant to protect. I sincerely doubt that will ever happen to her, but she fears it. This is why you should not fear her, Jame, because she needs someone not to, and unlike normal people who will always fear her power, you know with certainty that you have nothing to fear. Make _yourself_ feel better, Jame."

Jame nodded, and then thought of a question.

"Father, do the other Tier know that if they have a talent in a Circle it allows them to do real magic?"

The Father frowned and looked thoughtful for a long moment.

"Yes. They know, but they also know that using true magic like that always has a cost. I assume you are referring to what Kinas did here?" The Father gestured to the bands of light running down the road. They branched off onto other streets, able to lead the Tier wherever they wanted to go in the Center. Jame nodded.

"Kinas did this at the end of his life. He knew he was dying and wanted to leave something behind to help future Tier. This was a great magic, and it cost Kinas his life. Be mindful of how you use your powers, Jame. Do not squander them by overstepping your limits," the Father said, and then he was gone.

Stars had wandered to a stop without Jame directing her, and he gently spurred her into motion again. He thought about what the Father had said about Ales. He realized that his instincts were right about Ales, but that shouldn't really matter. He was more than his base instincts. He looked back to the colored bands of light in the road. He could pick them out now, and he could tell what they meant. He focused on the one that would lead him to the Clan Clai ancestral home, and followed it to its end. What he found when he got there he would never forget for the rest of his days.

Mina woke to the sounds of silence. The Clan Clai home had never been this quiet in as long as she could remember. Even in the darkest hours of the night, there was always someone doing something. She didn't move from beneath the covers of her bed, but she knew that something was dreadfully wrong. She waited a long time for some sound to make it to her ears. When nothing came, she pulled back her blankets.

The floor was cold despite the carpets covering it, and she shivered in her white shift. She went to the large wardrobe on the wall and took out one of her simple dresses, the ones she never wore. It was just a simple one-piece dress with a long skirt that hung to her shins. It was dark blue, and had a simple ribbon of green silk around her waist, which she tied in the back with nimble fingers. She wasn't used to dressing herself, so she didn't know if she got the bow right, but that really didn't matter to her then. She took a pair of warm, round-toed shoes with fur around the tops and slipped them on. She did up the buckles, and then went to her door.

She turned the latch as slowly as she could, and the click was almost inaudible. Just outside the door was one of the housekeepers. She was an elderly woman with tan, thin skin like old partchment. She had on her normal long cleaning dress, but she was lying in the hallway as if she had tripped and fallen. Her pale hair was a golden wheat color, and it was in a long braid. Her pale green eyes had something wrong with them. Mina went to the woman and shook her a little.

"Miss Nuin?" Mina said quietly.

She shook the woman again, but she didn't respond. Mina realized that the woman was cold, just like Ahldal had been. She was dead. Tears welled up in Mina's eyes. She staggered back from the corpse. She stumbled down the hallway towards her brother's room. When she found his door still closed, she had hope that he was fine. She turned his door knob as silently as she could. As soon as the door swung open, she saw his eyes. His head was turned on his pillow, and he was looking right at the door. His eyes were clouded just like Miss Nuin's. She swallowed back a scream, but she could not stop a sob from escaping.

She went to the next room down, which was where their little sister slept. She had just been moved here a few spans earlier. She was old enough for her own bed, but a caretaker, Minder Linn, slept in her room. Mina almost tripped over Minder Linn's body. She had died in front of Lila's bed, and Lila, too, was cold. Her tiny chest did not rise or fall.

Mina lost track of time. She knelt to the floor and wept uncontrollably. She wept as only a child could. Her nose became raw from rubbing it on her sleeve. Finally, she thought of her parents. She stumbled to her feet gasping, almost in a panic. She turned around, tears streaming down her face, and ran towards her parents' rooms. Down the silent hallway, she took a right. She ran, her shoes squeaking on the polished sorstone floor. She skidded to a halt outside of their room. The door was open. They were both sleeping in their bed just as they always did. She went to the bed and climbed up onto it, tears streaming down her face. She shook her mother, but she didn't respond at all. Then she shook her father, trying to wake him. Still no response.

"Mum, please wake up. Please," Mina sobbed.

She shook her mother's dead body. There was nothing, no response at all. She laid down in the bed between her mother and father and began to cry in earnest. There was no one to see her anymore, no more reason to feel like her mother would come in and scold her. She never saw the tall black figure coming through her parents' door until it was far too late.

The creature was roughly human-shaped, but that was where the resemblance ended. It had night black skin that shimmered as if it were made of made of polished sorstone. Its fingers narrowed to sharp claws. Its feet ended in two large toes that narrowed to sharp points that dug small furrows in the stone floor as it walked. Its head was a featureless ball with a short snout, like some breeds of hiluk that she had seen before. There were no ears or eyes at all.

Mina opened her mouth to scream and the creature darted forward. It mashed its hand over her mouth. The hand stretched impossibly, like the sheets of rubber that Ahldal used to seal jars overnight to keep the food fresh. It engulfed her head completely, and she scrabbled at it with her fingers for a moment. Then something latched onto her wrists and pulled them down and behind her back. Then the thing was all around her. It crushed her arms to her sides and her legs together. She felt herself being lifted from the bed and carried out into the hall. She started to gasp for air, and then there was a tiny opening over her nose allowing her to breath. She struggled, but it did her no good. When she did, the breathing hole over her nose disappeared. Her head swam as she tried to draw in breath. Finally, she passed into unconsciousness.

PART 4

35

Ales stepped up to the door of the Clan Clai mansion. She opened her Vision and peered through the wood of the door. She saw a man lying in the entry hall on the other side of the door. She pulled open the Circle of Light and focused on the infrared. No heat rose from the body. She switched from Light to Breaking and rapped the door on three points in rapid succession. It crumbled almost to dust, falling into the entryway. Ales pushed open her constraints to the fourth level and darted inside. She knelt next to the body, but whoever it was had been dead for hours. She did not recognize him. She heard someone coming up the walkway outside. It sounded like the hooves of a mavae.

"It is just me, Ales. I have made three circuits around the house and the surrounding streets," Jame said.

"We are too late," Ales hissed.

She furiously slammed her fist into the stone floor. It exploded away from her blow as if her fist was a bondsteel sledge. There was a massive crack in the stone floor and a chunk missing twice the size of her fist. A tiny bit of blue blood marked the center, but a moment later, the cut across her knuckles had knitted. She stood and stalked off into the house. Jame stood for a long moment, staring at the corpse in front of him. There were no signs of injuries. It was as if he had dropped dead for no reason at all.

"Can you tell why he died?" Jame called out as he jogged to catch up.

"Something injected a bubble into his bloodstream at the neck. It caused a blockage of blood in his brain and he had a massive stroke. The injection site is so small that I can't imagine what sort of instrument could be used without destroying it. It has to have been the Intruder, because only the creature or one of the Tier could use an instrument with such precision," Alex explained.

Jame realized that he was no longer afraid of Ales, and he never would be again. She was furious beyond all reason, and he knew that when she found the creature that had done this, she would stop at nothing to destroy it. But the Father had been right. Ales' fury was contained by a rigid code that made it clear who was to be protected and who deserved to be the outlet for her fury.

Jame's horror increased as they searched the manor, finding nothing alive within. Each room revealed only more silent corpses. When they began to find bodies in the hallways where they had been about the nighttime tasks that kept the manor clean and running, it was clear that no one here had survived whatever had swept through the Clan Clai ancestral home. Ales continued to search every room methodically until she came to a room decorated in pinks and yellows. Ales stood at the threshold for a moment, looking into the room. Her eyes swept the room and the glow of her Vision intensified.

"This is her room and she hasn't been gone very long. The bed is still warm. I truly wish I could make this a learning experience for you, Jame, because being a Lighteye, you can likely do this much better than I can. Eventually, you will be able to adjust the Circle of Light to allow you to see into many more spectrums than just the visible. If you combine this power with your Vision, you can actually see scent trails."

"Is that how you know this is her room?"

Ales nodded. Ales could see her scent trail. It led in and out of this room over a dozen times, but it was clear that one trail was more recent than the others. It stood out brightly as a wavering line of pink light in her Vision. She turned and followed it. The line went to several rooms before it streaked off down a hallway. They followed it to a room where Ales confirmed that the two people in the bed were Mina's parents, the Prince and Princess of Clan Clai. Ales turned in a circle a few times, searching the floor for the scent trail.

"It's gone. Whatever took her from here was able to completely mask her scent trail without a single molecule of scent left behind," Ales said confusedly. She went to the door and knelt down. She examined the ground for a long moment. "But it wasn't nearly as clever about hiding itself." Ales stood there for a few moments longer, and then she walked off down the hallway.

"This thing is made of some sort of elastic composite material that I do not recognize. It doesn't leave much behind, but there is enough to follow it here," Ales said.

She walked down the hallway and then turned left at the end. She followed it out of a door to a courtyard with a winding garden pathway. It was a well tended garden, with beautiful flowering plants lining the path and a number of twinebark trees, given their name because of their bark, which resembled twisted twine. She trailed it out of the courtyard, through another hallway, and then to a door into the yard between the house and the outer wall.

"Jame, go back and fetch your mavae. Head back and help them hold the fort until Lia is awake. When Lia wakes up, she will be well enough to trail me," Ales said.

"I need to stay with you," Jame protested.

Ales shook her head.

"I am sure you would do as well as you could, but I do not know what I am trailing here, Jame. Until I do, I don't know if you would be a help. Besides, neither you nor Stars can run fast enough to keep up with me. And I must go fast, Jame, because I don't think this thing has anything good intended for little Mina."

Jame grunted. "Alright. That's a blow to my ego, but I understand."

Ales grinned. "Besides, this is a good opportunity to test out something that Lia and I have been trying to reactivate. Further, someone needs to tell everyone about what has happened here."

"Do you think you can catch it?"

Ales looked down the street. The thing had long strides. "It's fast, but I'm faster."

Jame disappeared back into the house. It would be much faster for him to go that way than it would be to walk the streets. Jame found Stars standing right where he had left the mavae. He pulled himself into the saddle, and turned her back towards the workshop. He had gone only two streets before a tall black figure stepped out into the path in front of him. It was roughly human shaped, but something about it was very wrong.

Jame opened his Vision and examined the thing. It had a dull red aura around it, as if it had some sort of powerful energy source within. Jame took no chances. He drew his lancer, aimed, and fired, all in one smooth motion, just like Cole had drilled him to do. The thing moved in a blur, taking one perfect step to the side. Jame continued to fire the weapon, calmly adjusting his aim, but the creature shot towards him easily, evading each subsequent shot without an issue. It was almost on him when a silvery blur slammed into it.

The two figures rolled across the ground in a ball of wildly flailing limbs. Then the silver figure kicked the black one away. It smashed into the stone wall of an official looking building across the street. The stone shattered with the force of the hit. The silver figure came to its feet. It, too, was roughly human-shaped, though it was much smaller. Jame didn't bother looking at that figure. It was Kiltik, and likely, the diminutive synthoid had just saved his life, but there was no time to dwell on that now.

He reloaded his lancer and took aim on the creature. If it dodged his shots before, that probably meant that the lancer could hurt the creature. He focused on the creature's center of mass. It dodged to one side, but the lancer bolt smashed into what passed for its shoulder. It staggered, and then Kiltik was on top of it. In the moments that Jame had concentrated on aiming at the creature, Kiltik had taken the shape of a katali. It landed on top of the creature with all six paws flailing madly. Kiltik's claws bit into the creature, leaving ruinous tears in the surface of its body. It bled red light from each new slice. Its hands stretched impossibly and wrapped around Kiltik's throat. It mistakenly thought that Kiltik was a normal animal that needed air. Kiltik did not even slow. His front paws continued to tear at the creature feverishly. Tentacle-like limbs sprouted out of the creature's torso and latched onto all six of Kiltik's paws.

Jame dismounted and walked over to where the creature was struggling against Kiltik. He pointed his lancer at the creature's head and began pulling the trigger. The tentacles released Kiltik and began to whip around madly. Jame jumped back and released the magazine from the lancer. He loaded a fresh one. He was worried about running out of ammunition. He only had two magazines left.

The creature squirmed free of Kiltik's claws. Its featureless face split into a maw of needle-sharp teeth. It screeched its frustration into the sky and then turned. It began to run away, but in a display of amazing power, Kiltik moved so quickly that even with his Vision Jame lost track of the Mind. The silver katali landed on the creature's back, driving it to the ground. Kiltik's claws elongated, and he wrapped them around its throat. He twisted his body, and what looked like powerful muscles bulged in Kiltik's shoulders. A moment of resistence passed, and the creature's head was torn free from its body.

"You will not escape This One!" Kiltik roared.

It looked as if some sort of gruesome machine was convulsing out of control atop the creature's body. Chalkboard sounds of claws scoring the paving stones filled the air as Kiltik literally tore the creature limb from limb. Sprays of shattered stone flew away from each swipe of Kiltik's claws as they sliced through the creature's body, smashing through to the paving stones below.

Jame ran to Stars to pull her back away from the commotion. A jianfruit sized orb of dull grey metal flew free from the black body, and smashed into one of the nearby buildings. It crumpled flat on one side, and was embedded in the stone. Fluids leaked out of it that melted the casing. When it finally stopped moving, Kiltik stepped off of its motionless body with a very human snort of derision. Kiltik padded back to where Jame was standing next to Stars around the corner of a building.

"Are you unharmed, Jame? This One apologizes for taking so long to find you. This One has news," Kiltik said, his oddly metallic-sounding voice the best thing Jame had heard all night.

"I'm not hurt, Kiltik, but I think I would be without you. Thank you."

"This One was glad to be of assistance. This One spoke with Giri. That One has expressed regret to inform us that That One believes that That One's particular structures are far too dangerous to be used in our fight. However, That One will share That One's knowledge with This One on all topics that do not relate to That One's creation of Antistructs. That One also wishes to join with the Tier once again, but not until those that That One watches over are made safe."

Jame's head spun a little bit trying to decipher exactly what had been said, but he finally worked it all out.

"So that's good news, sort of."

Kiltik bobbed his head in a very human nod.

"I was just on my way back to the workshop to make sure everyone is alright," Jame said. Kiltik turned back the torn-apart body of the thing that had attacked them.

"Cut away a piece of this thing and bring it with us, Jame. This One would very much like to examine it."

Jame did as he was asked.

"Is Ales going to be all right fighting a thing like that?"

Kiltik turned back to him, arranging his six paws into a sitting position. Then he began to laugh. It was a bizarre metallic sound, not unpleasant, but so very strange to listen to. "Alessandra Family Katane?" He continued to chuckle as if he was amused beyond his ability to speak. "Alessandra would destroy a creature like that with a single touch. This One has extraordinary physical abilities that are likely close to matching hers, but This One is not like her. She has the ability to be destruction incarnate when she choses to unleash it."

"But once I got past my fear of how incredibly powerful she is, I don't think I've ever felt safer than with her near me," Jame said.

Kiltik nodded. "That One fears her own strength because she fears that she will somehow misuse her power. She always has. Having said that, woe be to the foolish thing that we fight against. When the creature is finally revealed to Alessandra, you may see why she names herself Destroyer." Kiltik sounded very sad.

"She's broken," Jame said solemnly.

Kiltik nodded. "A little, and she may always be broken. Mortal minds were never meant to hold even a fraction of the power of a god, but she has more than a fraction. Not the full power of the Father or the Mother at all, but her power has always been far beyond that of other Tier. People thought that her fight with the Traitor was a display of her full abilities.

It was not even close. She sacrificed herself attempting to reason with the Traitor. It would have been far easier to simply crush him. Alessandra has never taken the easy way. Believe this, Jame, if Alessandra is struggling in a competition of strength, it is with herself. There is nothing short of the gods themselves that could stand on even ground with her in a fight."

"How do you know all of this?" Jame asked. He remounted on Stars, and began to walk her back to the workshop.

"Unlike a human mind, the storage capacity of an artificial Mind is near limitless. Minds such as This One cannot store as much information as The Core, but This One has thousands of cycles of Tieran memories and knowledge at This One's disposal. That includes the complete memories of Alessandra Family Katane up until the time of her injury. This One has been assisting Alessandra in filling the gaps in her personal memories when time permits. This One has studied every fevered moment of that battle. You cannot imagine how hard she tried not to harm him," Kiltik explained.

"How can one person have that much power, even one of the Tier?"

"Alessandra Family Katane has ever worked harder than any Tier This One has ever seen to master her powers. If This One is being honest, we do not understand why Alessandra is so powerful. If the Gods are aware of the secret of her power, they have not seen fit to disclose this information. Unfortunately, This One cannot tell you more, Jame Family Katane. The rest of her story is a secret that belongs only to Alessandra Family Katane. If you desire to know why Alessandra feels that way, you will have to ask her yourself."

Jame got a pained look on his face. "I'll do that when I can ask her from as far away as possible, maybe when Warran invents a device that will let us talk from the other side of the planet. I'm not afraid of her anymore, but that doesn't mean I am going to invite her to teach me what her boot against my ass feels like."

"That was humor?" Kiltik asked.

Jame grinned. "Yes, Kiltik, that was humor."

It took them a few more minutes of silence to reach the Workshop. When they arrived, everything seemed in order. Lia had fallen asleep in her bath, and Ilsa was also still sleeping.

"I'm glad to see you back. I'm feeling woefully inadequate with everyone either out of the building or down for the count. Is Ales with you?" Juran asked.

"Alessandra Family Katane has gone hunting. This One is certain she will return soon," Kiltik said.

"How can you be so nonchalant, Kiltik? You killed that thing like it was nothing. You were amazing!" Jame said.

"This One would like to examine the sample of the synthetic being that attacked This One. Do you have it, Jame Family Katane?"

Jame produced a folded cloth and held it out. Kiltik's body reshaped into something much closer to human. He took the cloth and headed for the work rooms at the other end of the building. Jame launched into telling the story of what had happened to him on the way back from Clan Clai. Before he could get too far into the story, a soft voice came from the doorway.

"Would one of you two be so kind as to help me dry myself? I would rather not drip dry, and while I would prefer to sun myself dry, it is a bit late in the day for that." Lia was standing in the doorway. Her fur was dripping wet and thin streams of steam rose from her body from the heat of the bath water.

"Um..." Juran said. They both hesitated for a long moment. Jame began to turn red with embarrassment.

"I'm not asking you to fondle my private parts, you imbeciles! But since I have no thumbs, if you could towel off the larger patches of fur perhaps?!" Lia said with amused irritation.

Jame coughed spasmodically and pounded his chest.

"I will help you," he finally said when his coughing fit passed. He followed her down the hallway which had a few odd drips of water, but even though she was dripping wet, there wasn't much water tracked behind.

"How come there isn't more water?" Jame asked.

"I pulled down a towel, wiped my paws, and rolled on a couple a little. It didn't work very well, and my Cellstructs were not pleased with me for my further attempts to joggle my insides," Lia explained.

"Doesn't that hurt?"

Lia shook her head. "Pain is not a concern of the Tier. Once you say the words, it will open your mind to control over your mental landscape. When that happens, pain becomes a far more useful tool in terms of managing your own body. You can choose whether or not to even feel it. You must use caution, though. At that point, pain is an indicator that something is not functioning correctly in your body."

Jame picked up the towels she had rolled on and tossed them into the laundry with the rest of the dirty towels. He took down a clean one and began to dry the fur of her back.

"You ran into something on the way back from helping Ales?" Lia prompted him.

"Yes, some sort of monster. Kiltik called it a synthetic being. We brought a piece of it back for him to examine."

Lia hummed and laid down on her side to let Jame dry one side of her. "I trust Kiltik didn't have much trouble handling it?"

"Not at all. I was worried for a moment that Ales might have trouble with one of them. Kiltik just laughed and told me that she's way scarier than I could have ever imagined. Then it just made me feel like an ass for pressing her about the Circles."

"Don't be silly, Jame."

"Can you tell me why she is so frightened of her own abilities? I feel like I am missing something, and Kiltik wouldn't talk about it when I asked him."

Lia sighed. Most Arcangineers disliked talking about their exploits, but every single one ended up with a number of names. She, herself, had several that she was known by even to this day.

"It's a very old story, but it survived even to this time in some places. It's a story about a little girl who discovered she had a very dangerous power and became one of the greatest heroes our world had ever seen. I bet Kinas told it to your people. She had many names, and she earned every one, even if she wasn't proud of them all. Wind Tamer, Firekeeper, Path Maker, Breaker of Bonds, but most notably, everyone knew the little girl as the Heart of Balance."

"Alessandra is the Heart of Balance?" Jame's voice held awe.

"If anything, the stories probably do not live up to half of the things I have seen her do. She'll try to downplay the things she did, and so will I if you ever discover any of my names. It is our prerogative. We did those things because they needed doing, nothing more. They are extraordinary to normal people, but normal quickly becomes a subjective concept once you gain more of your Tieran abilities."

"But the story of the Heart of Balance said that when she was little, she almost killed a lot of people when she discovered her powers. It was an accident, but a lot of people were hurt. I only heard the story once. Gods, she..." Jame stammered to a stop. "She collapsed a volcano," he whispered, awestruck.

Lia let out a chuff. "That's the one that stands out for you? Not the story about defeating an entire army entirely without assistance, or how she crushed the corrupt governments of seven kingdoms on the moonward continent in a single night?"

Lia rolled over onto her back, and Jame toweled off the last of her fur on her stomach.

Jame shook his head. "Those are just people. The volcano was a force of nature. How does a person attack a volcano?"

Jame tossed the last towel into the laundry and Lia rolled back onto her feet. She laid there and looked at the floor.

"With the knowledge that you are all that stands between the people in surrounding countryside and awful death." Lia began to chuff with amusement again. "You should have seen what she looked like when she came down from the mountain top. She was entirely black with soot head to toe, and her clothing was burned through in a hundred spots. She lost most of her hair. She was so angry about that. She wouldn't go near Ahal until it all grew back. She wouldn't let Bann see her. It took almost an entire cycle." Lia shook her head and finally got to her feet.

"Who was Bann?" Jame asked. Lia just shook her head sadly.

"He was Ales' mate. He was one of most brilliant Fixers among the Tier. When the Cataclysm happened, he was among the first to die. He was right next to the device when it exploded." Lia's face twisted in pain that had nothing to do with her injuries. "Come on. Everyone needs to know what you found at the Clan Clai manor and I need to eat something."

36

Ales had followed the creature's trail to a massive complex just outside of the Center. It was well defended, manned by hundreds of the Ryhim. Ales jumped to the top of the wall with ease. It quickly became clear that this complex was terribly odd. It seemed like a prison complex, but it was far too large to house the relatively small number of criminals that the Ryhim were forced to imprison.

She called up the Circles of Distance and Finding, melding their powers to examine the building. She had known it was here. They had maps of the entire center, but the scale of the building did not show well on a map. The complex was massive, and information from the Circle of Distance made it clear that there was something wrong with the way the building was made. She opened the Cicles of Breaking and Repair, as well. With that extra information, she quickly realized that the building had at least four floors beneath the surface. That meant the building had eight floors in total.

The synthoid's trail lead straight into the building. She walked the circumfurance of it, shutting down her other Circles and pulling up Taking to let her walk between the guards entirely unnoticed. The trail did not leave the building anywhere, so the creature, or at least its trail, was somewhere in that building. Ales made her way within. She had to pick three locks to get to anyplace interesting, but she needed to know the layout of the facility. Her vision let her see one whole floor at a time, and she could probably pick out the other floors, but if it was a prison then the warden was sure to have a map of the building. She made for his office.

She finally got to the top floor, and looking around the walls, her eyes snagged on something in a room to the left of the stairwell. It lit up in her Vision like a firework. It was her Fixer mark. Every Tier who employed the Fixer's powers could leave a mark on something that would glow in the presence of the Vision. Peering through the walls, she focused on her Fixer mark. It was a recent mark, too. She focused through the haze of the objects between her and the mark. The image resolved, and Ales had to control her anger. The Fixer mark was on a pair of lancers. Cole's pair of lancers.

Ales walked straight towards them. When she encountered a wall, Ales simply drew back her fist and smashed it. The holes were oddly perfect in their squareness. Her precision was not an accident. No matter how angry she was, there was no reason to destroy the building and kill anyone within. The noise drew shouts, and she saw scrambling guards, but they were of no consequence, not right now.

She was finally standing in the store room, her fists clenched at her sides. She stared at Cole's clothing and his lancers. The door burst open, and a fiery haired man with a neatly trimmed beard came through. He was dressed in a grey and green uniform. He had a lancer trained on her, and at least half a dozen guards crowded the room behind him. She didn't turn her head. She drew her own lancer and fired six shots before the men could even react. With the aid of her Vision and Cellstructs, each shot was perfect. Swords and lancers shattered as bolts struck each one, knocking it from the hands of the person holding it.

"Where is Cole?" Ales demanded.

The man, apparently the warden, given his uniform, opened his mouth. "No, imbecile. You are a liar and a theif. I would like to kill you for the betrayal of your people, but I will let your own people pass judgement upon you. You, speak." Ales pointed her lancer towards one of the guards.

"He almost escaped a few days ago, but one of the guards knocked him out outside the wall by surprising him. He was taken to a more secure portion of the prison below. Only the Warden knows where he was taken," the man blurted out in fear.

Ales finally turned and grinned in a manic way.

"Is that so?" Ales said almost gleefully. "You men can go. I would have words with the warden." Ales stalked across the room.

"But..." one of the men stammered.

"I haven't the patience to explain to you why you should obey me. If you feel the need to fight me, I will understand,

and I will not kill any of you, but I cannot promise this will not hurt," Ales warned. She sighed in relief when they left.

"You are a traitor to your people, Warden. I can see into your mind, and you have given yourself to the Intruder. You did it knowing full well what the creature has planned for your people. Your greed is unforgivable. Tell me where they have taken Cole. Your putrid master cannot protect you from me. It may find you and kill you. If you keep me from my brother and he comes to harm, I will find you no matter where you hide." Ales said it very softly, but there was silence in the room. It couldn't have been louder if she had screamed it. She struggled with her anger. She felt so indignant that anyone would hurt her family. She tried to quiet her rage, and had some partial success. The man's face fell.

"It took him through the lower levels. It already knows you are here. It has been preparing for you. There was nothing I could do. It would have just killed me and replaced me with another," the warden said.

"I care not for your weakness. If it finds you, pass it the same message I have given it before. I will find it one day. It will never be safe from me."

Ales considered going into the bowels of the place right then. This was clearly where the creature had been doing its experiments. She couldn't go in alone, no matter how badly she wanted to. She took Cole's things from the shelf and made a bundle of them. She walked out past the warden to the outer wall of the prison. She smashed her fist into the wall, and a square doorway-sized hole disintegrated in the stone. She leapt back into the yard. She had no time to waste.

37

Lia closed her eyes and focused on the vibrational emissions coming from the satellites that remained around Ahlysim. In total, the Tier had launched thirty-one satellites into high orbit around their world for various purposes. After three thousand cycles, only twenty-two of them remained active. Some had been knocked out of orbit by debris. A few of them were research devices. Some, like the Probability Matrix, had been incredible tools but could be very dangerous in the wrong hands. Others were useful only to the Tier. That was one of the ones she was attempting to contact now. With the satellite, she could track the locations of anyone with both the Vision and Cellstructs. She made contact with the satellite.

{Access to this device is restricted. Idenitfy,} the device sent back across the vibrational wavelength.

Lia provided it with her unique helixical and energetic signature. A moment later, her mental landscape was presented with a three dimensional representation of Ahlysim. She mentally commanded the globe to spin gently on the vertical axis. The face of Ahlysim was covered mostly in blue, though there were some areas of brown, yellow, and orange. As the globe spun, the vast, dark blue expanse of the Black Wilds came into view. Inside of the irregular outline of the Wilds there were a number of glowing dots.

Currently, there were four dots. One was herself, one Ilsa, and one Ales. The other was Kiltik, who had a different connection to the system, indicated by a green dot. By her mental command, the orb grew larger, zooming up until only the Black Wilds were visible. Each of the dots were identified by mental energy signature, and they would only appear if the Tier in question wanted to be tracked. She would have to remind herself to explain to Ilsa how to block it if she did not want to be tracked.

Before she went any further, Lia checked the access log. Interestingly, the last Tier to access the tracking system had been old Kinas himself. She selected the only dot that was moving relatively quickly. That corresponded to Ales. It looked like she was coming out of a massive structure on the stoneward edge of the center. She was moving fast, too. Fast enough that the positional updates were causing the dot to stretch out along the map until she concentrated on how the dots were displayed. It resolved just as she entered the Center.

A few moments later, she was nearing the building. Lia turned her attention away from the map, and it faded as the connection was broken. She checked the list of her remaining injuries, but it was getting much shorter. It was down to minor muscle damage at this point. She wouldn't be doing any heavy lifting for a couple of more days, but it was good enough that she didn't have to worry about reinjuring her internal organs with every movement. She stood and went to the kitchen. Warran had returned, and was in the workshop when she passed.

"Ales is coming back. Please join us in the kitchen," she said.

Lia tried to make a mental connection to Ilsa. The rejection was normal, but her Cellstructs had taken enough of a hold that Lia at least got a response when she queried the girl's mind.

"I'll be right along," Warran responded as she went past.

She went up the stairwell at the end of the hallway and to Ilsa's room. She eyed the doorknob for a long moment. She didn't really want to knock. Ales had promised to replace all the door knobs with something a little more paw-friendly soon, but they hadn't had the chance. In a feat of willpower, she did not use her Vision to check if the knob was clean. She just turned her head and latched her teeth onto the doorknob. She twisted her head, and the door popped open. She nosed it open slowly, sticking her head inside. She wanted to let the girl sleep, but if she could give her a quick lesson, she could get back to sleep right away and still be part of the conversation. Lia sat down next to the bed and gently shook Ilsa awake. Her eyes slid open, and she took a sharp breath.

"Sorry," Lia said.

"No, it's fine. Your teeth are just really close to my face." Ilsa chuckled a little. She started to pull back the covers.

"No, don't get up. Your Cellstructs have reached your brain, and I wanted to give you a quick lesson on how to communicate with us through them. It is not difficult, and once I explain, you can go back to sleep. You'll be able to take part of the conversation while your body sleeps," Lia explained.

Ilsa closed her eyes again. "Go ahead."

"It's very simple. When another of the Tier tries to contact you on a purely mental level, you will hear a soft sound inside of your head. I won't try to describe it because everyone hears something different, but it will be a persistent sound. It will cut through any noise you might be hearing. This is called a handshake. To accept the handshake and begin a telepathic conversation, you simply think the word 'accept' in Tieran. To deny the connection, just think 'deny' in Tieran, but here is the key. You have to think it with the intention of communicating with your Cellstructs. As time goes on, we will teach you more about working with your Cellstructs, but for now, this will be enough," Lia explained.

There was a long moment of silence, and Lia was about to reach out to make sure she hadn't gone back to sleep when Ilsa nodded. Lia tried again to make a purely mental connection with Ilsa's Cellstructs. This time, the handshake was accepted.

{Well done, Ilsa. Keep in mind you have to be relatively close for telepathic communication to function properly. Now you can go back to sleep, but leave your connection to me open. I will bring you into the conversation in such a way that you will be able to hear everything I hear. If you have anything to add to the conversation, you can tell Ales, Kiltik, or I and we will speak for you,} Lia said.

{This is very strange. It sounds like you are whispering in my ear,} Ilsa replied.

{Yes, because your Cellstructs are feeding my words straight into your conscious mind. Eventually, with enough practice, you will be able to fit hours of conversation into a few moments, since everything happens at the speed of thought, but speeding up conversations like that takes some practice.}

Lia left the room and pulled the door closed by wrapping her tail around the knob.

{How do I tell if I am sleeping?} Ilsa asked, her mindvoice filled with amusement.

{Oh just ask your Cellstructs to put your body into a sleep state. I can explain more about how it all works later if you are interested.}

{Ales, are you listening?}

{I am. Excellent work, Ilsa. Be careful. You are the only other person in the world now who can hear Lia's mindvoice, and she is likely to talk to your ear off,} Ales said.

{What about Kiltik?} Ilsa's inquisitive mindvoice was so genuine. It took a long time for someone to learn to modulate their feelings in their mindvoice.

{This One is not much for human conversation,} Kiltik said.

{Well, Lia isn't human,} Ilsa replied. She felt Kiltik's focus on her for a long moment that made her feel very tense.

{This One is still new to the concept of human humor, but this one believes that you should avoid being a smart ass,} Kiltik said into their collective link.

Ales burst out laughing into the link and Lia joined her. Everyone had gathered in the kitchen. Warran, Jame, and Juran sat around the table. Kiltik was lying nearby, having kept the form of a katali.

{Icci, are you listening?} Ales asked into the mental link.

{Indeed. This One can hear both telepathically and audibly,} Icci replied into the link. *{Before we begin, This One has produced Warran's cellstruct initiator.}*

Icci was using a machine she had instructed Warran in building in the workshop. She controlled it remotely from her stand in the kitchen. Ales jogged down to the workshop and snagged the tiny blue sphere from the platform that had ejected from the machine. When she came back, she held it out to Warran.

"This is not the way we usually do this, but you are skilled enough with your Vision to make adjustments on your own personal Cellstructs. Since I do not believe you are going to withdraw from saying the words when you are ready, I am giving this to you now," Ales said. Warran took it reverently.

"Don't look at it with your Vision," Ales warned. "There is a lot of energy wrapped up in that little sphere, so trying to examine it will just blind you right now. When you get more experience using your Vision, you'll learn how to filter some of those things out. For now, just swallow it. Make sure you eat as much food as you can take. The cellstructs will need material to work with to replicate and integrate with your body, so they'll take some of the food you eat. The more you eat, the faster you'll be up to speed."

Lia spoke up, "Now that that is done, we have a lot to talk about. We have a theory about exactly what has been happening, and it's time we pull in all our resources. We have a lot to do and not a lot of time to do it in."

Ales continued. "We think that Rihanna is being used as a testing ground. The Intruder is attempting to replicate how our cellstructs integrate with our bodies. However, unlike our Cellstructs, which are carbon-based, the Intruder is attempting to base its Cellstructs on Black Sol Alloy. If it can accomplish this, it will be able to control everyone in the world that doesn't already have Cellstructs, since we cannot give cellstructs to everyone in the world in any effective way."

"But didn't you say that even we have to adjust our Cellstructs over time so that our bodies don't reject them?" Warran asked.

"Yes, but that isn't because there wasn't a way to make it work. It's because it works better this way. It gives our Cellstructs the flexibility to do things that they couldn't otherwise do. If we made them perfectly self-balancing, they wouldn't be able to stimulate our own immune systems, for instance. The trade-off for flexibility is that from time to time, we adjust our Cellstructs to integrate properly with our systems," Ales said.

"Can't we give lesser Cellstructs to normal folks, though?" Warran continued.

Ales frowned. "Warran, this is not the time for this discussion. There are numerous issues with giving Cellstructs to people that do not have the Vision and understanding to work with them. We will discuss this when we have resolved the current situation." Warran subsided, and Ales went on.

"This situation has been made worse by the fact that Cole has gone missing, and we know for a fact that the scion of Clan

Clai has been taken by the Intruder. Lia, are you up to using Finding to go through Clan Clai's manor? My Finding tells me that they were the ones operating the Probability Matrix. It's not there anymore, but the solar banks on the property were far more substantial than what was necessary to supply the manor house. But that is secondary. The first priority needs to be storming the prison complex outside of Rihanna. Cole is there now, I am convinced of it, especially since Mina was taken there as well. We can't wait, but there are other things that need to be done. I am going to go into the prison with Kiltik, and there are other tasks you will all need to complete while I am doing that."

Lia opened her mouth to protest. Ales could see it coming. She held up a hand.

"I am not suggesting that we do it this way because it is easier for me. I'm suggesting that we do it this way because this is going to be dangerous no matter what we do. Kiltik and I are the best equipped for fighting right now. You are injured, Lia, and Ilsa is still spans away from being ready to use her new strength. Do you remember what it felt like to use your Cellstructs for the first time? No? Neither do I, because we were born with them. She wasn't, and she's going to be lucky if she doesn't break everything she tries to pick up for the next few days at least. It'll take that long to teach her how to place the mental blocks necessary to control her new strength." Ales felt a mental sending from Ilsa, like she wanted to say something but was holding back.

{Please speak your mind, Ilsa,} Ales sent mentally.

{She's right, Lia. My Cellstructs are telling me that I need to help them place mental blocks or I will be operating at full strength at all times,} Ilsa said. Ales relayed what was said to everyone who couldn't hear it.

Warran got up and started to make a sandwich, opening the cold box to take out meat and cheese. Ales grinned because he clearly didn't really know what he was doing.

"If you're making food for yourself, spread it around, will you?" Ales asked. She chuckled when Warran looked down at what he was doing.

"I'm happy to," he stammered.

"Don't worry, that will only happen for the first few hours until your Cellstructs reach your brain. Then you'll be able to control the things they might do with your body," Ales said.

"I take it that they are telling me that I need to eat something a little more forcefully than my stomach did," Warran said.

Ales nodded and continued explaining.

"Kiltik and I will take the prison, and retrieve Cole. If we are lucky, we will find Mina there, as well. The unfortunate news of what has happened at the Clan Clai manor must be disseminated to all of the Ryhim. Juran and Jame, that task will be yours. Warran, take them to the Travelers Grove and teach them how to use the Lightleaf trees. Go to your own clans first.

Jame, since you are a member of the Outriders, you will have the bigger burden. You will need to get an audience with the five Banners. They can give you the authority to command audiences with the rest of the clan chiefs. Tell them that the Tier request that they come to Rihanna with all haste. Lia, I think that you will be best suited to speak with the Royal Families here in Rihanna. Inform them of what has happened with Clan Clai, and also tell them that we mean to make our home here in Rihanna. I don't know how they will react to that declaration, so you are best to do it."

"How am I the best one for this? I just frighten people," Lia said.

"Don't be dense on purpose just because you don't want to do something," Ales said.

Lia sighed. "I'm never going to be able to just find a nice rock to sun myself on again am I?"

Ales chuckled. "I suspect you retiring to a quiet life sleeping on rocks and doing nothing most days is some cycles away. But if you can convince Ilsa to take on the memories you have of all of your ambassadorial experience, she can take your place."

{If you can transmit memories like that, why don't you teach us all that way?} Ilsa asked. Lia repeated her question out loud, and everyone looked on a little more intently.

"Because it doesn't work very well. We experimented with transmitted learning a great deal. It only ever works properly with people who are extremely young, and even then, only for pure, factual knowledge such as mathematics. Even if Lia gives Ilsa all of her memories related to her training in being an ambassador, it is only going to accelerate her learning process by about twenty percent. There is a lot of body language and facial expression that someone has to be able to understand to be good at talking to people. Some people get it naturally. Ilsa is not one of these, unfortunately. Her mother is quite good at it, but Ilsa is a little too straight forward, though she has learned a lot from her mother," Ales explained.

{Hey! I tried to learn everything she taught me!} Ilsa protested. Lia repeated her words.

"The point is, it isn't a viable tool for teaching or we would use it. Lia has different tools to help her get through a conversation these days, but I'm sure she still remembers all of those lessons if she digs deep enough," Ales explained. "Still, we are getting off the topic."

Warran put a plate of sandwiches down on the table, and everyone took one.

"I agree that I am in no shape to go into a battle, but what is Ilsa going to do? And what about the little ones? Who is going to protect them while we are doing all of this?" Lia asked.

"You, Warran, and Ilsa will all be here. Warran still has a lot of work to do on his projects, and I have a task for Ilsa, something that should give the Intruder fits."

Lia tilted her head, and dropped one ear in clear question.

"Something that I should have thought of when we first decided that the Probability Matrix was being used here."

38

Cole woke in a similar cell to the one he had been in before. He touched his head, but there was no blood there even though he was certain there should have been. This room was well-lit by a glow bulb at the center of the ceiling. There were no doors that he could see, only a bench and a hole to use for the bathroom. In annoyance, he opened his Vision. It took him only a moment to find the door. this door, though, was just a stone slab that slid down from the ceiling. When he increased his focus on his Vision, he could see that there was some sort of counterweight system that allowed the slab to slide up into a channel in the ceiling.

Cole touched his arms and legs and was pleased to find his captors had still not found the thin pouches of tools that were bonded to them. He felt vindicated from the argument that he had had with Ales. If someone tried to remove them, he stood to receive a painful injury. The only way to take them off without his permission would be to rip away the skin they were bound to. Ales had warned him away from the idea, but Cole had said he would risk the injury. Cole was about to perpetrate his second escape when the door slid open.

Behind the door was a black figure. Not a figure dressed in black, but a figure with shining black skin. It wore no clothing and had no real definition. It looked like a simulacrum of a person. Even the face had no features. It was like someone had placed a misshapen melon atop the thing's neck. Its face split in a sinuous line along what passed for a short muzzle, and it opened a mouth full of needlesharp fangs.

"The Tier are dead. You cannot remake them." The hiss was in Tieran. It had a metallic twang near to Kiltik's voice.

It was unsettling to watch it speak. It did not have lips or any other corresponding facial expressions. It simply opened its mouth and the sound issued forth. Cole's grasp on Tieran was quite good, but it spoke the language with an insane raspy accent of madness. Maybe he was the one who spoke it with an odd accent. He didn't bother answering, though. He had no way to know how to destroy this creature yet, so he had nothing to say.

"This world is ours! It was given to us!" the thing continued. It was extremely odd, because it did not move. It drew no breath, and was motionless as a statue. "It cannot be returned to this world! Only we can access it. Only we speak the language of void. You will give it to us!"

The thing was making no sense now. Cole just eyed it and made a rude gesture. The thing lashed out an arm at him, and Cole's hand came up. He pivoted smoothly and dragged the thing from its feet. He threw it at the wall with every bit of strength he had. It smashed into the wall and then melted. It ran down the wall like he had splashed a bucket of black sewage against it. It reformed quickly into the rough shape of a man.

Cole's eyes widened and he took a step back. He examined it with his Vision and understood. It was made completely of bondstructs of some sort. He couldn't tell exactly what they were made of, but it was clear that without much more powerful weapons, there was no way for him to stop it.

Tentacle-like barbs shot out of the creature's body, lashing towards him. Cole fell backwards into a roll, tumbling through the cell door and into the hallway. At least this time, they had left him his clothing. He came to his feet and darted down the hallway. He had only made it about five steps when something wrapped around his throat and dragged him backwards off of his feet. Then the creature was crouching over him, choking him into compliance.

"You will give it to us!" the disturbing metallic voice issued forth from the creature's maw.

"I'm not giving you anything," Cole rasped.

The creature shook him violently, and surprisingly, it didn't hurt when his head bounced off the stone.

"You will give it to us, or we shall use the prediction device to destroy the Ryhim," it hissed.

"You're already destroying the Ryhim. Ales will crush you if you reveal yourself. You're afraid, and you should be. You can't hide yourself behind these puppets forever. You deceived her once before, but now she knows you. She will find you, and she will end you. Even if you kill every one of us, you'll never be able to stop her. Against her, you stand no chance," Cole challenged.

"We will gain access to it. It makes you all nothing!" it screeched angrily.

Cole couldn't figure out what this insane creature could possibly want from him. Two spikes grew from its shoulders and approached his eyes. He closed his eyes and mentally prepared himself for the torture to come. He wouldn't feel the pain, but the damage it could do to him without killing him was its own kind of torture.

"This will not persuade you like it does the rest of the pawns. You will not feel this pain," it hissed. "We will use another kind of pain. We will kill those you care about."

It climbed off of him and dragged him back to the cell. It whipped him into it, and his breath was driven out of him when he hit the wall.

"We will kill each of them, and we will ask again after you watch each of them die. How many are you willing to lose?"

The massive stone slab slid down between the creature and Cole. It was exactly what he wanted. If the thing went after his friends, it was sure to encounter Ales watching over them.

39

Ales watched the prison complex. She didn't like what she saw milling about in one of the prison yards. The space between the outside wall and the prison building had been divided into relatively smaller areas with walls as high as the outside wall. Two of the yards on the bloomward side of the prison had no guards on the walls. Inside, there were at least twenty of the creatures that Kiltik had described.

"How strong are they?" Ales asked.

"This One estimates that their strength would be a match for Ilsa in strength in her current state," Kiltik explained.

"And they are made of Black Sol?"

"This One's examination indicates that is the case. Before the sample we took broke down, This One was able to capture many details of the construction. These creatures are self-replicating, but they require a source of Black Sol Alloy to do so."

"I think the best approach here is a smash and grab. If the Intruder has these things to do its bidding, I suspect that we will not find anything living on the lower levels of the prison. It may call them in, but we are not dealing with soldiers in bondarmor, here. Not yet, at least. Even if we were, I can dispatch them without harming them. After Vilhena, I am sure that soon it will learn that we must be more careful with humans, so it'll start trying to use them against us whenever it can. But I think that these things are something it is attempting to develop in efforts to find something that can defeat us. I want to deal a crushing blow to that idea," Ales said. "I will simply destroy all of these."

{Will you be alright?} Kiltik switched to his mindvoice. He knew that destruction like this upset Ales. It upset her how good she was at destroying things. She took a long, deep breath.

{I will be. This thing is a rot, Kiltik, an infection. I name it Blight. We have seen its madness, and I believe it means to control or destroy us all. We must stop it. If it costs me a small piece of myself, I will give it. Wounds heal, Kiltik, but if I let this Blight run

Ales stood. Kiltik saw the telltale shakes of Ales' body as she released the constraints on her Cellstructs. They infused her body, and it tightened with power beyond the human. Ales dashed down the hillside towards the walls in a blur. They never saw her when she lept over the wall. She ran towards the far wall, which bordered the section where the synthoids were milling about.

She did not jump this wall. She called up the Circle of Breaking, and it overlayed her Vision with dots ranging from white to bright red. She drew back her fist and smashed it into one of the red dots close to the bottom of the wall. The stone exploded into dust, opening a hole twice the size of a person. Ales held her breath, closed her eyes, and dashed through the cloud of dust. She burst through it and opened her eyes.

The creatures had turned in unison to her, and they did not hesitate. They threw themselves at her with a combined screech of rage and madness. To Ales' eyes, they appeared to be moving through thick syrup. They were much faster than a human, but they didn't even approach her speed. To her horror, the creatures' limbs reshaped into weapons. Further limbs grew from the bodies of the Blighted until they were flailing numerous blades. It was clear they had extra senses as well, as they were able to track her movements despite their relatively slower speed.

She ducked and twisted her body as the first one dove at her. She made a knife blade of her hand, smashing her fingertips into the brightest of the red dots on the creature. It literally exploded. The bondstructs lost all cohesion as the magic of Breaking flowed through her into the creature. She spun to the right as the next creature dove at her, blades thrashing. She continued to turn, letting her Vision encompass all of her surroundings. She slipped her arm between the spikes sprouting from the back of the creature in front of her. Her elbow crashed into the gleaming red dot on its back. It blew apart, making a popping sound as the bondstructs lost their ability to cling to each other.

The remaining creatures jumped back from her warily. They seemed to realize that they were not going to be able to even touch her. Ales gave them no further chance. She had been working with three levels of constraints open. She opened two more levels and dashed forward. She ducked and dodged through the sluggish creatures as they attempted to flee. When she finished, she was standing at the doorway leading into the prison. There was no point in being less flashy now. Even though the fight had taken less than a minute, soldiers had gathered on the walls with weapons in hand, but as soon as they saw her glowing eyes, they lowered their weapons.

The door exploded into metal dust at her touch. The heavy bars that acted as locks inside of the door clattered to the ground as the metal sand gathered around them. She walked through the door, leaving the men gaping behind her. Kiltik came through the door a moment later.

{This One thinks that those ones will be telling stories about this for some time,} Kiltik said telepathically.

{Good,} Ales' mindvoice was resolved. *{I think we'll need to go below this floor to find what we are looking for. Let's go.}*

Ales took a few steps inside the room, looking down through the floor until she could see there was open space below her. Then she looked around the floor a little to find the place that would be best. She tapped a foot on a spot slightly off the center of the hall. The stone there turned to dust and a hole opened. Ales dropped through it and Kiltik followed.

Here, things were clearly different. The walls were bondstructed of perfectly polished stone. There were no lights at all on this floor. This impressed on Ales the fact that humans probably didn't make it to this floor very often. The machines wouldn't need light to operate down here any more than she and Kiltik did. Ales dropped down to one knee and focused on looking through the walls, but found that the walls had been bondstructed with metal plates in the middle. The mixed materials made it nearly impossible to see into more than the rooms nearest to her. Obviously, the Blight thought it would stop her from easily mapping the facility.

She scaled her Vision back so that she could see all of the air molecules. Then she slid her Windblade from its sheath in her coat. She rapped it smartly against the stone wall and watched as everything vibrated with the sound. She felt a mental rush as her Cellstructs pulled in information from the way the sound moved through the materials and air around her. A three dimensional representation of most of the floor appeared in her mind a moment later. She rapped the wall again, letting the echoes die out. More of the floor filled into the map. The lower floors filled in some, as well. She couldn't see everything that those floors contained, but she could see that there were three others below this one. She mentally sent this to Kiltik.

{This One thanks you. This One will stay one floor above you until you reach the lowest floor,} Kiltik assured her telepathically.

Ales nodded.

{If we pass close enough to each other, I'll pass you further knowledge of the layout,} Ales angry mindvoice vibrated with barely harnessed violence. She wanted to just level the entire building; such was her anger over Cole, and especially over Mina being taken.

{Be thorough, Kiltik. Cole and Mina are foremost, but I want to glean as much information from the building as we can before I destroy this place. I'll not let this place do any more harm,} Ales said.

{This One will record all possible information,} Kiltik replied.

Ales left him then. She slowed as she went to the end of the hallway. The facility was vast, and the mental map of the facility showed that there were people spread within, as well. This was far less help than she would have liked. There was no way to tell if any of them were Cole, though she did know that none of them were small enough to be Mina. There were dozens of the creatures laced throughout the four floors of the facility, and the layout seemed designed to intentionally confuse people moving through it. This was not uncommon for any well-designed prison, and many other facilities that needed to be defensible in a less than traditional way used a layout like this to help separate and isolate any invading force.

Ales made her slow way through the inky blackness of the facility. She stopped outside each pair of cells to examine the people within. She stopped to focus on each of them, and not all the cells were filled with people that belonged there. Reading the surface thoughts of a person was more difficult then peering through the thick wooden doors of their cells, but Ales managed it in most cases.

Reading a person's entire history was not something that she had the talent to do. Though some of the most talented Seers could extend their magic to do so, it was not within her power. Still, surface thoughts were enough in most cases. People in prisons tended to focus on what got them there enough to indicate whether or not they deserved to be there. Clearly, some of the people in the cells had done terrible things, but many just exuded a general malaise of confusion about how they had ended up where they were. She would free those who deserved to be free, and the rest she would deal with later.

{Ales, This One has an idea for what to do with our current bondstruct stores,} Kiltik said into her mind.

{I'm sure it's an excellent idea, Kiltik, but please hold it until after we have retrieved our wayward Taker?} Ales' mindvoice was exasperated.

{Yes, Arcangineer.} Kiltik's mindvoice held clear amusement.

Ales thoroughly searched the entire floor, which took some time. The hallways doubled back, and by the time she was done clearing the floor, she was nowhere near any of the stairwells. Surprisingly, she didn't encounter any more of the creatures. Perhaps Blight realized that it had no chance to stop her. She smashed a hole in the floor down to the next level. She paused for a moment to tap the hilt of her Windblade against the wall after she had dropped down. The map of this level showed that the cells here were more secure than above. They had thick bondsteel doors with single-sided locking mechanisms. Here, she did not take the time to scan surface thoughts. From the occupants of the first floor, she knew that everyone here would have to be reviewed. That was when she heard a noise.

Something small was moving through the hallways towards her at a fast pace. They were coming from both sides, at least a dozen creatures. She spun and whipped her Windblade down the hall in one direction. The blast of wind that came from the weapon was bone crushing. It carried the half dozen things approaching her back down the hallway in a flash, slamming them into the wall at the end of the hallway. None of them rose, and she slid the Windblade back into her coat. When she turned back, the remaining half dozen were almost on top of her.

They looked like large breed hiluk with stocky bodies and six strongly muscled legs each. Her Vision told her these were a different form of the creatures than she had fought outside. These were made of several layers of interlocking bondstructs, unlike the ones outside that had been roughly human shaped and had bodies made of a single pool of bondstructs. The design of these made it clear that the Blight was attempting to find technologies that would allow it to effectively fight the Tier. The principle here was that the layered construction would allow the creature to function even after the first layer had been destroyed. Against another of the Tier, it would have actually been somewhat effective. However, her ability with Breaking went far deeper. She could see where to hit them to cause a chain reaction that would destabilize their entire system.

The first one lept at her, and she ducked beneath it. The second of the small pack anticipated her dodge and was already in the air. She stood up, launching the first one towards the stone ceiling at speed. She drew her Windblade in a blur and smashed it into the face of the next one. Her follow-through knocked it to one side, into another of the pack. They slammed into the wall to her right. She let her body follow her swing, spinning to the right. The fourth one passed her harmlessly. She jumped, and the fifth of the creatures slid beneath her. She landed on its back, slamming her foot into a precise spot to one side of what should have been its spine. The creature disintegrated into a pile of black and silvery dust. The last of the creatures ran head-first into her fist. She completed the punch, driving the creature violently down the hallway through an explosion of bondstruct dust. The spot she had hit on its head had shattered only its outermost layer. The creature was slightly smaller when it hit the wall.

She cursed herself for a moment when she realized she'd hit the derivative break points instead of the primary deconstructor. If Blight was monitoring the data coming from these, it would know that it was at least partially successful. Then she grinned at a stray thought. If she made sure to destroy the rest of them in one hit, then the creature might think that the one she had missed on was special in some way when it really wasn't.

She forced open her constraints back to the fifth level, and everything seemed to slow down to another degree entirely. Levels of constraints were not a linear progression, but rather somewhat multiplicative. The jump between her fourth and fifth level was immense. She dodged to the left, and as the automaton passed her, she smashed her fist into the vulnerable spot to one side of its spine. The creature shattered, and she backed across the hallway giving her a wall to her back. She could also see the remaining four creatures.

The other six had not recovered, and Ales wondered if she had been more forceful than she had thought with her Windblade. The compact space of the hallway may have multiplied the force of the wind. She didn't have much time to consider as the remaining four creatures came in like a hunting pack. Their intent was clearly to attack her from multiple directions, making it impossible for her dodge. The smaller dull silver automaton jumped first.

This one she smashed with the spine of her Windblade. She turned it to strike another of the derivative break points which caused its second layer to shatter when it hit the stone floor. The second one was the one that ended up behind her when she turned to strike the first. This one landed on her back, and she whipped her entire body around, dodging the third one that came in from her left. She crushed the body of the one on her back between herself and the wall. When she stepped away, she spun to the right and slammed her elbow into the spot on its side near the spine. It blew apart into a cloud of black and dull grey metal fragments that immediately dropped into a pile on the floor.

Two quick swipes of her Windblade shattered the remaining automatons, save the small one that had been partially destroyed. She raised her Windblade and faced the remaining synthoid. It turned tail and darted down the hallway as fast as it could manage. She could have caught it, but she hoped that it had taken her bait and was trying to preserve the one that had survived.

She slid her Windblade into her coat and turned down hallway in the direction she had sent the blast of wind at the beginning of the fight. She could see that her wind had scoured the hallway, and the other synthetic animals had hit the wall with such force that they had been utterly obliterated. Ales shook her head. She was certain to have damaged the compression chambers along the length of the blade.

"Father's Stones, I didn't mean to push the weapon that hard."

She paused for a moment and examined the weapon with her Vision. Sure enough, it was showing signs that maintenance would be necessary. She sighed in annoyance, and continued her search of the floor.

40

Warran touched the interface panel in the large machine that Kiltik had constructed on one side of the workshop. It was designed to allow him to make large quantities of self-aware bondstructs. These were somewhat harder to work with because they had their own ideas about how to do things, but they were immune to energetic infections. The interface panel lit up and Tieran script began to run across the panel, indicating different things that he could request the machine to do. He touched the option indicating that it should start production on a new stockpile of bondstructs. The machine had only been finished a span earlier and already, it had produced hundreds of millions of bondstructs. Ales said they should stockpile as many as they could in the days to come. He wasn't sure what she was planning to do with so many.

He began to notice a sensation in the back of his mind that had gone unnoticed while he was working with the bondstruct manufactury. The bracelet around his wrist was pulsing, giving him a sense that Kayna was feeling very frightened. Warran dashed out of the workshop, heading for the courtyard behind it. He opened his Vision as he burst through the door.

The double doors to the street had been broken down. Somehow, someone had managed to cut the hinges on them. Still, the defenses had incapacitated two of the people who had tried to breech. The alarms should have gone off. He had no idea how they had bypassed them. That wasn't important now. These men were in heavy plate armor with few weak spots. The armor was not made of bondstructs, but it had a telltale design that made him think of Bondarmor. Each man carried a lancer of odd design.

Warran startled when glowing letters started to appear in his Vision, giving him data on what he was seeing. The weapons were long bondsteel swords sporting thick crossguards with turned up quillions. The armor had been lacquered green with a broad white stripe running down the chest and between the legs. He had never seen soldiers like these before. They certainly were not the Ryhim. One of them was carrying a struggling Kayna. The second one came from behind the stables, carrying Manat. The little boy seemed unsure as to what he should be doing.

Lines of light appeared in Warran's sight, indicating weak points in the armor. It was not Breaking. He could not begin to achieve the kind of destruction Ales would visit upon these poor fools. To his Fixer abilities though, the armor was just a simple machine. Well within that magic's ability to understand. The only weakness that his lancer would penetrate properly, though, was the eye slit across the front of their green-lacquered barbute helms.

He froze for a long moment. They had not noticed him yet, and his knees went weak with the rememberance of the pain he had felt in Vilhena when killing the soldiers who had come to take he and his daughter. He had left his Sparks inside in his haste and there was no more time. They would notice him at any second. He struggled with the knowledge of what it would feel like if he had to kill these men. He couldn't be useless again. The words he had not said yet echoed inside of his mind.

"Kill him," the man holding Kayna said.

{I shall protect those who cannot protect themselves.}

The words echoed inside of his mind and broke his indecision. The gain was worth the cost. He drew his lancers. He pointed one at the man holding Kayna and the other at the man holding Manat. There were half a dozen men in total, and the ones not holding children drew their swords.

"You will not take those children," Warran's voice held calm certainty.

The four unoccupied men stepped forward. Their armor began to shimmer like a heat haze, and then they vanished from sight. Clearly, that was how they had passed the Ryhim, but it was a poor imitation of what Cole or Lia could do with Taking. It took only a moment for his Vision to pick out the disturbances in the air as they moved. His Cellstructs began to overlay his Vision with shadowy figures, showing exactly what the men were doing. Warran lined up his shots. He thought about killing the men holding the kids first, but it was clear that if he did that, the remaining men might split off and grab them. He didn't want any of them to get away.

The first man came forward, holding his sword high. Warran raised his lancer and squeezed the trigger in one smooth motion. To his amazement, the bolt ricocheted off of some sort of perfectly clear material that covered the eye slit of the helmet. He hadn't noticed it in his cursory inspection, but his Cellstructs pointed it out to him now. Whatever it was it was obviously extremely strong to deflect a shot from a lancer. Still, no material that was clear enough to see through that easily had the proper density and tensile strength to take repeated hits to the same spot.

The man had obviously trained with the armor extensively as he didn't flinch back when the bolt bounced off of the visor over his eye slot. Warran jumped back as he swung the sword. What amazed him was that the impact from the lancer bolt did not seem to have any effect, either. Usually even wearing armor that could stop a lancer bolt was not complete protection from the impact. Clearly, this armor was reinforced for such things. He wanted badly to examine how the armor functioned, but he didn't have time for that now. His back hit the wall of the workshop, but he didn't hesitate. He hadn't had much time to adjust to his new levels of strength, but he could easily jump over these men. Before he did, he wanted to make sure his theory about the visors was correct.

He raised his lancer and snapped off three quick shots. Each one was perfectly aimed to strike the exact same spot on the first man's visor. The first shot pinged off the visor and the man continued forward. Warran moved to one side in a blur, but it wasn't fast enough. The man's sword cut a thin gash into his arm. The second shot resounded in a sharp crack. The third shot shattered the visor completely and smashed into the man's skull. He dropped like a stone. The rest of the men in the armor goggled at his body as it slumped inside of the armor. Warran tried to brace himself for the pain as it struck his mind like a hammer.

Then he saw his daughter struggling to free herself from the grasp of an invisible captor. The pain didn't diminish, but it became less important. He mentally shoved it aside and raised his other lancer and fired off three perfect shots. He needed to make some room to work. They dropped the next man in line, and this time, when the pain crashed into his mind, it hit a buffer he had created. He realized that he had to endure the pain at some point, but now was not that time. The remaining two men seemed to realize that their armor wasn't nearly as effective as they had thought, and turned and ran.

Warran slid his lancers into their holsters and then felt woozy for a moment. He wobbled as a red warning flashed in the upper right corner of his vision. He focused on it, and the tiny red letters grew into a small paragraph of text. It indicated that he had been poisoned by the man's blade. His Cellstructs only knew what he knew plus some inbuilt knowledge from Icci. They could identify the chemical compound, but he had no idea what those words meant in Tieran. His study of the language had not extended to scientific terms, and even if it had, he likely did not know what the chemical was. It didn't matter.

All that mattered is that they were cleaning the poison from his blood and the cut was already being knitted. The men were getting away, and he would need a moment to steady himself enough to chase them. That was when Lia slid out of the back door in utter silence. She looked up to him. She saw the fear on his face, and the anger, and the pain.

"It is time. Follow as quickly as you can. I'll bring them down," Lia said. She moved to the door and snuffled around. She meant it was time for him to say the words.

"Are you up to it?" Warran asked.

"I will have to be. Freedom to those who have had freedom taken from them," Lia said and trotted off into the night.

Warran sat down and thought about the words. They had appeared in his head as if he had known them all of his life, but he knew that if he said them, one day it might force him to chose between his duty and his daughter. That was a choice that he wasn't sure he was prepared to make.

The red warning overlayed on his field of vision lightened to pink, and then a moment later to white. The text changed to let him know that the poison had been cleared from his system. He stood up, and Ilsa came through the door.

"Can I help?" Ilsa asked.

Warran shook his head. "I think it would be best if you finished what you're working on. Lia and I should be able to handle this."

Ilsa's eyes lightened to two bright points of illumination in the dark, one blue, one amber.

"Something is different about this. The men outside are not in bondarmor. Did they hire some Ryhim to attack us? If so, how did they know that the defenses were so dangerous? These men are not from Vilhena, or from any of the Ryhim clans."

Warran shook his head. "And their armor is something else entirely. It bends light to make them invisible. Think you can repair the doors while we're out?"

She turned her eyes towards the doors. After a long moment, she nodded. "I don't like all these unanswered questions. I feel so unprepared for what's happening, like the whole world is starting fires around us and we're just putting them out instead of stopping the people starting them," Ilsa complained.

Warran nodded once more. "I feel the same way, but right now it's all we can do. Our numbers are too small to do anything more."

Warran shook himself and then dashed off through the doors after Lia. He didn't want to let her get too far ahead. She herself had said she would not be fully recovered for days yet. It didn't take him long to catch up with Lia. She hadn't waited for him, but she was only trotting. She had their scents now. There would be no escape for them.

"They're not far," Lia said.

"I can take them," Warran replied.

She nodded. "Of that, I have no doubt, but now that we are both here, we won't need to. I want to know who these men are. They are not from Vilhena, and they are not Ryhim.

While I am certain that the creature has allies the world over, I am not sure that is what we are encountering here." Lia's voice was full of annoyance. "As if there need be one more thing for us to deal with at this point."

"What makes you think this isn't the Intruder?" Warran asked, increasing pace out of worry for Kayna.

"The armor is reminiscent of a technology that we released 180 cycles before the cataclysm. On the shores of the Stormvale, it is impossible to make glass that is sufficient to withstand the rotational wind storms, so we taught them to make wall sections that would bend light. This allowed them to have windows that were of sufficient strength to weather the storms."

Lia trotted down the street, picking up speed as Warran seemed to be getting a better feel for his increased strength. They caught up with the men carrying the children a few minutes later. Lia circled around in front of them by taking an alleyway at top speed. The men turned a corner and found her sitting in the middle of the path, her eyes glowing with her Vision.

The four men skidded to a stop. They were well-trained and did not hesitate. The two not carrying children came to the front, drawing their swords. She was somewhat surprised that they did not pull the lancers to fire at her. Maybe the men thought that the poison on their blades would aid them, but the Tier had spent intervals making sure that poison would be less than effective against them. Once Warran's Cellstructs were fully integrated with him, they would do the same.

"Who are you?" Lia enunciated each word carefully. The men did not startle. They simply came forward, the swords held in a ready posture. "You have no chance of defeating me, and if you did, my companion would cut you down before he let you take his child from him. I sense somehow that you feel you are doing something correct, and while I have no idea how you found us, I would rather know why you are attempting to take these children from their rightful place."

The two men took quick steps forward and swung their swords. Lia took one perfect step back. The swords missed her completely and clanged into each other.

"This is your last chance to see reason. I can tell from the workings of your minds that you understand my language," Lia said.

The men came forward again. This time, they attempted to attack at an angle from each side. She rolled her eyes and took a step to one side, letting a sword swing pass. Then she spun in a circle, smashing the off-balance soldier into his companion. The second sword clanged loudly off the man's armor as Lia used him as an impromptu shield. It was so odd. When she looked into these men's minds, she didn't see murderous intent, nor did she find any sort of chaotic influence that would mean that they killed for senseless reasons. She saw only fear and resolve.

{These men are not working for the creature that they know of. They are here for another reason. I don't know what,} Lia said into the mental link.

{I killed two of their companions. I highly doubt they are going to listen to reason,} Warran replied bitterly.

The sympathetic pain of those deaths was still clawing at him, but he was holding it at bay. Warran stayed back from the fight. Once again, they had not noticed him, but this time it was because Lia was drawing all of their attention. She dodged the men almost politely, and it quickly became clear that they couldn't even touch her, much less harm her.

{This is getting us nowhere. If they will not talk, we'll have to capture at least one of them to find out what is going on here,} Lia said.

{What about the others?} Warran asked.

{Take the two with the children. Do not kill them yet.}

Warran felt uncomfortable leaving her behind if she still wasn't in full fighting form, but she didn't seem to be having any trouble with the men. Finally, after dodging a few more swings of the sword, she drove forward. She hit one of the men with her shoulder, smashing him into the stone wall surrounding a house on one side of the road. The wall cracked from the impact, and Warran heard the telltale clang of the man's skull rattling on the inside of his helmet. The man slumped to the ground, unconscious. The second man stepped up behind Lia and lunged smoothly with his sword. She sidestepped, and the point of the man's sword slammed into the stone wall, sending stone chips flying. Lia circled around behind the man and he spun to face her, sword held high.

{Did I have to kill those men earlier?} Warran's mindvoice was somber.

{You didn't make that choice. They did,} Lia responded with confidence.

Lia dodged back in forth in a pattern designed to decive the eye, and the second man lunged again. Warran examined the armor. It had odd locking clamps holding it in place. Both helmets had two clamps, one on each side where it attached to the pauldron. They were nearly impossible to see, but they showed up in his Vision easily. The clamps were recessed, making it difficult to unlatch them. Warran didn't bother trying to reach for them. He aimed carefully and took two precise shots. He was standing to their left, so the bolts hit the clamps on the left side of the armor. Much weaker than the armor itself, the clamps shattered. He was already moving when they turned to look at him, and much faster than he could have ever moved before. In a blur, he was on the other side of them. He fired two more shots, shattering the remaining clamps.

Each man dropped the child they were holding. Kayna and Manat hit the ground. At some point, the men had stopped to bind them hand and foot. Immediately, Kayna began to struggle against her ropes. Manat, though, didn't seem to know what to do. It was odd that he didn't react with a higher level of panic. Maybe he had been knocked unconscious. Warran stayed behind the two men as they drew their own lancers and tried to find him.

He spun his Lancers in his hands and used each one as an improvised club. He used the grips to knock each man's helmet off. They were well-trained, spinning calmly and lifting their lancers. As soon as they faced him, Warran smashed the grips of his lancers into each man's forhead. They began to fall backwards. Warran holstered his lancers in a blur and caught each man by the collar of their chestplate so that they wouldn't fall onto the children. He yanked them forward and let them fall onto their faces. He knelt and found he had been right about Manat. The young boy was unconscious. He took a knife from the sheath on his belt.

"I tried, Daddy, but they were so strong." Kayna seemed more angry than upset.

"I know, Kayna. I know you did. You did good."

Warran cut the ropes at her wrists and ankles. Kayna got to her feet and balled her little hands into fists when she looked at the men. The look on her face was cold and hard, even though tears were streaming down her cheeks. Warran did not like it at all. He hugged her to his chest for a moment.

"You're safe. Will you cut Manat loose?"

He handed her the knife, and she nodded. That was the best way to help Kayna. Give her something to do so she didn't feel useless.

A clatter rang out. Lia had knocked the sword from the man's hand. He went for his lancer and she lifted her paw in a blur. Her claws sliced through the belt holding his lancer and it fell away out of his reach. She gave him a small push with her shoulder, and the man fell onto his back. She climbed atop him and sat on his legs with her middle set of paws on the sides of his torso. She laid down and clicked her claws into the clamps holding his helmet in place with a pert, jerky motion. She pushed off his helmet and bared her teeth a bare finger-length from his face.

Warran looked around, but the rest of the men were down. At some point at least two more had come into the fray. He hadn't noticed being so occupied with the children. Only three of them were left alive. Something had changed. Lia had gone from merely angry to a cold fury. She had seen something that made her judge these men guilty of crimes enough to merit their deaths.

"Now, let us resume our parlay," Lia said with a ripping growl of fury in her voice.

41

Repairing the doors had not taken Ilsa very long. A little help from the mavae to hold the doors up while she fastened new hinges was all it had taken. She had gone back to her work in the the shop with some reluctance. Warran and Lia were more than capable of handling a few men in fancy armor, so she wasn't truly worried about what would happen with the children. They would get them back. What worried her was that Ales and Kiltik had been gone for almost a full day now. Ales had expressed to her the urgency of completing the device. The problem was, she wasn't sure how to do what Ales had asked her to do.

Making the outer shell for the device of Sol alloy had been fairly simple with Kiltik to help her. Ales had given her the schematics for the device and assured her that it would work. A proper piece of crystal to put inside had taken her an hour and several Lightjumps to find. Warran had given her one of the solar cells that he had made for lancers and showed her how to get energy from it. The rest was up to her.

The device was fairly simple. It was a hollow sphere of Sol alloy, about three times the size of her fist. It was split down the middle to allow her to work inside of it. Inside, formed into the metal, were two cavities. One was a place that the solar cell would fit perfectly into. The second was a place for the crystal to fit securely. Her task was to build a small device that would be powered by the solar cell and when turned on, would give off the natural light of the sun. Ales had said it had to be exact, and to do it properly, she would need to push her Vision all the way down to the sub-atomic level.

Ilsa had practiced zooming her Vision all the way down to that level, and while she could accomplish it, the act quickly gave her a pounding headache. Worse, she didn't have much time to work with. Ales had told her she should finish it as quickly as possible and bring it to the prison as soon as it was done. She had followed the schematic and constructed the device, and the two tiny emitter panels had been fitted into their slots on either side of the crystal. She had constructed the elementary energy transmitter and placed it between the solar cell and the piece of crystal. Four braided wires coated in an insulating material ran from the transmitter to the emitter panels, two to each panel. Two wires ran from the emitter to the contact points on the top of the solar cell. She could see the power running along the wires with her Vision when she triggered the transmitter, but the panels were not giving off the light properly.

She leaned back, folding her hands in her lap and staring into the device with an anxious look on her face. She remembered then that she had some help. She queried her Cellstructs for what the problem might be. Immediately, information flashed in her field of vision. The wires were highlighted in two colors. Three of the wires were blue, three were red. Tieran script ran across the top of her vision, explaining that the order in which the wires were attached to the contact points was important.

"Could it really be that simple?" Ilsa mumbled to herself. Surprisingly, her Cellstructs answered her with an incredibly complex explanation of the directional flow of elementary energy. She didn't understand the full explanation, but she laughed to herself. "Fair enough, it isn't simple." She carefully detached the wires and rearranged them per the instruction of her Cellstructs.

{*This One wonders what that one is creating?*} Icci asked into their mental connection.

{*I'm not entirely sure what it's for. Ales said she needs it right away,*} Ilsa replied.

She triggered the transmitter once again, and the two panels started to emit a warm light into the crystal. The two halves of the sphere were made so that they would interlock with a twist. The trigger on the outside of the device was a point that created a neural interface by touch. Only a Tier could mentally trigger the device to work.

{*This One can infer from the design that the crystalline matrix seems to concentrate the light,*} Icci said.

{*But what good is that?*} Ilsa wondered.

{This One is not certain what such a device could be used for. This One does not think that Alessandra Family Katane would have set you to create this device without reason.}

Ilsa twisted the two halves of the sphere together, and they locked into place. She sighed. She was still exhausted, but she was better off than Lia had been. She would be able to get into the prison without much issue, but she would have felt better if she didn't have to go alone. A bang came from the door downstairs. Ilsa put the device into a small hide satchel and attached it to her belt. She exited the room, went downstairs, and then walked across the lower floor of the workshop. She went to the door and pulled it open.

Standing behind the door was Warran, Kayna, and Manat. She stepped back out of the way and let them enter. Warran's face was extremely hard, like a wall of stone. He looked to be in great pain, and she realized he had been forced to kill someone. How she knew, she had no idea. Killing another human wasn't something she had experienced yet, and she hoped it was a long way off for her.

"Who were those men?" Ilsa asked.

"We don't know yet. They refused to talk, surprisingly, even after Lia was most persuasive, and even when they realized that they were not going to survive the night. I thought Lia had been angry with Cole when we first met, but that was like a candle next to the bonfire that I saw tonight. She said that she would find out where they had come from another way. I didn't stay to watch, but I think she may have bitten that last man's head off. His scream cut off rather abruptly. She said that she had a sense that you would need me, and that I should come back," Warran said.

Ilsa tilted her head in a motion that many of them seemed to have somehow picked up from Lia. It was a question. "I'm not sure I've done this right. When I look at the light particles, they seem to be identical to natural sunlight, but considering Ales did not tell me what this device is for, I have no idea if I've done it right."

"Show me the schematics," Warran said. His mental handshake was a sound like a small metal tool breaking. Ilsa grinned.

{*It's a sound that will absolutely get my attention,*} Warran said hearing her surface amusement in his mind.

{*True enough.*}

Ilsa sent him the schematic. He nodded, and she took out the device and handed it to him. They broke the mental connection.

"Now, my Vision is not strong enough to allow me to examine the particles coming out of the emitters here, but what I can do is tell you if you have constructed the device exactly as the schematic called for."

Warran touched the security contact on the outside of the device and the shell unlocked. He twisted it, and it popped open. He opened his Vision and examined the the emitters. He took a small metal pick from a small hide case on his belt. He prodded the inner workings of the device and activated the elementary energy transmitter. Light bloomed, and the crystal glowed brightly with it. Warran followed the process backwards, and moments later, held the device out to Ilsa.

"It is perfect," Warran said. "It functions exactly to schematic. We'll have you building a Windblade in no time, young Fixer." Warran grinned when Ilsa blushed. Warran's face then turned serious.

"Do you think you can get it to her?" Warran looked like he wanted to offer help, but then he looked down at the children.

"I am no Taker, but I think I can manage it."

"Just, don't kill anyone." Warran grimaced.

"You seem to be doing better," Ilsa said.

Warran nodded. "It still hurts, but I'll not hold myself responsible for the decisions that other people make any longer."

Ilsa slid the device back into the pouch at her waist. She donned her long black coat from the rack. It hung down past her knees, hiding her skirts. The coat had many pockets on the inside containing a variety of tools. Every one of the Tier developed an affinity for the equipment they carried over time. Hers had been secreted away into the coat over the previous cycle and change. He was surprised that she didn't wear it more often. He thought after her ordeal with Lia, she probably would from now on. She folded the front of the jacket over itself and it stuck closed. It had a bondstruct closure that allowed her to open the jacket through mental command. This meant that it was easy to use it to hide her weapons, her clothing, and to a certain extent, her gender if she chose to wear a hat.

"I had an idea," she said as she finished checking her coat.

"Oh?" Warran asked.

"I think we could make clothing that will stand up to lancer bolts. We could infuse the cloth with bondstructs made of Sol alloy. We could instruct them so that when a lancer bolt hits them, they interlock in reaction to the movement energy."

Warran eyed her for a long moment. "That is... brilliant." Warran's awe was clear in his voice.

"Thank you, but I think I'll need your help to actually make it happen. It's beyond my current Fixer abilities to conceptualize a machine that could produce cloth like that."

"Mine too, but I think Kiltik can help us both."

"I'd better get going."

"Not quite yet," Lia said as she came through the door. "There is something you can do to make our lives a little easier. You can help Warran say the words." Lia's voice was solemn. Warran looked to her.

"I would be honored," Ilsa said.

Lia opened her Vision and looked Warran over to make sure his injuries had healed properly. He was free of all injury and poison. His Cellstructs were functioning extremely well. She started to look away, not feeling particularly happy that she had killed those men. She had looked into them, though, and they were steeped in the blood of innocent people; people they had killed because of their own personal beliefs. To those men, their belief was more important than the truth, so they had killed without question. She still wasn't sure they were not connected to creature, and her Vision was not strong enough to invade their deeper thoughts. It was a mystery that she would need to tell Ales about, and they would have to solve it together. Then her eye caught on something Ilsa had attached to her belt. Her gold and orange gaze glowed with her Vision, and then went very wide.

"What is that?" Lia used her nose to touch the pouch at Ilsa's side.

"I'm not sure. Ales gave me the schematics to build it, but she didn't tell me what it was," Ilsa explained.

"Gods all around us is that what I think it is?" Lia asked. Ilsa took the device out of the pouch. She unlocked it and twisted it open again. "But no one ever made one work," Lia said as she examined the internals.

"It was fairly simple to make," Ilsa said with confusion.

Lia shook her head. "We have to be quick. If Ales had you make this, then she is sure it will work. If she is sure it'll work, then she needs it badly. Get out your Lightleaf."

Ilsa's face became even more confused. She fished in an inner pocket through the neck of her jacket. Her hand came out with the crystal leaf a moment later.

"Alright, trigger the device and then use it like it's an exposed crystal to make a Lightjump back to the Traveler's Grove."

"I'm so confused," Ilsa complained.

"Ilsa, what you are holding is legend even to the Tier. It is a Lightgate. If it works properly, it will allow you to transport back to the Traveler's Grove no matter where you are. No one could ever make an emitter that produced a perfect replication of the sun's energetic particles, so no one could ever make a working Lightgate." Lia's voice was awed. She held up a paw and touched a single digit to the device.

"You too, Warran," Lia said. He touched the device, and Ilsa held up her leaf. There was a bright flash of light, and they appeared in the Traveler's grove. Lia gasped in astonishment.

"She did it," Lia whispered. She made a whooping sound of pure enjoyment and both Ilsa and Warran jumped. "She

did it!" Lia roared in laughter. She composed herself a
moment later.

"Let us induct Warran," Lia said.

The ceremony was short, but it left Warran overwhelmed
just as it had Ilsa. They had seated a large crystal at the
workshop behind the stables where the sun would shine on it
every day. Lia activated the Lightjump to get them back.
Then she scolded them both not to overuse the Lightleaf trees
as if she hadn't been the one to make the jumps.

"But you were the one who did it," Ilsa complained.

Lia scowled mightily at her.

"She has a point. Besides, didn't the Father tell us that the
stored energy in the Lightleaf trees was nearly limitless at this
point after three thousand cycles of disuse?" Warran said.

Lia rolled her eyes. "Fine, yes, he did. But near limitless is
not limitless. If we did more than a hundred or so Lightjumps
in a day, the trees would start to die, but we grew the grove
and began to use it as soon as it was strong enough. We never
even knew that they <u>could</u> store energy over long periods of
time like that. Go on with you. Ales has been gone for an
entire day. If she doesn't already need you, she will soon."
Lia shooed her out the door. "There is a crystal near the
prison. It's stoneward of the prison about a quarter length.
Use it."

Ilsa opened her mouth to rib her a bit more about scolding
them on the use of the Lightleaf trees. Lia gave her a look that
shut her mouth. Ilsa slid her leaf back out of the inner pocket
and hurried out into the courtyard.

"Are you sure she'll be alright?" Warran asked.

Lia shook her head. "No, but someday soon, you all are
going to have to work on your own without us. She needs the
experience that we don't have the time to give her partnered
with one of us. Neither Ales nor I like to do this.
Unfortunately, we don't have the luxury of hundreds of Tier
and Arcangineers to train you all the way you should be
trained." Lia's voice was seeded with deep regret.

"You don't think we are all going to make it, do you." It
wasn't a question, but Lia answered it anyways.

"No, Warran. I know we will not all make it through this. I am frantically trying not to think about the fact that even when we were strong, we still lost Arcangineers and Tier in dangerous situations." Lia's voice and expression were laced with remorse.

"We chose this, Lia. You didn't choose for us."

Lia sighed. She turned and headed down the hallway towards the room that she and Ales shared. Warran remembered something Lia had said to him after he had killed the soldiers in Vilhena. No one could convince her that she had done something right by taking them into the family of the Tier. She had to convince herself.

42

Ales had cleared three of the four floors. Upon getting to the fourth floor, she found that it was partitioned off into two dozen massive rooms. Each one had a single person inside. Peering through the walls had been useless because the construction was designed specifically to interfere with her Vision. Different densities of materials had been layered on the inside of the walls of each room. It made it impossible to look through the walls, but having seen Cole's scent trail before, it did not take her long to find the correct cell.

She eyed the door. This one was just a large slab of rock that slid into place from a channel in the ceiling. She thought about just destroying it, but something told her she should be more subtle here. She examined the wall for a moment then paced along it, using Breaking to find the right sort of weak point. The spot she was looking for was about knee height, and she crouched down to peer at it. She touched the spot very carefully, and a hole the width of her fingertip appeared as the stone was turned to dust. She cupped her hands around the hole and very gently blew air through it to clear the dust.

Through the hole, she could see the situation. Cole was strapped to a chair with thick hide belts. Around his neck was a wide collar. She squinted and discovered that it was made of Black Sol. Ales grimaced. She couldn't get a fix on what that collar was supposed to do, but she guessed it wouldn't be good. Then something else caught her eye, something so terrible that she almost gave herself away with her gasp.

Sitting near the back of the cell cloaked in the shadows was a miniaturized version of the device that had destroyed Ahal. It was a device that collected antimatter until there was too much to maintain the elementary force field separating the antimatter from the matter. She wasn't sure that the original device that Alizar had built was designed as a weapon. The information they had on the device was incomplete as the Tier had only had about a day to examine the device before it had exploded. This one, on the other hand, certainly was.

She examined the configuration of the machine. The solar cell powering the device was also there. It was the largest solar energy container she had ever seen outside of the central collector in Ahal, which had been the size of a building. This one took up at least half the large room. Blight must have built a collector panel somewhere outside to feed the massive solar cell. There was no way it could have been exposed to enough light or heat down here to charge it properly.

"We go to destroy your friends even now. Unlock it for us and you can save them. You will unlock it for us even if your friends die." The black figure next to Cole was not like the others she had encountered as she swept the prison for Cole. This one had a human inside of it. It appeared to be an amalgamation of all of the technologies that they had encountered both here and in Vilhena.

Ales examined the man more closely. She quickly realized that there was no control interface between the armor and the man. It meant that the man was cooperating with the Blight of his own free will. The armor was just a way to enhance his strength and physical abilities. Ales gaped at the figures that came back when she queried her Cellstructs concerning the power of the armor he wore. It was a leap forward compared to the bondarmor they encountered in Vilhena.

There was more to see. At least a half dozen of the synthoids she had destroyed earlier were also standing at the back of the room. One of them in particular was unlike the others. It also contained a person, but this person was much smaller. She was bound by the body of the synthetic monster surrounding her. It was clearly Mina. Ales took a deep breath. This was a trap meant for her. She tried to compose a plan that could possibly resolve this situation. That was when she felt Kiltik's mental handshake. She sighed in relief.

{This One assumes from your anxiety that you have discovered a situation that you are not sure how to handle,} Kiltik said.

{We are not in a good situation here. I can handle this, but there are two things I need you to do. Otherwise, this is going to become a true massacre.} Ales' mindvoice was hard with anger. She quickly explained what she had seen in the room.

{We cannot clear this building, Kiltik. I fear if we do, the creature will set off the device, but there is a way we can save all of the people here. Gather them in the yard. The dawn is coming on so it is not terribly odd that all the prisoners be moved there. If Ilsa arrives in time, we should all be able to get out of here alive. I doubt the prison will survive this night, as when it realizes it cannot defeat me, it will attempt to set off the device. Breaking the device will only set it off, and even I am not fast enough to diffuse it before a signal arrives to disable the energetic field to release the antimatter. They are using elementary energy signals, which means you should be able to jam them for a short time. That will be the short time I need to destroy the minions of Blight, free Cole, and join you both in the yard. Ilsa will carry something that will get us all out of here before this place is destroyed.} Ales' mindvoice was worried as she laid out her plans.

{This One can jam all elementary energy signals in the area. This One does not know how long This One can maintain such a signal before This One will need to stop to repair the transmission capabilities of This One's body,} Kiltik replied.

His form melted from that of a katali into a small humanoid shape. The shape took on a more human appearance a moment later. Clothing appeared from his body to flow about his shape. A moment after that, a very human-looking man stood before her. He had tan skin and bright orange hair that hung to his shoulders. His clothing was a simple black tunic and pants. He was barefoot, but it somehow did not look out of place. The only real give-away that he was not human were the pupilless orange orbs that served as his eyes.

{I'm sure you will do the best you can. I think that you should take on the clothing of a guard. It'll make it easier to convince them that they should listen to you,} Ales said.

The clothing shifted from the plain black tunic and pants to the uniform that she had seen on the guards earlier: tight-fitting green pants with hide armor plates over his shins and thighs and a deep grey tunic covered by a hide chestplate. A moment later, a helmet formed around his head.

{Excellent. Give me a count of two hundred before you start jamming signals,} Ales said. Kiltik nodded and then trotted off silently down the hall.

Ales took a deep breath and gathered herself. She drew her Windblade and, increasing her concentration on Breaking, she rapped a knuckle on the door. It split with a loud crack both vertically and horizontally. The slabs of stone collapsed into the room. There was an earsplitting crash as the counterweight for the door crashed to the floor inside of the wall. She moved in blur, swinging her Windblade with rhythmic violence. Blasts of superheated air smashed four of the six synthoids to dust before the black figure that had been interrogating Cole appeared in front of her. Its fingers wrapped around her Windblade and attempted to wrench it from her grip. Ales just grinned and held onto the hilt of the blade as the man struggled with it.

"I was crushing corrupt armies for intervals before your parents were even thought of, Child," Ales challenged.

"And even then you were stale," he growled.

Ales slowly and deliberately pulled the Windblade screeching from his crushing grip.

"What's the matter, boy? Finding that what your master provided you is not all that it claimed?"

The man bore down on the Windblade even harder. Still it continued to slide from his grip under the sheer force that Ales was applying. She could see his eyes go wide through the helmet's visor. She reached behind her and pulled a throwing knife from a brace hanging from the back of her belt within her jacket. The man released the Windblade and jumped back.

One of the remaining synthoids slid between Ales and the man. It was the one that had Mina inside. Clearly, he intended to use her as a human shield. Ales lifted the knife and her hand whipped forward. The knife zipped past both of them and struck the thick metal collar around Cole's neck. A sharp metallic sound resounded through the room and the collar shattered. The knife spun end over end and landed perfectly in Cole's lap. Both of her opponents turned toward him as he grabbed the knife with his bound left hand.

"Over here," Ales gibed.

She slashed her Windblade forward, blowing both the man and the synthoid across the room. She was careful to control the power of the wind so that Mina would not be damaged. They skidded to a stop before they hit the opposite wall, but it was already too late to stop Cole. He spun the knife in his hand and cut the bonds on his left wrist. Then, he quickly slashed at the rest of his bonds and stood. He staggered for a moment, clearly injured, but then he steadied. He came towards her and then stood beside. She leaned over and whispered in his ear.

"I am sorry, Cole. Your work is not done this night. Make your way upstairs and find Kiltik." Ales slid the small pack off of her back where she had slung it. She handed it to him. "Your things are inside. I'll take care of this, but you must go."

Cole looked stubborn for a moment, but then he looked back at the the three figures still remaining in the room. He knew he was not ready to fight these things. "Sorry I caused so much trouble." He slung the pack over his shoulder and turned to go.

"Everyone makes mistakes, Cole, but you didn't make one here. Go up to the prison yard. Kiltik will be waiting for you there." Ales gripped his shoulder for a moment in a gesture of comfort, but her eyes never left their opponents.

"You know they have the girl?" Cole asked very quietly.

Ales nodded.

Cole got through the rubble of the door, and then one of the two synthoids darted forward after him. Ales' structures had marked that one as the one that did not contain Mina. She let it pass, because while Cole was probably not ready to fight these things hand to hand, his lancers would be more than a match for it. He needed to get some of his confidence back.

Ales slid her Windblade into the scabbard inside of her coat. The armor the man was wearing made him more durable than she was, but it did not make him stronger. Further, the layers of the armor made it very difficult to find any points weak enough to penetrate with Breaking. It had a self repairing nature. Ales raised her fists into a guard position and darted forward. The synthoid attempted to interpose itself between her and the man in armor. She had anticipated this, and spun to one side. The creature's arm became a blade and it slashed at her. It was too slow and the blade passed by her.

Ales came at the armored man from the side and threw a punch at the left hand side of his face. His arm came up, and there was a deep thud when her fist struck his arm. The armor protected him, but he had severely underestimated the force behind her blow. It blew him off of his feet and slammed him violently into the opposite wall. He gasped out a breath and slid to the floor. Ales completed the motion, diving smoothly into a forward roll when the synthoid attempted to take advantage of her change in balance from the punch.

She came up and immediately spun to her left when her Cellstructs warned her that the armored man had drawn a blade. He executed a perfect thrust that went right through the air where she had been standing. Abruptly, he twisted the blade in a motion designed to fool the eye. Ales danced quickly out of the way, but the blade sliced through her shirt and left a line of bright blue blood across her ribs.

She growled in anger and pushed open the fourth level of her constraints. The shallow cut knitted itself closed almost immediately and Ales took two quick steps away before the synthoid, coming up from behind, could strike at her again. She danced backwards to give herself some space and examined the synthoid again. She could see that the creature was changing the position that Mina occupied within its body. Now she was being held spread-eagled with her legs inside of the legs of the creature and her arms stretched towards its shoulders.

She couldn't strike the creature in such a way as to destroy it without damaging Mina as well, so she disregarded the creature for now. If she wanted to get outside in time to save everyone that Kiltik was gathering, she couldn't leave this man behind to trigger the device as soon as she was out of sight. She had no more time to waste. Then she saw the elementary energy waves flowing through the room, disrupting the signals running between the armor and the device at the back of the room. The man in the armor recovered himself.

"You cannot find it without us, and we will not give it to you! You will unlock it for us. This world is ours, now. You cannot return it to what it was. You are dead! Why will you not admit it?!" The man was clearly repeating words being fed to him through the armor somehow.

"Do I detect fear, Blight? I will not yield, not to you, nor to your puppet. You have proven yourself mad and hellbent on our destruction or enslavement. I will allow neither. Protect those who cannot protect themselves." Ales said the admonition with conviction.

The man waved off the synthoid and held his blade up in a challenge. The synthoid walked toward the exit. The tone of the fight had changed. Before, it had felt like they were trying to stall, but now it seemed as if the creature wanted to escape with Mina. Ales could not stop it and fight the man without risking harming Mina. She needed to be able to focus her whole attention on the creature if she were to extract the girl without harm. Sure enough, as the android reached the door, it blurred into a run. So she did the only thing she could. She pushed open the fifth level of her constraints and dashed towards the retreating thing as fast as she could.

Neither the man nor the synthoid were prepared for her speed. She struck the creature precisely on one of the derivative break points on its back. Her fist penetrated through the outer layers until her knuckles just brushed against Mina's skin. In that split second, she transferred some of her Cellstructs into Mina's body. If it somehow managed to get past Kiltik, Cole, and Ilsa, there would be no escape. She would find the girl by tracking her own living Cellstructs and free her. The synthetic monster tumbled away to fetch up against the opposite wall of the hallway. It immediately lept up, the hole in its back closing almost as quickly as she made it. It darted away down the hallway, and she let it go.

She turned back to the man. He was running towards the antimatter device. Ales shot across the room, appearing between him and the device in a flurry of motion. She smashed the wrist of the hand holding his short sword. The sword flew from his hand and skittered away across the floor.

"It cannot be returned to the world without us!" the man shouted.

Ales just drew her Windblade. With growing disquiet, she realized that the 'it' that the creature kept shouting about was The Core. She thought for a moment about how to respond. She decided it might be best to let the Blight think that perhaps she might need it. She latched onto the ridge between the chestplate and the helmet of the man's armor. She lifted him from the ground and held him in the air effortlessly. His feet swung a mark off the floor.

"You cannot keep me from The Core. Where have you hidden it?" Ales growled.

The man just laughed. "Only we speak the language of the Void. Once we have unlocked its secrets, you will be nothing!"

Ales pulled the helmet closer to her face, and grinned. "You need us to unlock it, and we will never help you."

In response, the man slammed his fist into her left side. She locked her muscles, but the damage had been done. Broken ribs punctured her lung. She gasped, but did not release the man.

"Enough!" she screamed.

The pain of her ribs was nothing in the face of her fury. She spun violently in a circle. She pushed her constraints open to the sixth level, increasing her strength substantially. She whipped the man through the air and threw him at the wall of the room next to the exit. She did not think it would kill him, the armor was far too strong for that, but he was unlikely to remain conscious through the impact. His body smashed into the stone wall with a thunderous crash. The stone exploded, his body smashing through the wall as if it were tissue paper. He slammed into the wall on the opposite side of the hallway with a second earsplitting crack.

Ales stalked towards the man, fully dismissing the pain of her broken ribs. She could already feel the bones shifting back into their proper positions. The violent impact had definitely knocked him unconscious. She shifted her Vision to see the elementary energy waves that Kiltik was projecting. She could see that the waves were getting weaker. She couldn't risk that the man would wake and set off the device any earlier.

She thought for a long moment about killing him. It was clear that she would have to do it at some point anyway. He had given himself to the Blight, and she highly doubted he could ever be trusted again. He had betrayed not just the Ryhim, but the very world in which they lived. She shook her head and slid her Windblade back into its sheath. She slung his body over her shoulder, and started to jog towards the hole she had made at the opposite end of the floor.

43

Cole ran, strapping his belt around his waist. He shrugged into his coat and opened his Vision. He looked back down the hallway and then scanned through the walls. He was not surprised to see one of the two synthetic monsters trailing him. He was glad to see it was not the one carrying Mina. He skidded to a stop and drew his lancers. These things had attempted to break him. It was time to gain a bit of recompense. He invoked the Circle of Taking and stepped back into the shadowed corner at the end of the hallway by an open cell door.

The creature came speeding into the hallway, and just as it was about to pass him, he stuck his foot out in front of it. It stung his ankle, but the creature was flipped from its feet. It cartwheeled head over heels and spun through the air, smashing its head on the floor. Finally, it smashed into a closed door at the opposite end of the hallway with a piercing crack.

Cole turned and began firing. Bolts zipped down the hallway, colliding with the creature at a dozen different points on the creature's shimmering black body. They tore through its body, leaving a multitude of holes. Cole reloaded his lancers and then slipped them into their holsters. He slid his short sword from the scabbard on his back and produced a long, single-edged dagger in his off hand. He reversed his grip on the dagger so the blade faced back along his arm. The holes began to close, but he knew from experience that the creatures could be destroyed if you inflicted enough damage upon them. Cole raised his sword to a guard position.

"You may be faster than I am, but let us see the depth of your skill, creature," Cole said.

The creature's arms shifted shape into a pair of sharp blades. The creature drove at him, impossibly low for any human trying to strike at his legs. Cole lept into the air, flowing into a perfect flip. As the creature passed beneath him, he lashed out with his sword, scoring a line down its back. He landed and took one step back, bringing his sword

back up to guard, anticipating that the creature would be able
to attack him at superhuman speeds. He had been right, and
the thing's blades smashed into his sword. The strength of the
blow nearly tore the weapon from his grasp, but Cole had
trained with Ales. Compared to her physical power, this thing
was but a child.

He pulled back as the creature bore down on its blades,
overpowering his single arm. Cole pushed as hard as he could
for a split second. Then he relented and spun to the right. The
creature stumbled forward, and Cole took advantage. He
slashed at the thing's arm just above the blade. The Sol alloy
blade slid through the monster's arm with barely any
resistance at all. Its bladed arm fell to the ground, and
anticipating its next thrust, Cole took one flawless step,
turning his body further sideways to allow the thrust to pass.

He kicked away the bladed arm on the ground so that it
skittered through the open cell door and away from the
creature. Cole whipped his other hand up, slashing upwards
at the creature's other arm. It yanked its blade back with
inhuman speed, and Cole's dagger struck the hardened blade
edge with a clang. This put Cole somewhat off balance, but
not as badly as the creature. It rolled back away from him, and
Cole stabilized his stance, moving back to the middle of the
hallway.

The creature's arm grew back and lengthened into a blade.
Cole noticed though that it was slightly shorter than it had
been. He examined the creature with his Vision and realized
that it had an extremely serious flaw. That was how Ales had
destroyed them so quickly. Floating inside of the mass of the
creature was an orb about the size of his fist. This was the
solar cell that powered the creature's bondstructs. That was
why when part of its body was dispatched, it instantly lost the
ability to move, because the low level elementary energy
current necessary to power the tiny machines was coming
from that solar cell. If he destroyed it, the creature would be
destroyed. It seemed to be continually moving inside of the
thing's body.

He spun his long dagger in his hand to make it easier to thrust with. The creature came at him in a blur. It slashed at him madly. He parried the first slash with the short sword in his right hand. The second slash, he tried to push aside with his dagger, but the strength of the blow bound the dagger against the creature's blade. It pushed with far greater than human strength, pushing the razor edge of its blade into his arm.

Cole shoved with his dagger and rolled backwards, out of the reach of the creature. It dashed forward to attempt to catch him before he was set. Cole came to his feet, slashing his dagger left to right in front of him. It pushed the two blades aside just enough to let him spin out of the way. He drove the short sword into the creature's hip. The tip of the sword struck the orb and stopped cold. The solar cell had some sort of armor casing around it, probably Black Sol alloy.

Cole dodged away instantly. He flipped backwards into a roll that brought him to his feet several marks away from the creature. The creature reached down to the weapon its blade returning to a hand, and Cole darted forward. The creature released the blade and dashed forward to meet him. Their blades clashed, and Cole latched onto the blade in its hip. Its hand shot forward toward his throat, latching around his neck, and began to bear down.

Cole yanked the dagger free and slashed through the creature's arm. It tried to swipe at him with its other arm, but he caught the blade on his own. He slashed at the creature's stomach as it pressed its advantage in strength. The blade of its arm descended towards Cole's neck. Its off arm began to reform, but just as the fingers split from each other, Cole made a cut that laid open the creature in a wide swath, right down to the orb. Cole slammed the dagger into its chest and thrust his hand into the hole he had made before it could close. His fingers wrapped around the orb. He pulled at it with all of his might.

At first, it did not budge. Then he jumped. It pushed him off balance as the creature's sword slid towards his face. He tilted and lifted his short sword, then slammed his feet into the creature's stomach and straightened his legs with a shout of effort. The solar cell gripped in his fist ripped free from the creature. He fell backwards and immediately rolled away from the creature. Ripping the cell free would kill the creature, but it might take a long moment for it to run out of power.

"Too late. We have broken your sister. She will unlock it for us," the creature rasped in a final effort to do him harm. Then it melted into a shimmering black puddle on the stone floor.

He was certain the thing did not mean Ales. The man in the armor was powerful, but he had seen Ales do things that were impossible. She had told him the story about how she had become known as the Breaker of Bonds. No mere human could match up to that, no matter how powerful his armor made him. It had to be talking about Ilsa. He picked up the solar cell on the off chance that the creature might somehow reclaim it. He turned and dashed away down the hallway headed for the exit. He had to get to Ilsa.

44

Ilsa appeared in a flash of light not far from the walls of the prison. She could see the massive building through the gaps between the thick stonebark trees. She had moved the Lightgate to a more secure location in the small pack slung across her back. Even though it was protected by a Sol alloy shell, she did not want to chance that the device could be destroyed. She queried her Cellstructs as Lia had taught her. She requested their assistance in running at full speed, since she had not yet become used to using her body at its increased strength.

She began to run, and the sensation of being a passanger in her own body overcame her. Then she was moving at a speed that she could scarcely believe. She shot towards the prison, almost deafened by the roar of the wind as it blew past her. As she neared the wall, she found it odd that she saw no guards on patrol atop it. She queried her Cellstructs to see if she could make the jump over the wall. They indicated that it would not be a problem, and when she got close enough, they took her body into a massive leap that threw up clods of dirt when she left the ground. She landed on top the wall with a deep thud and amazingly, it didn't hurt at all, despite the massive force required to propel her. Her amazing new strength took her breath away.

She paused to scan the walls. It was clear that the yard was separated into numerous areas, she assumed to help with management of the prisoners. She opened her Vision and cast about, looking through the walls until she spotted an odd gathering of over a hundred people. She considered the distance and whether it would be better to jump from wall to wall or to run around. She wasn't sure that she could jump from wall to wall. Each space was at least eighty marks wide. Her Cellstructs indicated that currently it was slightly out of her jumping range, so she ran around the top of the wall.

The intersections of walls were locked guard houses. She didn't bother with going through them. When she got close enough, she jumped across the corner to the next wall. She

quickly made her way towards the collected people. They
were huddled to one side of the large space. It was peculiar
because it appeared that there were both guards in uniforms
and prisoners among the people. On the opposite side of the
space, Kiltik was lying on his back in his human form.
Struggling against him was a roughly human-shaped creature
made of shining black material. She drew her lancer and took
aim. She squeezed the tigger.

"Stop!" Kiltik let out of shout of warning noticing Ilsa a
split second to late.

The sound of the lancer discharge seemed to blow away all
other sounds. He yanked the creature to one side, but the bolt
from her lancer smashed through the creature. Ilsa gasped in
shock and horror. Pain lanced into her mind unlike anything
else she had experienced in her life. It was not physical pain
because she could not block it out. It was like she could feel
herself dying for a long moment. She fell to her knees and let
out a short, stricken sob.

Kiltik threw the creature from atop himself. He shifted
form to that of a katali. She watched, gripped by terror as the
body of a small child emerged from the chest of the black
creature. The creature let out a screech of triumph as the body
fell unmoving to the ground. Then Kiltik landed on top of it.
He roared in rage and tore the thing apart. He moved so fast
that Ilsa lost track of him. She stared at the tiny body and
knew that she had killed an innocent child. She lost all track of
reality as tears filled her eyes and streamed down her face.

"Ilsa, please respond. This One requires your assistance."
Kiltik was sitting next to her, still wearing the form of the
miniature Katali.

"I killed her," Ilsa whispered. "I didn't mean to," she said
frantically. She repeated the words, beginning to sound
hysterical.

"Ilsa Family Katane. You are of the Tier. This One calls
you to uphold your oath."

Kiltik did not shout, but his metallic voice cut through her
jibbering like a razor parted cloth. She blinked once, and her
Vision faded from her eyes. She could not deny the call Kiltik

had made. She had said the words, and she had to stand up to her oath. She pushed away the jibbering part of her mind. If she had broken her oath to protect, then she would answer for that when there was time.

"What must I do?" Ilsa asked.

"This One is not sure what Ales summoned you to do here," Kiltik said.

Ilsa got slowly to her feet, took out the small device, and held it out to Kiltik. Kiltik examined it, and his eyes went wide.

"This One did not think it was possible to create a Lightgate. There were hundreds of attempts. None were successful. Come. This One knows why you are here."

Kiltik lept from the top of the wall. Ilsa jumped after him. They landed almost together, and Kiltik led her across the yard towards the large group of men. Just as they reached them, Cole burst through the open door to the prison. He looked at Ilsa and his face became pensive.

"I'm too late. What has it done to her?" Cole asked.

"Caused an accident. There is no time for discussion now, Cole Family Katane. Where is Alessandra?" Kiltik asked.

"She's coming. She said that there was not enough time to run," Cole said.

"She was correct. This One's elementary energy transmission functionalities are reaching their limit to jam the Blight's ability to detonate the antimatter collector below. Prepare for a Lightjump. If Ales does not return before I fail, we must go without her."

Kiltik went to the small body of the child and began to examine it. Ales came through the door a few moments later with the unconscious armored man over her shoulder.

"Alessandra Family Katane, please come here. This One believes this damaged child may yet be saved," Kiltik said.

Ales knelt down to watch what Kiltik was doing. He had two small tendrils inside of the bolt hole in the girl's back and was doing something delicate inside of her.

"Oh Gods, what happened?" Ales asked, but she immediately shook her head. "No time, no time! Bring her. We will see what can be done once it is safe."

Ales strode towards the mass of people on the other side of the courtyard. She began to shout when she stood in front of them.

"There is little time, so I'll brook no questions. If you want to live, do as I say. Line up in rows. Each man put a hand on the shoulder of the man in front of them. Quickly, now! There is no time."

The men exchanged glances, and Ales shouted.

"Move or die!"

The men, both guards and inmates, began to line up as she said. She noticed Ilsa staring listlessly off into space, fresh tears streaming down her cheeks. She frowned unhappily. She had seen that look before, and she had fervently hoped never to see it again. She went to Ilsa and put her arms around the girl because there was nothing else she could do. Only Lia might be able to help her. She reached out mentally to Kiltik.

{Kiltik, I hope you have made the girl stable enough for a Lightjump,} Ales said.

Kiltik came closer, carrying Mina's unconscious form on his back. Ilsa immediately turned away, though she said nothing.

{This One would inform you that This One's transmission is failing.} Kiltik's calm in the face of the impending disaster was utterly unnerving.

"Everyone at the front of the line reach out to touch one of us!" she shouted frantically. She almost had to drag Ilsa to the front of the lines. She put her hand on Ilsa's shoulders.

"Ilsa, we need to save these people," Ales said. She wasn't sure how much the girl was hearing right then. When she didn't respond, Ales shook her. "Now, Ilsa!"

Ilsa's eyes snapped up to her, and she nodded. "Right. Lets go."

She took her leaf out of an inner pocket. Ales sighed in relief. She held out her hand to three of the guards at the heads of the lines. Kiltik stood and held up his tail to the other three.

"This One will not harm you. Please grab This One's tail."

They did, and Kiltik reached up and put a paw on Ilsa's hip. Time seemed to slow as Ales watched the elementary energy waves emanating from Kiltik's body cease.

"Go!" Ales shouted.

45

Lia's eyes snapped open. She sensed something was about to happen, something enormous and terrifying. Her instincts told her to hunker down into the nice warm spot against the wall of the store room adjacent to the forge. The stones absorbed the heat from the forge on the other side of the wall and radiated it into the room quite nicely. Despite the safe-feeling location, somehow she knew that whatever this was, it was going to scare everyone else in the building.

She arranged her paws beneath her and pushed herself to her feet. She went to the door and hooked a claw into the latch that Ales had installed especially for her. The door popped open and she slunk out into the dark hallway. She went to the children's rooms first. She nosed Kayna awake. Kayna's eyes opened slowly, and unlike anyone she had ever seen, she did not draw back from Lia's muzzle.

"Mmm, whasamatter Lia?" Kayna asked softly.

"I don't know yet. Something, though. We are safe enough here. It feels far off. I'm not going to wake Manat, but if you hear anything scary, don't be afraid. I'll be nearby," Lia said.

Kayna nodded and then reached out, scratching Lia between the ears in her favorite spot. She drew her blankets back up over her and closed her eyes. Lia slipped silently out of their room and went down the hall. Before she could tap on Jame's door, it popped open quietly. He startled when she was sitting in the hall outside.

"Oh, Lia. Something's wrong. Do you feel it? Like the world is holding its breath," Jame whispered.

A moment later, Juran's door popped open. He had his Vision open and his sword in his hand.

"What is that?" Juran asked.

"I'm not sure. Something is about to happen. Something big," Lia said. She felt a vibration in her paws, and then she froze. Her face went slack with terror.

"No no no no." She just repeated it hysterically. She turned around and ran down the hallway back towards the children's room. She burst through the door, and both of the little ones started awake.

"On my back right now."

She laid down. Kayna didn't hesitate. She jumped out of bed and swung her little leg over Lia's back. Manat was a little slower, and the vibrations got a little stronger by the time he was behind Kayna on her back. Jame and Juran had just made it to the door when she darted back out into the hallway.

"Jame, you get Icci! Then get to the crystal! Now!" Lia roared.

She dashed down the hallway towards the the second story door that lead out onto an open air deck. She crashed through the door, making sure not to dislodge either of the children. Kayna knew to hold tight to her collar and she made sure to keep one hand on Manat. Lia leapt over the balcony railing. She landed in the courtyard and waited a long count of ten.

She was about to go to the crystal when Jame and Juran burst out of the back door of the workshop. Jame was carrying the jet black orb that was Icci. The glowing green lines crossing her surface were very dim, showing her own fear. Lia went to the crystal. She had no need to take the leaf from her pouch. Apparently, being in the pouch was the same as being out in the open and touching her body. It was as though somehow Avaara had made the pouch a part of her just like the collar was.

"Grab on!" she shouted, holding her tail up in front of Jame and Juran.

Both grabbed on. The Lightjump to the Travelers grove made Lia a little queasy, but it passed quickly. No sooner had they appeared than their bodies were assaulted by a stiff wind followed by an earth-shattering boom. The sound was of such deep volume that they felt more than heard it. The ground shook in a violent quake, knocking them all from their feet. Lia looked up to the Lightleaf trees with concern that they might be displaced from the ground. Even she did not have the strength to hold up a Lightleaf tree. Thankfully, there seemed to be no danger of any of the trees falling.

"What's happening?!" Jame shouted. Lia could barely hear his voice over the roar of the wind.

"It's a massive explosion!" Lia shouted back. She could see a trickle of blood running from one of Jame's ears. "We should be fine here!"

Lia hunkered down next to one of the trees out of the wind, and the rest of them followed suit. After a moment, the wind died down and Lia raced around the tree, knowing that with an explosion of that size, there would be an implosion afterwards. The rest of them followed her with nary a word. The wind reversed itself, though thankfully, it was not quite as violent as the wind from the explosion. Suddenly, they were surrounded by hundreds of other people, all fighting to keep their balance. They, too, failed, but it was not long before the wind and quake subsided. It was not natural.

Lia blinked her eyes rapidly, trying to dislodge the grit forced into them from the blast of wind. She licked her paw and rubbed it across her face reflexively. She repeated the behavior until she felt like all the grit had been cleaned from her face. She saw Alessandra then, but Ilsa was the one who immediately drew her eye. That utterly empty expression was like looking in a mirror across thousands of cycles. She remembered when she looked like that.

"Jame, quickly bring Icci here!" Ales shouted. She took the small body of a child from Kiltik's back and laid her down on the ground. She immediately took a small knife from a pouch on her belt. She made a cut on her own palm and dripped a bit of her blood into a bolt hole on the girl's back.

{Icci, we'll need some temporary healing Cellstructs for this girl's helixical structure. Kiltik and I have done what we can to keep her alive. It isn't going to be enough. The bolt struck her heart, and she has already died once. Kiltik improvised a stitch on her heart muscle and used an elementary energy burst to restart her heart, but it is barely functioning. She is slowly bleeding out,} Ales said mentally.

{This One will prepare them right away, but This One will need to return to the workshop to produce them. The internal mechanisms that This One's previous body enjoyed do not fit into This One's new body,} Icci replied.

Ales held out her hands and Jame handed her over.

{What are you attempting?} Lia asked.

{To save this girl. And maybe that one, too.} Ales nodded her head at Ilsa. Ilsa's eyes were filled with pain, and tears were making tracks in the dust on her face.

{You know that there is only one thing that will save her now,} Lia said.

Ales sighed. *{I know, but I have to try, Lia.}*

Then, she and Icci vanished in a flash of bright light. Lia grunted. She reached out to Kiltik. He accepted her handshake.

{Can you tell me what happened to Ilsa?} Lia asked. Kiltik related the story through his own memories. She felt his desperation to stop what had happened, and his sadness at failing to do so. *{It isn't your fault, Kiltik. There was no way either of you could have stopped this.}*

{This One is well aware, but that does not seem to negate the feeling that This One should have done something more. If This One had noticed her one second sooner, This One could have prevented the damage. This One will be fine, Liassa Family Katane. This One will make peace with this failure,} Kiltik responded.

Lia padded over to Ilsa. She noticed the massive dust cloud rising into the air from where the prison had been, but she put it out of her mind. The men and several women were milling about. Some of those who were clearly inmates of the prison were looking about as if they might slip off in the confusion. She sighed and turned away from Ilsa. She raised her voice to a volume where everyone could hear her.

"Some of you may be thinking that this is an opportunity to escape your crimes. Know this. If you attempt to run before we review whether or not you belonged where you were, I will personally hunt you down. I'll return you to where you belong, and if you put me through the inconvenience, I will not be gentle about it." She bared her teeth and saw several of the inmates shiver. She flicked her tail once, and then turned back to Ilsa.

Ilsa had not moved, and was staring blankly into the distance. Kiltik was sitting with Mina, and Jame had started speaking with the prison guards. Lia sat down in front of Ilsa.

She reached out to her mentally, but her handshake was refused. There was another flash of light. Ales appeared with Icci in one hand. She had a small blue marble in the other. She looked at Lia and nodded. Lia nodded back, and Ales went to work.

Ales knelt over the girl. Icci had told her that there was not enough time to both make the structures and tell them what they had to do. Ales would have to guide them to make the repairs to the girl's body. Ales dropped the marble into the girl's wound and it immediately melted to fill the opening. She opened her mind to the structures, and they immediately queried for their purpose. Ales began to desperately work to try to save the girl's life.

"I'm not going away, Ilsa, but I'll wait until you are ready." Lia walked around Ilsa in a circle and finally curled her massive body protectively around the girl. A long few minutes later, Ilsa abruptly collapsed to her knees and began to sob. She tipped to one side and lay against Lia's body.

"She was innocent and I didn't protect her, Lia. I killed her," Ilsa sobbed.

"You acted to protect Kiltik when you thought he was in danger. It was not you who hurt that little girl. It was the creature holding her," Lia consoled softly.

"But it hurts so much, Lia. I don't think if it was someone that was trying to hurt someone else for no reason, or for reasons that were out of balance, it would hurt so much."

"Maybe for you it wouldn't, but that didn't matter for me. It still hurt more than I ever imagined it would."

Ilsa finally looked up at her. "How does Ales do this? I can't. How did I do that to her, Lia? She's part of me. They're all part of us, even the ones who would hurt others."

"Ales has ever been sure of her place in this world, Ilsa. Ever since she was six cycles old, she has known that she would do anything to follow the path of the Tier. It protected her from the things she has done in the pursuit of her duties. She doesn't suffer doubts, and I have yet to see her make a mistake that resulted in someone being injured without cause. It is not something that very many of the Tier could ever do.

Even without her Vision and Tieran powers, Ales is super human, but we mere mortals all suffered some effects of doing what was needed." Lia's voice held both amusement and deep admiration for Ales. "Each of us coped with it in different ways. Some couldn't cope the way they were. We needed help."

Ilsa burried her face in Lia's fur. "That's how you become one of the Wild," she whispered.

"That's how I became one of the Wild."

"But I can't do that, Lia." Ilsa sniffed, and then the tears began again. She couldn't seem to stop them. The pain did not seem to fade, and she couldn't believe she had done what she had.

"Ilsa, there is no shame in distancing yourself from that pain. Do you think I am less because I wear a body that is not human?" Lia asked.

Ilsa shook her head. "I..." She seemed to have run out of words. She just cried. Lia purred soothingly. Ales' mental handshake buzzed inside of her mind.

{How is she?} Ales asked.

{It's not good. She's not talking. Just like I wouldn't. We can't let it get as far as it went with me, Ales.} Lia's mindvoice held slight shame and deep concern.

The story that she never told was that she had tried to do harm to herself before she became one of the Wild. She had mistakenly thought that it would be better to not bring shame upon her family by becoming one of the Wild. She couldn't keep her oath in the state that she had been in. That had depressed her more than all of the pain and doubt put together. She had not known that they had only worried about her because being one of the Wild was a hard life. She knew now that they had never been prouder.

{If it hadn't been someone so clearly innocent of any wrongdoing, I think she might have been hurting, but she might have been able to cope,} Lia said.

{The girl is going to make it, Lia. Do you think that will help?} Ales' mindvoice was extremely concerned.

{I don't think it will help in the way we would both hope. The damage is done. We will just have to see how she recovers. Keep an

eye on her, because this kind of damage is not going to go away on its own. This is far more profound than what happened to Warran. What happened at the prison?}

Ales explained everything and finished with their escape. She had found the man she brought with her. She had stripped the man out of the armor by carefully destroying each individual layer. There had been ten layers to it. They shifted continually to ensure that no single strike from Breaking could destroy the armor without destroying the man inside.

Warran had identified the man as being the assistant the Ryhim had given to him. His name was Kavan, and devested of the armor, he was not much of a threat. Ales did not know if he would wake up. She had not wanted to kill him, but he had been unconscious much longer than he should have been. She had assigned Juran and Jame to watch the man so that one of them could fetch her if he woke up. He definitely was not just a Fixer. His fighting skills had been far better than average.

{Alessandra Family Katane, we should inspect the damage done by the device. Mina of Clan Clai is stable and comfortable. The situation with the prisoners needs our attention,} Kiltik spoke into their mental link.

{I'm aware. Kiltik, what is our bondstruct stockpile like?} Ales asked.

{This One would have to express the size of the stock pile in exponential terms. It is sufficient to construct incredibly large physical objects in a few days, properly managed.}

{Prepare them to construct this structure on the site of the prison.} Ales mentally passed him schematics and diagrams for a massive building easily the size of the prison structure, and then some. *{Please estimate construction time when you are able.}*

{This One will begin immediately. We must examine the site to decide how to handle this.}

Ales nodded.

"Mother, I beg your council," Ales whispered, and suddenly she was there. She had not seen the Mother in over a cycle. She was in her fall guise. Her body was the most human it was over the course of the cycle. She was not thin, but she had lost much of her summer weight and curves. Ales went to one knee and noticed that the only figures around her were the others of the Tier, and Tier to-be.

"I will give you my council if I can, my Child." Her sultry voice was a little sad, and Ales noticed that she was looking at Ilsa and Lia.

"You honor me with your presence, Mother," Ales said, and the Mother smiled beatifically.

"Please, my Child, say your piece."

"If it pleases you, Mother, we would make this place our home. I seek your blessing to do this thing," Ales said reverently.

The Mother looked around to see the rest of the Tier.

"My blessing upon you, Children. It would please me greatly for you to have a place in which you may feel safety." The Mother knelt, hovering a mere tick off the ground. She reached down and touched Ales' face. "You go beyond all we have ever hoped you would be."

Then she vanished, and the world around them returned. Ales took a deep breath, and got back to her feet.

"Jame! What did the Banners say?" Ales asked.

"That they are willing to meet with you," Jame replied.

"Good. Take the Lightleaves and return them here as quickly as possible. Juran, you do the same. Go to the Chieftans and Chieftesses of the clans. Return them here as quickly as you can. I do not wish to force anyone to agree with us, and I will not, but I will not be denied a chance to convince them. If they do not agree to meet with me, you may tell them that I will fetch them personally. I think they will come, though. They will have felt that explosion for hundreds of lengths in all directions. They will want news of what has happened. I think they will take the offer of travel by Lightleaf."

They each nodded.

"Lia, will you two be alright?" Ales asked.

Ilsa looked up at her, and Ales knelt. She put a hand on Ilsa's cheek.

"Take all the time you need, Sister, and whatever your decision, you will always be our Sister," Ales said.

{We'll be fine in time,} Lia said. *{Be careful. I somehow feel like you will find more among the rubble of that place than we know of.}* Lia's mindvoice was concerned, but not just for Ales. She was worried for all of them.

{Finding?} Ales asked.

Lia just sent a mental shrug. *{Likely. We are still missing things. There were no laboratories in there, but we know things came from there. Finding does tell me that.}*

{I promise, but if there was something there, it is likely gone now. The antimatter accumulator will have vaporized that entire facility, and probably left quite a crater. Just like in Ahal. Lia, how close are you to being fully recovered?}

Ales moved to Kiltik who was still hovering over Mina. She was quickly growing stronger as the Cellstructs repaired her internal organs and tissues.

{Close enough to handle anything that might go wrong here. My Cellstructs are telling me that the damage is eighty three percent repaired. I'm fine, Ales,} Lia assured. Her mindvoice, though, held real confidence that she could handle whatever might happen. That was more reassuring than anything else that Lia could have told her.

{Alright. I won't mother you any more. When you think she is ready, you should tell Ilsa that Mina will survive. She likely won't wake up from the shock for a day or more, though. She lost quite a bit of blood,} Ales said.

{Why did you summon the Mother for that? You knew she would approve.}

Ales turned her eyes to the guards and inmates. They had not been included in the conversation for their benefit, since many of them would have been rendered unconscious by her voice and influence. Ales knew, though, that they had seen the Mother.

{For the same reason she came. To make it clear to the Ryhim that we have the favor of the Gods. I do not want to force these people, Lia. I want them to know that we mean for our taking residence here to be mutually beneficial. We are few, and even with the defenses I am planning for our stronghold, we would be hard

pressed to hold the area without the cooperation of the Ryhim. But I'll not be denied a place of safety for us all.}

She sent the memories of what she had been planning to build here to Lia. Lia's mental nod came with a suffusion of approval. The defenses of the stronghold she had planned were impressive. It was likely that it would be completely impenetrable, save for an orbital strike. Since no one in this time had the capability of building something like the Taker's Eye, or even a more primitive Orbital Striker, that meant that their home would be safe.

Lia shivered at the thought of the orbital deterrents that the Tier had once controlled. They had never used them to hurt anyone, though the Striker weapon had been fired a few times to stop a war somewhere on the planet. The effect of the weapon was devastating, and while the Taker's Eye was still in orbit, it was completely inaccessible even to them. The possible impact from the Taker's Eye would be far worse than the Orbital Striker. Ales made connections to all of the Tier with Cellstructs and a moment later, she was sharing her memories of what had happened in the prison. They all gathered around Lia and Ilsa. Kiltik even carefully lifted Mina and brought her closer.

"This is not over. There are things we all have to do before we can truly rest. Jame and Juran, you already have tasks to accomplish. Cole, I am loathe to ask you to do anything further as I can see that you are exhausted and somewhat physically and mentally damaged, but I am also loathe to leave you in your current condition." Ales paused when Cole stood up a little straighter and held out his hand to stop her.

"Please stop. I'm not your responsibility anymore. I am your brother, and you are not my keeper. I was captured because I was careless, and your training was the only thing that kept me alive. I'll forgive you for taking so long to come find me. What do you need from me, Sister?" he said with a worn smile. Ales sighed.

"Smartass. Fine. I'm trying to say that you are ready to say the words, and I need you to do it. Right now. I would like to induct you myself, but Kiltik and I must secure our new home.

Go with Lia. She will help you. Also take this." Ales held up the small blue marble that comprised Cole's Cellstructs. He took it from her hand and held it up where he could see through it.

"What am I supposed to do with...?" Cole trailed off. "These are Cellstructs, aren't they? Are these mine?"

"They are perfectly in line with your current helixical coding," Ales said. "You swallow it."

Cole did so without hesitation.

"Make sure you get as much food into you as you can stand. Warran has been eating six or seven meals a day. They'll chew through as much food as you can get into you until they let you know that they are at full capacity. Stay with Lia and Ilsa. They will be happy for your company and protection, brother."

"I'm sorry I was so careless," Cole said solemnly.

"None of us are perfect, Cole. Experience will remedy your mistakes, just as it does for all of us."

"Warran?" Ales asked.

"I'm here," he said from where he sat up against one of the nearby Lightleaf trees. Kayna was sitting between his legs with her back against his chest, and Manat was there curled up under his arm.

"We will go back to the shop first. I need you to stay with the manufactury and make sure the stockpile gets replenished," Ales said.

"When I was fighting the synthoid, it seemed to think it had broken one of us. It acted like it had accomplished something," Cole said with confusion.

Ales pulled Cole gently aside. "That is why my instincts are telling me this is not over. Ilsa reacted to defend Kiltik without knowing that she would be hurting Mina. She has taken severe emotional damage. Damage so severe that she may choose to take the Wild. I don't know why the Blight would think that it would give them some advantage, but it was not an accident." Ales shook her head.

"And these prisoners?" Cole asked.

"You take care of it."

Cole stared at Ales, slackjawed. "I don't even know where to start."

"You shouldn't have any trouble telling if someone is lying. Just question them on whether or not they have ever committed any crimes. Start with the guards. I don't think that most of them were involved, but we have to be sure of who is and isn't trustworthy before the Banners arrive here. We didn't destroy the prison, but that is going to be the perception. While I know we can convince them of what is happening, I would rather do more," Ales expounded.

Cole looked at the large group of men and women skeptically. "Ales, you realize that not long ago, they would have thrown *me* in that prison."

"Cole, are you the same man you were a cycle ago?" Ales asked with annoyance.

Cole shrugged. "Sometimes it feels like I am."

"Stop being a child. You were hand-chosen by the Mother," Ales scolded. There was no doubt that Cole had come a long way in the last cycle, but his doubts about his criminal past were pulling him down in a terrible way, making him vulnerable.

Cole took a deep breath and nodded. "I'll take care of it, but I think before I do, we all need food and rest. What are we going to do with them?"

"Lia and Ilsa will be staying here for the time being. Ilsa is not ready to move yet. She is still too mentally damaged to deal with anything outside of her own mind. The weather inside of a grove is always perfectly climatic, no matter what is going on outside. Everyone will be comfortable here for the few hours that we need. If they all ran in different directions, I doubt that even one of them would make it out of the city before Lia caught them. Don't ever underestimate Lia. She may not be as powerful as I am in terms of direct combat abilities, but she earned the name Thieftaker all on her own."

Cole looked at Lia with slightly wide eyes. "Theiftaker? She's the one who single-handedly brought down every Thieves guild across all of Ahlysim?" Cole's disbelief was palpable.

"It took her three cycles of planning, but she systematically destroyed every organization of thieves across the world. It took her almost two cycles to complete. Her planning was nothing short of supernatural. Her intelligence is far more terrifying than anything else about her, Cole." Ales looked upon her little sister with a smile filled with pride.

"Theiftaker," Cole said. Theiftaker was just a legend. "No one could do that on their own," Cole whispered.

"No one except her. Lia has even more names that I do," Ales confided. Cole looked a little dumbfounded. "Back then, the Thieves Guilds were responsible for all of the slave trade. Slave trading was a well-kept secret because the Tier had outlawed it. When it was decided that it was time to put an end to it, Lia took on the task herself. The things she did may not have been as flashy, but some of them were far more impressive than many of my own accomplishments. Though I think I topped her permanently with the Volcano," Ales chuckled.

"Volcano?" Cole asked bewilderedly.

"Long story from a long time ago," Ales said and strolled away towards one of the Lightleaf trees. Cole's eyes went a little wide. She turned back and gave him a sardonic grin.

"We don't have time for old legends right now, Cole. If you want something to eat, go with Lia and then have her show you the path to the workshop crystal. There is plenty of food in the coldboxes at the workshop," Ales said.

Kiltik trotted over to her and sat down. He put a paw on the the same tree and they both vanished. Cole turned to Lia.

"Is it true?" Cole asked. Everyone knew the story of the Firekeeper.

"Which?" Lia was stroking Ilsa's hair comfortingly with a paw.

"Either," Cole said.

"Yes. Once, a long time ago, people called me the Thieftaker. Once, they called her the Firekeeper." Lia spoke quietly, sadly. Lia looked around at all the people milling about, and then looked at Ilsa worriedly. Then she shook her head. "This must be done privately."

"Cole, carry Ilsa over here. She can stay with us, and I will go back to the workshop after you are done," Warran said.

"Careful," Lia cautioned. "Her conscious mind is elsewhere and if she feels threatened, she might defend herself."

Cole nodded. He came closer, and instead of picking her up, he knelt in front of her. He touched her face and gently turned her head until she was looking at him. He held out his hands, inviting her into an embrace. Slowly, she held up her hands. She was small enough that he could lift her as a father does his child. He picked her up and she clung to him. Not desperately, but clearly, she needed someone to be near right then.

He took her over to where Warran was resting with his back against a tree. He set her down, and she seemed to realize that she was safe with Warran. She closed her eyes and sighed. She put her face against one of the trees, and that seemed to comfort her. Lia got her paws under her and stood. She walked off into the trees, and Cole followed her.

46

The crater left behind when the prison exploded was massive and perfectly circular. It was much larger than the the prison complex had been. The dust cloud that had been blown into the air by the explosion was still settling, but enough had settled to let Ales and Kiltik explore. What they had found within the massive hole in the earth had disturbed them both. In the stoneward facing side of the crater was a large hole that looked like the entrance to a cave. When they managed to climb down to the hole, they had found a large hallway made of glittering black sorstone that extended into the darkness.

Ales opened her Vision and walked into the hallway. There was far less debris than Ales had anticipated, and her Cellstructs informed her that it was likely that the area within the crater had been utterly annihilated by the matter antimatter reaction. That was what gave the crater the perfectly smooth appearance, as if a giant ice cream scoop had dove into the earth and removed the land that had disappeared. She slid her Windblade out of her coat and tapped it on the wall. She watched the pattern of the vibration. Whereever the hallway went, it was more than five hundred marks away.

"We are going to need to have a talk to see how this complex was built. Some of the Ryhim had to know. The complex was one quarter as large as Rihanna itself."

"It appeared to This One that the facility was constructed during Kinas' time among the Ryhim."

"A mystery for another time. What is your maximum speed, Kiltik?" Ales asked.

"This One can sustain travel at two hundred marks per second without risking damage to This One's body," Kiltik replied.

"Good. Keep up with me." Ales pushed her constraints open to the fourth level. She blurred down the hallway, focusing on the Circle of Observance to make sure she was not going to run into any sort of trap. The passage was far longer than five hundred marks. It was almost half a length long.

When they got to the end, they found that the door was disturbingly made of Black Sol alloy. Ales became extremely worried that what she had destroyed of the Black Sol alloy had been far less than what she had thought it had been.

"Kiltik, considering the effective conditions here in the Nexus, how much Black Sol alloy would you calculate could have been produced in the last two cycles if maximum theoretical output was achieved?" Ales asked.

"This One estimates it would be possible to produce approximately thirty thousand sphere of the material," Kiltik replied.

Ales had destroyed nearly ten thousand sphere in that warehouse. That meant that there was still enough to do massive amounts of harm. Thirty thousand sphere could create thousands of armor interfaces, or other horrifying devices that the Blight could use to control people.

{Alessandra, This One is concerned about Ilsa Family Katane. The mental disturbance she has suffered could be permanently scarring.} Kiltik's usual calm tone was nowhere in evidence in his mindvoice. His concern was almost palpable.

{I agree. I never imagined the Blight would know to use Mina against us in this way. It is not a secret that there are checks to our power that it hurts us to kill, but no one outside of the Tier has ever known the exact specifics of those checks. We have never made it clear to anyone that we experience each death as if it were our own, and more specifically, that even mistakenly harming those we are attempting to protect can cause us damage beyond any other thing we might do.}

{This One believes this may confirm a long-held theory posited by This One. It is known that Alizar Family Istina was controlled by the Blight. This One has long suspected that the Blight was able to mine Alizar's mind for many facts about the Tier. This One suspects that Alizar Family Istina held back much from the creature, telling it answers only to those questions it asked directly.}

Ales nodded in response and then focused on the Circle of Breaking. She examined the door for a moment, and then in a blur of motion, she struck several points on it. She stepped back, and the door crumbled to dust. Kiltik was amazed at her power with Breaking. The fact that she could Break Sol alloy so completely was amazing, considering the relative strength of the metal in terms of sheer physical durability. Ales scanned the room inside with her Vision.

It was a large room, perhaps twenty marks square. There were rows of tables holding various pieces of equipment that Ales recognized as Structure manufactures and devices used for microscopic image enhancement. This was definitely the facility where the Blight had been attempting to study and improve upon its ability to impregnate creatures with Cellstructs. There were two doorways at the far end of the sparse room.

{Catalog this room, Kiltik. Leave nothing unknown. I want to know exactly how successful the creature's experiments have been,} Ales said.

She ground her teeth with frustration. This was never going to end. This thing had had thousands of cycles to infect their world. She felt overwhelmed with the idea of ridding their world of all of it. If it was an energetic infection, the only way to destroy it completely would be to either destroy absolutely everything that carried the infection, or to design some sort of energetic vaccine that could be transmitted to the entire infection at once.

She was certain that if she could reach the source of the infection, she could use her power to accomplish its destruction, but finding the source was the greatest challenge she could imagine. It could be literally anywhere. Warran was trying, but she had no idea how successful he was going to be. She feared that they were going to have to locate and retrieve Fahmor to deal with the Blight.

{What's the likelihood we can find Fahmor?} Ales asked.

{Unlikely with the data available. Considering the predictive model that This One has produced, Fahmor likely plunged into the Grey Tide around two hundred and seventy lengths off shore. Lia has reactivated the orbital tracking devices, but after three thousand cycles, they are in disrepair. Before we can reestablish the full viability of the tracking grid to locate the remaining minds, repairs must be made. The orbital vehicles are running self checks on the stores of structures meant to maintain them now. We suspect we

may have to arrange to deliver new structures to bring them to full operation,} Kiltik explained.

Ales went to the two doors at the other end of the laboratory. She picked the door on the left. It too was locked, and she didn't waste any time destroying it. There was a short hallway of polished sorstone behind it and another door. This one, though, was unlocked. She slid the door out of the way. It made a hissing sound as air escaped the sealed environment. Her breath misted into the freezing air of the room beyond. This room was smaller than the first, perhaps ten marks square. It had two rows of tables with equipment that she didn't recognize initially. There, sitting on one of the tables, was a large, square black box with a glass panel that made up most of one side. It was the Probability Matrix. That, though, was not what was most interesting thing in the room.

At one end of the black stone room was a large metal tube sitting on top of a large metal box. She inspected it with her Vision and it became quickly clear that it was a high-power cooling unit. Considering the wear on the clasps holding the tube closed, it had been opened many thousands of times. Ales went to the tube and found that it looked as if opening them shut down the cooling unit. Ales popped open the clasps and the sound of the cooling unit faded away. Fog billowed from within the container as the lid swung open.

Ales waved the condensing fog away from the lid, and her eyes widened at what she found inside. Inside was the body of a large animal, not something Lia's size, but something closer to the size of a human. It was an animal that was known only to the Tier. Her eyes went wide as she saw the glowing symbol on the back of one ear, the symbol that appeared on every one of the Wild.

She looked on in mounting rage. The animal was four-legged, with a long tail that had been curled around its body. Instead of fur or skin, it had thick, opalescent scales covering its entire body. Its head was wedge-shaped with a wide muzzle. It had large, diamond-shaped white ears. Its eyes were glittering violet jewels that stared sightlessly ahead. Its forepaws had retractile claws and long digits that looked like they would be good for climbing. That was exactly what they were.

The tentai had been able to climb literally anything, and they could quickly expand their lungs, taking in enough air to slow their descent enough to make it almost impossible to take damage from a fall. They had also been extremely rare. So rare, in fact, that the Tier had brought the last twenty-eight of the extremely intelligent animals to Ahal. They had been in the process of carefully manipulating their helixical structure to attempt to repopulate the species. Ales assumed that they had been killed in the cataclysm. Kinas had loved the animals, and when he chose to take the Wild, it was an easy choice of which animal he would take the shape of.

Ales fingered the collar around the neck of the body, which was strangely free of ice. She trailed her finger across the nameplate. The body had belonged to Kinas. Ales took a deep breath to stave off tears. She examined the body more closely, and was happy to see that his Cellstructs had followed their disposal routines. There were none present in this body. She narrowed her eyes. Why would the Blight keep a body like this one? It held no secrets that the Blight could use. She shook her head and clenched her hands into fists.

{Kiltik, I have discovered something disturbing here. Kinas' body is in cold stasis here. I have no idea how the Blight would have obtained his body and frozen it fast enough to keep it. It seems the disposal routines that should have caused his body to be deconstructed were interrupted somehow. I have also found the Probability Matrix.}

Ales closed the lid. She would keep his body frozen until they could properly honor him in death. Perhaps they could even honor him further by using his helixical coding to finally repopulate the tentai species.

{If it has his Cellstructs, why has it taken the creature so long to reverse engineer them?} Kiltik asked.

{I don't believe that Blight was fast enough to freeze him before his Cellstructs destroyed themselves. Without seeing how they were interacting with his body, I think the mystery has escaped the creature,} Ales explained.

She left the room and went to the other door. Kiltik was still cataloging what they had found. She opened the second door, and found another, longer hallway. She followed it to its end. Here, there was no door, and the doorway opened up onto a massive space. The ceiling was forty marks high, and the room was at least two hundred marks wide and three times that long. The room was filed with countless cages. There were four rows, stacked from the floor to the ceiling, and they extended into the darkness to the other end of the room. There were several ailses made up by the stacked cages. Hanging from the ceiling was some sort of automated loading system that looked as if it were meant to pull cages at the request of some unknown Searcher. The cages were of various sizes: some small enough to hold a shoovu, some large enough to hold Lia. They were all empty.

Ales switched to focusing on the Circle of Light so that she could see in infrared. There, she noticed that a large number of the cages still had lingering heat signatures. Her Cellstructs calculated that there were a little over ten thousand such heat signatures left behind. She had just missed them. Not that even she could have easily stopped so many on her own. Thousands of animals that were likely to be infected had been unleashed. There was only one place they could be going.

47

{*Lia, wake up.*} Ales' mindvoice was deeply stressed. Lia had rarely heard her so upset. She immediately got to her feet in alarm. Sunddenly, Ales was much closer to her. She had used a Lightjump to get back.

{*Wake up everyone, even Ilsa too, if she is able. The Blight has released thousands of infected animals. I can only think that with its defeat, it has decided it would be better to destroy Rihanna and as many of the Ryhim as it could, rather than leave behind anything that the Tier might be able to use against it. Get everyone ready for a fight. I will try to rouse the Outriders in the city to defend it. We don't have much time.*}

Ales did not bother to come into the workshop. She had left Kiltik behind to protect the hidden laboratory. Despite the fact that he would have been a massive help to fight the animals, they could not risk that lab disappearing while they were distracted without a complete catalog of what was there. He would join them as soon as he was sure he had everything.

A moment later, Ales jumped again to the Traveler's Grove. The Outrider Dispatch Center was one of the four story glass and bondsteel buildings that surrounded it. She dashed through the grove at speed and did not stop for even a moment. She smashed her fist into the doors of the Dispatch Center. She twisted her punch at the last second so that the doors still exploded into harmless dust, but the sound was a thunderous boom that was sure to have jarred everyone from sleep. The two Outriders sitting at a table just inside of the door were playing some sort of game with dice. They jumped to their feet and drew lancers. They blanched when they saw her eyes flaring with lambent energy.

"Rihanna will soon be under attack. Wake everyone and alert the guards to prepare to defend the wall."

Ales turned and dashed out of the door. There was no point in bogging herself down with trying to justify what she had done. It would have taken precious time that she could spend attempting to slow down the animals so they couldn't reach Rihanna. Ales jumped back to the workshop. There she found Lia, Cole, Warran, and Ilsa waiting. Mina was standing at the back door, looking out worriedly. She would not be fully recovered from her injuries for many days yet, but it was good to see that she had survived.

"Listen to me, all of you. I don't want to have to kill these animals. They are innocent in all of this. Their lives are just as valuable as all of ours or the Ryhim. That being said, we do not have nearly the resources needed to cleanse them all, and considering the awful things the Blight has done to those of them who cannot be saved, I strongly suspect that at this point death will be a release."

Ales went to Ilsa. She offered a mental handshake, and Ilsa accepted. Ales put her hands on Ilsa's shoulders and let her love for her sister flow through their mental link.

{You don't have to, Sister. You can stay here and protect the children. It would be better to leave a minder behind,} Ales said, projecting her confidence through the mental link. She didn't want Ilsa to think that Ales thought her weak. That was the furthest thing from Ales' mind.

{You need me. If I don't come and do what I can, a lot more are going to die than just those animals we are forced to kill. I don't know if there will be anything left of me when this is over, but I have to help,} Ilsa replied. The sadness in her mindvoice ate away at even Ales' will, but the resolve that also came through was overpowering. This young Tier would destroy herself to keep her oath if she had to.

{I will help you, Sister,} Ales said. She put her hand on Ilsa's head.

"Mother, I beg for your blessing. Let my Sister's pain be mine for this night that she may have the time she deserves to recover," Ales spoke, and the Mother faded into view nearby. She hovered a few ticks off the ground with a grave expression on her face.

"You know what you ask of me, daughter? To bear the burdens of another Tier even for a single night could break you beyond repair." She spoke slowly to insure that she was being clear. Ales nodded.

"To see my Sister kept whole, I'll endure," Ales said. Ilsa started to protest. *{Hush, now. I'll be fine, but if I don't do this, you will not. We need you, Ilsa, whether you wear this shape or another, we need you. I'll not lose you to something like this.}* Ales' mindvoice was resolute.

The Mother nodded and put her slender fingers over Ales' hand on top of Ilsa's head.

"Are you certain, Daughter?" the Mother asked. Ales nodded in response. A soft blue glow surrounded the mother, suffusing the room in sapphire light.

"For this night alone, you carry the Oath of two, my Daughter. I wish you luck this night, for you will all need it." The Mother put one slender finger under Ilsa's chin and lifted her face so their eyes met.

"Remember your Oath, my Child. If you survive this night, you may seek my council and I will help you understand the answers to your questions," the Mother promised.

Ilsa shed a few tears and gave a short nod. "Thank you, Mother," Ilsa whispered, and then the Mother faded away like the light at sunset.

Ales turned and went back to the endpoint crystal. She held out the Lightgate to Warran.

"Take this, Warran. If any of us are injured and can no longer fight, it will be up to you to get us back here to recouperate," Ales said. "Cole, how is the progress of your Cellstructs?"

"They have reached my brain, and I believe I understand how to utilize them, for the most part. I've a long way to go," he said.

"But the added strength, you are feeling it?"

Cole nodded. "Yes, and my Cellstructs are helping me adjust to it. I can fight."

Ales put her hands on the endpoint crystal, and so did the others.

"Wait!" A tiny voice pipped up from behind them. Ales turned to see Mina standing nearby, looking lost. "Can't I do anything to help?"

"Staying here with the others is the best help you can give us right now, Mina. When Jame and Juran get back, you and Kayna must tell them what is happening so that they can do their part." Ales smiled, and the little girl nodded. She spread her skirts in a curtsey and went back inside, closing the door behind her.

Ales transported them to the Traveler's Grove, and then from there to the endpoint crystal nearest to the ruins of the prison complex. It was several lengths from the remnants of the complex, and with any luck, ahead of the animals. It had taken them bare minutes to make what preparations they could. Ales opened her Vision, and the others did as well. She peered through the trees, examining the ground nearby.

"Either they haven't passed, or they are not heading for Rihanna," she said a moment later.

"They are coming," Lia said with certainty. Her large ears were twitching one way then the other. She nodded. "We have two minutes or less. They are coming fast."

"Ilsa, we need to slow them and break them up. We cannot stop or kill them all, so we need to break them up to make them more manageable. Run as fast as you can stoneward, and I will go bloomward. We will create a break by downing a line of trees. Use Breaking to cause a chain reaction that will down trees in a mostly straight line all the way back to this spot," Ales explained. Ilsa looked skeptical. "You can do it, Ilsa. Focus." Ilsa nodded and turned stoneward.

"The rest of you know what to do. I can only hope that the Outriders heeded my warning and are prepared for those that get past us," Ales said.

"There are only five of us," Warran said.

"Countless times, we of the Tier have done the impossible. Now we must do so once again. Trust in yourself, Warran. Our job is not to stop this from happening. It is to do what is necessary to protect those among the Ryhim who cannot protect themselves. To do that, we must stop just enough of these animals that those Ryhim defending Rihanna can fight the rest. I shall gift defense to the defenseless," Ales said.

"Must we kill them?" Ilsa asked without turning back. Lia laid her ears back unhappily when Ales started to speak. Ales quieted and held out her hand to let Lia speak.

"Not all of them. You and Ales have the skills necessary to render them immobile long enough to cage and cleanse them, but you must know that they have been infected with Cellstructs that are slowly destroying them from the inside. You can use your Vision to tell the difference between those that can be saved and those that cannot. Be warned, operating your Vision at that level will strain you at your current skill. But our Sister is right. To many of these animals, death will be a release. We absolutely must thin their numbers," Lia explained. Ales' mental handshake buzzed in her mind.

{You're right. I should have been clearer about that earlier,} Ales said.

{You have a lot on your mind,} Lia said, her mindvoice filled with warmth and support for her sister.

"Lia is right. We do not have to kill them all. Remember, though, the primary goal is to defeat as many animals as we safely can before they can reach the Center. Ilsa, lets go," Ales said. Ilsa nodded and turned. She darted into the woods at top speed. Ales did the same.

"The rest of you prepare yourselves. This is going to be bad. Spread out and attempt to stay out of Ales' way. For the most part, she will be moving too fast for even us to follow. Just do the best you can," Lia advised. Warran reached for his lancers first and Lia spoke up.

"I think it best to save your lancers in case you run into something you can't handle with a sword. Everyone open your mental link. Talking in battle is inefficient, and at the speeds everyone will be moving, it is far too slow," Lia said. She reached out to everyone to establish a central link.

{Can everyone hear me?} Lia asked. She received a mental affirmative from everyone. Lia could feel Ales' mental disquiet over having to harm trees. Flora was closer to the Mother than fauna. Trees did not have individual souls, but rather were part of the spirit of the Mother. Kill a tree, and you did a small harm to the Mother, so the Tier treated all flora with reverence.

{The smell is getting much stronger. If you are going to do it, Ales, it must be now.} Lia's mindvoice was filled with growing concern.

{Ilsa, we have gone far enough to make a large enough break. Do it now.} Ales' mindvoice was unhappy, but resolved.

{Alright.}

A long moment passed in silence, and then from a distance came a loud boom. Less than a second later, a second rang out. Then, with increasing speed, the crashing sound of massive trees being felled swelled in the forest. The massive trees began to fall like dominos. It was not a perfectly straight line. Each tree came down at just the right angle to strike the next tree, toppling it into the ground. As the last few leaves settled to the ground, a line of black figures crested the horizon. All of them had crouched down behind the massive line of trees. Lia was using Taking to keep them invisible until some had passed. Depending on how thoroughly they were being controlled, the trees would allow them to easily split the group at the very least.

{Remember, be safe. If you are gravely wounded Warran will use the Lightgate to take you to safety.}

She received affirmative replies from everyone. Then, the ground began to vibrate beneath them as the herd of snarling animals rushed down the incline towards them. Black shapes began to fly over their heads as the freshly downed trees were trampled by paws and hooves. Some of the animals stopped in the flow of the herd and looked around warily.

{Wait,} Ales spoke into all of their minds.

Suddenly, Ales was there. She dove into the fray at the perfect moment when a massive set of laranic hooves hit the ground in front of them. She had thrown a massive log towards the creature, and then she had used her super human speed to run fast enough to jump atop the enormous projectile. The creature was covered in an oily black coating of bondstructs, and the log hit it with such force that the bondstructs burst away from its body in a disintegrating cloud. Ales jumped back off the log as it plowed the large animal into a deep furrow in the ground. The log flipped over and landed ontop of the animal, crushing it.

{Now!}

Ales darted away, drawing her Windblade. She searched the crowd of animals, which had stopped moving forward while the first half of the herd continued. She tried to seek out the groups that were the most damaged; those that she knew she could not save.

{Ilsa, you try to clear the ones that can be saved. I'll destroy those that are too damaged. The rest of you scatter and stop as many of them as you can,} Ales sent.

{Alright,} Ilsa said.

She had already downed dozens of animals in the time it had taken them to recover from Ales' entrance. Ales whipped her Windblade forward, and there was a roar. A large group of black bodies were whipped into the air with bone breaking force. They smashed into trees, the sound of crushed bones and snapped necks filling the air. It was brutal work, and Ales' face was set in a grim mask of determination.

Cole drew his sword and dashed towards Ilsa. He staggered for one short moment when his first steps carried him much further than he was prepared for. Then he steadied and drove into the fight right behind Ilsa. He whipped his blade in a well-practiced pattern that sliced through necks and severed spines. Each kill was precise and resulted in a quick painless death. The confusion did not last nearly long enough, and before Lia and Warran could join the fight, the animals had already started to organize themselves into ranks. There were just so many that Lia wasn't even sure where to start. Warran drew his sword. He did not get too close to Ales, but rather began his fight in her general direction.

{Be our reserve, Sister?} Ales asked. *{If any of us get bogged down, you can step in and use Taking to give us some breathing room.}*

Lia gave her a mental nod and sank back into the shadow of the line of downed trees.

Warran cut a path towards where Ales was standing on a small hillock nearby. Each precise cut killed hiluk and marskok. The hiluk were all large breeds, and Warran wondered where it had found so many big ones. It was possible that it had been breeding them. The marskok were a surprise. They were far more dangerous than the hiluk. The larger breeds were easier to fight, despite their high strength. The marskok were small animals with stout, long bodies and retractile claws on the toes of both fore and hind paws. Each one had a mouth full of fangs, and they attacked in coordinated packs, sometimes as many as twenty together. They were supernaturally fast, and they had killed many people who carelessly entered forests where they lived. Warran froze in place as a pack of them squirmed out from between the other, larger animals surrounding them. He brought up his sword and focused on his Vision, which allowed him to track even the ones that were behind them. They bared their razor fangs at him and lept.

He spun his sword in a pattern that Ales had drilled into him a thousand times in their cycle of training. He placed his feet carefully to turn his body full circle, creating a cage of blurring steel between him and the marskok. His blade cut through their bodies in a confusing circular pattern. Some made it through. He could not get them all. Most of them, though, fell to the ground dead. One landed on his calf, sinking in its fangs and tearing away a small chunk of meat. Warran gritted his teeth as claws sunk into his shoulder. He whipped his blade around in a tight circle at his side, stripping away the one who had taken a chunk out of his calf. Twisting around, he slammed his back into a tree, crushing the one climbing his shoulder. He spun as it fell towards the ground stunned. His blade separated its head from its body as it fell. He felt more than heard when a line of superheated air blasted past him. He had already been turning to engage the large hiluk that thought to take him from behind. It was cut cleanly in half by a strike from Ales' Windblade.

She said nothing, and he marveled at her awareness in combat. She had swung her blade like it was all part of some massive plan she had concocted in her head before the battle had even begun. She never stopped moving, her body whipping in a circular pattern as she blew away another group of animals with such precision that eight out of a group of ten were smashed flat. The other two ran towards Ales, and Warran reached for his lancer to cover her. It was completely unnecessary. Ales darted out of the way, and he realized that she had been communicating silently with Ilsa, who arrowed towards the two animals. She hit them almost gently, and they collapsed into unconsciousness. Warran could feel his calf being knit together by his Cellstructs, and he tested it to make sure he could move without doing more damage, but it was almost fully healed.

{Help Cole. He's getting bogged down, and there is a katali stalking him,} Ales' thought sounded inside of his mind.

He took a mental accounting of where everyone was. He found Cole a hundred marks behind him. Warran turned and ran towards his brother. Ales had been right. While the smaller animals did not seem to be giving Cole trouble, it seemed that some of the larger ones had isolated him. There was something else large stalking him in the woods, but it was keeping between the trees. That made it hard to figure out what it was, even with his Vision open. The katali had climbed a tree, and some of the other smaller animals were attempting to force Cole to back up beneath it.

{Be careful, they are gathering in larger groups to try and rush us a few hundred marks away,} Lia warned.

Warran drew his lancer and shot the katali as it prepared to jump down on Cole.

{Watch your head, Cole. Body falling behind you,} Warran warned.

{I'll take care of that,} Ales said in response to Lia.

It had been only a few short minutes, but hundreds of bodies were down on the ground around them. Warran went to stand by Cole as they both felt daunted by the number of animals still moving through the trees around them.

Cole did his best to watch everything around him. He had used some tricks of Taking so far to make it seem as if he were attacking from out of nowhere, but the animals were getting really thick. He looked up to see a writhing mass moving towards him, and he knew he could never successfully hold it back. He felt more than heard the incredible sound scale up nearby. The roar of sound struck him like a physical thing, and he clapped his hands over his ears to protect them. What went past him was like a brick wall made of air. It slammed into the mass of animals and scattered them like leaves. Bodies cartwheeled in every direction as if an incalculably huge battering ram had smashed through their formation. The roar came again, and Cole crouched down, trying to figure out what was going on.

{What's happening?!} Cole shouted into their mental link.

{Ales is breaking up the larger formations so we don't get bogged down. You don't have to yell into the link. The volume of external sound does not affect how well we can hear you.} Lia's mindvoice was calm and collected, with overtones of worry.

{Just keep your ears covered. Three more blasts,} Ales said into the link.

True to her word, a moment later, the sound died down. Animal bodies had been scattered everywhere. Some had been killed in the blasts, and there was one sizable crater about a mark deep that looked as if a giant hand had scooped out the earth. Whatever had been there was simply gone, trees, dirt, and all. There were no animals within twenty marks of it.

Cole stared in disbelief at Ales as she held her Windblade poised, ready to strike again if she needed too. The devastation she had wrought with her Windblade was vast. He tried to compare his strength against hers, but looking around at what she had just done, the gap was so enormous that he had no way to measure it. His mind boggled trying to work through the problem, and he gave up to just stare in awe at her.

"Destroyer," he whispered, but he made sure to keep it too low for her to hear. He knew it hurt her.

{Those were almost dead already,} Ales spoke into the link as her lambent eyes searched the forest. She growled and turned away to walk back towards where Lia was crouching

protectively over Ilsa. Ilsa was already stirring, but she had a bump on her head where something had struck her.

{What happened?} Cole asked as he got to his feet, regripping his sword in a defensive posture.

{Accident. I don't know my own strength yet.} Ilsa's mindvoice was muzzy, somehow conveying a feeling of dizziness.

{She lept into a tree branch that she would not normally have been able to reach. She will be fine in a few seconds.}

Cole cut down a black hiluk that lept at him from the shadows, and then he backed away as a massive form lumbered out of the trees. It was an animal Cole had never seen outside of the one that Ales and Lia had saved. It was at least twice Lia's size, and had six legs tipped with nonretractile claws. Four horns came from the top of its skull. Two were straight pointing backwards, and two of them curled around its large triangular ears. There was no fighting that monster with a sword in any normal sense, but his muscles were tight with new power, and he queried them to compare his own strength to that of the animal. His Cellstructs assured him that he was more than powerful enough to lift the creature if he so desired. He reached for his lancer.

{Do not shoot that animal,} Ales said.

She jogged over as Cole backed away. She eyed the animal then bent and snatched up a rock off the ground. She whipped her hand and the rock shot forward, whacking the creature in the skull with a loud crack. It immediately collapsed onto the ground.

{It will survive this,} Ales said.

Cole eyed her suspiciously.

{The one we saved had a mate. Banics mate for life, Cole, and this one may be her mate since she told us that he was with her.}

Ales eyed the creature unhappily. The same sorts of steel tines had been driven through its eyes. It must have been in horrible pain from the modifications. Cole eyed it warily, but Ales waved him away.

{No time for staring. It won't awake for hours, yet,} Ales said through the link. She turned and ran off towards a large

group of animals that she had knocked down. They were getting back up now. Cole turned back to his own portion of the battle.

Ilsa pushed away the dizziness as her concussion subsided. Her Cellstructs had warned her a moment too late that she was going to strike her head on the branch. They now informed her that it would take eighteen seconds to cool her damaged brain tissues, and thirty-eight seconds until the synaptic connections could be restored. Until they were, she might experience difficulty in speaking, as she had done minor damage to the speech processing centers of her brain.

She picked herself up from the ground and startled back when a black shape dove at her. Lia flew past her and smashed into the large black shape like a boulder flung from a trebuchet. She crushed the large hiluk to the ground, raking her claws through its spine, killing it instantly. She spun back to Ilsa, and her Vision enfolded them both in the sphere of her Taking abilities.

{I'll give you a moment to recover,} Lia said.

{I'm fine,} Ilsa said a little too quickly.

{No, you're concussed, but your Cellstructs will take care of it in a moment.}

A moment later, Ilsa stood on wobbly legs. She steaded a moment after that as her dizziness actually subsided.

{There's no end to them,} Ilsa said.

{Actually, we have killed or incapacitated around three quarters of the number that remained behind. I fear that the Blight will soon realize that this is a losing battle since I so quickly killed the ones of its minions that were true dangers to us.} Ales' mindvoice sounded worried and a little harried. She jumped back out of the way as a large hiluk with blue and white skin lept at her. She landed on top of the downed trees.

{Everyone listen. My Cellstructs have now marked and identified all twenty two hundred and forty eight remaining animals. I'm giving you all this data. Your Cellstructs will display which of these animals can be saved and which need to be killed. There is no more time to waste here. Back in here, close to Lia. This is the first time I'm sending memories to all of you at once. Only Lia and I will not be a little confused for a moment after this,} Ales said.

They all slowly backed towards the shadowy space beneath the line of downed trees. They struck at the animals that closed in around them as they backed up. Lia lept forward and made the animals pay for getting too close. Ales distributed the information, and they all staggered for a moment. When they rose, each animal was outlined in their Vision with either a red outline or a blue one.

{Blue can be saved. Those are for you, Ilsa. The rest cannot be. Their internal deterioration has gone too far for us to be able to prepare Cellstructs quickly enough to save them. They are in deep, horrible pain. Let's get this done,} Ales said.

She lifted her Windblade and whipped it towards a large group of animals that had red outlines. A roar rang out, and then the animals were smashed to bits by the force of the blast. Ales cringed at the pain of so many deaths. It did not hurt her like it did when she judged someone. These deaths were not her decision. These were a mercy.

Ilsa had been especially careful not to kill any that night, and Ales felt grateful that she had tried so hard not to add to Ales' burdens. She made a decision to trust them to take care of the rest here in the woods. They had only done so well because she had been able to use her Windblade to full effect at the beginning of the fight. Those defending Rihanna would stand little chance of defeating the overwhelming force that likely already had reached them.

{I have handled the largest animals. I'm going to Rihanna while you all clean up the rest here,} Ales spoke into their mental link. She received mental affirmatives from everyone. Ales whipped up a wind that blew back all of the animals around them to give them some breathing room. Then she dashed towards Warran. Her hand dove into the pouch at his side. She vanished in a flash of brilliant light.

{Yes, she's annoyingly amazing at everything. Focus, please,} Lia said sarcastically into their mental link, snapping them back to the task at hand. *{Without her whipping that Windblade about, we have a real fight ahead of us.}* Lia's mindvoice was stark and realistic. They each nodded. Each of them drove into the

fight at a different point, exercising their new abilities to their fullest extent.

48

Ilsa watched Ales go and sighed. She could only feel the horrible sense that she was now going to have to kill more. The pit the grief had dug into her stomach was just going to get deeper. Ales had been right. If she had had to bear the weight of this night alone, it would have destroyed her. She felt utterly useless, no matter how much Ales insisted that they needed her. She could never trust herself to keep her oath ever again. It really didn't matter that Mina had survived. That was nothing of her doing. She had killed that innocent child. Lia's admonition drew her back to the present. Ilsa looked around at her friends fighting for their lives against hundreds of animals. Ilsa focused herself.

{Will she be alright on her own?} Ilsa asked into the link. She felt a mental affirmative from Lia. At the beginning of the fight, Ilsa had been using fist-sized stones to render those animals that could be saved unconscious. That was not going to work any further. Ilsa reached for the sword on her hip but hesitated for a long moment.

{Try this,} Lia spoke into a private mental link just between them. She came closer and touched a paw to the bag hanging around her neck. From the top of the bag, a short metal bar rolled out onto her paw. It was less than a mark long, and made of polished Sol alloy. She held it out to Ilsa.

Ilsa picked up the short bar, and she could feel that it had a mental interface. When she touched it with her mind, the bar extended into a staff that was nearly as tall as she was. It was lighter than it should have been, being made of Sol alloy, and she could see the way it was weighted to better balance the implement. Simple knurling was raised along the center of the staff, and gave her an excellent grip. Ales had drilled her with the staff for the whole of the cycle for reasons that Ilsa had not known at the time. But now, as she hefted the staff, it felt so right in her hands.

{Thank you, Sister.} Ilsa's mindvoice was so thankful that Lia almost laughed.

{Thank Ales. She knew that you would need it.} Lia sent support across their mental link.

Ilsa spun the staff, and then turned to the fight. She assessed where her brothers were fighting, and she moved toward them to support them as best she could. They fought savagely against the odds, dodging the animals outlined in blue and cutting down those outlined in red. Ilsa danced around them, smashing down the animals outlined in blue. Corpses of various animals began to pile up around them. They would soon become a hinderance, and so they began to retreat away from their position. In the end, though, there were too many for them to handle on their own.

Lia had been circling them the entire time, attacking from the shadows, taking large groups of the animals out of the fight. She had managed to open a path for them to retreat by some miracle, and Ilsa thought that they might be able to do what Ales had asked. Then a small pack of marskok dove out of a tree.

Their black bodies swarmed with clouds of bondstructs. They landed on Ilsa in a biting, clawing swarm. She screamed, enraged, and smashed at them with the staff. Then she was suddenly choking on bondstructs as they flowed into her mouth and nose. The haunting image of the things flowing into Lia's mouth filled her mind. Then the world went away as she was somehow drawn back into her own mind.

She was standing in a white room with gleaming white walls. The room was hexagonal, and on each of the white walls were flowing groups of ever-changing letters and figures. After a long moment of reading each wall, she realized that this was a constant flow of information about her own body. The writing on each of the walls was scribed in shades of blue and purple, except for one. When she turned around, she found the wall that seemed to be outputting her brain function was written in a stark blood red.

"What is this?" she asked. Her Cellstructs replied.

{This space is your Mindscape. These Ones have brought your mind here because there is a problem that you cannot address from the confines of your conscious mind. Our body has been infiltrated

by structures that are attempting to Cut themselves access into your mind. They seek to control you through the connection that These Ones possess to your mind. If they are successful, you will cease to be able to control your own body.} The words chilled Ilsa to her core.

"What must I do?!" Ilsa gasped frantically.

{You must direct These Ones in defending against this threat. Elementary Energy is being injected into These Ones in an attempt to overwrite current operational instructions.} She felt them feeding information about Elementary Energy infections into her mind. She still didn't understand what to do.

Lia roared in panic as Ilsa was burried under a swarm of marskok. Small, writhing bodies drew blood with bites, and claws. But that was not the true issue. She swiped one massive paw at them, smashing most of the group away from Ilsa's body before they could do any real damage. The issue was that her Cellstructs had slammed closed their mental link. They had created a barrier around her mind, and Ilsa had gone completely unresponsive. That meant that something was attacking her Cellstructs directly, somehow. They were defending themselves, and in turn, Ilsa. Lia latched onto Ilsa's dress with her teeth and pulled the girl into the shelter of the felled trees.

Cole and Warran backed towards her as they were slowly overwhelmed by the hundreds of animals that attacked relentlessly. Warran dropped his sword and drew his lancers in a blur. He began firing into the mass of writhing animal bodies rushing towards them. They dropped in a huge wave as he emptied his lancers into them. His reload was so fast that it appeared as if the magazines lept from his belt into the weapons. He began firing again, and Cole spun behind him, cutting down the animals that tried to come at Warran's back. It was a frantic blur of motion, and Lia knew she needed to help them, but she did not dare leave Ilsa unprotected lest the creatures try to pour more structures into her body. Lia gasped in relief when Kiltik bounded into sight over the trees. He spun towards Lia and fluidly joined their mental link.

{Go help them. This One will assist Ilsa Family Katane. The Blight wishes to control her to use her to unlock the knowledge of The Core. This One will not let that happen,} Kiltik said frantically.

{I'm leaving her in your care, Kiltik,} Lia responded.

She jumped from her spot, leaping high into the forest canopy, twisting to miss branches and limbs. Her paws hit the trunk of a massive stonebark tree a hundred marks off the ground. She clearly had opened all of her Constraints, because when she pushed off of the trunk, she shot towards the ground like a missile. She was a blue blur when her paws hit the ground. She claimed she wasn't anywhere near as powerful as Ales, but she was a power in her own right. The sound of her hitting the ground was a deep thud that was more felt than heard. Dirt and black bodies flew away from the impact site as if an explosion had blown them away.

Kiltik turned back to Ilsa. Having taking the form of a katali, he arranged his six paws carefully for comfort and reached out towards Ilsa's mind. The elementary energy barrier Ilsa's Cellstructs had constructed around her mind was substantial. Kiltik sent a Tieran confirmation key to the access point of the barrier. The energetic barrier irised open to allow him to make a connection. Then he was standing in the stark, white room of her Mindscape. She was frantically trying to direct her Cellstructs to attack the energetic infection coming from the bondstructs that had gotten inside of her.

"Oh gods, oh gods, it is going to take me," she was mumbling. She didn't notice Kiltik when he faded into view.

"Ilsa," Kiltik said. When she did not respond, he moved closer and put a paw on her shoulder. She jumped and her eyes darted up to him.

"What do I do?" she asked frantically, and Kiltik's Katali muzzle morphed into what looked like a comforting smile, at least, as much of one as his animal muzzle could produce.

"This One will not let the Blight harm you. This One will teach you how to defend yourself against an infection like this. You have already begun. You simply need to learn how to strike back," Kiltik explained.

She waved her hand, and the displays on the six walls changed. The blue and green displays vanished, and the red display expanded to cover all six walls. The compressed information spread out into a more useful display. Kiltik examined it.

"I don't know what all of this means. I can read the Tieran just fine, but all of this about Energetic Transfer and Elementary Redirection Barriers... I don't know what it all means. My Cellstructs are trying to advise me, but they aren't making much sense," Ilsa said with distress.

"This One understands. You do not yet have the proper grounding in Elementary Energy theory and manipulation to understand what your Cellstructs are attempting to convey. Your Cellstructs are attempting to instruct you on how to position them to counter the energetic infection that is attempting to spread to your brain and the Cellstructs contained therein. They have already erected a defense barrier to prevent this from happening, but that is only a short term solution.

Elementary Energy holds the information that allows the bondstructs that have infiltrated your body to function. What you are attempting to do is surround those bondstructs with overwhelming numbers, allowing the collected Elementary Energy to surpass the collected Elementary Energy that the bondstructs hold. Once you have done this, your Cellstructs can project their own data into the bondstructs. This will overwrite whatever instructions they were given and allow you to take control of them. They will continually move within your body to attempt to wear you down.

You have to set a trap for them. Remember, they are not completely autonomous. They have a set of instructions that they are following. They can be baited to rush to one space within your body where you can quickly surround them. Make note that this is only true of those structures that do not have an omnipositional connection to the Blight. Those with a connection like that have full access to the self-awareness of the creature. It will be far cleverer than these structures," Kiltik explained.

"So if I make it look like there is an opening in my mental defenses, these things will drive for it and leave themselves open to being surrounded?" Ilsa asked.

"Good thinking, but take it further. Their instruction set will be much more complicated than that. It'll hold back some of its mass to make sure it is not surrounded," Kiltik said.

"Multiple openings still isn't going to do it, then. We need to make it look innocuous. An opening in the Cellstructs that could allow them to travel closer to my brain," Ilsa said a little feverishly.

As distressed as she was over what had happened with Mina, Ilsa still did not want to let the Blight win. She waved her hand at the wall and a schematic of her body displayed, surrounded by Tieran script. She drew a circle in the air around her chest and made a beckoning gesture. The display zoomed in to display her heart pumping blood throughout her body. She stood up from her kneeling position and she looked like she was going to walk across the room. She realized, though, that her mind was creating this place. Then she was just standing in front of the wall. She ran a finger over the image. The image changed to show just veins and arteries inside of her body.

"Can my Cellstructs pass through the walls of my veins and arteries without damaging them?" Ilsa asked.

Kiltik did not answer, but a monotone voice sounded in the room. "These Ones have unfettered access to all areas of your body. These Ones are you." The response was immediate.

Kiltik nodded. Ilsa drew three quick circles, one around each artery in her neck and one around the thickest one above her heart.

"We'll setup a weak line of defense here, and leave the arteries unblocked, but gather a large number of Cellstructs around the arteries so that they can rush into each one through the artery wall front and behind," she said.

"This is dangerous as it will temporarily cut off the flow of blood to the brain," the monotone voice of her Cellstructs warned. They sounded very much like Kiltik, and she wondered if all Tieran technology had the same odd metallic voice. Thoughts for another time, she admonished herself.

"Leaving these things loose in my body is more dangerous. We'll have to finish the fight quickly. I assume we don't have much time, anyway. Line the artery wall with defenders so that it cannot damage the artery wall itself," Ilsa said, and looked at Kiltik, concern plain on her face.

Kiltik seemed to know what she was thinking. "They are doing well enough. Cole was severely damaged, but has been safely evacuated. Most of the animals are dead or down. Warran and Lia were both damaged in minor ways. Warran lost a finger to a bite, but it will be replaced within a day or two. Lia has let out what she has been holding back. She is shy about her killing power. She doesn't like to scare people," Kiltik said with some dour amusement.

"This One cannot tell you how well Ales is doing. Rihanna is too far distant for a mental link. Please try to focus on this, as your life is quite literally in the balance here," Kiltik finished.

Worry crossed Ilsa's face. "You can't let me go if it takes me," Ilsa said shakily.

"This One cannot. This One will not let what befell Alizar befall another of the Tier. This One will not let the Blight torture another of This One's family," Kiltik said plainly.

He was not threatening, and there was no ill will in his voice. He was simply stating a fact. If anything, he seemed sad that it had come to this. Ilsa realized how serious the situation had become. This was a fight not just for her life, but to keep her oath to her gods.

"I understand, Kiltik," Ilsa said.

"Your plan is a good one," Kiltik said.

Ilsa began to put the plan into action like a general moving pieces on a map. She waved her hand to the right, and a second display appeared on the wall. The bondstructs that had invaded her body were in two groups: one centered in her lungs, and the other in her stomach. They showed up on the second display as nebulous black clouds in those places in her body. Her cellstucts were fighting a losing battle to keep them contained in those organs. She left those where they were, but the rest of her Cellstructs, she pulled back through the various parts of her body until they gathered at the base of her neck. They followed her plan, gathering around her arteries and veins. And that was when things went terribly wrong.

The bondstructs swirling inside of her lungs broke through, and she could feel them moving inside of her. They went through the thin capillary walls in her lungs and into her bloodstream in a rush. The trap at her arteries was not nearly ready. If the bondstructs managed to strike through to her brain, it was all over.

She instructed her structures to block the arteries right then. She dove into the minds of her Cellstructs to share in their frantic fight. The bondstructs were like tiny sea naks, spherical bodies with eight spindly legs, and two spindly arms with pincers at the ends in the front. Their pincers looked massive to her Cellstructs, which were about half the size of the terrible attackers. Her Cellstructs were similar to tiny insects, but their spherical bodies had twelve spindle-like legs. The front four legs were each tipped with a small pincer, the same as the four on the opposite end of their oval-shaped bodies. They were designed so that they could interlock with each other and quickly knit muscle and bone. They were quickly being destroyed, eaten through by the bondstructs. It was not a completely one-sided battle, but she was losing more than five Cellstructs to every bondstruct destroyed. It was losing ground, and then she had a thought.

"How come these have not been attacked by my own immune system?" Ilsa asked.

"They are giving off an elementary energy pulse that is driving back your immune cells," Kiltik replied.

"Can we disrupt them?" Ilsa asked.

"I can, but it is problematic. I can run an elementary energy current through your body. It will render your body unusable for a few minutes."

Ilsa jerked and stared at the diagram in horror. The trap had failed on one side of neck. The bondstructs were pushing through a gap in her Cellstructs.

"Do it!"

She felt the nauseating feeling of an elementary energy charge going through her body. Her body reacted immediately. She could feel herself going limp and falling over onto her side. Within a moment, her Cellstructs stimulated her lymphatic system and immune cells poured into her bloodstream. She made a last-ditch effort to block the few bondstructs that had gotten past her trap by moving the specialized Cellstructs from her brain into the arteries as a last line of defense. Ilsa held her breath and chewed her lower lip for a long minute in fear that she had been too late with her idea. Then, the zoomed in diagram faded from deep red to orange as her immune cells engulfed the bondstructs in her system. Then it faded to a light purple when her Cellstructs began to overwhelm the nebulous black cloud of bondstructs. Kiltik came closer to her in her Mindscape. She was gasping in relief and tears were streaming down her cheeks.

"You did it!" Kiltik yelped enthusiastically.

She realized that his mental form had reverted to the shoovu that he had been for so many spans when they were with the Navano. He lept into her arms, and she hugged him.

"This One has to go, but This One will leave this small part of This One's mind here with you until you come back to consciousness. This One will be somewhat unresponsive as This One attempts to help with the remaining small army."

Ilsa squeezed the mental representation of Kiltik and nodded. "Please go help them," she said with a sigh of relief.

Kiltik snapped back into his body and looked around to assess the situation. It was surprisingly better than he had hoped. Lia was dashing about, destroying stragglers. Warran was leaning against a tree. He was not in very good shape, but after a quick assessment, it was clear that Warran would surive. He was wobbly because a long, straight gash ran from his left shoulder across his spine to his right hip. Clearly, it had smashed through his spine, but his Cellstructs had knitted things back together for the most part. The tree was holding him up more than his legs, but he was taking aim on stray animals. He squeezed the trigger of his lancer, and the bolt downed a darting black body thirty marks away. Kiltik went to his side.

{Ilsa Family Katane will be up soon. It looks like Liassa Family Katane has this under control,} Kiltik spoke into their mental link.

Warran nodded grimly. *{Does she ever. I've seen the gap between us and her this night. I am intervals away from being able to do the things that she did.}* Warran's mindvoice was pensive. *{We almost died.}*

{Yes, and it is not done. This was only half of the army.}

Warran's eyes burned with his Vision, and he nodded. *{I need to replenish my ammunition before we go to the Center. I hope we are not too late.}*

Lia appeared in front of them. *{We have done what we can here. A few dozen of the animals have fled, perhaps towards the center. I chased them for three lengths, but they were driven to escape.}*

A mumbling sound came into the link, and then Ilsa spoke. *{Mother's end, I feel like...}* She didn't finish the thought. She leaned over the edge of tree she was laying upon and vomited what looked like black liquid. Warran pushed himself away from the tree and wobbled. Lia steadied him.

{Don't worry, she is fine. Her body is just expelling the leftovers of the bondstructs that got inside of her. We don't have time for this. Get us back to the workshop,} Lia said.

Warran nodded, and fished in his pouch for the Lightgate. The four of them gathered around, and they all put their hands and paws on the sphere of the Lightgate. They vanished in a flash of white light.

49

Ales yelled in fury and threw her shoulder against the massive gate that was the only one that had not closed in time. By amazing good luck, she had arrived at the Traveler's grove at the same time as the Banners. With the information that Jame had already given them, it had not taken much convincing to get them to lock down the city. They had closed all of the gates but the sunward one before the animals had rushed around the city.

She counted almost eight thousand bodies in the force. It made it clear that the group they had faced in the forest was the slightly smaller of the two. A few hundred had flowed in through the sunward gate before she had blown away a gap in the animals flowing through. The gate slammed shut with a hollow boom. Men pushed a massive bondsteel bar into place holding the banded gates closed.

At least a dozen animals slammed into her back before she could turn around. Claws scrabbled against her, cutting furrows through her flesh. Ales twisted her body in a blur, smashing her elbows in both directions, throwing animals off of her bloody back. She roared in anger and yanked her Windblade from the sheath inside of her long coat. The back of the coat had been shredded by the claws, and that made her angrier still. She whipped around and swung her windblade in a horizontal slash. Wind roared at a volume that was almost a weapon in itself. Black bodies were thrown away in a wide swath. The soldiers that had been helping her close the gate let out a cheer of support. Then they roared and dashed past her into the fray.

Men with longbarrels were shooting into the mass of animals that had made it into the Center. Many of them dashed away in every possible direction. They disappeared into alleyways and down cross streets.

"Chase them down! They'll kill anyone they find!" Ales shouted and pointed into the center.

Outriders in lighter hide armor dashed off into the streets behind the animals. Hundreds of men with lancers and swords flowed past her to follow her orders. Those on top of the wall turned back to the outside and started firing lancers into the large army of animals. Ales stood there for a long few moments, trying to master the roiling pain striking at her mind. She had killed so many tonight, and she was ready to collapse from the pounding in her head. So many deaths that she had bulled her way through with her anger. It was starting to fade now, though, as it looked as if they had secured the Center. Even the latest attack was not enough to keep her pushing through the pain. She would need to find a place to fall to her sorrows soon, someplace where no one could see. She saw the flash of the Lightleaf trees above the buildings.

{*Ales?*} Lia's mindvoice was a little frantic.

Ales sighed in relief. {*How many got past you?*}

{*Perhaps two dozen. How are things here?*} Lia asked.

{*They are probably going to run out of ammunition before they kill all the animals,*} Ales said.

{*How come there are so many soldiers here?*}

{*Jame and Juran nearly threw up their guts, but they managed to endure and Lightjump in almost five thousand Outriders from various clan camps. They are recovering in the Traveler's Grove.*}

Ales' head pounded, and she went down to one knee. Lia came out from a side street at a run, having felt Ales' distress through their link.

{*I'm fine, Lia. Just having to deal with the pain. I'm exhausted, and I'm not sure how much longer I can hold it together before I have to step away and process this.*}

{*Will the Banners work with me? I haven't had to kill as much tonight. You all took that burden off of me. I am fairly fresh.*}

{*They are set up in the guardhouse near the bloomward gate. Let's go speak with them. I think that now that the gates are closed, this is academic. I would like a Tieran presence here, just in case anything goes wrong.*}

{*Cole, Kiltik, and I can stay. You can head back to the Traveler's Grove. We have more to talk about. Kiltik tells me that the Blight tried to take control of Ilsa. It was a very close thing, and he says he is certain he knows how it was done.*} Lia's mindvoice was gently dismissive.

"Alright, Spook, let's go talk to the Banners,"

They made their way around the outer wall of the Center towards the bloomward gate. Kiltik had made brief contact to let them know that he would take a few extra minutes. He had run across a group of Outriders who had been outnumbered and were taking heavy casualties. He had stopped to help them. A group of the larger animals were attempting to break into the guardhouse. Ales grunted in clear displeasure when she saw the two massive balath slamming themselves against the heavy bondsteel doors. She drew her Windblade out and Lia put a paw on her hand.

{I can handle this,} Lia offered.

Ales shook her head. {No. I'll be a wreck after this for a while, but it is mine to do, Lia. Besides, they are in such pain. I want this over quickly.}

Ales pushed open her constraints to the sixth level. She swung the Windblade, and there was a roar of diffuse sound. It was different than the other sounds that had been made by her Windblade tonight. It scaled up into a hurricane force roar that lifted the group of large animals from the ground and flung them towards the wall. They crashed violently through a small empty building and hit the massive stone wall with bone breaking force. So violent was the impact that the animals were killed instantly. Ales slipped the Windblade back into her coat. She put her hand to her head, took a deep breath, and then let it out slowly. A tear rolled down her cheek, and she quickly wiped it away.

"Please open the door," Ales called through the thick bondsteel. A moment later, the sound of a bolt being thrown came from within. The door opened, and the soldiers jumped back when they saw Lia. She rolled her eyes at them and let Ales go in first.

"Please do not insult my Sister," Ales said, and Lia followed her inside.

They went to the left, and through a small door into a stairwell. They went up several flights of stairs and came out into a large room. There were maps hung on the walls, and a large table in the middle. Standing around the table were five men. Each one was older, perhaps thirty-five to forty cycles. They wore various uniforms that were immaculately kept.

"Gentlemen, how goes the battle?" Ales asked.

"Well, thanks to you. We have lost some runners in the city, so there are still animals loose in the center, but we will root them out. We have lost a few off the top of the wall to larger animals like Katali that have cleared the wall, but they were quickly killed or subdued by you," Banner Juka explained. He was the eldest leader of the Outriders, and it seemed that he spoke for all of them most of the time.

"This is my sister Liassa. I am exhausted, and I no longer trust myself to make solid decisions in the field. I am going to take some rest. She will be of as much assistance to you as I have been." Ales' voice was confident.

"If you could bring me up to speed?" Lia spoke up, and the men around the table all paused for a moment.

"Ah, yes, honored Tier." Banner Juka hesitated for only a moment. "We have distributed our Outriders in platoons of one hundred soldiers each to every section of the center to hunt any animals that were able to pass the wall. We have arrayed double ranks of soldiers who have been trained with lancers on the wall to defend it from any climbers."

Ales turned away from the discussion and went to the door. She headed back outside and followed a meandering path back to the Traveler's Grove. She avoided the fighting completely, and it took her only a few minutes of jogging to reach the grove. She passed the outer borders of the crystalline trees, and she felt the power of the Gods enfold her. Lightleaf groves were special places, suffused with the power of both the Mother and the Father.

When she was certain that the power of the Gods had taken hold, hiding her from anyone that might find her, Ales fell to her knees and let out a sob of pure anguish. She slammed her fists into the ground as the feeling of all those deaths poured through her mind. She felt each one she killed as if she were dying herself. Lives ripped away before their time, and it made her feel so useless for a long moment. Then the feeling passed, and she felt the touch of the Mother and Father on her mind, soothing her pains. She needed to feel the pain to know that when she made the decision to kill, it had to be the right one. The constant reminder was always necessary, but the touch of the Gods on her mind assured her that she had made the right decision, even if it hurt.

"Why? Why does this Blight hate us so?" Ales screamed at the sky.

"Even we are are not sure of that, Daughter," a deep voice spoke from nearby. There, a few marks away, were both the Mother and the Father.

"We have suspicions concerning its origins, and we have not told you only because we do not feel that it will help you defeat the creature." The Mother's higher voice held a note of confusion. "You know that we are not the only Gods in the universe. In the early times before we Gods attempted to create life in the universe, there was some disagreement amongst us about the idea of bringing creation into the void."

"So we agreed that we would use our power to create many dimensions and leave the void intact for those amongst us who did not wish to partake in the creation of life. It took us many millions of cycles to carefully construct each reality," the Father picked up the story. They did this sometimes when they were together.

"It has been countless aeons, but we recently became aware that energy was being bled out of some of the living dimensions. The energetic configurations upon which our dimensions stand are being degraded. The gods of the Void refuse to treat with us as in aeons past, and we have come to the grave conclusion that they have decided that our living dimensions are somehow a threat to them. They cannot attack us directly because the Eldrich Law prevents we gods from warring amongst ourselves. Further, our choice to surround ourselves with self-propogating life has made us much stronger. So they have created and sent attackers from the Void against our creations to weaken us. We do not know their goals. They cannot possibly destroy us, so we can only imagine that they seek to destroy only our creations to return all things to the Void as they once were," the Mother finished.

"So there is no end? We can't ever win? If we destroy this creature, they'll just send more," Ales said.

The Mother and Father exchanged a glance, some communication that went between them.

"We will not lie to you, Daughter, it is possible, but it is also possible that if we are given no other choice, we can lock the Void away from our realities for all time. But to do that, we will require cooperation from other gods and the denizens of other dimensions," the Father said.

"You are correct. It spoke of the Void to me. It said that was where The Core had been taken." Ales said. They paused for a long moment, exchanging a look.

"We cannot give you much further information, but this. Physical Matter cannot exist in the Void." The Mother said.

"Thank you Mother. But how can those from other dimensions help?"

"Before we can even attempt to reach out to other dimensions for more information, we must stabilize our own. Once we can you can find out how they may help. Your world is the last that is infected in our reality, and further, it is the greatest locus of our power. So, Daughter, now you know why we have charged you with finding The Core and returning the Tier to protect this world," the Mother said and touched her face with delicate care. She used a slender, elegant thumb to wipe away some of Ales' tears.

"I will do it, but I fear that when I do, there may be nothing left of me," Ales said uneasily.

"I think, my Daughter, that you will find that your resolve is more equal to this task than you know," the Mother said.

"Can you help Ilsa, Mother? She did not deserve what was done to her," Ales asked.

The Mother smiled sadly. "You know the answer to that question, Daughter."

Ales nodded, and then they were gone, leaving Ales alone with the grief and pain of what she had had to do that long night. Then she felt the warm suffusion of energy coming from the other Tier in the mental link with her. She felt momentarily ashamed to have forgotten. She was never alone.

50

Mina walked through the front door of what had been her home for all of her life. Her uncle was holding her tiny hand as they walked through the empty halls of Clan Clai's ancestral home. Clai was the smallest of the clans, with only a few thousand members total, and over a hundred had been in the house the night that the creature had invaded. It had killed everyone but Mina. Mina paused for a moment, and her uncle stopped next to her. Banner Juka watched her curiously as he waited for her to continue.

"You don't have to show me the way, little one. I can have my Outriders search the house." Banner Juka's deep strong voice was a comfort. It was what she needed.

"I can do it," Mina replied. She was the only person left who knew where the old underground passages were hidden. There were important things hidden in them that Mina had not really learned about yet. She just knew where the tunnel entrances were located in the house.

"The house will be full again soon. Your Aunt would love to have you stay here," he said, and she led him down the hallway. Mina shook her head and shivered. The place she had called home felt cold and terrifying. She only felt safe with Ales and the other Tier.

"I have to go with the Tier." Mina shivered again as she looked around. "I will not be far away, uncle."

"You are the Princess of Clan Clai now. We will need you here," Juka said a little sternly.

"Banner Juka, you are pressing a very young child into something that is no longer meant for her. Can you not see that she is terrified of this place? You haven't the faintest idea what was done to her," Lia said from her spot not far behind. She had lingered outside to make sure that there were no straggling infected animals that might attack them, but she now trotted down the hall with a grim expression on her face.

The man scowled at her, but said nothing. He was deeply respectful of the Tier, but he had not liked it when they had declared that Mina was welcome to live with them and eventually become one of the Tier. He had been trying for the two spans since the battle for Rihanna had ended to change the girl's mind. Lia could tell he had been wearing the girl down. She was young and had no idea where her life should go. Lia didn't, either, but she wouldn't presume to know like Juka did. She had never liked the idea of hereditary titles in the sense that someone would be forced into something they didn't want, simply to satisfy some hereditary duty. Juka looked as if he were about to protest.

"I realize that you are accustomed to being in command, but Mina has made her decision, and she is fulfilling her duty to the Ryhim to allow the other members of Clan Clai to manage the center in the way that the clan always has. I would appreciate it if you would cease badgering her." Lia did her best to keep the growl out of her voice.

The man's jaw snapped shut, and he followed where Mina lead him down towards the basement floors. She stopped halfway down a stairwell and touched a tiny hand to the wall.

"It's right here. I don't know how to open it, though," Mina said. She didn't let go of Juka's hand.

Lia came closer, and as it became too tight for all of them in the space of the stairwell, Juka and Mina moved down the stairwell. Lia opened her Vision, and after a moment she touched the wall. She pressed a stone into the wall, and another stone popped out of it with a subtle snapping sound.

"This stone must be pulled out of the wall. I haven't the proper appendages to grip it." She stepped back, and Juka came back up a stair. He pulled the stone out until another snapping sound came. "Just go ahead and push it back in. The door will open," Lia explained.

Juka pushed the brick back into the wall. There was one last poping sound, and the outline of a door appeared as it opened slightly. Lia nosed the door open and found another stairwell within. The stairwell went down two flights before it opened onto a long stone hallway. There were six widely-spaced doors and the hallway went on for about five hundred marks. The rooms beyond the doors had to be massive.

Lia noticed that there was an air current in here. The smell of hide and old paper filled the air around them. It was a massive library, but there was more. There was a Tieran databank down here somewhere. She could feel the telepathic access point within. Lia followed the sense towards the first door on the right. When she went inside, her eyes went wide at what she saw. The room was large, perhaps a hundred marks square, and there were rows upon rows of shelves. Each shelf was divided into hundreds of cubby holes. Each of the cubbies had a small silvery cube inside.

"Gods, Kinas, what have you left behind here?" Lia wondered out loud. That was when she heard Mina's confused voice.

"Where did she go?" Mina asked.

Lia looked back to them standing in the hall. They were standing right there, yet it appeared that they couldn't see her. She narrowed her eyes and examined the door. That was when she saw it. The door had been enchanted by a Lighteye in such a way that it was entirely imperceptible to anyone without the Vision. Even if someone knew the door was there and attempted to walk through it, they would find themselves crashing into the wall. Not only that, if someone who was not Tier managed to breech the room, everything within would be destroyed. The silvery cubes were information storage devices, but these were not like a piece of The Core. These were of Tieran make. They trapped information in the form of light. They could be erased with a sustained burst of certain frequencies of light.

The enchantment had such power that Lia was one hundred percent certain that a Tier of substantial power had given their life to create it. Kinas had died crafting this enchantment. Lia was not a Lighteye, so she could not have possibly created this enchantment, but she recognized the power when she saw it. They would have to absorb whatever information Kinas thought so important as to leave it here. Whatever it was it had to be extremely important for him to have given his life to create this protective enchantment when he enchanted Rihanna. She was certain that the informational enchantment that was part of the streets of Rihanna was only a distraction for this. Lia returned to the hallway and Mina jumped when she noticed her.

"Where did you go?!" Mina asked excitedly.

"I'll explain it as soon as I consult with my Sister about what to do about it," Lia said. "This is a library, and I belive it contains all of the knowledge and history of Rihanna. I would be careful who you tell about this were I you, Banner Juka."

Lia put her huge paw on Mina's head and ruffled her hair affectionately. "You have done well, little one. You will make a fine Tier one day." Mina blushed a little and gave a proper little curtsy.

51

Jame stood on the open grass before the massive glittering white sorstone building. It had been a mere three spans, but the building had grown up from the ground as if it had appeared by magic. It took up the entire crater where the prison complex had been, and a large space beyond that. It had slid into the sky, surrounded by a dozen towers in a circular pattern. Inside those twelve towers were four larger towers in a square around an enormous central courtyard. A wall fifty marks high ran around the circumference outside of the smaller towers. In the center of the walls the four taller towers reached into the sky at least four hundred marks high.

"It's really is something, isn't it?" The voice was Warran, who had come out of the woods, where he had been playing a game with the children.

"How can such tiny machines build something so massive?" Jame asked.

"I could attempt to explain, but I think that the numbers would be somewhat meaningless to you, considering that I'm likely a hundred cycles from understanding it all myself. This is the true power of the Tier, the power to create things that we could never imagine."

"There are no words for it," Jame said, watching it.

Then Warran looked up thoughtfully at the massive structure. "I think I will call it home," Warran said meaningfully. Jame nodded at him.

The children and Ilsa came out of the forest to stand there with them. Jame put his arm around Ilsa in a comforting way. In the last three spans, he had rarely left her side. He had sort of taken charge of her, and while he didn't understand what she was going through, he acknowledged that she needed someone to make sure she would survive what had befallen her. Mina had come through it better than Ilsa had, for which Ilsa had been grateful. It didn't seem to help her feel as if she had broken her oath any less.

"Your parents will be here soon," Jame said, and Ilsa nodded.

"I don't know what I'm going to do. They won't understand," Ilsa said.

Jame just grunted, "So you are going to do it then?"

Ilsa had talked to him endlessly about what it had felt like when she had killed Mina. He wasn't sure why she had latched onto him when she could have talked to Lia, Ales, or any of the others that had known her much longer. The only explanation was that they were the same age, and he had just shut his mouth to listen to her. She had confided in him that the pain had not faded. It had gotten worse, and were it not for her oath, she might have thought of taking her own life. Whenever she slept, she writhed with nightmares of the moment when she had felt the pain of Mina's death. The girl had died, and she had had to experience that completely. It had only been the skill and power of the Tier that had pulled her spirit back into her body.

"I don't think I have any other choice. It isn't going to go away. I can't continue functioning like this. They won't understand, though. My parents are not Tier. They won't understand my need," Ilsa said.

Jame just shook his head. "I think that they will. If you explain it to them like you have explained to me, I think that they will."

Ilsa still seemed uncertain, but she nodded thoughtfully.

"I'm not exactly sure what I'm going to tell my parents," Jame said with a little laugh. "As far as they know, I'm still with the Outriders."

"Why wouldn't you tell them?" Ilsa asked skeptically.

"Because I am an idiot, and I'm worried that they'll be upset that I will not be one of the Outriders. They are both members. Just insecurity," Jame said.

Ilsa smiled. "I'm pretty sure that they'll understand. You'll be able to do a lot more for your people as one of the Tier than you would as an Outrider."

"Easy for you to say," Jame said, but he seemed content with what he had done for his people already.

The massive wall of their new home seemed to move and a portal irised open in the wall. When it closed behind Ales, it looked as if there had never been an opening at all. Only one of the Tier could open doors in the walls. The Ryhim had been calling the place the Tower of Life on account of all of the plants living within the tower.

"Would you all come inside? There are hundreds of places the kids can play in the tower. You're making me nervous out here," Ales said.

Lia came out of the tree line, and trotted closer to the wall. "It's safe enough for now," Lia called back. *{Let them have this small victory. There are worse times ahead, and they need this,}* Lia added privately into their mental link.

Ales sighed and nodded. *{Fair enough, Lia. Fair enough.}*

She wiped the smudges of black from her face. She had been in the forge with Juran, showing him how to work bondsteel. It was good work that had been a momentary distraction from what was to come. They needed some of the Tier to know how to work metal the old fashioned way in case something happened to the tower, as it had happened to Ahal.

Kiltik and Icci had been working non-stop on building the new Mind a body in the safety of the tower. It had taken spans to chase down all the infected animals, and amazingly, they had managed to cleanse almost half of them. They had used the Lightleaf trees to transport the animals back to their various habitats. The Probability Matrix had been locked away until they could examine it more closely. A cursory examination had told them that somehow the Blight had reconstructed the thing and had Cut into the orbital vehicle that partnered with the device.

Almost a span after the end of the battle, the Banic they had first saved came out of the woods. She did not have her mate. Ales had hoped that her mate had been among those they had been able to cleanse. She was still blind, but what Lia had taught her about using her other senses had obviously been enough. Icci and Ales had undertaken the task of restoring her sight, as to be inducted as one of the new Tier, the banic needed her eyes. Once they got Cellstructs into her, the Banic had explained to them that she had met with the three banic they had cleansed and none were her mate. She had returned

to search the fields, and found the remains of her mate
amongst those that had attacked Rihanna. The banic, who
they had given the name Unia after another Wild who had
been a banic, had taken her place among them. They had all
found their new home.

EPILOGUE
"Wild at Heart"

Lia lead the way down the glittering white hallway. The door at the end slid open of its own accord when Lia approached it. It opened onto a darkened room. Ilsa followed behind her and Lia turned to face her.

"Are you certain of your decision?" Lia asked.

Ilsa's face was a blank mask. The pain had not gotten better, and Lia supported her decision. The question was part of the ritual that Lia had to follow. It was the last chance for Ilsa to remain as she was now. Ilsa had spoken with her family and with both the Mother and Father. Her parents had not understood at first, but Lia had helped them grasp what had happened to their daughter. She had helped them understand that Ilsa would be their daughter, no matter what.

Two rotations had passed, and it had not gotten any better. She had distracted herself as well as she could. She had become their resident instructor in hand to hand fighting, and her ability with staves had surpassed everyone except for Ales. While she could not grow better than Ales, she matched her four times out of ten, which was impressive considering that Ales had honed her abilities over hundreds of cycles. Mina had even attempted to help her feel better. The girl had spent large swaths of time with Ilsa, attempting to bring her out of the malaise that had come over her following the battle for Rihanna. None of it had helped her, though. The pain in her mind did not fade. When sleep came to Ilsa, she would relive that horrible moment when she squeezed the trigger of her lancer. She hadn't been able to touch her lancer since.

"I've given it time, Lia. It doesn't get better. I think that I could take my own life and my oath would be unfulfilled," Ilsa said.

Lia nodded and turned her large katali body around, slipping through the doorway on silent paws. Ilsa followed her into the darkened room. The lights came up slowly as not to blind them, and Ilsa gasped at the sight of the room. The room was a perfect cylinder with a ceiling thirty marks high. It was at least a hundred marks across. The glittering sorstone floor ended a few marks into the room. The rest of the floor was bright blue grass. At the center of the room was a large tree. It was an odd variety that Ilsa did not recognize. The massive trunk was twisted as if it were made up of a dozen smaller tree trunks. The trunks had smooth, pure white bark and a wide canopy that reached almost to the edges of the room. It had odd star-shaped leaves in every color Ilsa could possibly imagine. The leaves seemed to change color as she turned her head this way and that. It was perhaps twenty marks high, and how it grew here without access to sunlight was beyond her.

Ilsa's eyes wandered to the walls, and she gaped at them in awe. They were moving, somehow. Ilsa went to one of the walls and circumspectly touched one of the carvings. The carving was of a marskok, rendered in amazing detail. She could feel its fur under her fingers. She could immediately understand the animal and all the facts about it: where it lived, how it lived, things it ate, and what its normal lifespan was like. She intrinsically knew everything about the animal, as if she had lived like one of them for many cycles. She realized her Vision had opened on its own, which had not happened in more than a cycle. She took her hand away from the carving.

As soon as she did, the marskok carving twitched its whiskers. Ilsa gasped when it turned and bounded off into the wall as if it were somehow an open space. It ran back up a branch carved into the wall that seemed to terminate right at the surface where the marskok had first appeared. She realized that the carving was not just the animals, but also a forest. Were it not carved in stone, Ilsa could have easily mistaken it for an actual forest, one that she could walk directly into from the room. Even with it clearly being made of stone, Ilsa touched the wall again, almost expecting her fingers to pass through into the space beyond.

"What is this place?" Ilsa asked.

"This room is one of the great marvels of the Tier, and only those who planned to take the Wild ever experienced its power in full. We call it the Archive of All Fauna, or just the

Fauna Archive for simplicity. It was constructed with the consent of the Mother, using some small bits of her own power. Because it is an exact recreation of the one lost in the Cataclysm, the sum total of the power of the Mother's hand on this world has not changed, so we receive the benefit of this sacred place," Lia explained.

"The tree is beautiful," Ilsa said.

"It is a sprig of the Heart Tree, the living soul of nature."

Ilsa's face went slack with disbelief. "Gods, it's real?"

"Of course it's real. It's the Mother's connection to nature."

"What does it do?"

"The room, for the most part, is a repository of knowledge of all of the fauna in the world. It teaches us about the motivations and abilities of all of the animals of the world. It helps us interact with animals so that we do not have to harm them. For one who is about to take the Wild, it also helps you choose the animal form that is best suited to contain your mind and Tieran abilities by giving you the experience of living as one of them. I am here to help you do this. The Mother encourages her Tier to take the shapes of predators since it makes it easier for us to protect ourselves, but that is not always suited to our abilities and personalities," Lia explained.

Ilsa ran her hands across the bas relief carvings that were moving in a loose cloud on the wall. Each one seemed to pause only long enough for her to touch it. Once her hand had touched and passed them, the animals would spring away back into the woods. Some sat and watched her with interest, while others went about their business as if they were real animals. Each one she touched filled her mind with a complete knowledge of everything the animal was. Ilsa turned back to Lia, who sat near the tree looking up into the branches in reverence.

"Is it going to hurt?" Ilsa asked.

"No, Ilsa. There will be no pain, but the change is overwhelming to your senses, and you'll have trouble at first because you'll lack the ability to speak human languages anymore, though that does depend on the shape you choose to take. Some animals have the proper voice box to speak human tongues, and driven by a human mind, they can speak. However, no Tier I know has chosen such an animal."

Ilsa had made her choice, but she deserved to know everything that would happen when she finalized the process. Lia would answer every question the girl had, even if it cost her secrets that she had not shared with anyone but another of the Wild.

"I didn't know that. You can speak," Ilsa said.

"I suspect my ability to speak human languages will not last much longer. The Father gave me this ability to simplify teaching you all until we could provide you with Cellstructs. Prior to my time teaching you, I had not spoken human language for thousands of cycles. Further, you are all quickly outstripping me as a teacher. I am adequate, but Warran is better than I'll ever be at it."

Ilsa nodded and touched more of the animals on the walls. "I'm sorry for all the questions. I already know I'm going to go through with this." Ilsa seemed to sense that there were questions that were sensitive to Lia.

"Ilsa, this decision will be part of you for the rest of your life. I'll answer any question that you ask to the best of my ability, no matter how long this takes or what the question is. You are worth any discomfort it may cause me. You'll just have to become used to the idea that vocalization is not your first form of communication any longer. You'll have to endure others gently reminding you that your vocalizations no longer mean anything to them.

Also, depending on what shape you choose to take, some of your animal instincts can be troubling to you. For instance, my personal grooming reflexes were deeply disturbing to me for a number of cycles before I became comfortable with them. Also, your food cravings could be a little much for you at first, depending on the form you choose. It took me some time to become comfortable with killing for my food, and eating raw meat at first was just..." Lia gave a little shudder. "But it all fades as you become used to the new body."

Ilsa touched more animals, slowly making her way around the room, but she didn't feel much of a kinship with any of them, at least not the way that Lia had described. The way they bounded away from her also suggested that she had not yet found the right one.

"Are they grouped any specific way?" Ilsa asked.

"The room responds to your mental request. If you want to group them a certain way, just think of it and touch the wall."

Ilsa touched the wall and animals darted about in the woods, lining up until the forest disappeared behind two enormous walls of them, hundreds of animals facing the wall. They watched her with curious attention. When there was no more visible space on the ground, the trees appeared to grow numerous new branches that streaked along the walls in beautifully organized lines. Smaller animals lined up on the branches in ranks to the right and left of Ilsa's hand on the wall.

"Predators and non predators?" Lia asked.

Ilsa nodded. "What are the limitations?"

"May I assist?" Lia asked. Ilsa stepped back from the wall and waved towards it. "You cannot choose an animal that is much smaller than an adolescent human, and it must share certain features of the human anatomy. You cannot choose cold blooded animals, for instance. I do not recommend something that procreates differently than we do, but that is not a true limitation. I just personally don't think laying eggs would be an experience I would wish to have," Lia said with a chuff of laughter, and a toothy grin.

Ilsa let out a genuine laugh, the first she had in a long time. "Yes, but most egg-laying species can fly. I bet being able to fly is really something."

"So I have been told. There are a couple of flits that are large enough for you to choose." Lia put her paw on the wall. Many of the animals on the wall moved away, clearing a small space. Two very large flit species swooped between the trees. They backwinged and landed gently next to each other with their backs to Ilsa. Each mantled their impressive wingspans, and both were the size of a small human child. They turned their heads to look back over their wings at her with interest.

"I didn't know we could still have children if we went through this process."

"Of course you can. Children of the Wild are rare, but there are still some in the world even today."

Ilsa shook her head and Lia took her paw away from the wall. The flits took flight and winged their way back into the forest. She did not want feathers, even if it meant she could fly. "What do I get to pick?"

"For the most part, you can choose how you want to look. It is best to stay within the colors that your species could possibly have. If you want to attract a mate and you are oddly colored, it could make things difficult for you. I personally was never sure I wanted a mate or cubs so I went with a color scheme that pleased me. Not that my coloring is drastically out of the ordinary, but female katali almost never have spots or markings. Our fur is usually completely composed of a single color, but others of the Tier were more circumspect. They had mates and children. Don't worry very much about your coloration. When you change, the Mother infuses your Cellstructs with the power to change your body, but they work from your will. You will look how you want to look."

Ilsa put her hand against the wall and tried to focus on the things she thought would be nice. The mass of branches receded, and the forest returned to normal. She knew of a few animals whose front paws were as dexterous as a human hand. There might be more that she didn't know about. Dozens of animals slid out of the underbrush. Some swung through the tree branches and then sat in the trees, waiting patiently.

"What's it like to have a tail?" Ilsa asked.

Lia turned her body to look at hers. "Uhm, well, it's interesting. There are advantages and disadvantages to it. The first thing you should know is that I am certain that humans evolved without tails due entirely to doors. You'll slam your tail in a door at least once in your life, and you'll feverishly consider chopping it off so that you don't ever have to feel that horrifying pain ever again. I have broken bones, dislocated joints, lost a couple of toes once on a very sharp rock in a fast-moving river, and been stabbed and burned numerous times. Nothing came close to how much pain I have to suppress if I slam my tail in a door," Lia said, "but the advantages of having a tail in balance, and if you choose something that has a prehensile tail, in the use of an extra limb, are undeniable."

"Do I have to pick something that eats raw meat?" Ilsa shuddered.

Lia chuffed a little. "I wouldn't change what you choose over eating raw meat. Most predators are designed to eat raw meat without harm, and believe it or not, it is actually quite tasty once you get past your human preconceptions. Besides, killing for food doesn't hurt us the same way killing to balance chaos does. Predators do not need Tieran powers to take prey. It doesn't trigger the check to our power the same way."

"It doesn't sound appetizing to me."

"It didn't to me, either. Try not to think about it for now. We can eat cooked meat just as easily, and if you stay within the walls of the Tower, you don't ever have to eat raw meat, but I suspect that after a cycle or two, you'll get a craving for something that bleeds. Instincts honed over hundreds of thousands of cycles cannot be denied."

Ilsa nodded and went back to focusing on the wall. Animals dashed and darted through the trees as she tried to feel her way through the process of deciding what she wanted to become. A few animals appeared in the cleared space. One of the flits she had dismissed earlier glided in to land on a large branch in one of the trees before her. Another was an animal about the size of a large breed hiluk or an adolescent human child. It bounced on a large branch not far from the flit. The resscall was a stoneward climate predator from the other side of the Grey Tide. It lived in mild climate forests in the stoneward areas of the continent. They were tree dwellers, with front paws that had an opposable digit. It wasn't exactly like a human hand, having only four thick digits instead of five, but it would give her most of the dexterity of a human hand. This appealed to Ilsa because she would still be able to do work as a Fixer. It had a stocky body, and its fur had several standard colors for females. It had a tail that was almost as long as its body. The tail split into three slender appendages about three quarters of the way to the end.

The more she learned, the more it appealed to her. The information feeding into her mind told her that the tail was considerably stronger than it seemed, allowing the creature to catch itself even in a bad fall. She received images of it with the three slender appendages curled around a branch. The animal swung from the tail, seeming quite comfortable. When she thought about the idea that there might be differences between the females and males, another resscall trotted out of the bushes. It scaled the tree with alacrity and joined the first. This one was male, and there were some distinct differences. The females had large round ears and shorter muzzles. The males had distinctly pointed ears, and their fur was plainer, with less markings. Ilsa had a silly thought.

"Can I change my gender?" Ilsa asked with a little smirk.

Lia chuffed. "You don't really want to, do you?"

"Not really, but I can't see myself ever getting to wear a dress again. I take it that most of my human femininity is going to be moot, and it seems that the males are physically more powerful. It might be an advantage I can exploit."

"Not as much as you might think. If you are feminine, which you certainly are, it isn't going to just flee. You're right to think that animals in general don't have the same sort of concepts, but you are not going to completely lose your humanity. We have not had much time to have formal ceremonies, but we will, and you would be surprised how much femininity you can convey with a few carefully placed ribbons in your fur, if you have someone with fingers to tie them for you. As for physical power, I wouldn't concern myself there either. With your cellstruct integration, pound for pound, you'll be nearly unrivaled in physical power."

Lia sat next to her. She sent Ilsa a mental image of how she had looked at the last Skyfire festival she had attended before Ahal had been destroyed. She had been festooned with bows around her tail, behind her ears, and some delicate ruffles on all of her paws. They had made Lia look decidedly effeminate. Lia tilted her head, peering up at the animal she was touching. Information about the resscall continued to flood into her mind, and she was a little startled to see that the animal was an ambush predator. It had razor sharp retractable claws on each paw. Each claw was over a tick long, but the claws used for climbing and holding onto prey were nothing compared to the teeth. The animal had a mouthful of razor-sharp triangular teeth designed for shredding flesh. It often ate smaller animals, but was also known for bringing down gantha and other larger animals.

"Mmm, a good choice. Just be careful with those teeth or you might snip off a bit of your tongue. I know I have, with these things." She ran a tongue across her own extremely sharp fangs.

"Do I have to eat only meat?" Ilsa asked.

"It isn't as bad as it sounds, but…" Lia drew out the word. "If you delve into the knowledge about the resscall, I think you'll find that they can eat some fruits as well without trouble."

Ilsa did so and found that Lia was right. There were some drawbacks to it. It had to do with what kinds of sugars and other chemicals were in the fruit. The animal's fur was soft and warm, but not shaggy or so dense that she would suffer horribly in the heat. Then it became clear that the animal had a summer and winter coat, so in the winter her coat would get far denser and a little longer to give her more protection from the cold.

"How does that work?" Ilsa asked.

"Just like it does for the animal. The length of daylight hours determines when your body is triggered to change coats," Lia said.

"Can I control that?" Ilsa asked.

Lia lifted a paw, and made a so-so gesture with it. "I honestly cannot say for sure. Katali don't have seasonal coats, and I don't have experience with other Wild who had them. I suspect the answer is no. I suspect that it will go for you just like for the animal."

Ilsa ran her fingers over the image carved into the wall. She lifted her fingers away, but the resscall did not bound away as the other animals had. She touched the other four animals, including the large flit, the Opani. It was a massive animal with extremely dexterous feet tipped with sharp talons. Ilsa lingered on it for a long moment, but eventually she lifted her hand and the Opani beat its wings, joining those Ilsa had dismissed in the amazing stone forest. Only the resscall was left.

"A fine choice, Daughter." The Mother's voice was a slow warm comfort to their ears. Lia bowed her body forward until her muzzle touched the floor. Ilsa turned and knelt. She bowed until her forehead touched the floor.

"Rise, Daughters. My blessing for your supplication." The Mother wore her summer guise, her body made up of beautiful curves. She floated closer to them. Ilsa stood and stared up into the Mother's night sky eyes.

"I see your worries, my Daughter. Let me ease those fears." The mother reached down with delicate, long fingers and touched her face. "Like so many of the Wild before you, you worry that wearing a different body will make you less. This is not true. This will make you more. It will allow you to do things that you could never do in this broken form," the Mother assured her.

"Can't you just fix me?" Ilsa asked.

The Mother paused and looked at Ilsa. Her eyes were sad, and her expression was filled with compassion.

"Let us say that I were to do that, Daughter. Let us say that I use my power to reach into your mind and alter the way you feel. What do you think would happen?"

Ilsa shook her head. She hadn't the slightest idea.

"It would destroy you, Ilsa. The core of who you are would be gone. All that would be left would be my will imposed upon your body. Personality develops organically, Ilsa, and if I were to alter the structure of your mind to make you more insulated from your feelings, you would no longer be yourself. Is that truly what you want, Child?"

Ilsa considered it for a long moment, and then shook her head.

"In this way, by making you your own unique form of life, I allow your mind to develop its own feelings of insulation instead of attempting to impose them upon you from the outside." The Mother touched the wall where the carving of the resscall rose from the surface of the glittering stone. When she drew her hand back, she held a glowing image of the animal. It tumbled, rolled, and climbed a tree where it sat on a branch, staring at Ilsa.

"Speak the words, my Daughter."

Ilsa bowed her head. The Mother placed her long, delicate fingers atop Ilsa's bowed head. A single sparkling tear cascaded down Ilsa's cheek, and a moment later in a quavering voice, she began to chant.

"I seek new life by leaving behind a broken body and broken mind." Her voice got a little stronger as she continued the chant. "By my free will, I make this change to shield my mind from endless pain. To keep my oath and persist stalwart, I forever remain Wild at heart."

The image of the resscall in the Mother's hand flared with a bright internal light. The image took on a solidity that it had not had a moment before. The Mother tilted her hand with the solidifying image of the resscall and brought it forward. She reached down and pressed the image into Ilsa's chest. Ribbons of blue white light exploded into existance and spiraled up from the ground. They cocooned Ilsa, and the Mother stepped back, withdrawing her hand.

The magic of transformation filled the room with azure light and a roar of sound that came with the power of the Mother to bend reality to her will. It was not just the magic that produced the transformation. The magic empowered the Cellstructs already in Ilsa's body with the capability to rebuild her body in the moments that it took for the ribbons of light to unravel. It started at the ground, and the uncurling ribbons disappeared into the air above Ilsa's head. Left behind as the ribbons of magic disappeared was a lavender-furred resscall. She had three lighter stripes of white fur running horizontally across her back, just above her tail. She had socks of white fur on her hindlegs and a band of white fur around her left forepaw. There were spots of white dotted across her cheeks and muzzle. She was wearing her winter coat considering how light the coloring was, which was interesting.

"Her winter coat, Mother?" Lia asked.

"I thought she might like to know what she will look like in winter. I have accelerated the summer coat change so that she will lose the extra fur for her summer colors within a few days. Normally, the change takes a number of spans," the Mother said with a smile. "She will wake up momentarily, and as with you, Daughter, she will be woozy from the change."

"I'll care for her, Mother, and see to it that she recovers properly," Lia vowed.

"She could not possibly be in better paws." The Mother ran her delicate fingers through the fur between Lia's ears comfortingly.

"Thank you, Mother," Lia said.

"Of course, Daughter," the Mother said. She looked about to depart when Lia spoke up again.

"Mother, can you return this to the Father? I don't think I need it anymore."

Lia touched the device hanging from the side of her collar lending her the ability of human speech. The Mother gave her a beatific smile. She reached down and touched the collar. She stood up, holding the round device. Lia bowed the front of her body in thanks, and the Mother faded away.

A moment later, Ilsa's two-color eyes slid open, one amber and one blue. Unlike her human eyes, the iris reached almost to the edges of her eyes. The round pupils dilated and then darted back and forth. She made a small rumbling, cooing noise of confusion. Her round ears tilted this way and that, trying to get a bearing on her surroundings. She put her paws over her stomach and made another lower pitched noise of confusion almost like a grunt. A moment later, the door darkened and Ales came into the room carrying a tray with a teapot. There were two small dishes on the tray, and steam curled from the spout of the teapot. Ales knelt down next to Ilsa and put the tray on the floor.

"Does every one of the Wild come out of it like this?" Ales asked. Lia's mental handshake chimed inside of Ales' mind, and Ilsa joined it a moment later.

{As far as I know,} Lia said. Ales looked at her quizzically. *{The Mother took my speech back. I was done with it.}*

Ales nodded. *{Ilsa, this is lisan tea. It should settle your stomach.}*

Ilsa fumbled with her forepaws for a moment, reaching for the dish.

{Like this, Ilsa.} Lia bent her neck and lapped from her own dish of the tea.

Ilsa made another noise between a coo and a grunt. She tipped forward from her sitting position, and wobbled a little when her front paws hit the ground. She put her muzzle down to the dish, and after a few false starts, she lapped rhythmically from the dish.

{Mmmm, I feel so muzzy,} Ilsa said into their mental link. Her mindvoice sounded as if she were mumbling.

{It'll pass soon. Your mind is acclimating to your new body,} Lia responded.

Ilsa let out a little gasp of surprise. *{It's fading. Still there, but the depression and horror are better. I feel whole again,}* she said excitedly. Then she wobbled and fell back onto her rump.

{You didn't think it would work?} Lia asked.

{I didn't think it would work so quickly.} Ilsa made a little cooing yelp of pleasure. She got back to her feet and hopped about a little before overbalancing herself. She tumbled over onto her side.

{You'll get better on all fours soon enough,} Lia said.

{I don't know how to do anything with my tail. I can feel it, but it doesn't seem to respond when I try to do something with it,} Ilsa said.

{That'll take a little more time. Your brain is used to having four limbs. You have to just start walking around and using your new body. Your brain will make the connection in time. It took spans for

me to get control of my tail, and it still seems to operate on its own sometimes to this day,} Lia assured her.

{I don't care how long it takes. I feel like I can be me again,} Ilsa said. Her lips pulled back from triangular razor teeth in a terrifying facsimile of a grin.

{Might want to be careful with that smile around your family until they get used to you,} Ales said with a little laugh. Ilsa carefully closed her mouth. Ales ruffed the fur between Ilsa's ears gently. Ilsa discovered that it was extremely enjoyable. *{I'm just having some fun with you, Ilsa. Are you ready to see your parents?}*

Ilsa looked down at her new paws and her ears folded back in a gesture of shyness. *{I hope so.}*

Ilsa walked a little circle to make sure she could move properly. She was still a little wobbly, but it was already getting better.

{Look at this,} Ales said with interest in her mindvoice. She lifted Ilsa's chin a little. Her collar was just like Lia's, made of light lavender hide to match her fur, with a golden colored nameplate. But unlike how Lia's collar started out, this one had a pouch attached to it just like Lia's. It had the same symbol for the Wild in the center of it.

"Is she alright?" The voice from the door was Ilsa's mother. Ilsa crouched behind Ales's legs like a small child. She was not as large as a full grown human now, but she was larger than a child. She was big for a resscall, and Ales thought that was likely the Mother's doing. Still, she was small enough to keep most of her body behind Ales.

"Of course, but she is understandably worried that her new shape will make you unhappy with her," Ales said.

"Is it alright if we come in?" Ellena asked, her voice uncertain.

"I think she'll survive her embarrassment," Ales chuckled.

Ellena and Lerand came into the room. They had not made it ten paces into the room when they slowed to a stop, staring at the tree and then the moving carvings on the walls. They stared in wonder for a long moment. Ales took the opportunity to turn and kneel in front of Ilsa.

"Ilsa, your parents maybe startled, but they'll still love you. I promise they will," Ales said.

Ilsa tipped herself forward from her sitting position and went back down to all fours.

{I'm afraid,} Ilsa said into their mental link. Ales sent warm affection down their mental link to help her.

{Who wouldn't be, Sister, but there is only one way to be rid of fear,} Ales soothed.

{Is there any way I can talk to them?} Ilsa asked.

{There is not, but I promise you we'll work on something. In our time, it was very infrequent that someone who took the Wild had those who were close to them that did not have their own Cellstructs. In this time, we'll find a way for you to be able to speak to your loved ones. Warran and I will do it ourselves,} Ales said.

Ilsa bobbed her head in a nod, and then padded around Ales and walked towards her parents, who were still too busy with the room to notice her. Ilsa very carefully sat down in front of her mother and father and waited for them. When her father finally looked down at her and their eyes met, the recognition was instantaneous.

"Oh, Ilsa, you look so worried, but I would know you no matter what." Her father knelt down to get to her level. He put his arms around her neck and held her lovingly. Then her mother was kneeling down. She looked a little more disconcerted than her mate, but it didn't seem like she was appalled.

"Are you better? Are you whole?" her mother asked uncertainly.

Ilsa lifted her muzzle from her father's shoulder and bobbed her head yes. Her mother threw her arms around Ilsa and squeezed her in a way only a mother could. Ales smiled at them, and knew that Ilsa was going to be just fine.

GLOSSARY

Sphere	A sphere is a weight of measure that is equivalent to 2.25 lbs on earth.
Interval	100 Cycles Equivalent of the term century in English.
Long Interval	1000 Cycles Equivalent to the term millennium in English.
Cycle	Language equivalent to a year in English. 1.51 Years Earth Time (550 Earth Days) 440 Days on Ahlysim On Ahlysim a cycle has 10 rotations.
Day	Same as the earth concept. Equivalent to 30 hours in earth time.
Rotation	Language equivalent of a month in English. A Rotation has 44 days.
Span	Language equivalent of a week in English. A span has 11 days.
Falling	English language equivalent of Afternoon, or the middle of the day. After the sun has reached its peak and is falling.

Break	English language equivalent of morning, day break. Language Equivalent Examples in the morning: at breaks morning: breaking(alt. breaks depending on phrasing)
Ends	Dusk, the end of the day. Language equivalent to evening in English. Language Equivalent Examples evening: ending (alt. ends depending on phrasing such as at dusk would be at ends)
Night	Same as night in English. The time between full dark, and morning.

Curses	Mother's End: General curse, referring to the end of the world, the death of the Mother Avaara. Father's Stones: General curse, no explanation needed. How in the howling abyss(?): The howling abyss is one of the deepest canyons on all of Ahlysim. No normal person has ever made it through the howling abyss. It is said that there are supernatural creatures in the abyss making it impossible to pass. It is a phrase used to express frustration, or impossibility of a task.
Moonward	The direction from which the moon rises on Ahlysim. English language Equivalent of East.
Sunward	The direction from which the sun rises, it is directly opposite the moon rise. English language equivalent of West.
Stoneward	Generally on Ahlysim the lands in the stoneward hemisphere tend to be more mountainous, and are generally associated with The Father. Hence Stoneward. English language equivalent of North

Bloomward	The lands in the bloomward hemisphere of Ahlysim are generally a little more temperate and covered in blue than the planet to the north and so is generally associated with The Mother. Hence Bloomward. English language equivalent of South
Peb	Unit of measure. 1/36th of 1 sphere. Or roughly 1 ounce.
Fixer	Fixer is a blanket term for anyone who repairs anything. This could be carpenters, mechanics, smiths, as well as physicians. There are different terms used but Fixer is the general term.
Mender	Mender is a specialized term for a Fixer who repairs the human body. A doctor, or physician.
Flit	Flit is a common word. It is used interchangeably with the Earth word: bird
Streic	A heavy fabric with elastic properties used for the manufacture of clothing primarily in Vilhena.
Length	English language equivalent of a mile. Equivalent to 6,000 marks.
Mark	English language equivalent of a foot. Equivalent to 10 ticks.
Tick	English language equivalent of an inch. Equivalent to 1.5 inches.

Jianfuit	The Jian is a small green fruit that has a salty skin with sweet green meat of the fruit inside. It is rare, and hard to find.
Sorion	Sorian is a metal that is found only in deposits of sorstone. It is rumored that there is a counterpart metal that can be found in norstone that has magical properties. There is no evidence though that this metal exists.
Lacal (Tree)	Lacal trees are some of the hardest wood available on Ahlysim. It is a deep brown, with veins of very light blue running through the grain.
Stonebark (Tree)	Stonebark Trees have very specific capilary filters that deposit the minerals that they draw in with water into their bark causing a petrifying effect to their bark giving it incredible durability.
Twinebark (Tree)	Twinebark trees are a common soft wood tree with bark that closely resembles braided rope. They often grow in clumps where the trunks of many trees twine together into a single tree.